A Soldier's Hell
One Man's Journey into the Darkness

William A. King

KSLEH Publishing— Dinwiddie County, VA
ISBN: 979-8-218-50447-2
Library of Congress Control Number: 2024920521
A Soldier's Hell: One Man's Journey into the Darkness
Author: William A. King
Digital distribution | 2024
Paperback | 2024

This is a work of historical fiction. While many of the characters, names, places, and events are based on history, some of the characters, names, incidents, places, and all of the dialogue are products of the author's imagination, and are not to be construed as real.

Dedication

To my children and grandchildren with the hope they may better understand our family history and the sacrifices of our ancestors.
And
To all who have worn a uniform and experienced their own personal "Soldier's Hell."

Semper Fi

Prologue

"And when I get to Heaven, Saint Peter I will tell.
Another soldier reporting Sir, I served my time in Hell."

Anonymous

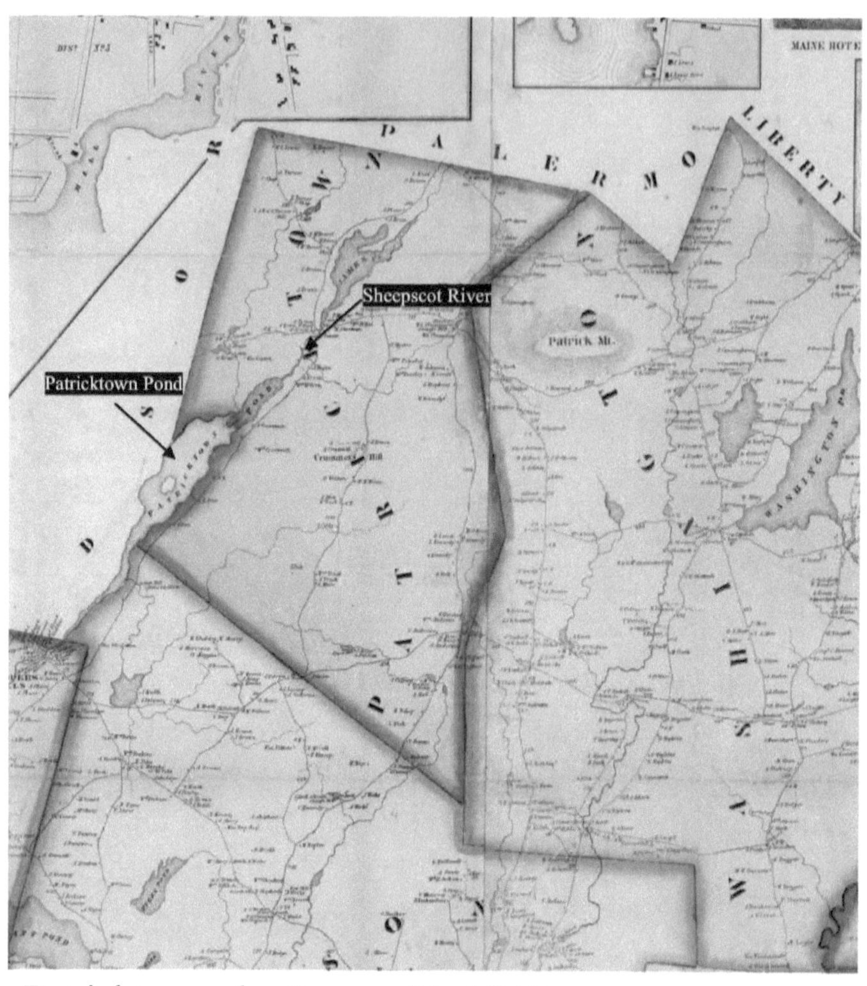

Patricktown aka Somerville 1857

September 1864 – Petersburg, Virginia.

The fall in Maine is the very best time of year, when the green shades of the pines and cedars mix with the reds, oranges, yellows, and browns of the hardwoods to create a palate of incredible beauty on the surrounding landscape. Warm, brightly lit days marry with cool, crisp nights and serve as the harbingers of the cold harsh winter yet to come.

The fall in Maine is that time after the crops have been harvested, the orchards picked, and the cooking, salting, smoking, and preserving complete. County fairs are in full swing and the air is filled with a general mood of thanksgiving for another successful season.

The fall in Maine is a time for hunting. Game is extremely essential to fill the larders and storehouses in preparation for the hard months to follow. How vividly I recall the thrill of those fall hunts when frost and snow at the higher elevations drove the game down in search of food. I learned to shoot as a youngster under the watchful eye of my father as we hunted squirrels, rabbits, and wild turkey. The harvested fields also provided a wonderful source of pheasants and grouse. My proficiency with his .36 caliber percussion cap musket and black powder shotgun provided some of the much-needed food for our growing family. As a teen, I graduated to hunting larger game, first with my father and later with one or two friends I considered equal as hunters. During these fall hunts there was always an abundance of deer and occasionally a moose, to augment the smaller game. I became a crack shot and seldom missed.

The fall in Maine is also a time for fishing. The Sheepscot River runs through Lincoln County and feeds the Patricktown Pond. This waterway provides a bountiful source of trout, pike, bass, and musky. Not far downriver are the seaports of Boothbay and

Southport Island where striped bass, flounder, lobsters, and crabs are caught, cooked, and salted for the coming winter.

The fall in Maine really is the closest thing to paradise on earth. How well I can remember it. With eyes closed it was as if I was there, living in the memories of my childhood. I can see everything about the area: my family, the people, and the beauty of the landscape.

But as my eyes slowly opened and began to focus, the splendor of Maine started to disappear. What remained were the harsh realities of my current surroundings and the horrors of the life I knew for the past three years. It wasn't Maine. It was Virginia. It was war, and I was a soldier.

Scarcely a living thing grew in the blood red clay soil of the Petersburg battle line. There were no trees left. Only charred stumps remained where majestic white and red oaks, pines, maples, hickories, and poplars once stood. The wood was used to erect shelters for soldiers, Union and Confederate alike, or form the fortifications and bomb-proofs that protect us from unremitting artillery and mortar bombardments.

After four months of siege activities around Petersburg, the fort where my unit was garrisoned and the surrounding terrain were pockmarked with the craters of thousands of exploded projectiles, all of which contributed to this apocalyptic nightmare. No green grass or woodlands; only red clay that turned into an ocean of mud during rainstorms or a barren, dusty wasteland during dry times. Even the sun contributed to this surreal world as it set in the evening. Its blood red rays cast an ominous glow over the battlefield: not the paradise of Maine but an accurate vision of hell on earth. The hell that was Petersburg, Virginia: a Soldier's Hell.

I was certainly no stranger to the concept of hell in the religious sense. Back home, the Reverend Mr. Hardin preached on the subject regularly. The sins committed in this world are determining factors for assignment to a specific level in that spiritual realm of evil and suffering. Even refusing the faith could commit one to the land of limbo with others deemed unfaithful or unbaptized.

In school, I learned of the literary existence of hell. Our teacher, Mr. Parsons, was quite fond of the subject particularly as it pertained to the various cantos from Dante's Inferno. Guided by the Roman poet Virgil, Mr. Parsons, playing the role of Dante, would escort the class through the various levels of hell he experienced, pausing only to introduce the people he encountered.

Over the course of my three years in the Army, I have had a lot of time to contemplate the true meaning of hell, specifically the hell that surrounded me. This was a particular brand of hell brought about by man's inhumanity to his fellow man. This was not the hell to keep the masses in line or to scare small children into behaving. Rather, it was a unique kind of hell created exclusively for a soldier.

In a soldier's world, this was that special hell born in the experiences and desires of youth; cultivated by the methodical preparation and drill of basic training; fueled by an unholy baptism of fire; fortified by subsequent campaigns; and reinforced in the memories and dreams of old men. Unlike the hell of religion or literature that starts when life ends, a soldier's hell is created during life and ends only when life ends and the eternal darkness of death releases the soldier from his burden.

The Seduction

"The hottest places in Hell are reserved for those who, in times of great moral crisis, maintain their neutrality."

Dante Alighieri

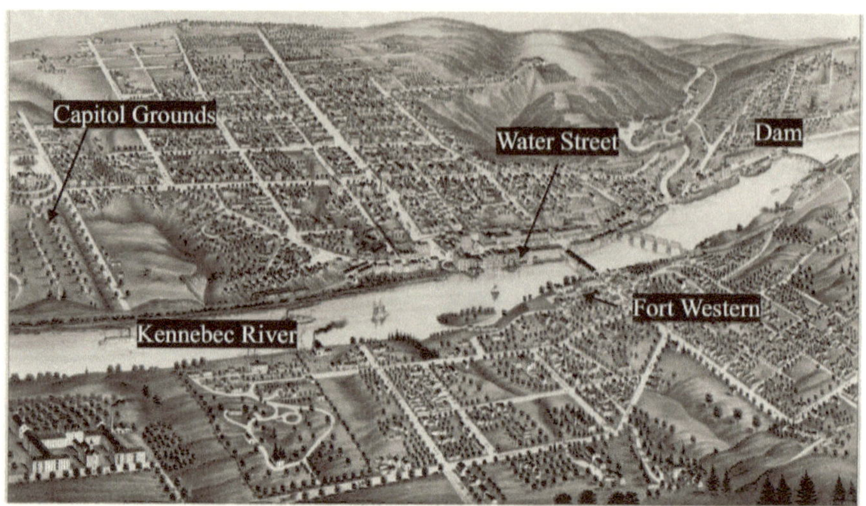

Augusta, Maine circa 1860

Chapter One

May 1859 – Somerville, Maine

Like so many young men of this era, my descent into a soldier's hell began at a young age around the family dinner table. At each clan gathering or holiday meal there was always talk of the heroes of our ancestors. This became extremely intoxicating conversation for a young impressionable mind. To hear the stories of William Wallace at Stirling Bridge or other Scottish heroes was truly awe-inspiring.

After these family gatherings, I would recreate images of the various stories over and over in my imagination. I became the avenging angel for Wallace and other Scots who were betrayed and executed by the British. In another scenario, I was mounted atop a large, gray charger striding across the Belgian countryside to reinforce the collapsing line. This advance saved the Gordons from certain annihilation and protected the entire British flank. Then, with saber flashing, I led the Scot's Greys headlong into the French square, routing it. I saw myself capturing the eagle from the 45th Regiment of Line; Frenchmen fleeing everywhere from the boldness of the charge; the Emperor Napoleon soundly defeated at Waterloo.

There was always a somber mood of reverence when the discussion turned to Robert the First of Scotland. Now there was a man, a fellow clansman, and a true patriot. What an honor it would have been to fight with The Bruce in the First War of Scottish Independence. How glorious it would have been to stand with him at the Battle of Bannockburn when the heavily outnumbered clans united to defeat King Edward II and earn Scottish independence.

And, of course, there was the glorious victory at Prestonpans before the crushing defeat at Culloden. Like many of my family, I can still taste the agony of that defeat. I often visualize what it must have been like to stand in the battle line at Culloden. Culloden: the very mention of the name sends chills down my spine. Culloden: the end of the Jacobite Rebellion of Bonnie Prince Charlie. Culloden: the death knell of the clans in Scotland.

Not all of the tales of bravery and patriotism were of our ancestors or the clans in Scotland. The family also had a noble history of service in wars here in America that provided additional fuel for my over-active imagination. My father spoke proudly of Great Grandfather Isaiah, who heeded the call from Paul Revere and his riders and joined the other "embattled farmers" at Concord Bridge and Lexington. Another ancestor, Grandfather Barnard, shouldered a weapon with the militia during the War of 1812 and defended what was now the Maine coast from the invading British.

My mother was inclined to proudly remind everyone of the patriotism on her side of the family as well. Great Grandfather Squire Bishop, and his brother Isaiah marched with the Massachusetts Line from Boston to Yorktown and both were pensioned for wounds received in battle. What great stories of the heroes in my own family; the tales of their desperate struggles to create a free country independent of British tyranny or preserve the new nation from all enemies. This was a tough pedigree for a young man to live up to and the start of my seduction down the path into a soldier's hell.

Surprisingly, it was my mother who provided the impetus for the next step in the seduction process. When I was about four, she insisted that I, and later my brothers and sisters, learn to read and write. At first, the reading lessons came from the family bible, but the bible soon gave way to a host of other reading materials. I read everything I could lay my hands on, from the local newspapers to penny novels from the general store. I found not only a degree of comfort in reading but also an escape from the daily routines of farm life.

These penny novels further stimulated the formative imagination of a young, naïve farm boy. There were the stories of heroes from the American Revolution and the War of 1812 and tales of the men who made America. I fantasized about fighting Indians with Daniel Boone on the Kentucky frontier or Mexicans with Crockett and Bowie at the Alamo. I was there with Washington in the cold at Valley Forge or fighting alongside pirates with Jackson at New Orleans. There were even exploits at sea with John Paul Jones, another Scotsman, or aboard Old Ironsides. These were truly powerful stories for my impressionable mind.

At school, my teachers recognized this zeal for reading and began to introduce me to the wonderful world of real literature. There were stories of mythology and tales of ancient civilizations. I saw myself riding into battle with Alexander, or with Caesar crossing the Rubicon. These stories paled in comparison however, to my favorite, fighting side by side with Leonidas and the brave three hundred at Thermopylae. The accounts of ancient times and places further awakened a deep-seated desire for adventure in the great world outside of Maine.

When I was a teenager, our teacher, Mr. Parsons, introduced me to authors from the first golden age of American literature. I was soon absorbed in a variety of new adventures or thinking about innovative ideas and theories. There were great stories from Washington Irving and James Russell Lowell depicting experiences in the American wilds, although in a very romanticized way. There was the assertion of personal independence and the spiritual discovery of simplistic living as Thoreau described his life at Walden.

Emerson's Concord Bridge became a favorite because of our family's connection. I was also an ardent fan of the works of Edgar Allen Poe and his tales of the macabre. But it was Mr. Parsons who introduced me to the greatest of all possible adventures, the works of Herman Melville. Battling a goliath sea creature halfway around the world or interacting with native populations capped an already hyperactive imagination and further lured me towards a life filled with travel and adventure. During my teen years, it was literature that provided an outlet for exploration and discovery but the real impetus for the move along the path toward a soldier's hell came from Maine itself.

Early in its history, the part of Massachusetts that became Maine was predominately agrarian. Only after achieving statehood in 1820 did the forest and mineral products industries as well as the shipbuilding and fishing industries experience tremendous growth. Farming, on the other hand, did not flourish as did those other industries. Maine's geographic location coupled with its poor soil conditions, extensive forests, and wholly unpredictable weather were substantial obstacles to any farmer.

For most Maine farmers there were no true cash crops like those found in other areas of the country. The potatoes grown in Aroostook County were the only crop actually exported outside of Maine. Since most of the farms in other regions of Maine were relatively small, family run operations of around one hundred to one hundred fifty acres, farmers relied on what could be grown and harvested to provide enough foodstuffs to see the family and the livestock through the long winter months. If the winter was especially long or severe, farmers were often forced to turn to other sources of income to survive. Many of the menfolk sought work in the forests harvesting trees, in the quarries harvesting granite, or making bricks. Still others turned to more craft-oriented sources of income: making furniture, barrels, shingles, or farm related implements.

The women also pitched in, making brooms, baskets, and other crafts to earn additional income. They wove cloth or sewed fabric and leather into clothes and shoes. Men and women alike bartered various goods and services in an effort to limit outside purchases and maintain a self-sufficient lifestyle. Blacksmithing, weaving, dressmaking, health care, and carpentry were all highly sought after skills that were easily bartered, all in the name of subsisting through the harsh Maine winters.

I was ten when my mother passed away from the rigors of childbirth and the hardships of Maine living. The baby brother she bore before she died followed her to Sand Hill Cemetery a year later. After waiting a suitable period of time, my father took a new wife. Although our stepmother was a pleasant enough sort, she was twenty years younger than my father. Soon enough, new brothers and sisters began arriving at the rate of about one per year. As the eldest male child, the responsibility for the farm and the family fell to me.

By the time of my eighteenth birthday, any aspirations I had about becoming a farmer were at an all-time low. The family had grown with the birth of five new half brothers and sisters. Two others joined my mother in Sand Hill Cemetery and our stepmother was once again in the family way. My formal schooling was at an end and that ever-present adventure bug was, once again, gnawing at my soul. After some serious discussions with my father, we agreed that my two younger brothers would assume additional responsibilities around the farm along with our half brothers and sisters. This freed me to start planning a future away from the farm.

Unfortunately, the options for eighteen year olds in Maine at the time were somewhat limited. Workers in the fishing and lumber industries suffered from many of the same issues as the farmers when it came to winter and work. Another option was to use my carpentry skills and apply as an apprentice boat builder at one of the many maritime shipbuilding facilities along the coast. If I felt really daring, I could travel to New Bedford, Massachusetts and follow Herman Melville into the whaling business. In the end, on the counsel of my father and Mr. Parsons, I left the family farm and traveled fifteen miles from Somerville to Augusta to become an apprentice in an apothecary shop.

Chapter Two

July 1859 – Augusta, Maine

The next phase of my seduction into a soldier's hell began in late May 1859 as I boarded the stage for Augusta and began to experience and understand the national political climate of the late 1850s and early 1860s. Somerville was far enough off the beaten path to remain fairly isolated from the outside world. If it didn't concern farming, or the local and state elections, it wasn't really that important. Augusta, on the other hand, was front and center in knowledge and communications concerning not only what was happening in Maine, but also the politics and policy of the nation. Decisions made there impacted not just Maine, but the rest of the country as well. I was about to become a part of that world.

It really wasn't much of an adventure to take a stage ride to the State Capitol. I had been there several times before with my father. However, this time I was going to Augusta to become an apprentice in the apothecary shop of Henry Hartwell. Mr. Hartwell was a lifelong friend and classmate at Bowdoin College of my old teacher, Mr. Parsons. On the ride over, I took time to reflect on what I remembered about Augusta from our Maine history classes in school.

It was hard to believe that members of the ill-fated Popham Colony had first explored this area of Maine in 1607. After the colony was abandoned some fourteen months later, Augusta reverted to the wilds until 1628 when it was inhabited by settlers from the Plymouth Bay Colony and served as a trading post on the Kennebec River.

Originally called Cushnoc, after the Indian term for "head of the tide", the area remained a critical trading station for lumber and furs until it was incorporated into the City of Hallowell in 1771. In February of 1797, the Cushnoc area was set off and included into the newly formed Town of Harrington. Later that year, the name was officially changed to Augusta after the infant daughter of Henry

Dearborn, Revolutionary War General, former Marshal of Maine, and Secretary of War under Jefferson.

The stage passed old Fort Western and slowed to cross the bridge into the station. The traitorous Benedict Arnold and his troops visited Fort Western on their way to attack Quebec during the American Revolution. These days, the old Fort was the home for some of the local mill workers and their families. As the stage lumbered into the station and I climbed down, I could see the dam across the Kennebec River and the multitude of sailing ships, mostly coastal freighters, tied to the quay walls along Water Street.

Walking up Water Street to Green Street I spotted the Arsenal across the river and the top of the State Capitol. Normally a peaceful city of about seventy-five hundred residents, Augusta became a different place when the legislature was in session. Taking the turn onto State Street my destination lay ahead, Hartwell's Apothecary, Henry Hartwell, Druggist. As I approached the shop, I realized that this trip would be much different than any other previously taken. On this trip, I would be starting an adventure away from the farm. On this trip, I would not be returning home.

Working in Hartwell's Apothecary was not at all what I expected. Mr. Hartwell and his family were decent, Christian folks who welcomed me into their home and their business. Mr. Hartwell's wife Mary tried to make me as comfortable as possible during my tenure as their apprentice. There was a pleasant attic room to live in and a place set for me at breakfast before work and at dinner after the shop closed.

The Hartwells had two children, William, aged twelve, and Elizabeth, aged ten. They also went out of their way to make me feel at home and welcome. After a time, they began to view me as the older brother they did not have.

Mr. Hartwell was a fair employer, taking a couple of hours of each day to instruct me in the various tasks associated with being a druggist. These sessions included some detailed discussions about the various medicines kept in the shop. What did this drug heal? What did that drug prevent? Which of these drugs could be sold outright and which required a physician's prescription?

After a while these instructional sessions began to include aspects of running an apothecary business. How did you order this item or that medicine? What kind of paperwork was required to order and sell what medicines? How do you keep track of what had sold in order to keep a well-stocked inventory?

When the apprentice training sessions were over for the day, my responsibilities were to clean up the shop and stock the shelves. After a short time and under the watchful eye of Mr. or Mrs. Hartwell, I began to interact with customers. I listened to their maladies and made recommendations for their treatment. I also assisted Mr. Hartwell in preparing special medicines that were prescribed by the customer's doctor. I learned which of these special medicines required close supervision when administering or using, which caused what side effects or hallucinations, and which became addictive if not used properly.

In the afternoon when things were slow in the store, William and Elizabeth would come by after school for a visit or stay with me if their parents had business outside the shop. I especially liked helping them with their schoolwork when I could. Both children were avid readers and I found myself enjoying the times we spent together discussing various books. William had developed a fascination with the world of Greek and Roman mythology and other aspects of ancient times. Some of these discussions brought out old feelings about travels and adventures yet to be taken and awakened somewhat dormant yearnings brought on by years of the seduction.

Not all aspects of my current situation were work oriented. In addition to room and board, Mr. Hartwell provided me with a small weekly salary. I wasn't going to get rich on the money but it did provide an opportunity to go out and experience Augusta. The shop closed promptly at seven and after the evening meal I was free until the shop opened again the next morning. This was time I could catch up on reading, get to know Augusta better, or socialize with new friends at one of Augusta's quaint watering holes.

Since arriving in Augusta I made several new friends, all of whom were apprenticed in various trades. Charles Clark migrated upriver from Farmingdale in late 1858 to work for the Kennebec Journal as an apprentice typesetter and printer. Charlie, as his friends knew him, had aspirations of becoming a reporter or writer and exercised his desired profession regularly, often regaling his mates with stories and articles he had written.

John Lewis hailed from Boothbay and, after finishing school, had the choice of an apprenticeship or a career on the deep blue sea. John's father owned one of the coastal freighters that plied its trade along the Kennebec River and as far south as Boston, New York City, Philadelphia, and Baltimore. His education however, provided him with the opportunity to apprentice in one of the shipping offices working the quays off Water Street. John was a master in tracking shipments and with two older brothers to assist his father aboard ship, he was ordained to run the business aspects of the operation.

While Charlie and John were considered friends, I found a true kindred spirit in Jim Ross. We were both suckled on the hardships common to all Maine farmers and decided on other career paths. Unlike me, Jim was the youngest of six and held no hope of inheriting the family farm. Jim's family farm was larger than most by comparison, over two hundred acres in Androscoggin County not far from the city of Monmouth.

The four of us met two or three times a week to relax from the grind of our apprenticeships and, over a couple of pints, talk or argue about books, news, politics, girls, or any subject under the sun. Charlie would bring the group up to date on various stories from the Kennebec Journal or read aloud a story he was working on. When encouraged, John entertained us with tales of adventures aboard his father's ship and the ports of call she made. As my friends talked, I listened with great enthusiasm to the news or to John's adventures, while that old seduction bug once again began gnawing at my soul.

When the legislature was in session, I would tell my friends of the important people who frequented the store and the politics they professed. When things were quiet in the shop, I would ask Mr. Hartwell about the myriad of issues overheard when these politicians stopped in. While Mr. Hartwell harbored some definite Republican oriented opinions about various subjects, he presented both sides of most issues and enabled me to make up my own mind. Like many of the politicians who visited, Mr. Hartwell spoke of his utter distain for the government in Washington in general, and specifically, the Buchanan administration.

Chapter Three

December 1859 – Augusta, Maine

In the election of 1856, Democratic nominee James Buchanan of Pennsylvania defeated President Millard Fillmore of the American Party and John C. Fremont of the newly formed Republican party to become the fifteenth President of the United States. "Old Buck" wasted no time in fanning the fires of the opposition as he tried to bring an end to the slavery question.

In his March 4th, 1857 inaugural speech, Buchanan spoke of slavery as a state issue and not one for the federal government. His political position was to leave the people of the emerging territories free of all outside interference and allow them to decide their own destiny. In his speech, he also argued that the slave code protected the rights of slave owners and alluded to his support of the pending Supreme Court decision in the case of Dred Scott versus Sanford.

If Buchanan's inaugural speech fanned the flames of the slavery question, then the Dred Scott case stoked the fire into an inferno. Dr. John Emerson, an Army surgeon, took Scott and his family, slaves from Missouri, to the free states of Illinois and Wisconsin then back to Missouri. Scott claimed that under the Missouri Compromise, slavery was outlawed in both Illinois and Wisconsin and having spent five years outside of Missouri, he and his family were entitled to be free.

The case worked its way through the judicial system until, in 1857, two days after the inauguration, Chief Justice Roger B. Taney, himself from a slave owning family in Maryland, issued the Court's decision. In a seven to two vote the Supreme Court held that "people of African descent" were not American citizens and, therefore, Scott had no grounds to claim his freedom. Buchanan's inaugural remarks and his strong support of the Supreme Court's decision led his opposition to believe that Taney divulged the decision before it was publicly announced.

Buchanan's southern leanings were also very apparent in his Cabinet selections. In addition to Vice President John C. Breckinridge of Kentucky, four other members of the Cabinet were from the South: Secretary of the Treasury Howell Cobb of Georgia, Secretary of War John B. Floyd of Virginia, Postmaster General Aaron V. Brown of Tennessee, and Secretary of the Interior Jacob Thompson of Mississippi. One of the three Northern Cabinet members, Secretary of the Navy Isaac Toucey of Connecticut, was often viewed as a doughface or Southern sympathizer.

Another doughface was Buchanan's only Supreme Court nominee, Nathan Clifford of Maine. Clifford served as Speaker of the Maine House of Representatives and Maine's Attorney General before finding his way to Washington as a Congressman and in 1846, United States Attorney General. When Buchanan announced Clifford's nomination shortly after the Dred Scott decision, those who labeled Clifford a political hack due to his pro-slavery history met the President's choice with fierce opposition.

Another issue plaguing the Buchanan administration was the economy. The California gold rush of 1848 had ushered in a period of prosperity in the early 1850s, especially as it involved the westward expansion of the railroads. By the mid-1850s this overexpansion of the domestic economy coupled with a declining international economy caused the first worldwide economic crisis. This financial crisis, dubbed the Panic of 1857, spread quickly as over five thousand businesses began to fail. The banking industry was especially hard hit with the failure of over fourteen thousand state banks. The railroad industry also experienced heavy financial declines forcing hundreds of railway workers to be laid off. Hardest hit by these economic failures was the Midwest, the railway and banking hub of the westward migration. The largely agrarian South, with limited industry and no significant rail infrastructure, suffered the least.

The Panic of 1857 led many in the South to believe that the North needed Southern interests to maintain a stabilized economy. For a short period of time, the economic situation temporarily softened threats of secession in the South. By 1859 however, much of the economy in the North and the entire South had recovered with the exception of the banking industry. Opponents of the Buchanan government continued to cite the poor economic policies of the

Democrats in general and the administration in particular as the fundamental reasons for the economic woes that plagued the country.

In 1857, the slavery question in the territories also came to a head, particularly in Kansas. Anti-slave settlers established their government in Topeka while pro-slavers established their government in Lecompton. In October of 1857, Buchanan declared his support for Kansas entering the Union as a pro-slave state and backed the Lecompton government. Pro-slavery advocates then drafted the Lecompton Constitution, a document that included provisions to protect slaveholding in the state and exclude any and all free blacks from its bill of rights.

The government in Topeka rejected the Lecompton Constitution but Buchanan accepted it as the legitimate constitution of the state. After much discussion in Congress, a recommendation was made to allow the people of Kansas to put the Lecompton Constitution to a vote. In January of 1858, the people overwhelmingly rejected the Lecompton Constitution. Buchanan however, insisted Congress approve it and admit Kansas as a slave state. His dogged support alienated many Democrats, including Stephen Douglas, who felt any federal government support for the Lecompton Constitution violated the entire electoral process established by the law of the land.

Douglas' position represented a growing trend among northern Democrats in the late 1850s. It was becoming increasingly difficult for the Democratic Party to sell the concept of slavery as an economic necessity to northern voters. To this sect of the Democratic Party, Buchanan's insistence that Kansas be admitted under the Lecompton Constitution, when a clear majority of Kansas did not approve of it, was a clear indication of how powerful the slavery question had become and how it influenced politicians from local government all the way to the White House. Northern politicians, both Democrat and Republican, recognized that if Kansas came into the Union as a slave state, under the objections from its citizens, the Republican Party would dominate the midterm elections of 1858 and possibly the Presidential election of 1860.

If the actions of the Buchanan Administration lit the fuse for future events, one incident in particular galvanized the Country as the fuse burned. It was a Monday evening in mid-October when Charlie came racing into the tavern where we were meeting.

"There's been an attack on the federal arsenal at Harper's Ferry," he panted trying to catch his breath.

Instantly, he had the attention of the few patrons in the bar. "Where's Harper's Ferry?" asked an onlooker.

"It's in Virginia, west of Washington on the Potomac River," Charlie explained.

"What happened?" John asked.

Charlie went on to report what he knew. "It just came over the wire that late last night a group of about twenty whites and a few blacks seized the federal buildings at Harpers Ferry and cut the telegraph lines. They stopped an eastbound express and held it for a while before releasing the train and its passengers. People on the train reported the leader to be John Brown."

"John Brown of Kansas?" Jim gasped.

"The very same," Charlie replied.

We all knew about the notorious John Brown of Kansas and his rabid abolitionist activities. At this juncture, the raid appeared to be an attempt to provoke a general uprising of slaves in the South. The question yet to be answered was just how successful would Brown be at inciting open rebellion.

On Tuesday night we were once again gathered in the tavern to hear Charlie's update. "This morning the train and its passengers continued on to Baltimore. The train stopped in Monocacy, Maryland and telegraphed the B and O headquarters in Baltimore. The railroad president notified several people including Secretary of War John B. Floyd, and President Buchanan. There is also an unsubstantiated report that Brown has taken hostages, armory employees as well as notables from the surrounding communities. One is believed to be Lewis Washington, grandnephew of General Washington."

A hush fell over the patrons in the tavern at the thought of a relative of George Washington being held hostage by a bunch of radical abolitionists.

"What else happened?" one of the patrons asked.

Charlie continued. "During the day militia groups from both Maryland and Virginia began converging on Harpers Ferry. These militia groups succeeded in recapturing the bridges leading out of town and forcing the rebels into the fire station at the armory. There was a heavy exchange of gunfire between the militia and Brown's men and both sides took casualties. As of last night, the President dispatched Marines from the Washington Navy Yard under the command of Colonel Robert E. Lee. That group should have arrived late last night."

Charlie was bombarded with a thousand questions, most of which he could not answer. Debate about Brown and his raid sparked up throughout the tavern heated by the flow of alcohol that accompanied the discussion.

By Wednesday night, Charlie was a bit of a folk hero in the tavern, sort of the 1859 version of a town crier. His evening news report drew quite a following. Even Mr. Hartwell and a few of the other merchants from State Street showed up along with some of the politicians who were still in town.

"I am quite pleased to report this evening that the Marines from Washington succeeded in storming the fire house and capturing John Brown. We now know that the raiders numbered twenty-two men, ten of whom were killed including two of Brown's sons. Seven others were taken prisoner. The rest escaped and are being hunted around Virginia and Maryland. The Marines and the militia had five deaths and nine wounded. Brown was seriously wounded in the assault and has been taken to a jail in Charles Town, Virginia."

There was general cheering and back slapping in the tavern as more questions were fired at Charlie.

"He's got to be one raving lunatic," one patron remarked.

His drinking companion agreed. "Only a madman would take on the whole South with only twenty-two men."

Over the course of the next six weeks, Charlie regaled the tavern crowd with news of Brown's confinement and trial. Brown was charged with treason against the Commonwealth of Virginia, murder, and inciting an insurrection of slaves against their owners. After a swift trial, Brown was found guilty of all counts and sentenced to hang. On December 2nd, 1859, John Brown went to the gallows and met his maker. Six other raiders followed him over the next few months.

"Only a madman would take on the whole South with only twenty-two men." These words haunted my thoughts in the weeks after Brown's death. Was he truly mad? This was not the first time that slaves or those working to free the slaves had revolted. I recalled Nat Turner's rebellion of 1831. Turner and his followers murdered over fifty whites including women and children in their brief reign of terror. Many Southerners lived in mortal fear of another slave uprising.

In the North and West, opinions about Brown's success were varied. While many tried to continue to portray him as a madman, others started speaking of Brown as a martyr. At the gallows, Brown stated that the "crimes of this land will never be purged away but with blood". Were these the ravings of a lunatic or the prophecy of a martyr? It appeared that the only thing standing in the way of Southern secession now was the 1860 elections. There was still a small glimmer of hope that the nation could be healed.

Chapter Four

Spring 1860 – Augusta, Maine

By the spring of 1860, the radical abolitionist John Brown was dead and President James Buchanan announced he would not seek a second term. Tensions ran high as all eyes, both North and South, became focused on the upcoming elections. Debate around the country covered a multitude of issues, but the two at the forefront of everyone's minds were the preservation of the Union and the rights of individual states. The national stage was set and, on this stage, the final act of my seduction into a soldier's hell was played out.

Charlie Clark received a promotion at the Kennebec Journal. He was now an apprentice copywriter. While happy with his promotion, one night he lamented to the group that he knew more about the states of matrimony and death in Augusta than anyone else. Occasionally, he would get the chance to cover some real news and now he was fortunate enough to work with a veteran reporter who was covering the National Conventions.

The Democratic Party held its convention in Charleston, South Carolina on April 23rd, 1860. Charleston was noted for being the hot bed of pro-slavery in the South, so the galleries at the Convention were filled with pro-slave spectators.

"We all thought Steven Douglas would be the Democratic nominee," Charlie said.

"That was before the Southern Democrats ratified their pro-slavery platform. We all knew Douglas would never accept their arguments," Jim replied.

"That platform will be extremely unpopular anywhere in the North. I don't think the Democrats can carry a single Northern state in the election if they maintain that platform," John stated. "And if the Northern Democrats present an alternative platform, I don't think the South will buy it."

"They didn't," Charlie said. "The North did present an alternative platform today that was adopted by convention vote. As soon as the votes were tallied, the Southern delegations walked out of the Convention."

This was an interesting turn of events. Would Douglas have enough votes to secure the nomination? As it turned out he did not. After the fifty-seventh ballot, Steven Douglas still could not muster the required two-thirds majority to capture the prize. The ruling from the Convention Chairman stated that he needed two-thirds of all delegate votes, not just two-thirds of the members still present. This decision further hampered Douglas' chances. The end result was the Convention elected to adjourn and reconvene six weeks later in Baltimore.

Baltimore appeared to be a rerun of Charleston. Most of the remaining Southern delegates as well as a few from the North and West chose to leave the proceedings. After the voting procedures were amended to reflect a two-thirds majority of the delegates present, not the total number of delegates, Steven Douglas secured the Democratic nomination.

The Republican Party held their Convention in Chicago from May 16th to the 18th. Unlike the Democratic Convention, where delegates from the South walked out of the proceedings, at the Republican Convention there was no delegate representation from nine pro-slave Southern states.

"William Seward has got to be the front runner for the nomination," Jim said.

"True, but I think it's important to note his speeches about a pending war spooked a lot of folks. Even his longtime friend, Horace Greeley, supports Edward Bates," Charlie rebutted.

John countered, "But I think Salmon Chase is also a serious contender at this point."

"Chase has all the personality of that bar stool," Charlie responded. "Even delegates from his own home state of Ohio don't like him."

I listened intently to my friends. They seemed to believe that either Seward followed by Chase or Bates would secure the nomination. None of them, and few others around Augusta, gave much credence the other candidates: Abraham Lincoln, John C. Fremont, Cassius Clay, or Benjamin Wade.

The first ballot did not surprise anyone. Seward led by a wide margin followed by Lincoln, a distant second. By the third round of ballots however, the tables had turned and Abraham Lincoln became the Republican nominee for President.

The Republican Convention also gave the people of Maine something to cheer about. One of our own, Hannibal Hamlin received the nomination for Vice President. Hamlin began his career as a Jacksonian Democrat serving in the Maine House of Representatives. After two terms in the United States House of Representatives, he was elected to the Senate in 1848. Unable to find common ground with the Democratic Party over the issue of slavery, Hamlin switched his allegiance to the newly formed Republican Party in 1856. Elected Governor of Maine in 1857, Hamlin resigned the post to return to the Senate. Now, he was the vice-presidential candidate.

Henry Hartwell took the time to introduce me to Senator Hamlin shortly after my arrival in Augusta. Mr. Hartwell was an avid supporter of Hamlin's, even more so now that he was the vice-presidential nominee.

"That was a smart move by the Republicans to nominate Hamlin," Mr. Hartwell told me.

"How so?" I asked.

"Lincoln is from Illinois so it's good from a regional perspective. He will help bring home the New England states and his stand on the slavery question will bring some of the more moderate anti-slavery Democrats to the Republican side." But would it be enough to bring home the election and, more importantly, would it be enough to preserve the Union?

December 1860 – Augusta, Maine

On November 6th, 1860 Abraham Lincoln was elected as the sixteenth President of the United States in what had to be the most nerve-racking election in history. The race for the Presidency saw candidates from four different political parties competing to run the country. In Maine, as with the rest of the country, the concept of state's rights and preservation of the Union were high on the minds of politicians and voters alike.

The Republican platform centered on allowing slavery to continue in the existing slave states but outlawed it in the territories. No mention of the Dred Scott decision, the Fugitive Slave Act, or personal liberties of slaves under the Constitution was included in their platform. Some Republicans were uncomfortable with a mid-westerner as their candidate while others, particularly abolitionists, were upset at the selection of the more moderate Lincoln as the nominee.

After the debacles in Charleston and Baltimore, the Democratic Party found itself divided into two distinct factions, each supporting its own candidate. The Northern Democratic Party nominated Steven Douglas as their candidate and former Governor Herschel Johnson of Georgia as Vice President. When it came to slavery, Northern Democrats supported the idea of popular sovereignty as was seen in Kansas. Leave the decision of slavery up to the people in the territories and the newly admitted states.

The Southern Democratic Party consisted mainly of the delegates who left the Democratic Convention in Charleston and Baltimore. They convened a convention in Richmond on June 18 and chose the current Vice President, John C. Breckenridge, for President and Senator Joseph Lane of Oregon for Vice President. The Convention adopted the pro-slavery platform rejected at Charleston.

The Constitutional Union Party was formed in December of 1859 from the remnants of the Know Nothing Party, the Whigs, and others who were unwilling to support either the Republican or Democratic Parties. Their May Convention nominated Senator John Bell of Tennessee for President and Senator Edward Everett of Massachusetts for Vice President. The Constitutional Unionists desired to save the Union through universal compromise but under strictest adherence to the Constitution.

The election turned out to be a race between Lincoln and Douglas in the North and Breckenridge and Bell in the South. Even though the United States had no national voting standards, over eighty percent of the 6.9 million Americans eligible to vote did so.

I caught up with my friends at the tavern where Charlie was announcing the latest figures from the election.

"It looks like Lincoln was elected with less than fifty percent of the popular vote. Douglas finished second with Breckenridge a distant third. Lincoln also finished first in the electoral vote with Breckenridge second, Bell third, and Douglas last."

Charlie also reported the Maine vote. Maine had gone solid Republican. Over one hundred thousand Maine men cast their ballots and over sixty-two thousand of them voted for Lincoln, more than twice the number who voted for Douglas. Furthermore, Maine was one of only five states that allowed free blacks to vote if they met state requirements. Maine also voted for one of the founding members of the Republican Party, Israel Washburn, as Governor, rounding out the Republican sweep.

Even with the elections complete, tensions in the Country remained high. While the South threatened secession if Lincoln was elected, Lincoln's advisors suggested this kind of talk was only election trickery. Key military leaders, to include General Winfield Scott, also warned Lincoln of active military preparations all across the South. As 1860 came to a close, the Nation, and even the world, held its collective breath to see if the economy would survive and if the great democratic experiment that was America would be salvaged or torn apart by civil war.

Chapter Five

May 1861 – Augusta, Maine

In his acceptance speech at the Republican Convention in 1858, Abraham Lincoln stated that, "a house divided against itself cannot stand". Before the end of 1860, that house of cards that had been the United States began to fall. On December 20th, South Carolina passed an Ordinance of Secession dissolving its association with the Union proper.

By the time of Lincoln's inauguration on March 4th, 1861, six additional states had joined South Carolina and formed the Confederate States of America. The Confederate States established their government initially in Montgomery, Alabama, drafted a constitution, and elected former Senator Jefferson Davis of Mississippi as President and former Representative Alexander Stephens of Georgia as Vice President.

The now inaugurated President Lincoln chose not to take any offensive actions against the rebellious states. He emphasized that the Confederacy had no legal authority nor was it recognized by any foreign power as a sovereign government. After restating his policy of no slavery in the territories, Lincoln offered these states the opportunity to compromise in order to preserve the Union but his overtures were refused. When it came to those matters military, Lincoln steadfastly refused to turn over any federal properties located in the seven defiant states.

The Nation walked the proverbial tightrope for the next month awaiting a response from the Confederate States of America. On Friday morning April 12th, 1861 the response was heard loud and clear as the South Carolina Militia opened fire on the garrison at Fort Sumter, a federal facility in Charleston harbor. That night, Charlie updated us on the situation at Fort Sumter. "Firing began yesterday morning at 4:30 and has been going on fairly constantly since. There is a Confederate General named Beauregard who is in charge of the militia forces in the city."

"Is there any chance Lincoln will reinforce the garrison?" John asked.

"He said he would resupply them on April 4th but the Confederates said that sending ships to resupply or reinforce would be considered an act of war," Charlie said. "If the fort is not resupplied there is no doubt that it cannot hold for long." Thirty-four hours after the bombardment began, Major Robert Anderson surrendered Fort Sumter.

Over the coming weeks, the firing on and subsequent surrender of Fort Sumter galvanized the North. Gone was any empathy for the South or the southern cause. The people of the North were more determined than ever to sustain the government and preserve the Union. Governors of every state in the North promised troops to aid in putting down the rebellion as patriotic fever ran rampant in every city and town. This abnormal degree of patriotic enthusiasm also sparked a dangerous level of overconfidence throughout the North. Secretary of State William Seward predicted that the conflict would be over in a matter of two months. Others in power thought the South to be weak and incapable of supporting any standing army in the field for a prolonged period.

The same enthusiasm and overconfidence ran high in the South as well. Southerners felt the North would not fight or be reluctant to fight in order to keep Southern goods flowing through Northern markets. On the other hand, some Southerners feared the worst if more states did not join the cause. On April 17th Virginia, a state on the secession fence, voted to break from the Union and join the Confederacy. This action was followed by three more states breaking ranks with the Union: Tennessee, North Carolina, and Arkansas. The die was now cast. The players were now identified. Twenty states remained loyal to the Union. Eleven had joined the Confederacy. Four others; Missouri, Kentucky, Maryland, and Delaware, were considered Border States and provided support for North and South alike.

Shortly after the first of May, we gathered at our favorite haunt to discuss the gravity of the situation. While all Augusta was wrapped in patriotism, not all news was good. John had received a letter from home sent by the friend of the family who owned another coastal freighter.

"My father says that there really isn't a lot of freight to be hauled right now and things are getting even tougher with the blockade the Navy is set to impose."

"I would have thought there would be a lot of business for your family now that war is upon us," Jim said.

"I would have thought so too." John replied. "Unfortunately, a lot of coastal freighters have been hauling southern goods through Maine ports bound for European countries. So, with the blockade, that work is finished. To top it all off, apparently a large number of Navy officers, all southerners, resigned their commissions to serve in the Confederate Navy. The Navy is scrambling to find Captains and crews for the ships they have and leasing other ships to serve as auxiliary vessels for the combat ships. My father was offered a command of one of the auxiliary ships and my two brothers were offered key billets on two other ships. To keep the money coming in, I think they are going to take the jobs."

"I heard that a number of ships were located in southern ports and have become the property of the Confederate states," Jim replied.

"That follows some things I have been hearing as well," Charlie said.

"Like what?"

"In addition to the ships, the previous administration stored a lot of war supplies and equipment, to include artillery pieces, in federal arsenals in the South."

Given the number of southerners and southern sympathizers in the Buchanan Cabinet, I thought this was probably not so farfetched a rumor. "Governor Washburn came into the store today," I said.

"Probably needing something for his heartburn over the current situation," Charlie joked.

"No. Actually he was talking with Mr. Hartwell about the number of troops the President asked Maine for," I replied. "The Governor is asking some of the leading citizens of Augusta and around the state to assist in the recruiting and billeting of these troops before they are sent down to Washington to join the regular Army."

"How many are we going to be required to send?" Charlie asked.

"The Governor said thirteen regiments. Three of the regiments will be the ninety-day militia from around the state but the other ten will be three-year enlistees. One of the regiments will be raised right here in the greater Augusta area."

"When are they going to start recruiting?" Jim asked.

"Soon," he said. "The Governor wants to be ready to turn over these regiments to the Army around the first of June."

My friends fell silent as they pondered this news. Each was contemplating his future here in Augusta and considering the ramifications of enlisting. Since I heard the Governor talking with Mr. Hartwell this afternoon, that seduction bug began gnawing at my soul again, this time with a level of ferocity not experienced before. This was a chance for the adventures I always craved as a child. This was the opportunity to write my name in the family history and have future generations talk of my exploits at family gatherings.

"I also heard the Governor say that the federal government was going to pay one hundred dollars to anyone who enlists and that he was going to ask the Legislature to give land grants as an added bonus."

One hundred dollars was a lot more than any of us would make in our three-year period as apprentices. On top of that, the federal government would pay us thirteen dollars a month for our service. That would go a long way toward realizing my dreams of owning an apothecary someday, maybe not one here in Augusta, but somewhere.

The next morning the Governor of Maine announced the raising of ten regiments of infantry and three regiments of militia. He called on all loyal Maine men to enlist for the pending crisis. One regiment, the Third Regiment Maine Volunteer Infantry would be raised in towns from the Kennebec and Androscoggin River valley regions. Two companies would be raised from the Augusta area, two from Bath, two from Waterville, and one each from Skowhegan, Hallowell, Gardiner, and Winthrop.

That evening, I met up with Charlie to discuss the news before the others arrived.

"What are you going to do?" I asked.

"I've pretty much decided to enlist in the Third Maine," Charlie replied.

"Why?"

"Well, I want to be a reporter or a writer and it's hard to catch a break if all I get to write about is who died or who got married. Maybe the Journal will pay me for something I would write as a soldier or maybe I will keep a diary and write of my exploits after the war is over."

"That sounds like a pretty good idea. Do you think the paper will pay for your stories?"

"I have a meeting with the editor tomorrow to discuss the idea. Who knows, maybe I can be sort of a war correspondent."

"Private Clark's War. It has a nice ring to it."

Charlie laughed. "Yeah, if you're nice to me I will write something about you and some poor girl will take pity on you and you'll finally have a girlfriend."

We both laughed. "What about you?" Charlie asked.

"I talked to Mr. Hartwell today about enlisting. He said he would be sorry to see me go but maybe my experiences with him might serve me to get a position in the medical field. Wouldn't hurt to see another side of medicine."

We continued the small talk until Jim and John arrived. Jim already made up his mind to enlist for the one hundred dollar bounty and the promise of acreage after the war. John didn't really want to go into the Navy. His limited experience at sea with his family would have seen him relegated to being a common seaman and not a position of responsibility like his brothers or father were offered. After a couple of beers, the four agreed to go see the recruiters tomorrow.

I had a hard time sleeping that night. The seduction that I experienced since childhood finally consumed me. Although the Hartwells were very good to me over the past two years, I was growing tired of the daily grind now that war was upon us. This was my chance to escape Maine. This was my chance to be free from the farm and experience the adventures I only dreamed of.

The next morning, I went with my friends and spoke to the Sergeant serving as the recruiting officer for the Third Maine Regiment. In the end, I gave in willingly to the seduction. In the end, I joined I my friends as a member of Company I, Third Regiment Maine Volunteer Infantry. In the end, I cheerfully put my feet on the path to my own personal Soldier's Hell.

Metamorphosis

"It is a comfort to the wretched to have companions in misery."

Christopher Marlowe

Washington D.C. circa 1860

Chapter Six

June 1861 – Augusta, Maine

I was now a soldier. At least they called me a soldier. I certainly didn't look like a soldier nor did I feel like one. I was still wearing the same clothes I wore when we reported in. That seemed so long ago.

After the four of us completed the enlistment process and were assigned to Company I, Third Maine Regiment, we were given until May 21st to put our affairs in order and report to the camp being established on the State Capitol grounds. I took the stage and went back home for a few days to say goodbye. Planting season just finished so I got to spend a good deal of time with my brothers and sisters. Even my half brothers and sisters seemed pleased to see me.

They were all generally concerned about my welfare now that the war had begun. My father was proud of my decision to enlist but sorry to see the opportunity with the Hartwells coming to an end. My stepmother was, as to be expected, once more in the family way. As I boarded the stage to return to Augusta and waved goodbye to the family, I wondered if this was to be the last time I would see them. Were these the typical feelings of a soldier going off to war or were they the precursor of the hell yet to come?

After saying goodbye to the Hartwells, I joined Charlie, Jim, and John and we reported to the camp. We were shown to the Company I area and assigned a billet. The quarters reminded me of a church bell or one of those Indian lodges I had seen in books about the West. The Corporal called it a Sibley tent. The tent was about eighteen feet in diameter and twelve feet high and designed to house up to twelve men. Entrance into the tent was by a flap on one side. At the top of the bell was an opening about a foot wide that served both as a ventilation port and as an exhaust hole for a stovepipe in colder weather.

The grounds of the Capitol were festooned with a sea of these tepee shaped tents as well as other canvas shelters of various sizes designed for a variety of purposes. That afternoon we were taken to one of the larger tents that served as the receiving medical facility. Here all of the new soldiers were given a far more complete medical examination than the cursory glance we received at the recruiting office. In addition to Army doctors, there were several physicians from Augusta assisting in the physical exams.

Everything was checked. Nothing was left to chance. After removing our clothing, we were told to jump, bend over, kick with each leg, and other physical activities. Special attention was paid to our teeth and eyes. Apparently, it was hard to kill the enemy if you couldn't see him or if you couldn't bite the cartridge when loading your weapon to shoot him. After the jumping and thumping of the physical exam, I was pronounced fit for military service. The few soldiers found physically lacking or unfit for service were sent to another area to await reassignment to another noncombat unit or discharge from the Army.

That evening it was announced that there would be elections in the Regiment for key leadership positions. We were introduced to the men who were soliciting our vote to become the officers and non-commissioned officers of the Regiment. There were two gentlemen in the running for the position of Colonel of the Regiment, Oliver Otis Howard of Leeds and Isaac Tucker of Gardiner. While Tucker had the support of many of the soldiers as a generally affable man who enjoyed a good time, Howard was a graduate of West Point and had fought the Seminoles in Florida before turning to the seminary.

"Who are you going to vote for?" Charlie asked.

"I'm leaning toward Howard," I replied.

"In spite of his religious tones and temperance views?"

"I'll take a little religion and a little temperance in favor of someone who actually seems to know what he is doing. Howard has the experience and the expertise of being a soldier and leading men. It's very clear to me that most people in this Regiment view this election as a popularity contest rather than casting their vote for someone who is the most qualified to keep them alive in the coming months."

"I can't argue with that logic," Jim said. "Who do you like for Company Commander?"

"I kind of like Lakeman over Quinby," John replied. "He talks like a soldier and seems to be someone that could be a good leader when the shooting starts."

"That Quinby talks too much like a lawyer," Charlie said. "I don't know how far I would be willing to follow him."

"Denola Witman seems like a reasonable man," Jim said. "I think he would be a good Second Lieutenant."

"Here! Here!" John cried. "And a fellow in good standing from Augusta."

"Does it bother you that Lakeman is from Massachusetts?"

"No," John replied. "It wasn't that long ago we were all from Massachusetts."

"True, True," we all laughed.

When the votes were tallied the next morning, Oliver Otis Howard was elected to lead the Third Maine. It didn't hurt his candidacy that Governor Isaac Washburn and Speaker of the Maine House of Representatives James G. Blaine made impassioned testimonials on Howard's behalf. Isaac Tucker stayed with the Regiment as a Lieutenant Colonel and second in command under Colonel Howard. Captain Henry G. Staples, the commander of Company A, the Bath City Grays, was promoted to Major and assigned duties on the Regimental staff.

Moses B. Lakeman was elected as the Company Commander of Company I and appointed a Captain. Albus R. Quinby remained with the Company as the First Lieutenant. Denola Witman received enough votes to be chosen as the Second Lieutenant. As far as non-commissioned officers were concerned, Henry Lyon of Readfield was elected as a Sergeant to serve as our squad leader. While Lyon cut an impressive figure both in size and strength, his good-natured attitude and pleasant disposition quickly endeared him to the squad. Like a lot of the soldiers in the Regiment, Lyon had come from the lumber camps attaining the position of crew leader and foreman before enlisting.

All in all, we didn't fare to badly in the election. Colonel Howard seemed like a good choice, as did Captain Lakeman and Sergeant Lyons. Even Major Staples was impressive. The Bath City Grays were a militia unit that had enlisted almost to a man. Staples was their commander and, while he may not have seen combat, he was very familiar with the drill and training required to get the Regiment up to a satisfactory level of competence.

Colonel Howard's vow to train the Regiment to fighting shape began that very afternoon. The Regiment was issued Springfield Model 1822 percussion cap muskets with the promise that their weapons would be upgraded once they were accepted into active service with the U.S. Army. The Model 1822 was a smooth bore .69 caliber musket that weighs about nine pounds. The musket had an overall length of fifty-eight inches with a **forty-two-inch** barrel. For a musket, this was a very formidable weapon. The Model 1822 had a longer barrel than my father's old .36 caliber musket and probably a much better range. The .69 caliber ball the Model 1822 fired was almost twice as large as the one my father's musket shot and definitely a whole lot more deadly. I was really looking forward to firing that weapon.

Unfortunately, the chance to fire the musket did not come. Besides having to keep the weapon clean and free of rust, the Model 1822's primary purpose was to serve as a prop in teaching the new soldiers the art of close order drill. For the few remaining days we had in Augusta, military instruction began each morning after the morning meal and continued until midday. After a break for the noon meal, instruction began anew and lasted till about 5:00 pm when the trainees were finished for the day. Evenings were spent cleaning ourselves, our equipment, our muskets, and preparing for the next day's activities.

After the evening meal, the officers and non-commissioned officers of the Regiment gathered for classes under the tutelage of Sergeant William Burt, on loan from the Army and assigned as the Regimental Drill Master. Mr. Frank Pierce, a now retired graduate of the Vermont Military School at Norwich, assisted Sergeant Burt in his duties.

Once the Regiment was accepted into federal service, Sergeant Burt was promoted Captain and remained on the staff as Regimental Adjutant. After receiving instruction from Sergeant Burt and Mr. Pierce, the noncommissioned officers assumed responsibility for providing that instruction to their respective squads under the watchful eyes of the company officers. As new soldiers, we were first taught the rudiments of basic close order drill with a promise of more intense training to follow when the Regiment arrived in Washington.

When we had achieved a fundamental grasp of the basics of drill without weapons, the training was enhanced to include the Model 1822. Learning the drill movements, with and without weapons, as well as the other aspects of soldering to be mastered was strenuous work and all of us were pretty much spent by the end of the training day.

I certainly appreciated the necessity of the training and the drill. Give a thousand men Model 1822 muskets and you have a mob of a thousand armed men. Teach them how to use the weapon, how to move in an organized fashion, and how to look out for one another and you have the beginnings of a real army. I read of the discipline of real armies. Soldiers like the Spartans under Leonidas, the Romans under Caesar, or the Old Guard of Napoleon achieved a high level of discipline from drill, training, and a brotherhood with their fellow soldiers.

By the end of May, the Regiment's organizational structure was formally established and what little training that was conducted progressed to a point where the Third Regiment Maine Volunteer Infantry was deemed ready for active service. The time spent here at the State Capitol grounds encampment seemed somewhat surreal. We had no uniforms or ammunition for our muskets.

On top of that, the good citizens of Maine augmented our accommodations. Each soldier got a straw mattress to sleep on, the Sibley tents were erected with wooden plank floors to keep us out of the mud, and the messing facilities came equipped with wooden tables and chairs. Even the food was augmented by baked goods and sweets donated by local citizens and businesses. Augusta citizens routinely turned out to watch the day's activities and delighted in the colorful language of some of the Sergeants. Wives, girlfriends, and others waved at loved ones when they were spotted. It was like learning to be a soldier in a giant fishbowl.

On June 4th, 1861, the Regiment was officially mustered into the United States Army in a ceremony held on the Capitol grounds. Governor Washburn and other dignitaries from the State Legislature and the greater Augusta community attended the ceremony. As part of the event, the men of the Third Maine were sworn into federal service for a period of three years.

With the formality of the swearing in complete, Governor Washburn presented the Regiment with its battle flags. The national ensign was about six feet square with thirteen horizontal red and white stripes. A blue field took up the left corner of the flag and contained thirty-four embroidered white stars; one for each state in the Union including those states now part of the Confederacy. Across the center red stripe was embroidered the regimental designation in silver embroidery thread. It was truly a magnificent sight.

The Regimental flag was also about six feet square but dark blue and fringed with yellow silk, representing the flag of an infantry unit. In the center of the flag was the coat of arms of the United States with a red scroll beneath it and the regimental designation embroidered on the scroll. As the flags were presented, and the color guard accepted them, I felt a growing sense of pride. These flags would be carried wherever the Regiment was assigned and be a part of the Regiment in battle.

I now understand the honor that must have been felt by the Roman Legions as the Emperor presented them their eagles or the pride of the Old Guard under Napoleon carrying their beloved eagle in the cold, hard winter outside Moscow. The flags, just like the eagles, were symbols of our country and this Regiment. They were something that must not be disgraced. They were something to be protected at all costs.

The following day, the Regiment marched through the City to the train yards and boarded the train for Washington. All along our route of march, men and women cheered, children waved, and a band played giving the departure with a real sense of patriotic fever. We were leaving Maine for war. But before the hell of war, we were being sent to a camp of instruction in Washington. The hell of war had to wait for the agony of the camp of instruction.

Chapter Seven

June 1861 - Meridian Hill, Washington D.C.

The train ride to Washington was a mix of anticipation and apprehension. For me, it was the excitement of traveling to places only read about. I watched the landscape of central Maine give way to the coastal plain of Massachusetts and finally into the thriving City of Boston. After a break for food and a locomotive change, the train continued its journey through Rhode Island and Connecticut. The second leg of the adventure culminated as the train pulled into New York City.

The cars of the train were overcrowded and uncomfortable to say the least. While many of the soldiers in the Regiment began the journey in a boisterous, almost jovial mood, for most, as the miles from Maine increased, so too did their levels of anxiety and apprehension. By the time we had arrived in New York, the ranks fell quiet and a general feeling of depression overtook many of the men.

"We'll be out of New York soon," Charlie said. "But the real fun won't start until we reach Baltimore."

"How so?" I asked.

"Apparently when one of the Massachusetts regiments were being transported to Washington early on, the southern sympathizers in Baltimore took exception to them using their rail yard."

"How bad?"

"The Massachusetts regiment had four soldiers killed and on the anniversary of Lexington and Concord. Massachusetts men took the first shots of the American Revolution, I guess it's only fitting they take the first shots in this war as well."

Our passage from New York to Washington was uneventful. The locomotive change occurred far enough outside the City of Baltimore proper to dissuade any potential troubles. The train pulled into Washington on the evening of June 7th and the Regiment disembarked to begin its training on Meridian Hill.

The first thing I noticed about Washington, aside from the overwhelming heat and humidity, was the smell. Now that war was upon it, Washington was a city that never slept. Business was conducted at all hours of the day and night. Civilians came and went regardless of the time, and new Army units were constantly arriving from all over the North. There was a definite threat directed at Washington from both Maryland's southern sympathizers and actual Confederate forces across the Potomac in Virginia. One of the first orders of business for the Army was to expand the perimeter into Virginia and Maryland to safeguard the Nation's Capital. Militias from all over the North poured into the city as did newly formed Army units like Third Maine.

The level of activity and large number of troops in the city contributed to the heavy odor of burnt coal oil and sweat that hovered in the air like a blanket. This foul aroma was further compounded by the oppressive heat and crushing humidity that seemingly formed a continuous dome-shaped grey cloud that engulfed the entire Capitol region. I really yearned for the clean crisp smell of the Maine woods or the pleasant sea breezes that wafted across the coastal areas.

During his Presidency, Thomas Jefferson planted a geodetic marker on Georgetown Heights directly north of the White House to mark its exact longitudinal position. This longitudinal demarcation and marker became known as the White House Meridian. After the War of 1812, one of America's earliest naval heroes, Commodore David Porter, the former commanding officer of the USS Constitution "Old Ironsides", purchased the land and built his estate. Porter called the property Meridian Hill. At the start of the current hostilities, the Army assumed control of the property as well as that of neighboring Columbian College and established Camp Cameron, a camp of instruction for newly formed regiments coming into Washington. The Camp was named after President Lincoln's Secretary of War, Simon Cameron and considered part of the defenses of the Washington area. Camp Cameron was staffed with a training cadre from various units of the Army and a hastily implemented course of instruction was developed to train the incoming soldiers for the rigors of combat that lay ahead.

Saturday in the Army was usually the day of the week set aside for cleaning quarters and maintaining equipment. For the Third Maine

Regiment, Saturday, June 8th, was the day of uniform and equipment issue.

After the morning meal, the Regiment marched, by company, to the Quartermaster's supply point for issue of their US Army uniforms and equipment. After we were measured, a host of uniforms and accessories were tossed at us: coats, trousers, hats, shirts, drawers, and a pair of shoes they called Jefferson boots. The two uniform jackets I received, called sack coats, were of single-breasted design, dark blue with a single row of four brass buttons down the front. I was also issued three sets of dark blue "stove pipe" trousers designed to be worn loosely without any pleats. The trousers had suspender buttons but no suspenders were issued. Instead, we received a narrow black belt to wear with the trousers.

Aside from these articles of uniform clothing, I received something called a forage cap. The forage cap had a very stiff horizontal visor with a sharp, sloping top and could be fitted with the accompanying oilcloth cover for inclement weather. There were also three pullover type flannel shirts, three "long john" flannel drawers to be worn as undergarments, four pairs of woolen socks, and a black leather stock designed to keep the head erect.

The Jefferson boots, or "bootees" as they were called, were low cut brogan style footwear made of heavy leather with the rough side of the leather on the outside of the shoe. The bootees had a squared toe box with a leather sole and heel that was held on the foot by rawhide laces. We were also issued a wooden locker box with hasp to store any articles of clothing we did not need. This locker box would accompany the baggage train when the Regiment was on the move. Other items of uniform wear more useful in winter would be issued later in the fall when the Regiment went into winter quarters.

After depositing our uniforms back in quarters, Company I marched back to the Depot Armory section of the Quartermaster's supply point to turn in our Springfield Model 1822 muskets and draw Lorenz rifles. The Lorenz rifle was developed by Austrian Joseph Lorenz and came into production in 1854. Designed as a medium range weapon, the Lorenz rifle had an overall length of fifty-two inches with a thirty-seven- and one-half inch barrel. Its weight of nine- and one-half pounds made it comparable to the Springfield Model 1822. The Lorenz fired a .54 caliber projectile through a barrel with four-groove rifling that increased the effective range of the weapon to about two hundred and fifty yards. The rifle came with either a block style or a flip up rear sight. When equipped with the flip up rear sight, the rifle had a maximum firing range of well over seven hundred yards.

Along with the weapon, each of us received a sling, a wicked looking 18.75-inch bayonet, and a tompion. The tompion was a two-inch long wooden cylinder slightly smaller than the bore diameter with a lead plate on the top end and three or four layers of tallow cloth on the bottom. The tompion's primary purpose was to seal the muzzle end of the weapon and prevent moisture or dust from fouling the barrel. Along with these items we received a combination tool, a mirrored metal disk, as well as an iron wiper and worm. The combination tool was a triangular shaped device with a ramrod pull pin, a nipple wrench, and a screwdriver. Additionally, there was a cleaning kit with two cloth rags; one with tallow for metal parts and one with oil for the stock. The kit also included a longer flannel rag that was enhanced with tallow for cleaning the bore, a small rifle brush, some feathers, and a bottle of oil. The combination tool and the cleaning kit proved to be very handy items for cleaning and maintaining such a fine weapon.

The final stop at the supply point was the issuing station for all the necessary military equipment that we required. The first items I received were a black leather waist belt, a pouch for carrying percussion caps, and a scabbard for the bayonet. The belt was adorned with a brass buckle and had an embossed US on the front. The supply clerk said the pouch went on the right side of the belt and the bayonet scabbard on the left. The bayonet scabbard was held on the belt by something the clerk called a frog.

Next, I received a cartridge box and sling to hold the ammunition for the Lorenz rifle. The cartridge box was referred to as "forty dead men", indicating the number of rounds the box held or the number of casualties the rounds were intended to inflict. The sling was black leather with an eagle insignia on the brass buckle. Then came something called a haversack. This was used to carry our daily rations. The clerk referred to the haversack as the bread bag. It was about a foot square with a flap style opening at the top. With the haversack came a set of eating utensils and a tin plate and cup. There was also a canteen with cover and strap. The canteen was constructed of two iron and tin sides soldered together. On the top was a pewter or tin spout with stopper.

The last item issued was a knapsack to carry all of our extra clothing and personal effects and a blanket stamped with a large US on one side. The clerk at the Quartermaster's supply point indicated that additional equipment items would be issued later in the fall to those of us still alive to need them.

After all the equipment and clothing was issued, the Regiment spent the remainder of Saturday and all of Sunday marking and stowing the gear in accordance with Army regulations. All of our clothing was marked in very specific locations with the company letter and our number. All of the equipment, except for the rifle, was also marked with the designation of the regiment, the company letter, and our number. Any equipment requiring painting, or having the existing paint touched up, was painted. All leather accessories were blackened. Any other accouterments that required cleaning or whitening were seen to as well.

At Camp Cameron, as on the Capitol grounds in Augusta, the Regiment was housed in Sibley tents. The only difference was the Camp Cameron tents were laid out in a more prescribed manner than back home. The troop tents opened toward the area of the sinks or latrines and fronted the kitchens and mess facilities. Behind the kitchens were the noncommissioned officer tents, the sutler's store, and the guard mount tent. The Company officer's tents came next, then the Regimental officer's tents, the baggage train and finally, the officer's sinks.

Although designed for twelve soldiers, our Sibley tents were configured for eight with wooden floors, an arms rack, and eight bunks. The individual soldier's name was mounted on the bunk, the rifle stored in the arms rack, and all clothing and equipment set up in the prescribed manner. Weekly, generally on Saturday or Sunday, the floors of the tents were dry rubbed and swept, the bunks and bedding cleaned and aired, and the rifles and equipment cleaned.

With all of the equipment cleaned and marked, the uniforms marked and put away, and the tent put into some semblance of order, there was time for personal hygiene. We were expected to bathe once or twice a week in garrison. Hands and faces were to be washed daily. Feet were to be cleaned and socks changed at least twice a week. Hair was to be kept short and neat and those with beards were expected to keep them trimmed.

There were three roll calls daily, after reveille (usually at 5:30), at retreat (at sunset), and at tattoo (at 9:00 in the evening). The squad leaders reported all roll calls to the Company First Sergeant.

After the evening meal, if there was no training to be conducted, we were occasionally allowed access to the sutler's store. Sutlers have been an integral part of American military culture in every war and campaign since the French and Indian War. The sutler frequently sold his wares out of the back of wagon or out of a tent when the Army was on the move or in remote outposts. The sutler's wagon generally travelled with the Army's baggage and was often found in close proximity to the front lines. In garrison situations, like at Camp Cameron, the sutlers constructed a store within the confines of the camp. The sutler's store required the permission of the camp commander and was subject to his regulations. If the camp commander was mindful of the sutler's business, prices were generally fair and reasonable. Often times however, the camp commander's attention was directed elsewhere allowing the sutler a bit more latitude in his pricing.

For those who needed it, a drink of "oh-be-joyful" or "oil of gladness" could be found for some hard cash money or sutler's tokens. Sutlers were often the sole source for other, non-military items and goods like coffee, tobacco, and sugar. Depending on the morality of the camp commander, at some sutler's establishments gambling and "horizontal refreshments" were available to supplement the consumption of alcohol.

It had been a whirlwind weekend. I now had a uniform that almost fit, a lot of equipment, and a beautiful rifle, complete with a wicked "pig sticker", as I heard one soldier describe the bayonet. As I lay in my bunk, the tattoo roll call was just conducted and the camp was awaited the call for lights out. Tomorrow was the start of training. Tomorrow we would meet Sergeant Major Liam O'Toole and his drillmasters. Up until tonight, life in the Regiment was a transition from civilian life to the military. Tomorrow the real metamorphosis from civilian to soldier would begin.

Chapter Eight

June 1861 - Meridian Hill, Washington D.C.

"Stand at Attention!"

"My name is Sergeant Major O'Toole, Regular Army, and it is my responsibility to turn you bunch of Sunday soldiers into fighting men that can go out and face the enemy. You can forget everything you ever learned about anything. If these Sergeants and I don't teach it to you, you don't need to know it. Make no bones about it. Your souls may belong to God but your asses belong to the United States Army."

On Monday morning, after that delightful welcome, the Third Maine Regiment officially began the school of instruction. From sunup to sundown and beyond, the order of the day seemed to be drill, drill, and more drill.

Drill, or what there was of it, on the Capitol grounds in Augusta usually took on an air of cheerful indifference on the part of a majority of Third Maine soldiers. True, there were some who really didn't know their left from their right. There were also a few others who sought comic relief from over exaggerating the prescribed movements or intentionally fouling up. It was difficult to take any of it seriously, since the noncommissioned officers teaching the drill had only learned it themselves the night before.

Things were different at Camp Cameron. The Regiment was finally in the hands of trained professionals. These were men who knew the manual inside and out and had trained thousands of other soldiers in the art of war as it pertained to the infantryman. The Third Maine was the civilian mound of clay to be molded and fired into a regiment of infantry by the drillmasters and this metamorphosis was accomplished under the watchful eyes of Sergeant Major O'Toole, Regular Army.

Like many Irish immigrants of the 1840's, Sergeant Major Liam O'Toole found a home in the Army. He served with distinction in the Mexican War and participated in the battles for Chapultepec and

Mexico City. After the war, he remained in the Army serving in units assigned to pacification of the Native American population. Most of the Sergeants assigned to his cadre were also veterans of the Indian Wars, on loan from their respective units to train up new soldiers before returning to the fight themselves.

The officers and noncommissioned officers continued to attend evening tactics and drill sessions and oversaw or participated in the daily training under the all-seeing eyes of the Sergeant Major and his horsemen of the Apocalypse. No one was exempt from corrective actions. Drillmasters hovered around the drilling formations like birds of prey around a cadaver, quick to pounce on an unsuspecting soldier who wasn't taking the lessons as seriously as the drillmaster thought he should. The cheerful attitude of some soldiers had been replaced by a genuine concern about being the drillmaster's next victim. The indifference, while harder to modify, began to change as we now realize there were consequences for our lack of concern and those consequences were administered by professional soldiers. Even those who didn't know left from right receive specialized instruction to assist their understanding.

"This is your hayfoot!" screamed the drillmaster at the bewildered soldier as he stomped hard on his left foot.

"And this is your strawfoot!" as he stomped on his right foot.

"All of you repeat after me to help this kid glove boy understand!"

"Forward March!"

"Hayfoot, strawfoot, hayfoot!"

Even the officers and noncommissioned officers were not exempt from the wrath of the Sergeant Major and his drillmasters. They too were corrected in terms that would make a parish priest blush. In spite of his Christian demeanor, any and all complaints registered with Colonel Howard generally fell on deaf ears.

"Look around you, you bunch of slovenly soldiers," Sergeant Major O'Toole screamed. "I'm going to teach you to think as one man; to move as one man; and to shoot as one man. Look around! These are the only people on God's earth you can depend on."

The first week of training began with days of drill by squad: first without weapons and then with them. For men not used to Washington weather, the combination of heat, humidity, heavy dark uniforms that seemed to soak in sunlight, and a nine-pound rifle were more than some of us could bear. Even the farmers and lumberjacks, who were accustomed to hard work or not adverse to it, had a difficult time with the heat and humidity. Those who did not pass out from the heat, collapsed when the drillmaster called for a break. No one had any problems sleeping in those early days.

Toward the end of the first week, basic drill was enhanced by the inclusion of marksmanship and bayonet training. The initial portion of the marksmanship training consisted of learning to load and fire the rifle in a drill the Army called "Load in Nine Times".

After a couple of hours of pretending to load and fire our rifles, I started to believe that there were three ways to teach marksmanship: the right way, the wrong way, and the Army way. The Army way wasn't necessarily the right way or the wrong way, it was the way that best provided a standardized approach to loading and firing a rifle for all soldiers. Some soldiers, like me, had extensive experience in loading and firing weapons, while others, like John, never fired a rifle or musket before.

After we became proficient with the mechanics of loading in nine times, loading in four times was introduced. More often than not on the battlefield a soldier was required to load and fire quickly but in a controlled manner. Often, some of the steps of loading in nine times took on individual or situation-based modifications. Loading in four times forced us to focus on specific steps of the process that required the most regularity and attention.

After we developed some experience with load in four times, the instructor moved to loading at will. Loading at will follows the format of load in four times but without any outside assistance to designate any specific steps of the loading sequence. The goal of this drill was to develop the capability to load and fire a minimum of three well-aimed rounds per minute.

In addition to extensive time spent learning loading in nine times, loading in four times, and loading at will, our squad learned the procedures for loading and firing from both the kneeling and prone positions. Next came the procedures for volley firing by squads. In this drill, the squad aimed twenty plus rifles at the enemy and discharged their .54 caliber rifle bullets in a single volley. The squad then reloaded and prepared to fire again, on command, in a single volley. Volley fire by squad focused on those situations where the enemy was to the direct front as well as when the enemy was on the left or right oblique.

With the squad arranged in two ranks, next came the concept of firing by file. Both the front and rear rank fired when the squad leader gave the command "Commence Fire" and continued loading and firing at will until the command was given to cease fire.

If more controlled firing was required, the squad leader could command, "Fire by Rank". In this drill, the rear rank was given the command to aim, fire, and reload. The front rank was then given the same commands and the ranks would alternate firing until the command to cease fire was given.

After hours of loading and firing drills to simulate the actual firing of the rifle and the endless practice of sighting the rifle at various known distances, the time finally arrived for us to go to the makeshift rifle range and fire real rounds through our weapons.

"Today we will be firing six soldiers at a time in each relay. To make sure everyone is loading properly, you will begin by loading in nine times. Your squad leader will call out the times and give the command to aim and fire. Let's have the first six."

I was in the second set of six and waited anxiously. Each soldier would fire five rounds at a target with a black circle the instructor called a "bullseye" painted in the center. I watched the proceedings as the first group fired. Between rounds an armory corporal came to each soldier and made any necessary adjustments to their rear sights. After two rounds, the instructor told Sergeant Lyon to switch to loading in four times and for the final round, loading at will.

"Let's have the next six," Sergeant Lyon called. I moved up to the designated firing point and prepared to begin the loading process.

"Make Ready!"

"Load!"

Grasp the rifle with the left hand and bring it vertically to the center of the body. The right hand grabs the upper band of the rifle and places the butt of the weapon between the feet, barrel to the front. Hold the rifle three inches from the body with the left hand near the muzzle while the right hand moves to the cartridge box.

"Handle Cartridge!"

Reach into the cartridge box and remove one cartridge and hold it between the thumb and first two fingers. Place the end of the cartridge between the teeth.

"Tear Cartridge!"

Tear the paper wrapper open with the teeth and hold the cartridge in front of the rifle near the muzzle.

"Charge Cartridge!"

Empty the powder into the barrel, disengage the bullet from the paper, insert it into the bore, and press it down with the thumb. Seize the head of the rammer with the right hand.

"Draw Rammer!"

Draw the rammer half way out of its pipe with the right hand. Slide the right hand down the rammer to the muzzle and pull the rammer clear of the pipe. Rotate the rammer 180 degrees and place the small end on the top of the projectile.

"Ram Cartridge!"

Steady the rammer with the thumb of the left hand and with the right hand push the bullet down the bore as far as it will go.

"Return Rammer!"

With the bullet seated, withdraw the rammer halfway with the right hand and steady it with the left thumb. Slide the right hand down the rammer to the muzzle and remove it from the bore. Rotate the rammer back to its original position and install it into the pipe with the right hand.

"Prime!"

With the left hand raise the rifle. Grasp the small of the stock with the right hand. Turn half right, moving the rifle to the right side of the body. With the right thumb pull the hammer to the half-cocked position. Take a percussion cap from the pouch and place in on the nipple and press it down onto the nipple with the thumb.

"Shoulder Arms!"

Bring the now loaded rifle to the right shoulder while moving the right foot back into position so the body is facing front.

With the loading in nine times complete, Sergeant Lyon commanded "Ready!"

Raise the rifle slightly with the right hand and make a half facing movement to the right. Bring the rifle down with both hands, pulling the hammer to the cocked position with the right thumb.

"Aim!"

Raise the rifle and support the butt against the right shoulder. Sight down the notch of the rear sight, align the front sight in the notch, and place the sights on the target.

"Fire!"

Keep the sights aligned on the target and press the finger against the trigger.

The rifle barked and recoiled but I held the position until Sergeant Lyon was satisfied all six soldiers had fired. The Sergeant then commanded, "Recover". I withdrew my finger from the trigger and lowered the weapon to the ready position. I saw that the bullet hit the target just to the left of the black circle.

Sergeant Lyon repeated the load in nine time and the firing commands. I noted that the second round struck the target in close proximity to the first, just left of the black circle. The armory corporal asked me a couple of questions about my aim point and then, taking a small brass hammer from his bag, tapped on the rear sight. The Corporal told me to aim at the same location as the first two shots.

For the third round Sergeant Lyon had the relay execute the loading procedures for load in four. When the command to fire was given, I was pleased to see the bullet had struck the target in the black circle but again to the left of where I aimed. Once again, the armory corporal asked about my aiming point and made a small adjustment to the rear sight.

The fourth round struck the target exactly where I aimed, almost dead center of the black circle. My fifth shot was also in the black circle in the same location as the fourth. The armory corporal said the sights were dead on and no further adjustment was necessary.

"That's some seriously good shooting soldier."

I turned to see Captain Lakeman observing the live fire exercise. "Thank you, Sir," I replied.

"Make sure his name gets on the list, Sergeant Lyon," the Captain said.

"Yes, Sir," Sergeant Lyon responded and gave me a nod and a smile.

After the marksmanship exercise concluded, I sought out Sergeant Lyon for an explanation of what the Captain meant by having my name added to the "list".

"The Captain is planning on creating a group of our better marksman and outfitting them with a Lorenz rifle with the flip up rear sight. He feels with that a rifle with a flip sight in the hands of a skilled marksman; well, let's just say we'll be able to reach out and touch the enemy long before he can bring any of his rifles to bear on us. Seems like a good way to thin their ranks a bit or maybe reduce their officer corps by a few. Don't you agree?"

I couldn't disagree with the concept and felt somewhat relieved that I had actually done something positive that was noticed. "Yes, I do. And thank you Sergeant."

"I'll let you know when we will be exchanging that rifle for another and when you can fire the new one with the flip sights. Wouldn't hurt to start getting used to it before we actually get into action," Sergeant Lyon responded.

The rest of that day and most of the next was spent learning the fundamentals of bayonet training. This was the final component of our individual soldier training and, without question, the most arduous. Learning the various thrusts, jabs, parries, and butt strokes turned into some seriously hard work. When attached to the Lorenz rifle, the eighteen-inch bayonet was a formidable weapon in the hands of someone who knew how to use it. There was also the psychological factor of seeing your enemy coming with bayonets fixed and gleaming in the sun.

"When I have that bayonet on the rifle it seems like I could stand in Augusta and stab someone in Portland without striding very far," Charlie stated.

"I agree," replied John. "But after eight hours of stabbing at the air or jabbing at straw bales, I don't think I can move my arms."

"I only hope to God that I never have to actually kill someone with a bayonet," Jim stated. "That is killing up close and personal."

"But it sure is a handy tool when it comes to cooking dinner," Charlie joked. "You don't ever have to get close to the fire."

We all laughed the laugh of men too tired and sore to actually laugh. Jim did have a point about killing up close and personal. I had just been told I would be assigned a new rifle that could kill someone out to seven hundred yards and now, when I needed to, I could kill someone face to face.

Chapter Nine

July 1861 - Meridian Hill, Washington D.C.

"On the right, by file, into line"
"March"
With the individual soldier and squad training programs complete, the focus of training turned to the drill movements needed by a company to face the enemy in battle. I was beginning to understand that these movements by the squad or the company are predetermined by the disposition of the squad or company in relation to the direction of the enemy. The goal for either the squad or the squad as part of the company was to assume a line formation, or "line of battle", facing directly at the enemy. Union Army lines of battle called for two lines of soldiers standing shoulder-to-shoulder facing the enemy. These lines were called ranks and the officers and non-commissioned officers of the company went to great lengths to keep the ranks aligned. The goal of this aspect of the training program was to maneuver the company into a line of battle and then move that line of battle to the front, the flanks, the oblique, and even to the rear. All of this was done at quickstep and, eventually, at the double quick.

Lines of battle were rooted in the phalanx formations of the Roman Army and the shield walls of the Middle Ages. Gustavus Adolphus of Sweden and Maurice of Nassau, Prince of Orange pioneered the current concept of line formations in the seventeenth century. Their lines of battle varied from two to five ranks with three ranks being the most commonly used formation. Lines of battle were the principal formation of the American Revolution and the Napoleonic Wars, but it was the British Army who adopted two rank line of battle formations with great success against Napoleon. This two-rank line of battle became the standard instituted by the United States Army as part of its tactical training.

Line of battle formations provided the best configuration for maximizing a unit's firepower. Both ranks could fire simultaneously with the soldiers of the rear rank firing between the soldiers of the front rank. However, a line of battle was not well suited to maneuver, as movement in line formation was considerably slow and alignment proved to be difficult especially in uneven or wooded terrain.

With the advent of rifled weapons and their increased ranges, casualty rates for units attacking in line formation were significant, especially for a force attacking with only musket type weapons. Even a cavalry force attacking a line formation where the soldiers of the line were armed with rifled weapons was wholly ineffective unless the charge achieves the element of surprise or occurs on the flanks of the line.

"Company - Right Face"

"Forward"

"March"

When the company was in the line of battle formation it could very quickly maneuver to meet a new enemy threat by marching to the flank. In this formation, the company executes a facing movement and reforms in columns of four soldiers abreast, elbow to elbow. The columns then march off, changes direction as necessary, and quickly returns to a company line of battle in a location more advantageous to meet the new enemy threat.

The column formation was also the most common configuration for rapid movement of a unit not in direct contact with the enemy. In a column formation, a squad or squad operating as part of a company was divided into two files, with one soldier directly behind the soldier in front of him. Movement was quick and, with training, the transition to a line of battle became second nature to the squad members.

There was also a new echelon of command introduced during the company training: the platoon. Up to now the soldiers of Company I were aligned as squads operating as part of the company. Under the platoon concept, two squads constituted a platoon, each commanded by one of the two Lieutenants of the company. There were specific drill movements that enable the company to divide into its two platoons in platoon line of battle formation or in column formation and then quickly reform a company line of battle facing another direction or in another location.

As part of our maneuvers, Company I simulated contact with the enemy by executing various fire commands. Since we were now proficient at loading in nine times, these drills focused on loading in four times and loading at will. There was training in firing by company, firing by platoon, firing by files, firing by ranks, and even firing by the rear rank. When conducting firing by the rear rank, the entire company executed an about face and directed their rifles to the area behind them. After practicing firing to the rear a few times, I realized exactly how terrifying it would be to have the enemy at the direct front of the company and at their rear. I hoped to never have to put this drill into actual practice.

The final phase of training at Camp Cameron was devoted to the tactics and techniques employed by the regiment or a portion of the regiment operating independently. Key to maneuvering the regiment was the location of the colors and the company identified as the color company. The color company served as the base company for all formations and the other companies of the regiment took position based on the formation required and their relationship to the color company.

As with the maneuver of squads and companies, all movements of the regiment were based on the concepts of line of battle and column formations. The goal of these maneuvers was to place the regimental line of battle squarely in the direction of the enemy with the preponderance of firepower directed at the enemy.

Along with the maneuver aspects of regimental drill were the usual firing exercises that accompanied maneuver. In addition to firing at will, firing by files, and firing by rank, the regimental commander could designate firing by company, firing by wing, or firing by the rear rank.

When commanded to fire by company, the odd numbered companies in the line of battle aimed, fired, and reloaded on the commands of their respective company commanders. This action was followed by the even numbered companies and continued until the cease fire order was given.

When the command to fire by wing was given, all of the companies either on the left or right side or wing of the colors fired on the command of the regimental commander. The regimental commander then directed that wing to reload while the other wing of the regiment fired. The colonel then alternated sides or wings until the command to cease fire was given.

Also new in the regimental tactics portion of the training was the introduction of skirmishers as part of the overall regimental movement. Skirmishers served as the advanced guard, flank guard, or rear guard and screen the regiment from the enemy or provided early warning of enemy locations or advances. Skirmishers had the responsibility of harassing the enemy through use of sporadic actions designed to delay enemy movement, disrupt potential enemy attack, or force the enemy into a premature deployment. In essence, all of the actions of the skirmishers were intended to fix the enemy's location so the rest of the regiment could maneuver against the threat.

Depending on the tactical situation, the regiment could deploy one or two companies in the role of skirmishers. Skirmish companies assumed a loose line of battle formation that was more spread in length and depth than a traditional company line of battle. The skirmish lines took their assigned positions far enough from the regiment to be effective but close enough to the main body so as not to be cut off in the event of an enemy attack.

The day after the 85th anniversary of American Independence, the anguish that was the camp of instruction came to an end. At a Regimental formation that morning Colonel Howard made an announcement that the Third Maine Regiment was considered to be fully trained and ready to assume any responsibilities associated with the defense of Washington. The Colonel also indicated that our training was not over, it was just moving to another location. The Regiment would continue to train while performing any other duties as may be directed. Company commanders were instructed to prepare their companies for movement as orders were expected to arrive that afternoon indicating where the Regiment was to deploy.

The agonies inflicted on the Regiment by Sergeant Major O'Toole and his drillmasters were finished. They were gone from our lives. Gone to inflict similar agonies on the next regiment to arrive. As a result of the Colonel's comments that morning, the mood of the Regiment was particularly upbeat at the noon and evening meals. There was a heightened level of cockiness in the soldiers now that the training was complete. Since all of us hailed from Maine, there was none of the usual regional biases that sometimes entered into conversations with other regiments. Rather, the talk centered on whose company was better, whose squad had endured more, or whose Sergeant was the toughest. There was also the inevitable discussion of how bad Third Maine was going to whip the "Secesh". I thought that a lot of this type of talk went beyond the level of self-confidence expected of a regiment that had never seen action and entered the realm of pure hubris. Granted, there was a degree of confidence in our abilities and the abilities of the Regiment that were born of hard work, sweat, and the never-ending haranguing of the drillmasters. However, as Colonel Howard indicated, there was a lot more work to be done before we could successfully meet the enemy on the field of battle.

To a certain extent the drillmasters had done their jobs well. We now reacted to every command issued by the noncommissioned officers with a degree of precision and a level of enthusiasm we did not possess when Third Maine arrived at Camp Cameron. Back in Augusta the differences in backgrounds of the soldiers in my Company, particularly the ethnic aspects of the unit, were very obvious. There were some Scots like myself. There were Irish, English, French, German, and others from all over Europe. Talking with some of them proved to be, on more than one occasion, somewhat difficult. In a few short weeks at Camp Cameron all language barriers had been broken, at least when it came to aspects of training and drill. The Army, through the drillmasters, became the universal translator for the commands given and the actions required by the soldiers.

On the other hand, since the initial shots of the war were fired on Fort Sumter, many regiments, like the Third Maine, had been formed so quickly that there was a serious shortage of training materials that limited the soldiers' ability to learn how to fight. One specific area with glaring shortfalls was marksmanship. Due to a shortage of gunpowder and rifle ammunition, we were going to the front with very limited marksmanship training. Other than the endless drills to simulate loading and firing of weapons, the Regiment had fired only a pitifully few actual live rounds. Even those like me who were now armed with the Lorenz rifle with flip front sights had limited practice with our new weapons and very few opportunities for live fire.

For now, however, the United States Army had declared the Third Maine Regiment to be fully trained. Our metamorphosis was complete. The lump of civilian clay had been molded, as best as it could, given the time and circumstances. The men of the Third Maine Regiment were now soldiers and not just civilians in uniform. It was time to put the training into practice. It was time to step into the breach and experience a soldier's hell first hand. It was time to go to war.

The Eve of Battle

"If the Union is once severed, the line of separation will grow wider and wider, and the controversies which are now debated and settled in the halls of legislation will then be tried in fields of battle and determined by the sword."

Andrew Jackson

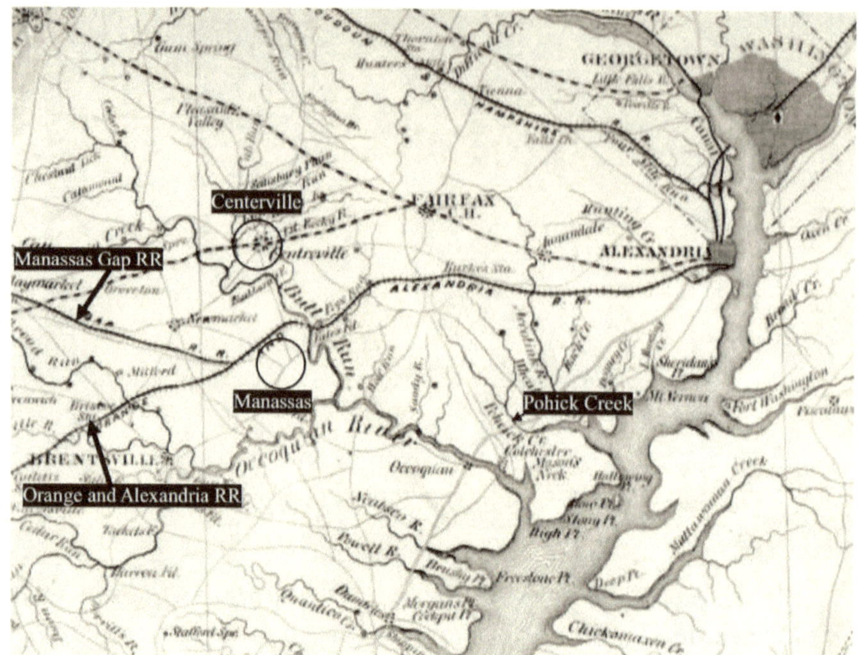

Northern Virginia Piedmont 1861

Chapter Ten

July 1861 – Alexandria, Virginia

Orders came down late in the afternoon of July 5th 1861. "The Third Maine Regiment will move to the vicinity of Fort Ellsworth and assist in the defense of the approaches into Washington". The rest of the day was spent preparing for the move and packing the baggage train.

As the Regiment stepped off on the morning of July 6th, the day broke sunny and warm with promises of yet another hot and humid afternoon. We said our goodbyes to the camp of instruction and began the climb down from Georgetown Heights. After a month at Camp Cameron, I became somewhat immune to the noxious smells of Washington but the thought of the fresh, all be it hot and humid, air of Virginia was something to look forward to.

The route of march took us past the National Mall, now festooned with newly arrived regiments from all over the North. Many of these regiments arrived trained and ready for combat while others were newly formed and lacked any kind of training at all. What I found interesting, as we passed the various units, was the assortment of uniforms, weapons, and equipment. It was as if no two regiments were outfitted the same or carried the same things. Probably the most flamboyantly dressed of the new regiments were the Zouaves. Hailing from Pennsylvania and New York, these soldiers dressed in red shirts, baggy trousers, open breasted jackets, and wore fez or turban styled headgear. They certainly were a sight. Still other units wore uniforms from or patterned after Army uniforms of the 1840's. There were even Union regiments who wore gray jackets. Seeing these gray clad Union soldiers, I imagine that in the chaos of a battle they could easily be confused with the uniforms of the Confederate Army.

The new units also carried a variety of weapons. One or two had the same Lorenz rifles as our regiment yet others still carried the Springfield Model 1822 muskets. There were a lot of soldiers who carried weapons I have never seen before. It wasn't hard to imagine the quartermaster's nightmare of providing ammunition for all of these different weapons.

There was a tremendous variety in equipment, accouterments, and accessories. Bayonets and knives of all shapes and sizes hung from belts of differing styles and colors, none of which was worn in anything resembling a consistent manner. There was great inconsistency in the types and wearing of haversacks, knapsacks, belts, and canteens, sometimes within the same regiment. To me, the Mall looked more like a large gypsy camp rather than a modern army preparing for war.

After passing the National Mall, the Regiment turned south and began crossing the Aqueduct Bridge into Virginia. The Aqueduct Bridge was one of the three main crossing points of the Potomac River along with the Chain Bridge and the Long Bridge. The Union soldiers who garrisoned the bridges had the primary task of controlling the rate and flow of bridge traffic across these critical access points into Washington, but also, checking the people and merchandise traveling into the Capitol from Virginia.

As the Third Maine started across the bridge, I began to feel a brisk, westerly breeze off the river. In spite of the fact the breeze was warm and by no means refreshing, the revitalizing river air competed favorably with the foul air of Washington. By the time the Regiment reached the Virginia shore and turned southeast toward Alexandria, the clean hot air of the Confederacy settled in.

While the Regiment was still geographically very close to Washington, we were, none the less, operating on the sovereign soil of a Confederate state and therefore, technically, in the war zone. As a precaution, Colonel Howard directed Company A to provide an advanced guard of skirmishers and, when applicable, flank guards as well. Two other companies were directed to provide flank guards and the last company assigned the responsibility for rear security. The remainder of the Regiment marched down the road in a column of companies, the soldiers marching along casually carrying on quiet conversations with their companions. It was hard to believe these men had been soldiers for less than two months. They certainly bellyached and complained as if they were grizzled veterans marching to yet another battle. I imagine that conversations like these had been commonplace in the Legions of Rome, Napoleon's Army, and among the patriots of the American Revolution.

As we marched down the Virginia road, my friends were deeply engaged in a debate over the relative merits, or lack thereof, of drums and bugles.

"I can see your point," Charlie said. "But without the drums or the bugles we wouldn't know what the Colonel wanted us to do or even what we should be doing and where we should do it."

"But they are so confusing," John lamented. "Especially the drums. If those drummers are off, even a little bit, you cannot tell what they are trying to beat out."

"That's very true," Jim said. "I much rather rely on the bugle. The only problem with the bugle is, aside from mess call, half of these men can't tell one note from another."

"And what if we are with other units?" John added. "One unit is blowing retreat and we are supposed to advance. With all that chaos and confusion, which calls do we listen to?"

The debate carried on as the Regiment moved along the Potomac toward Alexandria. As the miles fell away, so too did the soles of the many a soldier's Jefferson boots. Due to poor manufacturing, many of these bootees were literally coming apart. For some, the only things holding them together were the rawhide laces that were now wrapped around the soles of the shoes. By the second break, quartermasters began moving down the line replacing defective footwear as best they could. Shoddy boots and uncomfortable equipment became a hot topic of discussion for the soldiers, as did threats of physical violence directed at the manufacturers of the equipment.

Another interesting topic of discussion in the ranks was the never-ending war being fought against the insect life that bedeviled all soldiers, Union and Confederate alike. At home, the Maine men were all very familiar with numerous biting insects, particularly the black flies that plagued the population during the spring months. Black flies aside, nothing in Maine could compare to the assault of the common louse here in Virginia. Neither officers nor enlisted were exempt from their eternal torment. These little creatures were truly sent from Satan. Oh, the most fastidious in terms of personal hygiene lasted the longest, but, alas, even they succumbed to the attack of the brigades of these vile little demons that accompanied the army. "Gray Backs" was the term given the menace by Union soldiers and, so far, they were more threatening than any enemy.

Of course, no march would be complete without complaints about various members of the officer corps. The ranks went to great lengths to comment on the poor choices we made electing officers or how totally unprepared our officers were to lead. Pondering some of their comments, I realized that many of the prewar officers of the U.S. Army never commanded anything larger than a company. In fact, the only officer I could think of who did was General of the Army Winfield Scott. Any officer with brigade or regiment command experience was either retired, too old, too infirmed to take the field, or had followed their state into the Confederacy. Even Colonel Howard and the other officers of the Regiment had no experience in commanding a regiment and certainly most of the officers elected from civilian life had no real idea of how to lead men.

The hours passed and the miles slipped away but not without incident. While the distance from Camp Cameron to Alexandria was only about ten or twelve miles, for men not used to marching long distances, we might as well have been marching back to Maine. Given the weather, there were some heat related casualties that needed to be seen to, but for the individual soldier it was the plethora of blisters from ill-fitting boots, the chafing from stiff and uncomfortable pack straps, and unremitting rashes caused by our woolen clothing that, out of necessity, had to be endlessly endured.

The closer we got to Alexandria, the more we began to encounter some of the citizens of the Commonwealth of Virginia. Instead of being hailed as conquering heroes we were met with stares of pure hatred. Others made under the breath comments about the painful death that waited. Still others were more vocal in their comments. They directed openly violent and hostile comments at everything and everyone associated with the Union. As uncomfortable as these encounters made the march, finally in the early afternoon, the city of Alexandria appeared on the river and Fort Ellsworth materialized on the high ground west of the city.

Chapter Eleven

July 1861 – Clermont, Virginia

When the District of Columbia was first established in 1801, the city and county of Alexandria and the Georgetown area were included in the incorporation. In addition to being a rail hub for northern Virginia, Alexandria served as the seaport that serviced the entire Washington and northern Virginia area.

With this rail and sea access, Alexandria established itself as an important slave market, distributing its human cargo all across the South. Over the course of the next thirty years a stagnate regional economy, competition for goods and services with Georgetown on the north side of the Potomac, and talk of abolishing slavery in the District sparked a movement to return Alexandria to Virginia. Finally, in 1846, all of the parties agreed and, in addition to the city of Alexandria, all lands west of the Potomac were returned to Virginia's control.

Even before the attack on Fort Sumter and the onset of hostilities, security of the Capitol region was of paramount concern in the minds of Union military planners. On May 23rd, 1861, when the Virginia legislature confirmed the Ordinance of Secession that had been drafted on April 17th, the Union Army took action. Under cover of darkness in the early morning hours of May 24th, Union Army forces crossed the Potomac and seized the city without firing a shot. The citizens of Alexandria awoke that morning to find Union forces in control of their city.

Trouble began almost immediately when a close friend of President Lincoln, Colonel Elmer Ellsworth, commander of the Eleventh New York Regiment, the Fire Zouaves, attempted to remove a Confederate flag from atop the Marshall House Inn. After taking down the flag, Colonel Ellsworth was shot and killed by James Jackson, the owner of the Marshall House who, in turn, was promptly killed by the soldiers accompanying Ellsworth. As the first officer killed in the war, Ellsworth was hailed as a hero and the fort planned for construction outside Alexandria was named in his honor.

Immediately after the incident, a detachment of four hundred sailors off a Navy warship began the construction of Fort Ellsworth. Located on the high ground west of the city, the Fort commanded the river approaches to Washington as well as the Hunting Creek and Cameron Run sections of the Potomac. The Fort also controlled the landward approaches to Alexandria including the Orange and Alexandria rail line and the Little River Turnpike.

As designed by the engineers, Fort Ellsworth was built as an irregularly shaped Vauban star design of timber and wood construction with a perimeter of 618 yards. Sebastien Le Prestre de Vauban was a renowned seventeenth century French engineer for King Louis XIV. Vauban's star design, or some variation of the star design, became a popular defensive model for many French cities of the period. The star design also became very popular with U.S. Army engineers and formed the basic design of most of the coastal defense forts built on the East Coast and the Gulf of Mexico in the early nineteenth century. The basic design of Vauban's star eliminated any area where an attacker could move and not be brought under fire. This was accomplished by using a series of interlocking triangular bastions that commanded all possible avenues of approach.

By the time the Third Maine Regiment arrived at Fort Ellsworth, the naval force completed the Fort's construction to the point of starting to sod the landscape, whitewashing the buildings, and planting evergreens. The Sixth New York Artillery arrived in late June to assist in the construction and make the Fort operational. In addition to their defense duties, the New Yorkers were engaged in testing a new ten-pound rifled cannon for use with army artillery units and at other defensive locations around Washington. With the New York Regiment occupying the Fort, our Regiment assumed defensive positions outside the Fort oriented primarily south and west. It was easy duty for the most part. There were limited fatigue duties since the Fort was pretty much complete. Occasionally, a working party was required but for the most part, the Third Maine was occupied with picket duties.

Army units routinely posted pickets around their positions to provide early warning against infiltration or attack. The pickets, or picket line as it was called, was a chain of posts each with about six men. Each post on the picket line then placed soldiers at strategic points where these sentries could observe enemy activities during the day or listen for sounds of enemy movements during the night. If a unit was to be in a specific location for a significant period of time, the picket posts dug fighting positions for themselves and the sentries. Otherwise, the sentries found cover from observation using the local surroundings to their maximum advantage. Sentries were required to be fully dressed with belts on and rifles loaded and ready. Those soldiers not actually on sentry duty at the picket post could relax, eat, or sleep while waiting their turn on sentry duty. When the unit was in close contact with the enemy, the commander could also post a reserve force of platoon or company strength between the picket line and the main body for additional early warning and defensive support.

Unfortunately, the easy life of defense duty at Fort Ellsworth was short-lived. After only five days the Regiment was again on the move. On July 11th, Third Maine departed Fort Ellsworth and moved about three miles west to Clermont and established camp at the estate of former U.S. Navy Commodore French Forrest. Forrest was a forty-year veteran of the Navy who began his career as a junior officer with Oliver Hazard Perry on Lake Erie in the War of 1812. In 1847, he commanded all naval forces in Winfield Scott's landing at Vera Cruz during the Mexican War. Forrest's last assignment before Virginia seceded was as commanding officer of the Washington Navy Yard. He chose to follow Virginia and resigned his commission in the U.S. Navy to accept an appointment as Commodore in the newly formed Confederate Navy and command of the Gosport Shipyard in Tidewater, Virginia.

The original estate now called Clermont was built in the late eighteenth century by Benjamin Dulaney, a close friend of George Washington, and was comprised of 320 acres south of Little Turnpike Road on Cameron Run. After Dulaney's death, John Mason, the son of George Mason, one of America's Founding Fathers, purchased the estate. John Mason was a merchant and a banker who was instrumental in developing the Potomac Canal at Great Falls, Virginia. In 1807, Mason invested in Robert Fulton's naval engineering company and underwrote the development of the Clermont, America's first steam driven ship. Mason chose to name his estate Clermont after the ship and the estate of another Founding Father, Robert Livingston. The Third Maine Regiment now occupied Clermont. The Regiment established camp, picketed the area, and awaited the next step along the path toward their baptism of fire.

Chapter Twelve

July 1861 – Clermont, Virginia

In the aftermath of Fort Sumter and President Lincoln's call to arms, military planners began the process of reorganizing the prewar Army structure to meet the growing threat and the influx of newly formed regiments and other units. The prewar Army was grossly understrength and totally incapable of handling the current crisis.

There were a large number of Army and Navy personnel to replace. These were the men who elected to follow their home states into the Confederacy. Now, with new units from the Northern states arriving in the Capitol daily, the task became how to combine these regiments into larger sized units capable of conducting offensive operations against the enemy.

In May of 1861, after a careful analysis of the terrain and the threat, the War Department established two military departments to handle the two geographic approaches to both Richmond and Washington. The first approach to or from the very heart of Virginia was the rich and lush Shenandoah Valley. Mountains on each side of the valley could easily mask movement either north or south and bring an invading force into close proximity to either Richmond or Washington. The second, and most obvious, avenue of approach was the north and south corridor through the Piedmont area of Virginia. The existing rail and road networks in this region were more than sufficient to move and resupply any attacking force or move additional forces to forward deployed defensive positions.

Military planners determined that any operations conducted in these two departments could not be administrative in nature or operate from fixed locations. Instead, commanders needed to be given the freedom to conduct any offensive or defensive maneuvers they deemed necessary for success.

When it came time to actually select the commanders for these two areas, Secretary of War Simon Cameron was too engrossed with other matters to arrive at any decision. The political machinery in Washington also managed to suppress General of the Army Winfield Scott who, unfortunately, had little input or influence on the final decision. As the former governor of Ohio, Secretary of the Treasury Salmon P. Chase stepped in to manipulate the political machine and recommended George B. McClellan for command of the Department of the Shenandoah and Irvin McDowell for the Department of Northeast Virginia. While the geographic area of these two critical zones were called departments, both McClellan and McDowell would each command a field army in their respective departments.

Nothing in Irvin McDowell's military resume prepared him for the assignment he was offered. His command time with troops was minimal and he never commanded more than twelve soldiers at one time. Since his graduation from the Military Academy in 1838, McDowell served in a variety of assignments including instructor at West Point, aide-de-camp to General John Wool in Mexico, and a variety of other staff positions of an administrative or logistical nature. Yet now he was expected to command over thirty thousand soldiers in the Army of Northeast Virginia.

In spite of the fact his promotion to Brigadier General was politically motivated, McDowell's experience in the Mexican War caused him to detest what he called political officers. Rather than rely on those officers who joined the army from any political position in state or federal government, he tended to favor officers who were graduates of the Military Academy at West Point. After his assignment to the Department of Northeast Virginia, McDowell's choice of subordinate commanders reflected his Academy predilection.

When preparing his command, McDowell chose to organize the Army of Northeast Virginia into five divisions, each division composed of two to four infantry brigades plus artillery and cavalry. Brigadier General Daniel Tyler of Connecticut commanded the First Division. Tyler graduated from West Point nineteen years before McDowell but left the Army in 1834 to enter business. Although he did not participate in the Mexican War, Tyler received the appointment to his present rank when assigned to the Connecticut militia after Fort Sumter. The fifteen regiments that comprised the four brigades assigned to the First Division were from all over the north including the Second Maine Regiment out of Bangor. In addition to the infantry, the Division had four companies of U.S. Army artillery from prewar artillery units.

Brigadier General David Hunter commanded the two brigades that comprised the Second Division. Like Tyler, Hunter had graduated from West Point some sixteen years before McDowell. Unlike Tyler, Hunter remained in the Army throughout and had risen to the rank of Colonel in the prewar Army primarily as an Army Paymaster. Hunter's Division was composed of seven infantry regiments, one U.S. Army battalion, one U.S. Marine Corps battalion, a cavalry battalion, and two artillery companies.

Another prewar Army Lieutenant Colonel commanded the Third Division. An 1826 graduate of West Point, Samuel P. Heintzelman served with distinction during the Mexican War and in conflicts against Native Americans in the southwest. The three brigades of Heintzelman's Division included eleven infantry regiments and two companies of artillery.

The Fourth Division was the only Division not commanded by a West Pointer. In fact, the Division was so small that its commander, militia Brigadier General Theodore Runyon, chose not to brigade his regiments. Rather, he divided his eight New Jersey regiments into what was referred to as militia forces and volunteer forces.

Another veteran of the U.S. Army, Colonel Dixon S. Miles, commanded the two brigades of the Fifth Division. Miles had seen action in the Seminole War, the Mexican War, and had participated in several other campaigns against the Native Americans. Three companies of artillery supported the eight infantry regiments that comprised the Fifth Division.

About the time the Third Maine Regiment arrived at Clermont on July 11th, McDowell's organizational plan for the Army of Northeast Virginia was in full motion. At Regimental formation that afternoon, an announcement was made that we were now assigned to the Third Brigade of Heintzelman's Third Division. In addition to the Third Maine, the Third Brigade included the Fourth and Fifth Maine Regiments and the Second Vermont Regiment.

The Fourth Maine was raised from the Rockland area and mustered into service on June 15th, 1861. The Fifth Maine was organized from militia units in the state and left for Washington on June 26th. The Second Vermont was also composed of militia companies from around that state. Second Vermont mustered into service on June 20th, 1861 and departed for Washington on June 24th.

None of the three other regiments received the training provided to Third Maine at the camp of instruction.

It was no surprise that Brigadier General Heintzelman shared General McDowell's affinity for West Point graduates in key command billets. Colonel Oliver Howard was selected to command the newly formed Third Brigade. To assist in solving some of the myriad of logistical problems that plagued the Army, Colonel Howard selected Lieutenant Colonel Tucker as his Brigade Quartermaster. To the soldiers in the ranks, the reassignment of Lieutenant Colonel Tucker was met with mixed reviews. Those who knew him suggested that Tucker's influence with various politicians, to include Vice President Hannibal Hamlin, would serve the Brigade and the Army well in resolving some of their logistical issues.

Others, particularly those who observed his leadership, felt Tucker's departure as the second in command enabled Major Staples to assume temporary command of the Regiment. The Major showed himself to be a capable leader who understood his own shortcomings and worked hard to improve them. My friends and I all agree that if Colonel Howard should leave, Major Staples was the best man to replace him.

Chapter Thirteen

July 1861 – Clermont, Virginia

For the Army of Northeast Virginia to be successful in these early days of the war, control of the road and rail networks in the Piedmont area of Virginia became a critical necessity. Confederate military planners also saw the importance of the road and rail networks especially if they were required to operate on two fronts; the Piedmont and the Shenandoah Valley.

Unbeknown to the citizens of the sleepy little hamlet of Tudor Hall, Virginia their town was the strategic and tactical epicenter for planners on both sides, primarily because of the convergence of two major rail lines within their city limits. Astride the modest farmsteads lay the intersection of the rail lines of the Orange and Alexandria Railroad and the Manassas Gap Railroad.

The Orange and Alexandria ran from Alexandria southwest through lush farmland of the Piedmont to the city of Gordonsville in Orange County. From there, passengers and goods could link with other rail lines that travelled throughout the South. The Manassas Gap railroad was a sixty-mile line that connected to the Orange and Alexandria at Tudor Hall and ran through the farm country of Prince William and Fauquier Counties, across the Blue Ridge Mountains, and into the Shenandoah Valley.

If they were required to fight on these two widely separated fronts, Southern military planners realized that these two rail lines were critical. The railroad allowed for the rapid movement of troops and equipment between the Piedmont and the Shenandoah in response to any Union movement or to mass their own forces for a major offensive.

Unfortunately for the Confederacy there were few natural obstacles in the Piedmont region to seriously slow or block any Federal advance. The only real obstacles to any Union movement, especially for their artillery and baggage trains, were the numerous rivers and streams that flowed across the region. Many of these river networks could only be crossed using existing road or rail bridges or at specific points where the rivers could be forded.

What these bridges and fords, with their steep embankments, did provide the Confederacy was an unlimited number of strategic and tactical chokepoints that could be turned into defensive positions designed to slow or delay any enemy advance. These positions provided the South with its first line of defense against any Union assault through the Piedmont area directed at Richmond or any of the critical nodes along their road and rail networks.

By the late spring and early summer of 1861 both sides recognized the importance of the rail junction at Tudor Hall. The South began construction of a fortified camp at Tudor Hall complete with artillery, naval guns, and anything else that could fire on advancing infantry.

To supplement the forts and trench lines, the Confederates planned a series of defensive strongpoints along a meandering creek three miles east of Tudor Hall called Bull Run. Bull Run wasn't necessarily deep at any point, especially in the summer months, but its steep banks presented serious obstacles to movement except at very defined crossings. To counter Union advances in the area, the Confederates constructed defensive strongpoints at every crossing point along an eight-mile stretch of the river from the Warrenton Turnpike to the Union Mills Ford. Beyond this defensive line, Confederate cavalry and outposts patrolled the major avenues of approach from Washington to provide an early warning of Union advances.

By July the stage was set. McDowell presented his two-part plan for the capture of the rail junction at Manassas. Facing the 35,000 soldiers of the Federal army was the largest of all of the Confederate armies commanded by McDowell's former Academy classmate, Pierre Gustave Toutant Beauregard.

McDowell's plan recognized the importance of the rail lines at Tudor Hall, particularly the Manassas Gap railway, which would allow the Confederates to reinforce Beauregard's position with the four brigades of the Army of the Shenandoah under the command of Joseph E. Johnston. Part one of the plan called for Union forces in the Shenandoah Valley under the command of Major General Robert Patterson to engage Johnston's army and prevent any link up with Beauregard's forces around Manassas. The second part of the plan called for McDowell's army to attack and seize the rail junction at

Tudor Hall/Manassas while simultaneously destroying the rail bridge over the Broad River at Bristol Station in order to prevent any Confederate reinforcement or resupply from the Richmond area.

Unfortunately for those of us in the Third Maine Regiment our time spent at Clermont was to be of very short duration. After our assignment to the Third Brigade and the reassignment of officers, the Regiment was ordered to prepare for a march as the vanguard of the Brigade. As preparations were being made for the move, there was some time available for the soldiers to seek out friends or kin from the Fourth and Fifth Maine Regiments. That evening, after dinner, Jim and John left to see friends from the Fourth Maine, which enabled me to spend some time with Charlie and talk quietly about future events.

Private Charles Clark, the ever-vigilant war correspondent for the Kennebec Journal told me of the information he had learned while interviewing some of the staff at the Regimental Headquarters.

"I talked to a couple of the officers about where we're going," Charlie said. "Seems it's getting pretty crowded around here so they're sending us out to the west about five miles to a place called Springfield Station. It's on the rail line and should be a relatively easy march."

"Let's hope we don't run into any Rebs at Springfield Station," I replied. "I'm not sure this Regiment or even the Brigade is ready for a stand-up fight."

"You're probably right and I think McDowell agrees with you. The other regiments in the Brigade have even less training than we do. Fourth Maine got virtually none, and the other two, in spite of being militia, aren't much better off."

Charlie continued, "From what I hear McDowell is between a rock and a hard spot. He knows his troops are not ready. Hell, we're one of the better trained regiments in the army. McDowell also knows he has no senior leadership who have any experience at commanding brigades and divisions in the field. On top of all that, none of our troops are in any physical condition to operate in this oppressive Virginia heat."

"So why can't we get some more time to prepare? Maybe some more time to train and get used to this weather?"

"Two reasons. First, McDowell is being hounded by the President, by Congress, by the general public, and especially the press. They all seem to want revenge for Fort Sumter and want it done sooner not later. The second and more pressing reason is that large parts of this army are militia units who only signed ninety-day papers. By the end of July or early August they are going home."

That would be a crippling blow to the army. I wonder if the rebels have as many problems as the Army of Northeast Virginia. "If their army is anything like ours, I'll bet Jefferson Davis and the southern press are hounding their generals to toss these Yankee invaders off their land."

"At least the Rebels have no real advantage," Charlie said. "They are as green as we are and probably not as well equipped."

"The Rebels have one major advantage that we do not", I replied. "They are fighting on their home soil. I reckon you and I might feel different about this war if it was being fought in the woods of Maine rather than here in Virginia."

Charlie and I fell into a quiet reflection for the next hour until Jim and John returned. The four of us spent the rest of the evening preparing ourselves and our equipment for the movement to Springfield Station.

With the reorganization of the Army of Northeast Virginia nearly complete, the strategy for the campaign was put into motion that would bring the Army of Northeast Virginia on a collision course with Beauregard's Confederate forces at Tudor Hall. While the name Tudor Hall would be lost in the history books, the names of Bull Run and Manassas live on in many a soldier's remembrance of his baptism of fire and the hell that followed.

Baptism of Fire

"It is forbidden to kill; therefore, all murderers are punished unless they kill in large numbers and to the sound of trumpets."

Voltaire

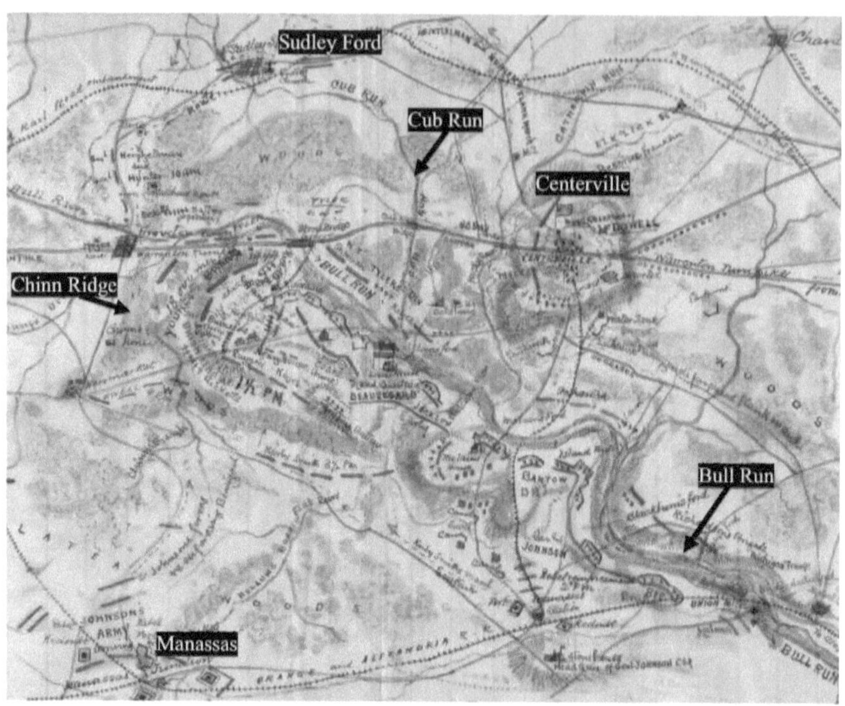

Battle of Bull Run/First Manassas July 1861

Chapter Fourteen

July 1861 – Pohick Creek, Virginia

The march to Springfield Station was relatively uneventful. The Regiment departed well before the heat of the day and made the trek in good time with a minimum of heat related casualties. The rest of the day was spent posting pickets, making camp, and preparing for the inevitable orders to follow. There was no real contact with the enemy although the area appeared to have been recently occupied. There were fresh signs that a cavalry unit and some infantry bivouacked near the station house but departed some time before we arrived.

The time was right to put McDowell's campaign plan into action. On July 15th, after his pleas for more time to train and prepare his army fell on deaf ears, McDowell ordered a general advance directed against Manassas and the rail junction.

In true Napoleonic tradition, McDowell's plan called for the Army of Northeast Virginia to move along several independent axes toward their first major objective, Fairfax Court House. On July 16th, Tyler's First Division would move into Vienna and prepare to relocate to the Germantown area on the morning of the 17th. Hunter's Second Division and Miles' Fifth Division would seize Annandale and the next day, Hunter would attack Fairfax Court House while Miles moved south of the Court House to block the southern approaches. On the 16th, Heintzelman's Third Division would proceed along the Old Fairfax Road and take up a blocking position along the Pohick Creek.

Our time at Springfield Station was spent in relative quiet. With the exception of a couple of sightings of Confederate cavalry, the Regiment stayed occupied manning picket lines and establishing defensive positions. On the 15th, the word was passed to prepare to move to the Pohick Creek area and be in position no later than the evening of the 16th.

The morning of the 16th was another of those hot, humid, and miserable Virginia days that literally sapped one's strength. My friends and I were packing our equipment when the word was passed that Company I was assigned the role of skirmishers. Our Squad was assigned as part of a Platoon under the command of Second Lieutenant Witman and tasked with screening the forward area along the designated route.

The rest of the Company was to follow a short distance behind keeping contact with the lead platoon and the Regiment. Company. I began their movement around noon. We hadn't gotten very far when our route took us down a slight hill and into a tree line where we encountered a series of trees purposely felled to block the road. The terrain surrounding the obstacle was an inhospitable and totally impassable marsh. While the infantry could easily move over the fallen trees, there was no way for any of the baggage trains or supply wagons to bypass the obstacle. Neither could they negotiate the soggy marshland without sinking up to their axles. Compounding this problem was a squad of Confederate infantry who thought it great sport to randomly fire at the halted soldiers.

After a conversation with Major Staples, Captain Lakeman ordered the lead platoon to move out and clear the front of the Rebel infantry while axmen from the rest of the Company began clearing the trees scattered across the road.

"What happened to you?" John asked.

"That last Reb round was awful close and I had to jump down the embankment into the swamp," Jim replied. "Went into that slimy water up to my knees. I was really worried that I wouldn't get my bootees out."

"Well, you smell almost as bad as some of those madams who frequented the tavern back home," John said.

"That wasn't the worst of it. I came to roost next to this three-foot black snake. He was a might agitated and opened his mouth and just hissed at me. His mouth was almost white except for those nasty looking fangs."

"I believe they are called water moccasins or cotton mouths," said Charlie. "Very common down here, especially in these marshy areas and very poisonous."

"Great!" Jim exclaimed. "I'll bet the Rebs put them here just to trouble us."

The rest of us just laughed at Jim's close call. Even Sergeant Lyon couldn't help but smile when he came over to see if everyone was all right.

As I prepared to move out, the sounds of the axmen starting to clear the road could be heard. Cutting trees in the heat of the day was miserable work. Our Squad moved through the fallen trees, past the swampy area, and formed a skirmish line on the next piece of higher ground about two hundred yards away. As we approached the crest of the hill, I observed about a dozen Rebel infantrymen retreating back across an open field and disappearing into a tree line three hundred yards further down the road.

Clearing the road took about an hour and a half. Our Squad was joined by the rest of the Platoon and once again set off as skirmishers across the field toward the tree line where the Rebels went. As we moved, I took notice the ground dropping off slightly toward the next tree line.

"I'll bet there's another swampy area along the road in that tree line", I said to no one in particular. Unfortunately, my prediction of the terrain in the trees was spot on. The road ran through another swamp with trees and other deadfall lying across it. As we approached, the Rebel infantrymen again started taking random shots at the advancing squad. While their rounds had no effect in terms of casualties, the sniping forced us to deploy and flush out the infantry before the axmen could begin to clear the road.

Rousting the infantry and clearing the road was serious work, especially under the blazing Virginia sun. For those unaccustomed to the heat and humidity, these delaying tactics had a significant impact. Over the course of the afternoon the heat and humidity, coupled with the wool uniforms, took their toll as more and more of the Company fell out as heat casualties.

Drinking water, or the lack of it, soon became a problem. An empty canteen forced many a thirsty soldier to dip his water bottle into the putrid waters of the swamps to quench his thirst. The stop and go movement caused by the delaying tactics of the Rebels also affected the discipline of the Regiment. Long periods of waiting under the hot sun and the close proximity of ripe, wild blackberries were too much for many to bear. It didn't take long for the foraging of the blackberry patches to begin in spite of orders from the officers and noncommissioned officers to maintain their positions.

What should have been an easy eight-to-ten-mile march from Springfield Station to the Pohick River turned into a marathon fiasco replete with scores of non-battle heat related casualties. Many more would wind up on the sick list from drinking the rancid waters of the swamps. The trek continued in this stop and go fashion until after 9:00 pm when the lead elements of Third Maine finally arrived at the Pohick River.

By the end of the day on July 17th, the first part of McDowell's plan was accomplished with a minimum of battle casualties. Tyler's First Division bivouacked around Georgetown; Hunter's Second Division occupied Fairfax Court House, while Miles' Fifth Division protected Hunter's left along the rail and road network south of the Court House. Heintzelman's Third Division held the extreme left flank of the Army of Northeast Virginia from Fairfax Station down to the Pohick River.

The next phase of the plan called for a move against the Centerville and Manassas area with the bulk of the Army. Simultaneously, the Third Division would swing around to the south of Manassas and seize key terrain including the rail bridge over the Broad River at Bristol Station. This move would deny Beauregard any reinforcements or resupply from the Richmond area.

As dawn broke on the morning of the 18th, McDowell's master strategy began to unravel. Around 8:00 in the morning, Colonel Howard and Brigadier General Heintzelman arrived at Regimental Headquarters for a meeting with Major Staples. Shortly after this meeting, several of the company commanders, Captain Lakeman being one of them, were summoned to the tent of the Regimental Commander. Upon his return, Captain Lakeman directed two squads be readied to conduct a reconnaissance of the area between their current location and a crossing point of the Occoquan River known as Wolf Run Shoal.

Sergeant Lyon's Squad was one of the two selected to accompany the captain on the reconnaissance and we set off about 9:00 am. From the beginning, the day was a repeat of yesterday's movement to Pohick Creek. At every low point on the road, felled trees and other obstacles restricted the trafficability to just foot soldiers. Artillery and the baggage train could not maneuver in the low, swampy area of the route without significant engineer support. Unlike yesterday's movement, the patrol noted no enemy activity until they reached the area around Wolf Run Shoal. Both sides of the shoal were covered with fallen trees and other man-made obstacles. A detachment of Rebels, probably dismounted cavalry, had assumed defensive positions on the south side of the shoal. Routing them out of that position would prove difficult assuming a force large enough to do so could actually reach the shoal without the Rebels being reinforced. The shoal was upriver from the Occoquan River, which was not passable and no other ford sites were available north of the shoal. After exchanging some fire with the Rebel force, Captain Lakeman ordered the patrol to return to the Company area.

All of the reconnaissance reports from the companies revealed the same situation on all of the routes observed. Low, swampy areas blocked by fallen trees and obstacles passable only to the infantry. As the word of the reconnaissance reached Heintzelman and McDowell, the original plan was modified. The Third Division would now move into the Centerville area as well.

About the time the Third Maine conducted their reconnaissance of the Wolf Run Shoal area, Tyler's First Division arrived in Centerville. Centerville was located about six miles from Manassas at the junction of the Warrenton Turnpike, the Braddock Road, and the road to Chantilly. In the eyes of the northern military planners, Centerville was a key strategic objective for the seizure of the rail hub at Tudor Hall. In reality, Centerville was a minor crossroads time seemed to have forgotten.

As the First Division arrived in the town they were greeted with fresh signs of a recent Rebel withdrawal. Information gleaned from the locals indicated a brigade of Virginians moved west along the Warrenton Turnpike toward the Stone Bridge. A second and larger brigade moved to the southwest toward Mitchell's and Blackburn Fords. These two fords provided crossings of the Bull Run on the most direct route between Centerville and Manassas Junction.

With the southern approach to Manassas in question, McDowell amended his battle plan and ordered the First Division to observe Confederate activity in the area with emphasis on the crossing points of the Bull Run. Tyler was to give the impression of moving against Manassas until such time as the situation with the southern route could be sorted out. Where McDowell desired a cautious approach, Tyler's open distain for the Commanding General manifested itself in a more aggressive approach that escalated into an outright battle along the Bull Run.

After receiving the information about the Confederate withdrawal from Centerville, Tyler directed Colonel Israel Richardson's Fourth Brigade to conduct a reconnaissance of the Blackburn and Mitchell's Fords. When the reconnaissance force was assembled, Tyler accompanied Richardson and his soldiers down the road leading to the river and Manassas Junction.

At the fork that led off the main road to Mitchell's Ford, the reconnaissance quickly determined that the terrain at Mitchell's Ford provided the Confederates a much stronger defensive position than did the terrain around Blackburn Ford. After assessing the situation, Tyler directed Richardson to continue his reconnaissance and push toward Blackburn Ford.

While the route appeared to be relatively clear, the Fourth Brigade was actually maneuvering directly into the center of the Confederate defenses. Shortly after 1:00 pm Richardson's Brigade engaged two Confederate Brigades: Colonel Milledge Bohnam's Brigade of North and South Carolinians and Brigadier General James Longstreet's North Carolina and Virginia infantry.

Our reconnaissance of the Wolf Run Shoal area complete and all of the patrols returned, we began our movement to join the rest of the Brigade at Centerville. The route was fairly easy with no obstructions or enemy activity but as the Regiment moved along, the sounds of a battle joined reached us from the direction of Manassas.

The closer we got to Centerville, the louder and more ominous the sounds of the battle became. The Regiment arrived outside Centerville shortly after 2:00 pm and took up positions southwest of the town along the same road to Manassas taken by Richardson's reconnaissance force. The order came down to give way to Colonel William Tecumseh Sherman's Third Brigade as they moved forward to support the now heavily engaged Richardson.

Shortly after 4:00 pm the sounds of the battle began to decrease. Rumors abounded about the situation and the outcome. Some said Tyler's Division broke through the Rebel positions and were now chasing the retreating Confederates. Still others said Tyler's Division broke and the Rebels were moving up the road in force.

Company I had set up their defensive area straddling the road to Manassas. As we prepared, an alarm was sounded that troops in gray uniforms were moving up the road toward us.

"Hold your fire!" screamed Sergeant Lyon. "They're friendlies."

Fingers came off triggers and rifles were lowered as the Maine men realized these gray clad soldiers were, in actuality, some of the walking wounded from the First Massachusetts Regiment of Tyler's Division. Company I was directed to fetch water and wagons from the Quartermaster for the wounded and render any assistance necessary to get these men to the hospital area.

"One of those Mass boys told me they mixed it up pretty good down at Blackburn's Ford" John said later that evening.

"Yeah, I spoke to one soldier who said they couldn't tell the Rebs from their own soldiers. Everyone was in gray," Jim replied. "He said their Lieutenant went out to see who was in front of them and when he told them they were from Massachusetts, about twelve Rebs shot him. It's a wonder there were not more casualties from this gray-on-gray action."

"I guess everybody from the First Division is back who is coming back," Charlie added. "The people on the picket lines better be extra careful this evening."

As the four of us lay there in the quiet of the evening, I pondered what had happened. The Army of Northeast Virginia had been bloodied but what will happen next? When will it be our turn? I heard some of the soldiers talking earlier and make reference to "seeing the elephant" which, when asked, meant to see combat. Now I wonder when would we "see the elephant" and who would blink first?

Chapter Fifteen

July 20th 1861 – Centerville, Virginia

On the Confederate side of the Bull Run there would be no blinking. Unbeknownst to McDowell, General Beauregard sensed a massing of Union forces around Centerville and sent a communiqué to President Davis asking for reinforcements. Davis responded by ordering one regiment from Leesburg and two from Fredericksburg to Manassas. Davis also dispatched Brigadier General Wade Hampton's Legion and the Sixth North Carolina Regiment from Richmond. The President then instructed General Johnston to make every effort to elude General Patterson's Union forces and start moving his army toward Manassas.

General Patterson's gross overestimation of Johnston's strength caused him to withdraw further up the Shenandoah Valley toward Winchester. This move gave Johnston the opportunity he needed to slip away and begin transporting his forces to reinforce Beauregard. At 1:00 am on the 18th, Johnston ordered Brigadier General Thomas Jackson's Brigade to Piedmont Station to begin the thirty-five-mile trip to Tudor Hall via the Manassas Gap railroad.

By the afternoon of July 18th, the Union consolidation around Centerville was becoming readily apparent to Beauregard and his military planners. Confederate engineers had done their job and denied the Union any possible move to the south of Manassas through the Wolf Run Shoal area. Forward elements of Beauregard's army also confirmed the movements of the subordinate divisions of the Army of Northeast Virginia toward the Centerville area.

By the evening of July 18th, all of the components necessary for the great battle were in place or in route to the Manassas area. Then, to everyone's surprise, McDowell balked. With his army now consolidated at Centerville, McDowell called for a halt to the movement. While the army waited, he directed his Chief Engineer,

Major John Barnard, to conduct a reconnaissance and find a suitable route around the Confederate left.

Major Barnard's reconnaissance was complete but by no means an accurate assessment. By midday on the 19th his efforts determined that the Confederate line extended along the Bull Run from Union Mill Ford to the Stone Bridge on Warrenton Turnpike. There were three additional fords to the northwest of Blackburn and Mitchell fords before reaching the Stone Bridge some four miles upriver. Island Ford, Ball Ford, and Lewis Ford, were mainly used for foot traffic and none were capable of supporting the movement of artillery or baggage trains.

Beyond the Stone Bridge and the Confederate left were two other crossing points, the Farm Ford and Poplar Ford, before arriving at a major ford at Sudley astride the Sudley – Manassas Road. Farm Ford was ruled out as being dangerously close to the Stone Bridge and not an acceptable route for the support wagons or artillery. The access at Poplar Ford was nothing more than a footpath through the woods and suitable for infantry only. Barnard concluded the ford at Sudley was the most advantageous from the Union perspective. The distance from the point where a unit was required to leave the Warrenton Turnpike, travel to the ford, and move down the Sudley Road back to the Turnpike was roughly seven miles. Unfortunately, Barnard provided no maps of the road networks, conducted no testing of the crossing points, or provided any markers delineating the best routes for the Union forces to take.

By midday on the 20th McDowell reviewed Major Barnard's findings and decided to move against the Confederate left using the Sudley Ford. The new plan called for a demonstration in front of the lower crossing points while two divisions would maneuver and cross at Sudley Ford and attack south along the Sudley Road. As the lead elements uncovered other fording sites they would be joined by units from the demonstrating force. This would free up the two attacking divisions to shift to their right and move against the Manassas Gap rail line.

While Major Barnard was off conducting his reconnaissance, the mood around Centerville was surprisingly upbeat considering the proximity of the enemy. Carriages and wagons were arriving by the hour filled with all sorts of folks who wanted to see the war firsthand. In addition to the people with their tents and picnic baskets, there were Congressmen and Senators mostly representing the states with regiments in the fight. There were even members of President Lincoln's Cabinet on hand. As I watched the political spectacle unfolding, I thought it was never too early for these people to start the old reelection handshaking.

"Who knows?" I thought aloud. "Tomorrow there may even be enough of us left to provide a few votes for the incumbents".

While the brass bands and the merchants hawking their wares provided a carnival like atmosphere around the Centerville area, not all camp activities were so frivolous. Charlie recently returned from a punishment formation in the Second Division. Two soldiers were caught in deserter status and returned to the Division for appropriate disciplinary action. After a hasty court martial, the two were found guilty and sentenced to receive fifty lashes and a branding.

"There were representatives from each unit in the Division as well as other divisions close by," Charlie said. "They were all formed in a square. The Adjutant read the results of the court martial and the prisoners were physically taken to the stock that had been erected for the flogging. Two sergeants administered the fifty lashes and these two seemed to know their business."

"Was it bad?" John asked.

"Not at first," Charlie replied. "But as the number increased and the blood began to flow, many in the assembly either fainted or lost their breakfast at the sight. Officers, too."

"Did the flogging kill them?" Jim asked.

"No. They were still alive at the end but cut up and bleeding pretty bad. After a doctor examined them the two sergeants proceeded to take hot irons and brand a "D" on one of their shoulders."

"God! How horrible," Jim gasped.

"I read about this once," I said. "When the British executed Admiral Byng for his failure and incompetence in battle, the French author Voltaire said 'this was for the encouragement of others'. About now, I believe word of this discipline has spread throughout the Army and those thinking about deserting are rethinking their actions."

The others all nodded in agreement. It may seem like a barbaric practice but it surely did serve to encourage others. It was a tough choice. On one hand, you could desert, be flogged, and then branded, or on the other hand, face the enemy and run the risk of being killed in combat.

On the morning of July 20th McDowell received more bad news. Enlistment periods for the Fourth Pennsylvania Regiment, a militia group from the First Brigade of Heintzelman's Division, expired. This Regiment was one of the ninety-day militia units called to active duty immediately after Fort Sumter. Their enlistments up, the men of the Fourth Pennsylvania, as well as Varian's Battery of the Washington Grays, chose to leave the Army and departed that afternoon for Alexandria. McDowell realized they were only the first of many and the exodus of militia units on ninety-day enlistments would continue over the coming weeks if he did not choose to act soon. On the afternoon of the 20th McDowell issued his plan for the coming battle.

McDowell's plan called for a three-pronged attack against the Confederate forces. Richardson's Brigade of the First Division and one brigade of the Fifth Division would demonstrate and fix Confederate forces at the Blackburn and Mitchell Ford section of the Bull Run. The rest of the First Division would advance along the Warrenton Turnpike to the Stone Bridge. The main attack would come from the Second and Third Divisions who would follow the route defined by Major Barnard to the Sudley Ford. After crossing the Bull Run, these two divisions would attack south along the Sudley-Manassas Road.

According to the plan, the Second Division with the Third in trace would move out at 2:30 am on the 21st and cross Sudley Ford by 7:00 am. The First Division would advance and open the battle at daylight.

As the Army of Northeast Virginia conducted its reconnaissance and prepared for battle, on the other side of the Bull Run, Beauregard's Army was also busy preparing and welcoming reinforcements. Brigadier General Jackson's Brigade arrived late in the afternoon of the 19th followed by Colonel Francis Bartow's Brigade and Brigadier General Barnard Bee's Brigade on the 20th. Colonel Theophilus Holmes' Brigade marched in from Fredericksburg on the 20th and Holmes was directed to form a reserve brigade with his forces and Hampton's Legion, recently arrived from Richmond.

With his forces flowing slowly but steadily into Manassas via the Manassas Gap railroad, Brigadier General Johnston arrived in Manassas around noon on the 20th and established his headquarters at the McLean Farm. Based on his seniority, Johnston assumed command of all Confederate forces in the battle area.

With only one of Johnston's brigades remaining in the Shenandoah Valley and due to arrive as soon as possible, the stage was set for this initial clash of wills. All of the players in the war's first major battle were in position. The plans had been made. The ultimate chess match was set to begin. It was time to "see the elephant"

Chapter Sixteen

July 21st 1861 – Manassas, Virginia

lthough McDowell's plan was risky and extremely complex, especially for untrained troops with inexperienced officers, it began as it was envisioned. At 2:30 am the two remaining brigades of Tyler's Division stepped off down the Warrenton Turnpike. The Second Division followed in trace of the First Division. Problems arose almost immediately. Between Centerville and the turnoff leading to the Sudley Ford was Cub Run, and the bridge over the Cub Run became a major choke point for movement down the Warrenton Turnpike. The Second Division quickly stacked up behind the First and by daylight, the Third Division failed to clear Centerville.

It took until about 5:30 am for the Second Division to pass the Cub Run and turn onto the country road identified by the engineers. Movement along this track was painfully slow, as pioneer units with axes were required to clear the route for the artillery and wagon trains. Back in Centerville, McDowell sensed the Union left was exposed. Any attack against the left would result in the loss of the supply trains and cut off any avenue the Army had to maneuver toward Washington. He ordered Colonel Howard's Brigade to remain at the road junction southeast of Centerville to defend against any Confederate attack on the left flank.

At 6:00 am the First Division's artillery opened the battle as directed. Unfortunately, the Second and Third Divisions were a good two hours behind schedule. To make matters worse, the Confederate signal corps detected their movement toward Sudley Ford.

McDowell's plan called for the Second Division to cross the Bull Run at Sudley Ford while the Third Division crossed further downstream at the Poplar Ford. In the early morning light, neither the civilian guide nor any of the Third Division staff officers could find the turnoff to Poplar Ford. As a result, Brigadier General

Heintzelman was compelled to follow the Second Division to Sudley Ford.

Johnston and Beauregard reacted quickly to the news of the attempted flanking movement. Word reached them that elements of Colonel Nathan Evans' Brigade were moving toward the once grand estate called Pittsylvania to counter the new threat. Newly arrived Bartow's Brigade and Bee's Brigade were sent to support Evans at the Stone Bridge. Hampton's Legion would follow Bartow and Bee.

It took until 9:00 am for the Second Division to cross Sudley Ford and begin its advance down the Sudley-Manassas Road. By that time, the Confederates moved forces to Matthews Hill astride the Sudley Road and north of the Warrenton Turnpike and to Henry Hill, south of the Turnpike, to counter the Union threat.

The chess match for control of the Bull Run was beginning to unfold but Howard's Third Brigade remained at Centerville. The noise of the battle became very evident to all.

"Everything that's going on and here we sit," Jim lamented.

"I think we are what's referred to as the reserve," Charlie replied.

"Did you fellows hear the commotion in the Second Division this morning?" John asked. The others nodded no. "Seems when the Rhode Island boys marched out, the Governor of Rhode Island rode out with them dressed in the uniform of the First Rhode Island."

"I think his name is Sprague," Charlie said. "Gutsy fellow in any case."

While waiting for an attack that probably would not come, the morning sun began to sap our strength. Suddenly, around 11:00 am our orders came. "With all haste, the Third Brigade will follow the route taken by the rest of their Division to Sudley Ford, turn south along the Sudley Road, and rejoin their division." With all haste generally meant periods of double quick or at least a forced march pace where the rear of the formation would be at the double quick anyway.

"This will be a brutal move," I said to my friends. "The Regiment is only about eighty percent due to the heat or soldiers drinking bad water and contracting dysentery." After checking my weapon and ammunition supply, I stored some of my extra equipment and possessions in the baggage train and prepared to move out. Around 12:00 pm the Third Brigade stepped off to join the battle.

Shortly before the Third Brigade began moving toward Sudley Ford, things heated up along the Sudley Road on Matthews Hill.

Bee's Brigade moved to reinforce Evans' at Matthews Hill and the Confederates were holding their own. About that time, Sherman's Brigade of the First Division forced a crossing of the Bull Run at the Stone Bridge. Sherman, marching to the sound of the guns, then turned his Brigade toward Pittsylvania and the right flank of the Confederates on Matthews Hill.

By 12:00 pm, mounting Union forces around Matthews Hill forced Bee and Evans to withdraw across the Warrenton Turnpike to Henry Hill. For the next two hours, elements of the Army of Northeast Virginia pushed the Confederates back to Henry Hill. Colonel Erasmus Keyes' Brigade of the First Division followed Sherman across the Bull Run and onto the heights overlooking the Warrenton Turnpike. About the time Howard's Brigade was reaching Sudley Ford, McDowell issued orders for an advance by the Second Division and the First and Second Brigades of the Third Division supported by the First Division to capture Henry Hill.

The seven-mile march to Sudley Ford was indeed brutal. The Brigade moved at the double quick for the better part of the way and our wake was littered with discarded blankets, haversacks, coats, and other equipment. Some even lightened their load by discarding canteens. The midday sun and humidity took its toll. By the time we reached Sudley Ford about half the Brigade was lost to either the heat or drinking the tainted water from the Bull Run. Third Maine fared somewhat better than the other regiments. We spent more time in the Virginia weather and were more acclimatized than our New England comrades.

In the town of Sudley the Union had set up an improvised field hospital. For the Third Brigade, this hospital was our first real glimpse of the horrors of war and the cost of battle. The dead and the dying lay all around the town. Piles of amputated limbs surrounded the makeshift hospital. Ambulances flowed back and forth to the front with gruesome regularity. As the Brigade moved down the Sudley Road toward the fighting, wounded men made their way back to the hospital area. Along the sides of the road in the few areas of shade available, gravely wounded soldiers, unable to make it to the hospital, made their peace with God and waited for their final moments.

It was 2:00 pm before the Third Brigade arrived at Matthews Hill. The ravages of war were all around us. Brigadier General Heintzelman directed Colonel Howard to move off to the right of the

Sudley Road near the intersection of the Warrenton Turnpike and await further instructions. As we passed the other regiments in the Brigade, I had a chance to look them over. The forced march took its toll. Many of the companies in one regiment were down to ten or twelve men per company.

The chess match now shifted to the Confederate positions atop Henry Hill. Realizing the Union was relying on their envelopment and subsequent movement down the Sudley Road, Beauregard stripped units from the Confederate right to reinforce Henry Hill.

With his artillery forward, about 2:00 pm McDowell ordered a general assault against the Confederate positions. Along the Warrenton Turnpike elements of the First Division, repelled by remnants of Evan' Brigade and Hampton's Legion earlier in the day, regrouped and moved out. After crossing the Turnpike, two regiments were once again repelled by Hampton's Legion and the Fifth Virginia Regiment from Jackson's Brigade.

Along the Sudley Road the fighting was fierce. Regiment after regiment attempted to storm the Confederate positions on Henry Hill. They were all beaten back in some of the hardest fighting of the day. The body count on both sides was climbing rapidly.

Around 3:00 pm Colonel Howard received orders to form his brigade and move against the Confederate left by seizing the long north-south high ground known as Chinn Ridge and the farm at the top of the ridge. Howard formed the brigade with two regiments forward: the Fourth Maine on the left and the Second Vermont on the right. Behind these two regiments came the Third Maine on the left and the Fifth Maine on the right.

As the Brigade formed and moved across the Warrenton Turnpike and Young Creek to the base of Chinn Ridge, I looked around the squad at the faces of the other soldiers. Some had the look of sheer terror in their eyes. Still others were mouthing prayers of self-protection. Surprisingly, there were many who just seemed anxious about the opportunity of finally going into action. I had spoken to many of the soldiers in the squad about what actual battle would be like. They talked about "seeing the elephant" and the "hornets" that would be "a-buzzing" around from the Secesh infantry. Many talked with a false sense of bravado not readily apparent now that the "elephant" was here and the "hornets" were flying.

The movement of Howard's Brigade to the Confederate left was spotted and the information relayed to Johnston and Beauregard.

They reacted by sending Colonel Jubal Early's Brigade from positions on the Bull Run toward Chinn Ridge. Joining Early was Colonel Arnold Elzey's Brigade, the last of Johnston's army to reach the railhead.

Colonel Elzey maneuvered his Brigade to the south of Henry Hill, across the Sudley Road and onto Bald Hill, a piece of high ground overlooking Chinn Branch. Chinn Branch was a small stream that tracked north, parallel to the Sudley Road, and joined Young Branch near the intersection of the Warrenton Turnpike. Beyond the Chinn Branch, Elzey could see Chinn Ridge and along the crest of the ridge appeared Howard's Brigade.

While Elzey moved his Brigade down the hill to the Chinn Branch, Early maneuvered his Brigade to Elzey's left, straddling the southern end of Chinn Ridge in the vicinity of Chinn Farm. Supporting the newly formed Confederate left was Beckham's Battery, positioned near the Chinn farmhouse.

As the Second Vermont and the Fourth Maine crested Chinn Ridge they received fire from elements of Bonham's Brigade and the Alexandria Light Artillery located on Henry Hill. From a range of over three hundred yards neither side actually inflicted any significant damage on the other. Suddenly, Elzey's Brigade joined the fight and began firing at Howard's forward regiments.

As the forward regiments engaged both Elzey and the units on Henry Hill, among the two rear regiments, panic and chaos started to build. The soldiers of the Third and Fifth Maine, who were waiting the call to move forward, became increasingly rattled at the volume of overshots directed at the ridge.

As I looked around, panic was evident on the faces of the soldiers huddled below Chinn Ridge. The sounds of the "hornets a-buzzing" could be heard everywhere.

"They are just overshots from the Rebs aiming at the Fourth Maine," I said. "Stay low and everything will be alright."

"It seems like it's raining lead," Jim replied. "And the noise of those artillery rounds striking the trees is frightening."

"A couple down the line in Company C got some serious splinters from one of those shots," John added. "It looks like our right and the Fifth Maine aren't holding up well."

Captain Lakeman and the noncommissioned officers valiantly tried to keep order but when a shell exploded in the Fifth Maine area, panic and confusion escalated. Three Confederate batteries were now engaging Howard's forward regiments. To add to the confusion of the battle, Union cavalry on the Brigade's right were misidentified as Confederate and in the resulting chaos, many from the Fifth Maine bolted to the rear. By the time Colonel Howard and others had restored order, over half of the Fifth Maine who actually made it to Chinn Ridge had withdrawn.

Colonel Howard was finally able to lead the rear two regiments up Chinn Ridge to join the battle. Third Maine relieved Second Vermont who moved back to the thickets behind the Ridge. What was left of Fifth Maine moved to the right of Third Maine and extended the lines to within a quarter mile of Chinn Farm, Early's Brigade, and Beckham's Battery.

As Company I crested Chinn Ridge a great deal of confusion ensued as to the actual location of the enemy. Many of the soldiers from all of the forward regiments were firing at shadows.

"The firing is coming from the low ground," I shouted at Sergeant Lyon. "They're down by the stream in that thicket."

Sergeant Lyon tried to redirect the Squad's fire, but in the confusion of the day, few listened.

"Some dang fool just fired his ramrod at the enemy," Charlie shouted.

"And I've seen a couple loading and reloading without ever firing a shot," Jim said. "They must have five or six rounds down those barrels. God help them or those around them if they actually fire those weapons."

As the Brigade engaged the enemy, real problems began when Colonel Howard ordered one of the wings of Fourth Maine to reposition itself to better engage the forces on Henry Hill. In the heat of the moment, Howard's directions were misinterpreted as a general withdrawal.

Rather than try to restore order to the other retreating regiments, Howard chose to continue the withdrawal. He ordered the entire Brigade to fall back into the thicket on the backside of the ridge.

"We're moving back," Charlie shouted above the cacophony of battle sounds. I acknowledged Charlie's comment and after discharging my weapon and reloading, I joined the squad in the move to the thicket.

Below the ridge, Elzey saw Howard's Brigade withdraw. With support from Early's Brigade and Beckham's Battery, Elzey now ordered his Brigade to advance up the ridge. Near the crest, Elzey sent out skirmishers to reconnoiter the top of the hill. Finding no Union soldiers, Elzey ordered his Brigade forward onto Chinn Ridge.

From my position in the thicket, I watched the rebels advancing across the ridge when the order came to fire. Howard's Brigade, or what was left of it, began a sporadic fire, which halted the Confederates for a while. Then, Beckham's Battery shifted its fire and began shelling the thicket.

Captain Lakeman and the noncommissioned officers tried to rally the Company to stand their ground. In spite of the Confederate artillery and rifle fire, Company I held its ground and returned fire. Suddenly, as I reloaded, I watched a regiment of Elzey's Brigade assault the thicket to my right. The firing from that sector became intense for a brief period. Then the unthinkable happened, the right flank of the Brigade collapsed and soldiers started running away from the fight.

Colonel Howard tried to stem the flow by ordering another withdrawal to the base of the ridge across Young Branch but his efforts were futile. Confusion, disorder, and wholesale panic began to grip the Brigade. Captain Lakeman and others managed to rally a number of Company I and, with the assistance of Sergeant Lyon, set about organizing a fighting retreat. Major Staples and others in the Regiment were desperately trying to stem the tide but the flood had started.

What was left of Company I fired off a few rounds to slow the enemy down, then withdrew to another location and repeated the action. As we crossed Young Branch and then the Warrenton Turnpike, I noted another Union unit engaged by the Stone House at the intersection of Sudley Road. Very soon this unit saw Elzey's Brigade charging from their right flank followed by elements of Early's Brigade and Confederate cavalry. This unit, which turned out to be Sykes' Battalion of Regulars, was forced to fall back from their position.

Any effort to stop the flow of men moving back proved to be futile. A few units like Company I maintained some degree of discipline, but more simply ran off and left the field. McDowell, now realizing the battle was lost, cobbled Sykes' Battalion and a few artillery batteries to cover the withdrawal and slow the Confederate pursuit.

Most of the retreating Army of Northeast Virginia returned to Centerville the way they came. The word was passed for Howard's Brigade to consolidate the positions they left earlier in the day. The remnants of Company I trudged along to Sudley Ford and turned onto the track leading back to the Warrenton Turnpike.

The march back to Centerville was not without its share of difficulty. In addition to the supply wagons and baggage trains, there were artillery units trying to move their guns and caissons out of harm's way. Compounding the movement of the Army wagons and units were the scores of civilian carriages and barouches carrying panicked onlookers to safety. The area around the Stone Bridge and the Cub Run Bridge, both natural chokepoints, became clobbered with soldiers, civilians, and wagons all trying to escape the advancing Confederates.

Johnston and Beauregard both realized what the Rebels desperately needed at this point in the battle was a true cavalry force that could exploit the Union retreat. Unfortunately, Beauregard could only muster only a force of about one hundred and fifty troopers of Colonel J. E. B. Stuart's First Virginia Cavalry. Stuart began to assault the Union rearguard and trailed the retreating Union forces toward Sudley Ford. Elzey's Brigade followed Stuart and advanced to the Poplar Ford while Early's Brigade secured the Farm Ford area.

South of the Stone Bridge, Johnston was able to send two battalions of cavalry across the Bull Run at Lewis and Ball Fords. Exploiting the cavalry successes along the Warrenton Turnpike, the Second and Eighth South Carolina Regiments, supported by the Alexandria Light Artillery, moved east along the Turnpike toward the Cub Run Bridge.

The withdrawal of Union forces and the chase by Confederates continued until around sundown. Beauregard, fearful of a counterattack near Union Mills Ford, called off the pursuit and ordered all units back across the Bull Run.

As McDowell's weary Army made it to Centerville, the Army reserve, the Fifth Division, took up position to support the withdrawal. The two brigades that were demonstrating before Blackburn and Mitchell's Fords returned to support the defensive efforts.

When the remnants of Company I returned to Centerville, they joined what was left of the Third Maine Regiment. Company commanders were absorbed in getting an accurate count of those killed, wounded, or missing and those fit for duty. Soldiers continued to straggle in, many with only the clothes on their backs: no equipment, no weapons, and no enthusiasm. Once these soldiers arrived in Centerville, the panic and confusion of the withdrawal gave way to anger and depression.

As we sat in the twilight back in Centerville, a parade of emotions washed over me. There was a lack of understanding and confusion over the events of the day that soon gave way to anger. There was anger at what had turned into an absolute rout. There was anger directed at those in Washington who sent an inexperienced, ill-trained, and poorly led bunch of volunteers into a meat grinder. There was enough anger left over for those in the Brigade who "saw the elephant" and chose to run away. After a while, the anger subsided and left in its wake only shame. I felt shame for letting my comrades down, for letting the people of Maine down, for disgracing my family, and for letting myself down.

As these emotions subsided, what remained was reality and a lot of questions. There was the reality that people had died this day. There was also the reality that I contributed to that death count. My ability with a rifle caused several on the other side to be lost. The final reality was that everything I owned I either wore or carried. Gone was the baggage train with all of my extra clothing and my red blanket from the good people of Augusta. Gone was my knapsack and haversack during the forced march to Sudley Ford along with just about everything else.

A light rain began to fall just as the orders for Third Maine arrived. The Regiment was to return to Clermont to reorganize and re-equip. As Company I marched out later that evening, a thousand thoughts raced through my mind. Among them was a newfound respect for the Confederate soldiers who fought and died so well. There was also the nagging question of what lay ahead. Yes, we have been beaten, but was this the end? Was the war over? Was this the end of the United States as we know it?

As we marched along, I also realized I had changed. The battle, the blood, and the chaos changed me in a way I could not describe. This day had changed us all. This was our baptism of fire and one thing was very clear: if this battle was not the end, a lot more blood would be shed before this conflagration was over.

Purgatory

"The only thing worse than a battle lost is a battle won."

Sir Arthur Wellesley
The Duke of Wellington

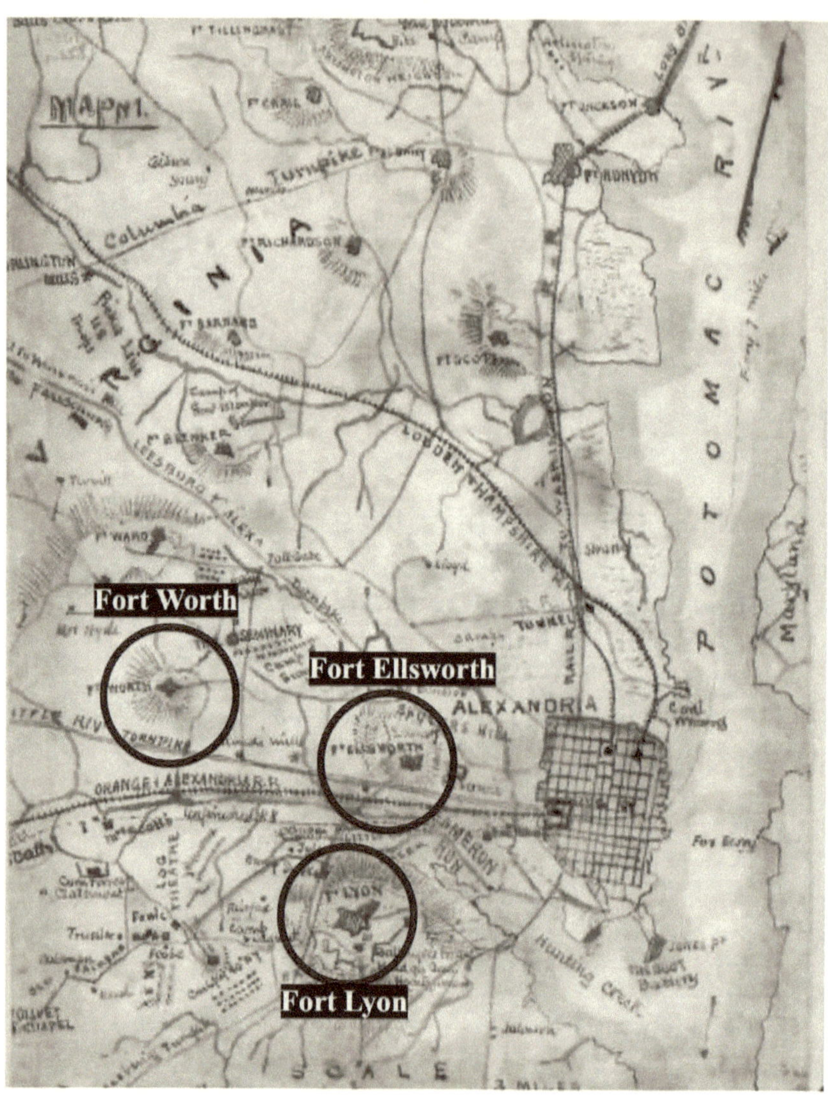

Defenses of Washington – Summer/Fall 1861

Chapter Seventeen

August 1861 – Clermont, Virginia

S ome religious upbringing teaches that after we shed this mortal coil, the souls of the less than righteous enter a realm of the afterlife known as purgatory. In this transitional world between heaven and hell, the uncertainty of time itself creates a state of limbo for tormented souls. My five-month stint in purgatory began when we marched away from the Manassas battlefield and returned to Clermont. This period would prove to be a difficult time for not only my comrades and I, but for our nation as well.

The twenty plus mile march from Centerville began about 9:00 pm and took most of the night. While the night air was somewhat cooler than the day, the humidity hung like a blanket over the entire route. At each break, fewer and fewer got back on their feet to continue, stringing the Regiment out for miles.

It was about dawn when the lead elements arrived at Clermont but it would take until noon before the stragglers and the walking wounded caught up. The rest of the day was spent counting our losses. Non-battle related casualties significantly outnumbered any losses inflicted by the Confederate army. As far as the battle was concerned, the Regiment suffered eight killed, twenty-nine seriously wounded, and twelve missing in action. One man from our Squad was listed among the seriously wounded. In addition to him, we had three others who sustained battle injuries, two from superficial bullet wounds and one from splinters of a tree hit by artillery fire.

The Company fared well as far as battle related casualties. However, when the non-battle casualties were figured in, our overall strength was now down to less than sixty percent of what it was when we left Augusta. We later found out over nine hundred had been killed on both sides during the battle and more than two thousand, six hundred sustained serious wounds.

"We certainly lost some good men in this one," Jim said as we relaxed in the morning sun.

"Did anyone know those who were killed?" John asked. None of us did.

As we licked our wounds and tried to placate our damaged pride, the administration and the country were reacting to the defeat. Aside from horror and dismay, many had the same questions about the war effort as we did. Some of these questions concerning the future of our country and President Lincoln's commitment to preserve the union were quickly answered. On July 22nd, the day we arrived in Clermont, Congress authorized another five hundred thousand volunteers for military service.

Even as bedraggled soldiers and wagonloads of wounded were returning to Washington, Abraham Lincoln demonstrated his resolve to preserve the union. He pledged increased funds for military procurement and development. He demanded better-trained and disciplined forces that would stand and fight. Additionally, in order to discourage the threat of European involvement with the South, Lincoln directed the Navy to proceed with all haste to make the blockade of Southern ports a reality.

Along with renewed efforts to curtail Southern commerce on the high seas, Lincoln communicated a three-pronged approach to the War Department concerning land operations. First, he called for an attack down the Mississippi River from Illinois, toward Memphis. Second, he defined a sweep across central Tennessee from the Cincinnati area. Finally, he directed an outright assault against the Confederate capitol of Richmond. Lincoln's strategies were a variation of General Winfield Scott's Anaconda Plan developed in early 1861. The primary difference now, with the increase in volunteers authorized by Congress and adequate leadership, the President's strategy might actually be put into practice.

As part of his renewed resolve, President Lincoln addressed the leadership question in the Army as well. On July 26th, the President replaced Brigadier General Irvin McDowell as the Commanding General of the Army of Northeast Virginia. Lincoln also formally activated the Army of the Potomac and called on Major General George McClellan to assume command. The Army of the Potomac was created earlier in 1861 but with no forces assigned. By July 26th, when McClellan assumed command, the Army of the Potomac included the Army of Northeast Virginia, the Department of Washington under Brigadier General Joseph K. Mansfield, and the Army of the Shenandoah under Major General Nathaniel Banks.

As the days following Manassas gave way to weeks, second-guessing about the battle raged on in the press, in Congress, in the Army, and in the court of public opinion. Routinely, journalists and reporters visited our camp seeking some deep philosophical reason for the loss. Among the soldiers, some blamed the civilian onlookers for the panic that ensued. Others blamed the press for all of the pre-battle propaganda. There were even a few who suggested we were defeated because we fought on Sunday, the Lord's Day of rest. Most agreed, in hindsight, that the army was inadequately trained and led by inexperienced officers.

The history books will no doubt reflect that the major contributing factor to our defeat was the inability of Major General Patterson to keep Johnston's Army in the Shenandoah Valley. This coupled with Brigadier General McDowell's pause in operations to conduct a reconnaissance of the Confederate lines seemed to be the primary reasons Johnston had the time and the opportunity to reinforce Beauregard.

From a purely military perspective, McDowell's reconnaissance itself was subject to much discussion and debate. There was little doubt in many people's minds that it was poorly conducted. No maps of the roads were developed or distributed. Additionally, there was no testing of any of the crossing points and no engineering enhancements made to any of the choke points, particularly the Cub Run bridge, to facilitate the movement of forces.

Finally, there was fault to be found, militarily, with McDowell's overall battle plan. Aside from being too complex for inexperienced troops, the plan called for the Second and Third Divisions to follow the First Division down the Warrenton Turnpike. Realistically, the First Division had about two miles to travel from the turnoff to Sudley Ford. On the other hand, the Second and Third Divisions were required to traverse over seven miles to cross Sudley Ford and return down the Sudley-Manassas Road. It was debated around many a campfire if the First Division followed the other two, perhaps the Second and Third Divisions would have been further along toward Sudley Ford and their movement might not have been compromised by the Confederate Signal Corps.

While the North debated, philosophized, and attempted to justify our loss, on the other side of the Bull Run, the Confederate press, Congress, and even President Jefferson Davis was reveling in victory. Davis' unannounced visit to the battlefield late in the day on

July 21st triggered a level of enthusiasm that echoed throughout the South. In spite of their stunning victory on that fateful Sunday, the Confederacy did not experience any additional jubilation in the days or weeks to come. There was no follow-up victory. There were no secondary battles. There was no final confrontation in front of Washington. For the average Confederate soldier, it was only the horror of a battle won. To celebrate their victory, they dug over nine hundred graves in the rain. For their glorious defense of Manassas, they assumed responsibility for the wounded of both sides, a task Confederate medical personnel and facilities were ill equipped to handle. Compounding this problem was the fact that captured Union medical personnel were given no parole to treat casualties. Rather, they were treated as prisoners of war.

It was over. The first major engagement of the war was over. For the North, it was a battle lost, the aftermath of which left us picking up the pieces, regrouping, re-equipping and readying ourselves for what was to come. For our Confederate counterparts, it was a battle won, complete with the praise and acknowledgments of the newly formed Confederate States of America. For both sides it was a brief glimpse of hell on earth, a firsthand view of the apocalypse. It was the sights and sounds of battle that all of us would carry to our graves, whether in this war or in post-war years yet to come. We experienced that special section of hell reserved for those who wear the uniform. The opening act of a soldier's hell was officially over.

Chapter Eighteen

August 1861 – Clermont, Virginia

Back at Clermont, the Regiment was somewhat isolated from any and all of the strategic thinking and manipulations going on in Washington. We were more concerned about our physical welfare. Most of us had lost everything except what we carried. The baggage train was gone, lost to the Confederates, along with our extra clothing and food supplies. In fairly quick order the Brigade Quartermaster and the Commissary began to flow food, replacement clothing, and equipment to Clermont. No one had much to eat since our time in Centerville so any food, even Army food, was welcome.

"I am convinced that in the post-apocalyptic world when mankind is no more, that the cockroaches who will still inhabit the earth will be walking over boxes and boxes of these hard biscuits", Charlie stated rather philosophically.

Jim nodded in agreement. "God this stuff is disgusting. No wonder they call it hardtack".

Hard bread or hard biscuits have been a part of military and seafaring times since the days of the Egyptians and the Romans. It was even said King Richard I travelled to the Crusades carrying a basket of hard biscuits as part of his kit. Since the onset of this war, bakeries in the North were churning out plain flour and water biscuits about three inches square and a quarter to a half-inch thick. The cooked biscuits were then packaged in fifty-pound boxes and shipped out to military units. Soldiers soon dubbed the biscuits hardtack so as not to confuse them with actual homemade biscuits or the "soft" bread that was sometimes issued.

"Remember that lot of hardtack we got at Fort Ellsworth," John asked? "It was so hard you had to break it with a rifle butt."

"Yeah, and when you finally broke it and soaked it in water, the dang stuff was as chewy as an old rain hat," Jim replied.

"I chewed on a piece of those biscuits all the way from Fort Ellsworth to Clermont," Charlie said.

"Well, this lot is full of bugs," I noted. "Some seriously fat ones at that."

It was not uncommon for boxes of hardtack to become infested with maggots or weevils. While the Quartermaster made good on any moldy or wet hardtack, they drew the line on the insect life. Unless the box was literally crawling with the little devils, we had to make due.

Although the nine pieces of hardtack we received daily were somewhat filling, they were not enough to sustain a man for the day. Our primary diet consisted of salted beef or salted pork. In addition to the meat and hardtack there were also canned foods, vegetables, coffee, sugar, and other foodstuffs depending on our location in reference to the Commissary and availability.

In a garrison type environment such as here in Clermont, fresh beef and occasionally "soft" bread supplemented our daily rations. Each company then assumed the responsibility for preparing and serving meals. However, finding a company cook was definitely harder than it seemed. Before joining the Army, the women in a soldier's family handled all of the cooking related activities. Men did the hunting and slaughtering but women prepared the meals. It was difficult then, to find anyone who had any serious cooking experience. In some units, company cooks were just assigned by the First Sergeant based on who was available at the time.

In our Regiment, being a company cook had its advantages and disadvantages. The major advantage was that cooks were relieved of any other duties except preparing food. There was no guard duty, no picket duty, and no working parties. The main disadvantage was the constant verbal harassment from soldiers before, during, and after meals.

When the Regiment was on the move each soldier received his ration of food, which was carried in our haversacks. The individual soldier then assumed the responsibility for cooking his own food or sharing the cooking duties with other members of his squad. When the day's march was done and the Regiment stopped for the night, the foraging for wood and wild foods began. Cooking fires quickly blossomed as the soldiers prepared their evening meal.

My time in the woods served me well at meal times. I was much better qualified to turn the "salted horse" or "sow belly", as we referred to the meat products, into something that was edible. Salted meat could be broiled over the campfire, held in place by a piece of green wood or a bayonet. The meat could also be fried with broken pieces of hardtack that soften nicely in the fat. Panfrying hardtack wouldn't force the maggots or weevils out of the biscuit but it sure made them easier to swallow. The only sure way to rid the hardtack of wildlife was to break it up and boil it with the coffee. The parboiled critters floated to the top of the coffee and could easily be spooned out.

One item of our diet that always fascinated me were the desiccated vegetables. These two or three-inch squares contained various vegetables that had been dehydrated and pressed together. When rehydrated, the vegetables swelled to a much larger size. "Desecrated" vegetables, as the soldiers called them, were a welcome addition to our soup or stewpot.

When the "artillery" of the company mess, that is the pots and pans, could not be unlimbered, many of us used the containers our canned foods arrived in as cooking pots. Canning food had originated with the Army of Napoleon in the late eighteenth century. In 1810 an Englishman, Peter Durand, introduced a method for sealing food products in tin cans. His idea was carried to America and by 1825 Thomas Kensett has a successful canning operation running in New York City. By the time the war broke out, canned foods were very common throughout the United States. The empty containers served as excellent cook pots and were easily outfitted with handles or other safety measures to protect the user from the campfire.

Our resupplying and refitting time at Clermont came to a close on August 10th. On that day the Regiment was ordered to an area west of Camp Ellsworth to assist in the construction of Fort Worth, yet another in the multitude of defensive works built to defend Washington. About this time, the reorganization of the Army also caught up with the Third Maine. We were now brigaded with the Fourth Maine Regiment and the Thirty-eighth and Fortieth New York Regiments under the command of Colonel John Sedgwick.

An 1837 graduate of the Military Academy, Sedgwick served with distinction in the Seminole Uprising and the Mexican War. At the outbreak of hostilities, he was the Assistant Inspector General for the Military District of Washington. Having recently recovered from cholera, which kept him from Manassas, Sedgwick was selected to command this newly formed Brigade in the reorganized Army of the Potomac.

Since our return from Centerville, the Regiment had undergone some reorganization of its own. As a result of actions at Bull Run, there was a shuffling of personnel throughout. Colonel Howard returned to command the Regiment. Unfortunately, most of us felt it would not be long until the Colonel was once again slated for command of a brigade. Major Staples remained as the executive officer but several of the positions on the staff changed. At the company level, Captain Lakeman had proven himself to be a capable company commander and remained in that position. Gone was First Lieutenant Albus Quinby. No one really knew where he went or even saw him leave. In fact, no one could recall seeing him after the Regiment marched for Sudley Ford. By the time we returned to Clermont, he was gone. Of course, rumors abounded as to his fate. Some said he was a prisoner, captured by the cavalry during the retreat. Others said he was wounded and in a hospital in Washington. Still others suggested he jumped a civilian carriage and was halfway back to Maine by now.

Both Second Lieutenant Denola Witham and Sergeant Lyon remained with the company. Sergeant Lyon received a commendation for his leadership during the withdrawal from Chinn Ridge and the march back to Centerville. We all felt the commendation to be well deserved. We did lose Corporal William Place of Augusta, our assistant squad leader. Corporal Bill, as he was known, contracted dysentery during the march to Pohick Creek that got progressively worse over time.

By the time we got back to Centerville, Corporal Bill was vomiting and defecating blood and was last seen being evacuated to hospital. In his place, newly promoted Corporal Frank Martin was re-assigned from Company H to serve as our assistant squad leader.

As we stepped out on that hot and humid Saturday morning for the relatively easy five-mile march to the future site of Fort Worth, a strange sense of foreboding overtook me. At the heart of this apprehension were feelings of depression that remained from the battle lost and an ominous inkling of what lay ahead. Instead of turning to face the enemy we were being directed to lay down our rifles and pick up shovels. Denied the opportunity to regain lost honor we were being relegated to chopping trees. This was agony in every sense of the word, although a respite from the hell of battle, nonetheless a journey to a soldier's purgatory.

Chapter Nineteen

August 1861 – Fort Worth, Virginia

nfortunately, my sixth sense of what lay ahead proved to be correct. After a short march from Clermont, the Regiment arrived at the future site of Fort Worth about the same time as the other regiments in the Brigade. Since the onset of hostilities, Union engineers and military planners had worked to ring the Capitol region with a series of forts and other defensive measures. This protective ring included a series of fortifications erected in Maryland and Virginia as well as in Washington itself. When he assumed command of the Army of the Potomac, General McClellan, himself an engineer, found the existing effort to be lacking and ordered immediate efforts begin to address the shortcomings of the Washington defenses.

The future location of Fort Worth was about three miles west of Alexandria and ten miles southwest of Washington on the former site of the Vaucluse plantation near Virginia Theological Seminary. Doctor James Craik, a surgeon of the Virginia Regiment and the Continental Army and a personal friend of George Washington, moved his practice to Alexandria after the Revolution and established Vaucluse. After his death in 1814, Thomas Fairfax, the ninth Lord Fairfax of Cameron, purchased the estate. When Lord Fairfax passed on in 1830, his widow remained in the estate with her two widowed daughters until her death in 1858. When war broke out, one of the daughters, Momimia Cary, lived in Vaucluse with her daughter Constance until the property was seized by the Union and the mansion destroyed to build Fort Worth.

When completed, Fort Worth occupied the high ground overlooking Hunting Creek and Cameron Run, the Orange and Alexandria rail line, and the Little River turnpike. From this location, the Fort's guns would control the southwestern approaches into Alexandria. The design of the Fort called for a log and earth structure with an overall perimeter of four hundred sixty-three yards and gun emplacements for about twenty-five artillery pieces. The Fort was a variation of the star design of Vauban and constructed in accordance with established Army engineering practices.

From an engineering perspective, the two fundamental components of any field fortification were the parapet and the ditch. In the case of Fort Worth, the parapet was designed as an earthen and log embankment intended to provide protection from enemy fire. The ditch, in addition to providing dirt for the parapet, served as a formidable obstacle to any attacking enemy force.

At varying points along the parapet, the Fort's design called for a series of bastions to be constructed generally at the corners or where the parapet made a turn. A bastion was an angular wall that extended outward from the parapet, and was composed of two flank walls and two face walls designed to provide flanking fire along the parapet between bastion locations. The overall size of the bastion depended on the number and type of artillery pieces each bastion was intended to support. While artillery pieces could be positioned anywhere along the parapet, the optimal employment of the guns was in the bastions. From these locations the artillery could effectively cover all areas of the parapet and catch any attacking force in a murderous crossfire.

Larger, long-range artillery pieces were housed inside the Fort proper in triangular fortifications called ravelins. Similar in design to lunettes and redans, the fundamental difference was that a ravelin was placed inside the parapet while redans and lunettes were generally employed as advanced works or as detached fortifications that covered a specific geographic area.

The final structures to be built were the bombproofs and the stockade. Bombproofs were sunken post and beam structures covered by timbers and four to six feet of dirt. The purpose of the bombproof was to protect soldiers from enemy shellfire, serve as magazines for the artillery ammunition, or safeguard other critical facilities such as the command post or the hospital.

The Fort Worth stockade was a log structure about twelve feet high with sentry positions called guerites at each corner. While the stockade was technically the last line of defense of the Fort, during daily operations it housed the offices and facilities that supported the assigned units. The stockade also housed all of the logistical services for the Fort and either a series of wells or underground cisterns that supplied the Fort with potable water.

Once the final design of Fort Worth was settled and the engineers had completed surveying the site and marked various locations, the actual work of building the Fort began. Our time working on the Fort was generally divided into two undertakings. First, there was the actual digging of the ditch surrounding the Fort and the shuttling of dirt to the parapet area. The second involved working in the surrounding woods felling trees, splitting logs, or cutting stakes to be employed as defensive obstacles.

If we were not laboring on the Fort then our days were spent on various working parties, foraging details, or conducting endless training about one thing or another. Of course, duty on the picket line was a seven-day a week activity. Once the defensive positions on the picket line were constructed, assignment as a picket actually became preferred duty to Fort construction.

As the construction of the main part of the Fort continued, the engineers began spending more time evaluating the terrain outside of the Fort and designing defensive countermeasures to thwart an enemy assault. Once that task was complete, any attack would have to cross several levels of defense before the attacking force could actually penetrate the perimeter of the Fort.

The first line of defense for the Fort was the picket line. Pickets and sentries were located about three hundred yards out from the parapet and concentrated on the likely avenues of attack. All along the picket lines, rifle pits or trenches with small parapets of earth and logs were constructed. These defensive measures were then concealed with brush or branches to hide the occupants from enemy observation.

Once past the pickets, an enemy force needed to cross a large open area that had been stripped of anything that might serve as cover for assaulting troops. All of the trees were removed and used for other purposes around the Fort. When possible, the engineers took advantage of any natural obstacles available such as a dammed stream or dense thicket to channelize the attacking force into the killing zones of the Fort's weapons.

In addition to the natural features that could be used as obstacles, the engineers chose to construct a series of particularly nasty looking, man-made obstacles called the cheval-de-frise. This type of obstacle consisted of a nine or ten-foot log that was pierced by two diagonal rows of sharpened stakes. When properly constructed, the stakes stuck out from the center logs about four feet. The stakes also allowed the cheval-de-frise to be free standing and, with little effort, be moved to where the threat was the greatest. Two or more of these obstacles could also be linked together to cover a larger area or better channel an enemy force.

Once across this open area, the attacking force entered the wide and sloping area called the glacis. The glacis was purposely constructed in a way to give the defenders of the Fort a clear and open field of fire in close proximity to the ditch and parapet. As part of the glacis, a second type of cheval-de-frise could be constructed to further slow or channelize the enemy. This obstacle consisted of numerous sharpened stakes lying atop a log. The stakes were placed at an inclined position facing the attacking force with the other end embedded into the glacis.

Similar to this second type of cheval-de-frise was the abatis. This form of barricade consisted of smaller felled trees that were stripped of leaves and small branches. The remaining branches were sharpened to a point before the entire abatis was staked to the glacis.

If the attacking force managed to reach the top of the glacis, the next major obstacle in its path was the ditch. Aside from being considerably deep and possibly filled with rainwater, the scarp (the wall on the parapet side of the ditch) often contained a series of palisading chevaux-de frise designed to prevent further movement up the outside wall of the parapet.

The final obstacle for the attacking force was the parapet itself. The defenders of the fort used the thick exterior walls of the parapet as protection from enemy fire. From ground level inside the fort, the defenders manned the wall by climbing the slope of the banquette to the platform or banquette tread in order to bring fire on the enemy.

This portion of the parapet was supported by a series of gabions and fascines that served to reinforce the parapet wall and provide additional protection for the defenders. A gabion was a series of open-ended cylindrical wicker baskets laid side by side along the banquette tread wall and then filled with soil for reinforcement. As a base for the gabions, fascines of tightly bound straight branches were emplaced to hold the gabions and keep the soil of the parapet from eroding. Another layer of fascines was placed on top of the gabions creating large dirt filled wicker frameworks designed to protect the defenders.

As the "dog days" of August slowly marched along, this became our existence, a monotonous daily journey spent digging ditches, moving soil, cutting trees, and building gabions, fascines, or other obstacles. When not working on the fort, there was drilling and training, foraging parties, or other working parties. Our only real break came when the squad was assigned to the picket line. Then we could relax between sentry tours and contemplate our existence.

As the end of August approached, my melancholy deepened. Like many of my comrades, I had enlisted to fight, not to dig. I was not alone in these feelings. The overall mood of the Regiment had begun to sour and it seemed like only a matter of time before what morale and discipline would surely waiver.

Chapter Twenty

August 1861 – Fort Worth, Virginia

The 27th of August brought with it a brief respite from the purgatory of Fort construction. At a Company formation Captain Lakeman told us of our new assignment.

"We will be moving about five miles from here to a place called Bailey's Crossroads. The enemy has been killing off our soldiers and seems to pose a threat to the northern born citizens in the area. Major Staples will be in command of our four-company battalion. For the march out, Company I will be in the vanguard of the formation. Sergeant Lyon – your Squad will provide skirmishers for the point. Be prepared to move out at first light".

That evening there was a good deal of excitement throughout the Company. We were finally going out to meet the enemy. Of course, there was a lot of good-natured bantering with the companies not selected to go. They would remain here at Fort Worth and continue the construction effort.

In 1837, Hachaliah Bailey, a noted northern circus showman, purchased a tract of land near Falls Church at the intersection of the Leesburg and Columbia Pikes. I remember seeing Bailey's circus in Augusta one year. There were some spectacular performances and animals that I had only read about. I've been told that Bailey's circus later merged with P.T. Barnum and the Ringling Brothers and went on to international fame and fortune.

As the Union Army retreated toward Washington after the fight at Manassas, the Confederate Army advanced behind it. The Confederates now controlled the city of Falls Church and a ridgeline running from the city southeast to the area of Bailey's Crossroads. Falls Church, once an original part of the District of Columbia, was now the headquarters of Confederate forces in Northern Virginia. On Munson's Hill, the southernmost high ground on the ridge, the Confederates constructed a log and earth position called Fort Munson. From the heights of Fort Munson, the Confederates turned

Bailey's Crossroads into their personal killing field. Their artillery was registered on the crossroads and their sharpshooters were killing any and all who carelessly exposed themselves on picket duty or conducted reconnaissance of rebel positions on the ridge.

In addition to Fort Munson, the rebels garrisoned two other pieces of high ground along the ridge, Upton's Hill and Mason's Hill. From these positions they commanded a view not just of Bailey's Crossroads but all the way to Capitol Hill in Washington proper. Having to stare at the large Confederate flag that flew from the ridge unnerved many Washington residents who became increasingly concerned that the rebels would use the Falls Church area to launch an attack across the river and into Washington itself. Union engineers worked feverishly to construct fortifications and defensive works in the area, but this direct route of advance into Washington needed to be shored up.

The Battalion from Third Maine arrived at Bailey's Crossroads about ten o'clock on August 28th. We fell into a defensive alignment near a blacksmith's shop on the left of a regiment from Michigan. The blacksmith's shop, although deserted, was peppered with artillery and rifle shots. Later that evening, after the picket line was established and our defensive positions constructed, we found out why.

Charlie Clark, the ever-vigilant correspondent for the Kennebec Journal, visited some of the Michigan boys and had returned with the news.

"The Michigan lads don't rightly know who is on the ridge," Charlie reported. "Some say it is a regiment from Longstreet's Brigade and some say its dismounted cavalry from Stuart's Brigade. Michigan has taken some casualties from artillery and sharpshooters but neither side appears to be in any hurry to attack the other. There are other regiments moving in behind Michigan to block the route to the river."

"What's with all the holes in the blacksmith shop?" Jim asked.

"From what I heard, Old Michigan wanted to show the rebels they meant business so they constructed a 'cannon' in the blacksmith's shop from a length of stovepipe and couple of wagon wheels. When it was finished, they rolled it out into the middle of the road and took cover. The Rebels got real upset about the Michigan cannon and proceeded to fire on it and the blacksmith's shop. The Michigan boys got quite a laugh out of that."

For some reason the thought of opposing sides fighting over stovepipe cannons seemed hilarious at the time. The story became the highlight of our time at Bailey's Crossroads.

For their part, the Rebels didn't appear to be conducting any real work to upgrade their defenses on the ridge. We routinely watched them lying around or strolling down the ridge to man their picket lines. At a certain point on the side of the ridge they became more cautious and began to disappear into the blind spots in the ground until they arrived at their posts.

Major Staples ordered sharpshooters to man our picket posts and engage the enemy when they became visible. As one of these marksmen, I spent a good deal of daylight hours on the picket line. We would routinely exchange fire with the rebel sharpshooters that would soon escalate into a full-blown skirmish. Although none of us ever got hit, the logs and dirt of our fighting positions showed signs of bullet marks. After three days of this cat and mouse hunting, our Battalion was pulled off the line and replaced by another Michigan regiment. Late in the afternoon of August 30th we marched back to Fort Worth to rejoin the rest of the Regiment.

Our time away from construction at Fort Worth was a pleasant diversion. We got the chance to engage the enemy and came away with no casualties from our operations. On the march back I listened with amusement to the conversations among the soldiers. To hear them tell it, we had repelled the whole Confederate army instead of engaging a few rebels on the picket line. Now we were back in purgatory: back to an endless parade of monotonous tasks: back to a soul stealing depression: back to a morale breaking existence that only promised to get worse.

————————❦————————

Chapter Twenty-One

October 1861 – Fort Lyon, Virginia

It seemed like the "dog days" of August gave way to the "dog days" of early September. The heat and humidity of these days was usually accented by a late afternoon or early evening thunderstorm leaving our construction efforts floating in a sea of red clay mud. As September progressed however, the oppressive heat began to give way to somewhat cooler temperatures, lower humidity, and pleasant bordering on chilly evenings.

By the first of October, construction work progressed on schedule but the Fort was by no means close to being operational. The engineers estimated at least another month before a New York Artillery Regiment could occupy the grounds and place their guns.

One evening in early October Charlie returned from the Regimental Headquarters chuckling heartily to himself.

"What is so funny?" Jim asked.

"I just came from regiment," Charlie replied. "Do you remember the fun time we had at Bailey's Crossroads?"

"How could we forget," John said as we all nodded in agreement.

"Seems someone finally decided to do something about all the rebels on the ridge. They brought in a couple of brigades and were planning a major attack against the ridge and the rebel headquarters at Falls Church for the morning of September 28th." With that Charlie began to chuckle louder. Now he had our undivided attention.

"What happened?" John asked.

"Well, it seems sometime the night before, the rebels up and left the whole area. The attacking forces didn't find a single one. The cavalry supporting the operation reported the rebels fell back toward Manassas." Charlie's chuckles now turned to outright laughter.

"The best part was when our infantry got on top of the ridge all of the artillery everyone was so deathly afraid of turned out to be tree trunks painted black and pointed out of revetments at our lines." By this point in the story, Charlie's laughter was contagious.

"I heard Major Staples telling a group of the company commanders the story. They all thought it was hilarious. One of the company commanders called them 'Quaker cannons' because they were about as harmful as a Quaker in a fist fight."

The humor of the Bailey's Crossroads story was a welcome relief from our daily existence. By the middle of October, morale in the Regiment hit rock bottom. Word had been passed that Third Maine would be moving from Fort Worth about three miles south to the area where a new fort was being planned. The sullen attitude of many soldiers festered into outright hostility. Fights broke out daily within squads, between squads, and between companies. Disrespect toward both officers and non-commissioned officers increased. It got so bad Colonel Howard addressed the men and conveyed to them that this type of behavior would not be tolerated. In spite of the Colonel's speech, the incidents continued.

While there was a recognized need for discipline in the Army, not all discipline was administered in a just and fair manner. In the Third Maine Regiment, most of our minor incidents were punished with extra work details or extra guard duties. In a location like Fort Worth there were always things that needed to be done or tasks that required additional efforts.

Jobs such as chopping wood for the company kitchens or digging and filling latrines were usually reserved for punishment details. Anyone who willfully disobeyed orders or was insubordinate could also be sentenced to write a letter of apology to either the injured party or the command as a whole. This type of punishment presumed the convicted soldier actually knew how to write.

For any event that went beyond an isolated or minor incident the company commander would forward the information to the regiment with a recommendation that a court martial be convened. There were four levels of court martial in the Army at the time. For the most egregious of offenses the accused would face a general court martial. Desertion was the most common offense but murder, rape, treason, or conduct unbecoming an officer all qualified to be judged by a panel of five to thirteen members of the court martial board.

A regimental court martial handed most infractions of good order and discipline. This form of justice would be ordered by the regimental commander and staffed with three members of the regiment. Like a regimental court martial, garrison courts martial were limited to army posts where a permanent garrison, fort or barracks existed and the troops manning the garrison were from more than one organization or unit. Garrison courts martial were initiated by the individual commanding the garrison and, like a regimental court, consisted of three members of the command.

The last type of court martial, the drumhead court, was limited to offenses committed during military operations in the field that required immediate justice. The name was derived from the fact early field courts used a drum as an improvised table and any writing or signing to be accomplished was done on the drumhead. Drunk on duty or sleeping on watch were common offenses for a drumhead court martial.

Many soldiers felt court martial charges to be a form of petty tyranny evoked by despotic officers and inflicted to tarnish a soldier's good name or reputation. For the most part, in the Third Maine the punishment generally fit the crime and the justice, while not necessarily considered fair, was impartial and in the best interests of the command.

For the more significant of crimes such as murder or desertion a soldier could be sentenced to death. This early in the war the death sentence was not usually handed out. Confinement in an Army jail, solitary confinement, and confinement at hard labor were the preferred methods of punishment. While flogging was outlawed in the Army in late 1861, branding of cowards, thieves, deserters, or soldiers deemed to be worthless was a common punishment usually before expulsion from the Army. The brand served to alert other units in the event the soldier attempted to re-enlist to collect a new bounty.

At all levels of courts martial, the accused could receive a reduction in rank, a reprimand, a fine or forfeiture of pay, or a host of other punishments that included loss of privileges, assignment to a less desirable duty, some form of hard labor, as well as expulsion from the Army. In addition to these types of punishments, at the regimental level most other types of punishment were meant to physically impact the soldier or humiliate him in front of his comrades. For first time convictions for petty crimes, the offender might be required to stand atop a barrel at regimental formation while the regimental commander read a reprimand outlining his crimes. Another punishment required the guilty party to actually wear a barrel as a shirt while conducting his duties. Another humiliating punishment was to hang a signboard around the offender's neck defining the nature of his crime.

More serious incidents or multiple offenses of the same type required a more physical form of humiliation. Carrying a log around camp until the guilty party could not stand was one such form of physical humiliation. If a soldier was a consummate straggler or was caught fighting, the punishment might be a ride on the Spanish donkey or the wooden mule. The convicted party would mount a narrow log or rail suspended high enough off the ground so his feet wouldn't touch. In some cases, weights would be tied to his ankles to exacerbate the discomfort. The soldier would then ride the donkey until he passed out.

Bucking and gagging was a popular form of punishment for chronic disrespect or disobedience. The guilty party would sit for long periods of time with his hands tied to his ankles and his feet bound together. A wooden rod or branch would be shoved over his arms and under his knees and he would be gagged with a knotted cloth. In addition to these physical punishments, the convicted soldier would have to endure all forms of verbal harassment and humiliation that would be doled out by his comrades as he went about his duties or they passed the punishment area.

Given Colonel Howard's Christian nature there were other punishments handed out in other regiments that were not practiced in Third Maine. Tying a guilty soldier by his thumbs from a tree branch or tying the soldier to a wagon wheel went beyond what the Colonel felt was good order and discipline and entered the realm of malicious infliction of injury.

Chapter Twenty-Two

Fall 1861 – Fort Lyon, Virginia

Our expectations for Colonel Howard proved to be true. In late September he was ceremoniously promoted to Brigadier General and transferred to another brigade in the Army of the Potomac. In a stroke of good fortune, Major Staples was promoted Colonel and assigned as the Commanding Officer of the Third Maine Regiment. We remained a part of General Sedgewick's Brigade and the brigade assigned to the Division headed by our old division commander, General Heintzelman. The General had been wounded in the elbow at Manassas but was now healthy enough to resume his duties as our division commander.

Our move from Fort Worth to Fort Lyon was without fanfare or any level of enthusiasm. We had traded one set of shovels and axes for another without any significant increase in optimism that our lot would be improved in the future. Fort Lyon would be a major undertaking as far as fort construction was concerned. Yet another log and earth fortification, Fort Lyon was located on Ballenger's Hill south of the Hunting Creek and Cameron Run areas. Ballenger's Hill was the highest point south of Alexandria and overlooked Telegraph Road, the Columbia Turnpike, the Orange and Alexandria rail line and the Little River Turnpike. The Fort was named for Brigadier General Nathaniel Lyon, who died at the Battle of Wilson's Creek in Missouri, the first Union general killed in the war.

When we arrived at Fort Lyon and observed the layout, all of us realized it was to be one of the largest forts south of Washington proper. The perimeter of the Fort would be over nine hundred and thirty yards with all of the appropriate engineering creations to make this a daunting structure from the enemy's perspective. The thirty-one guns scheduled for the Fort included a battery of four eight-inch Parrott rifled cannons and sixteen mortars. With this armament and its location, when complete, Fort Lyon would command the entire

Potomac River Basin south of Alexandria and control the river access into Washington itself.

Work on the Fort began in earnest in October. Our days were spent either engaged in some form of company, battalion, regimental, or brigade drills, manning the picket lines, or constructing the Fort. The fall weather of Virginia managed to soothe some of the tension of the long, hot summer but tempers and emotions that previously festered ran just below the surface in the cooler weather. Fall in Virginia was pleasant enough but nothing on the magnitude of Maine. The hardwoods began to shed their summer green for a modest amount of color before fading to brown and dropping off for the winter.

By the fall of 1861, the government in general and specifically the War Department and President Lincoln were becoming increasingly disillusioned with the leadership of Major General McClellan. It was a far cry from the tumultuous welcome he received from both the crowd and the government upon his arrival in Washington in July.

An 1846 graduate of West Point at the tender age of nineteen, McClellan saw service in the Mexican War as an engineer and served in various other capacities to include an observer to the Crimean War before resigning his commission in 1857 to become the vice president of the Illinois Central Railroad. In 1860, he was appointed as president of the struggling Ohio and Mississippi Railroad and used his burgeoning organizational skills to right a company hit hard by the economic crisis of 1857.

When the war broke out, political connections with Ohio Governor William Dennison and former Ohio Governor, now Secretary of the Treasury, Salomon Chase led to McClellan's appointment as Major General of Volunteers. Before his summons to Washington, McClellan oversaw the establishment of training centers for the processing of thousands of Midwest volunteers. Thanks to Chase's political connection, McClellan was then assigned to the Army of the Shenandoah and given a commission as a Major General in the regular army. The "Boy General" was only thirty-four at the time of his appointment.

By appointing McClellan to the Army of the Potomac, President Lincoln hoped to draw upon his youth and organizational abilities and couple those traits with the experiences and wisdom of General of the Army Winfield Scott. In spite of the fact McClellan brought an increased level of organization and training to the Army of the

Potomac, the relationship with General Scott that the President hoped for never truly materialized. Their personal dispute centered on McClellan's inability to accept any strategic guidance from General Scott. He openly opposed General Scott's Anaconda Plan in favor of his own strategic design. McClellan saw himself as the commander of an overwhelming force that would sweep across Virginia in true Napoleonic fashion and crush the rebellion in one grand campaign.

General McClellan felt his grand strategy required an army of about two hundred and eighty thousand men supported by over six hundred artillery pieces, numbers which rankled the War Department and General Scott. This estimate of the numbers required was influenced by an extremely overblown estimate of the number of Confederate troops opposing him. While McClellan's overestimation of enemy troop strength certainly influenced his strategic and operational decision making, it also had a serious negative effect on his initiative. Instead of displaying an aggressive level of operational and tactical maneuvers against the enemy, McClellan chose to be cautious in any decision involving contact with the Confederate army. As October gave way to November, this cautious attitude began to undermine the spirit of the Army of the Potomac and perplex both the War Department and the President.

McClellan's dispute with General Scott became personal in early October when he refused to discuss any of his strategic plans with either General Scott or the War Department. Scott became so outraged and disillusioned with McClellan that he formally tendered his resignation to Lincoln. On October 18th, after over fifty years of military service to his country, President Lincoln reluctantly agreed to allow the aging Commanding General to retire for "health reasons".

By November some of the impacts from the situation in Washington had trickled down to the regimental level. One of the not so enjoyable tasks that came down from on high was an increase in the ceremonial aspects of army life. General McClellan was quite fond of his assignment as Commander of the Army of the Potomac and went out of his way to show off his command to any and all that would spend time and watch. Parades, reviews, inspections, and just about any other type of ceremonial function he could imagine made their way down to the ranks. Little Mac's crowning achievement on the ceremonial front was a troop review he orchestrated for President Lincoln and his Cabinet at Bailey's Crossroads on November 20th.

Bailey's Crossroads came to be selected as the site of the grand review because of the proximity to Washington and its large, uninterrupted plain that was capable of housing the thousands of soldiers involved. The President and the entire cabinet came out for the event along with about sixty thousand spectators. Although Third Maine was required to send a representative detachment of soldiers and our colors, Company I was one of the fortunate companies not to be selected to participate.

Those who actually participated told us that the parade consisted of troops, artillery, cavalry, and wagons that took all day to pass the reviewing stand. Another, unconfirmed story about the review said that a young, New England poet named Julia Ward Howe attended the ceremony. She was so impressed by the spectacle that she returned to her hotel that evening and penned words to the "Battle Hymn of the Republic" set to the tune of "John Brown's Body".

With the grand review behind us, Third Maine settled in for a long winter of Fort construction, training, and mind-numbing working parties. This would be a true winter in purgatory with no interruptions to the monotony that would provide even the remotest glimmer of hope for any of us.

By December I was resigned to my fate, at least for the coming months, when an unexpected reprieve landed in the Regimental Headquarters. This pardon from purgatory came in the form of a new draft of people for duty in a unit assigned to the Navy on the Mississippi River, the Western Gunboat Flotilla. As Captain Lakeman read the directive at a formation, that old seduction bug, which had been somewhat dormant of late, began to gnaw away at my soul once again.

The directive requested artillery personnel familiar with the workings of naval guns and infantrymen who were accomplished marksmen to assist in ship board defense as well as soldiers with an administrative or medical background. This was my chance to see the world outside of Maine. While not the Plains of Marathon, the fields of Waterloo, or the frozen wasteland outside Moscow, the Mississippi River was a fair distance from home. This was also a chance to volunteer for something besides the tedium of Fort construction.

That evening, I had the chance to discuss the situation with my friends. They seemed to understand my need to do something different even better than I did. I would certainly miss them. The next morning, I spoke to Sergeant Lyon and Captain Lakeman about volunteering. Both said while sorry to see me go I was indeed qualified to volunteer and submitted my name to the Regimental Adjutant.

Shortly before Christmas 1861 I received orders. I was to detach from Third Maine in January and report to the processing center in Washington for further transportation to the Commanding Officer of the Army Detachment assigned to the Western Gunboat Flotilla. Unknowingly, I was trading the purgatory we lived in since Manassas for a new kind of soldier's hell; a brown water inferno over two thousand miles long and dubbed the "Father of Waters".

War on the River

"There are no extraordinary men… just extraordinary circumstances that ordinary men are forced to deal with."

William F. Halsey

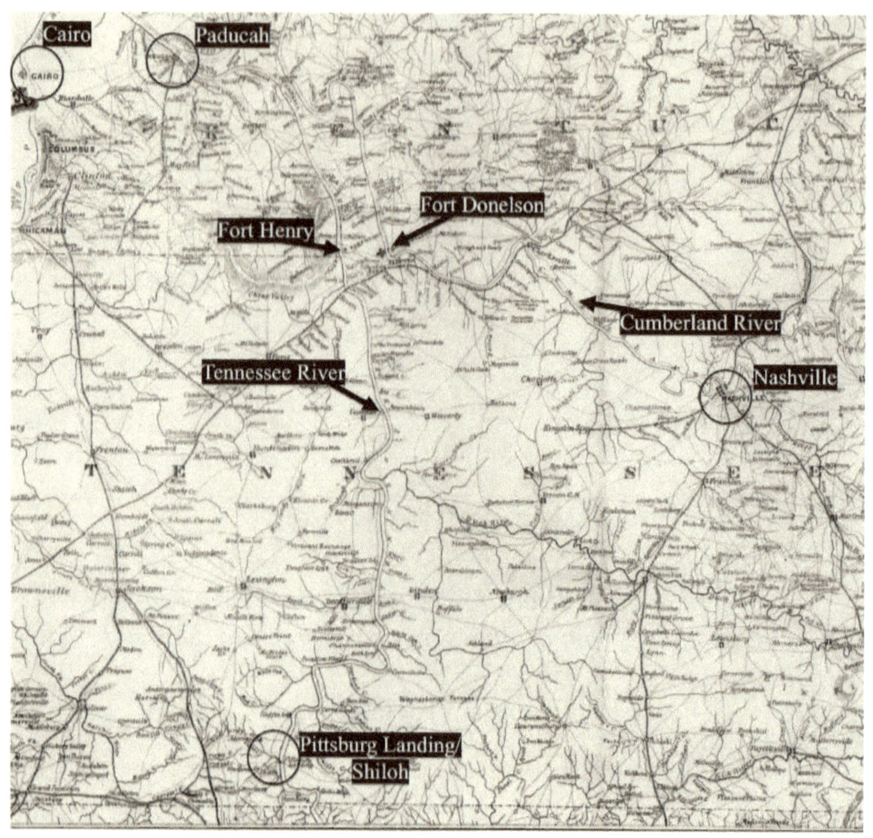

Tennessee/Kentucky River Network 1862

Chapter Twenty-Three

January 1862 – Cairo, Illinois

wo weeks after the start of the New Year, I departed the Third Maine Regiment with orders to "report for duty with the Western Gunboat Flotilla" in Cairo, Illinois. From Fort Lyon, I travelled back to Washington and reported to the designated transit facility. After spending a couple of days waiting for transportation, I was finally booked on a train bound for the West.

As I waited to depart, I read several editorials in the newspaper about a newly formed agency in the War Department taking control of the rail lines. In addition to rail lines captured from the Confederates, this takeover included any rail lines deemed critical for the movement of troops and equipment throughout the North. Unfortunately, by the time our train pulled out, the takeover had not happened. As a result, soldiers like me, traveling by rail from one area to another, remained at the mercy of civilian railroad workers.

About forty of us were herded into a boxcar for the journey. The small stove in the corner did little to alleviate the winter air that flowed freely through the car. After bouncing around in that frigid environment for four days, sustained only by cold Army rations, the train lumbered into Cairo and I stepped off to join my new unit.

Leaving the train station, I asked some of the locals for directions to the Army Detachment of the Western Gunboat Flotilla. The locals spared no time in informing me that the city name was pronounced "Kay-ro" and not Cairo as in Egypt. That blunder corrected; they were very happy to provide me with directions to the Flotilla offices.

The original charter for Cairo was granted in 1818 but it wasn't until 1846, when land was purchased for the Illinois Central Railroad, that the city started to grow. The railroad was completed in 1855 and Cairo became a major hub and transshipment point for steamboats delivering goods all along the Mississippi and Ohio Rivers. Cairo riverboats traveled as far south as New Orleans and as far east as Pittsburgh.

Now, as I stood on the pier overlooking the busy port and the Ohio River, I could look down to the right and see the convergence of two great rivers, the Ohio and the Mississippi. Even from this vantage point, the Mississippi appeared to be enormously wide compared to any of the rivers in Maine or the ones I encountered in Virginia. Turning north on the Mississippi and traveling about one hundred and fifty miles upstream, a ship could turn west into the Missouri River above St. Louis and follow the path once explored by Lewis and Clark. Turning south, a ship would pass the Confederate cities of Memphis, Vicksburg, Natchez, Baton Rouge, and the major port of New Orleans before reaching the Gulf of Mexico.

To the left was the Ohio River. A short distance upriver is the major naval shipbuilding and repair facility at Mound City. The Ohio then follows the Illinois and Kentucky border past Paducah, Kentucky to the mouth of the Tennessee River.

The Tennessee River begins in eastern Tennessee and flows southwest to Chattanooga. The river then dips into Northern Alabama, moving westerly then northerly across Tennessee and Kentucky until it joins the Ohio River.

Still further up the Ohio was the confluence of the Cumberland River. The Cumberland begins in southeastern Kentucky before entering Tennessee. The river then flows westerly across Tennessee into Nashville before flowing back northerly into Kentucky. Once in Kentucky, it runs somewhat parallel to the Tennessee River before turning and joining the Ohio River.

The major river networks of the Mississippi and Ohio Rivers were on the minds of military planners from the onset of hostilities. As part of General Winfield Scott's Anaconda Plan, as amended by President Lincoln after Manassas, these rivers and their principal tributaries were regarded as critical to Union success in the West. The Union strategy called for an attack down the Mississippi from Illinois toward the Confederate centers of Memphis and Vicksburg. Simultaneously, a second effort would drive up the Mississippi from the Gulf of Mexico past New Orleans and split the Confederacy. Success in this effort could give the Union control of all ship movements on the Mississippi River.

A second aspect of the Union strategy in the West called for an attack across Kentucky and Tennessee from the Cincinnati area. An essential element of success for any operations in this area was control of the Ohio River and its major tributaries, the Tennessee River and the Cumberland River.

While grand in design, the Union strategy was not without its share of issues. The amended Anaconda Plan also called for the Navy to blockade Southern ports and conduct riverine operations in the Western Theater. After Fort Sumter, the United States Navy was in no shape to conduct a meaningful blockade of Southern ports or any realistic and effective operations on western rivers.

Since the War of 1812, the American Navy sought to develop more of an international presence and made great strides to modernize its ships and weapons systems to meet that goal. This meant the Navy needed to keep pace with the European navies and not concern itself with the possibility of internal conflict. From 1854 to 1859 in a shift away from sails, the Navy commissioned the construction of thirty steam-powered ships with new and improved armament systems. In spite of some innovative technological advances, the Navy faced serious limitations as a force in readiness when it came to the preservation of the Union. Nowhere was this more evident than in the proposed conduct of operations on western rivers. With the exception of a few auxiliary ships, all of the operational capital ships in the inventory were too large or had too deep a draft to conduct viable riverine operations.

Personnel issues also plagued the Navy and hampered many a promising officer's career. Since there was no mandatory retirement age for senior officers and therefore limited promotional prospects, countless young and capable junior officers, many of them graduates of the newly established Naval Academy, chose to depart the service for the civilian sector rather than become mired in a stagnant promotion system.

At the time of Fort Sumter, the United States Navy had no rank above Captain and a very top-heavy roster of senior officers many of whom were unfit for sea duty. These officers also showed no willingness to retire, a factor that prevented promotions for worthy juniors. Additionally, when the dust settled and the individual states declared for either the Union or the Confederacy, over twenty-five percent of the Navy's effective officer corps left to join the Confederate Navy.

Although Secretary of the Navy Gideon Wells did not wholly agree with General Scott and the amended Anaconda Plan, he set about to create an effective blockade force and a "brown water" capability. To assist in the project, Wells and Attorney General

Edward Bates invited James Buchanan Eads to Washington to discuss his ideas on creating a riverine capability in the West.

James Eads was well known along the Mississippi River. His ideas and designs of shallow draft vessels earned his company numerous contracts along the river and made Eads rich. After Fort Sumter, Eads discussed his latest idea with Bates; the conversion of existing shallow water vessels into ironclad gunboats. Bates passed Eads' viewpoints on to Wells and the Secretary invited Eads to Washington to discuss implementation of his concepts.

Secretary Wells also enlisted the assistance of noted a naval architect, Samuel Pook, to assist in the brown water project. Working with Eads, Pook designed the United States Navy's first ironclads; seven ships to be built from the keel up at facilities in St. Louis and Carondelet, Missouri, Cairo and Mound City, Illinois, and Cincinnati, Ohio.

With the concept of a brown water capability gaining traction, on May 16, 1861, the Navy Department established the Western Gunboat Flotilla and appointed Commander John Rodgers as its commanding officer. Under an internal War Department agreement, the Flotilla was under the control of the Union army with Rodgers reporting to Brigadier General George B. McClellan, the commander of the western region.

In addition to overseeing the construction of the "City-Class" gunboats, Rodgers worked with Pook overhauling three steamboats, the Tyler, the Lexington, and the Conestoga, and modifying them to carry some heavy armament. Unlike the gunboats, they were clad with wood instead of iron as their armor protection. This earned them the nickname of "timberclads."

In July of 1861 General McClellan was relieved and sent to command the Army of the Potomac. The fiery tempered and often-obstinate Major General John C. Fremont replaced him. Troubles between Fremont and Rodgers began almost from the first day. To keep the project on track, in September, the Navy Department transferred Rodgers and brought in newly promoted Flag Officer Andrew Foote.

With the construction of the brown water navy underway, it was James Eads who recognized the importance of Cairo in the overall strategic picture on the rivers in the West. Union military planners were quick to agree with Eads and recognized the criticality of the city to their efforts in the region. Located at the confluence of the

Mississippi and Ohio Rivers, Cairo was the critical node for control of these rivers as well as the Missouri River, some one hundred and fifty miles upriver at St. Louis. Based on Eads' recommendation to the Navy Secretary and Secretary of War Simon Cameron, work quickly began to fortify this key part of the river network.

Union naval activities on the rivers were not lost on the Confederates. In an effort to keep Kentucky and their portion of the Mississippi River under Confederate control, Rebel forces under Major General Leonidas Polk crossed into Kentucky, an action that negated Kentucky's border state neutrality.

In September of 1861, as the Confederates built up forces in the region, General Albert Sydney Johnston was assigned as the area commander. General Polk was reassigned as a corps commander under General Johnston and placed in charge of that section of the Mississippi River from Kentucky down to Tennessee.

General Johnston, a former general in both the Texican and United States Army, saw the value of the river networks, particularly the Mississippi, but also the Tennessee and the Cumberland. To counter the Union buildup at Cairo, Johnston ordered the construction of fortifications at key points along the Mississippi River from Belmont, Missouri south to Vicksburg, Mississippi.

Confederate military planners also saw the value of the Tennessee and Cumberland Rivers in supporting Union army operations in Central Kentucky and Tennessee. As a deterrent to Union advances in this area, General Johnston ordered the construction of additional fortifications at key locations on these rivers.

As the summer of 1861 gave way to the fall, General Polk busied his forces building fortifications at Belmont, Missouri and across the river at Columbus, Kentucky, an area only about twenty miles downriver from Cairo. Polk also began to mount heavy guns further downstream at Island Ten, that is, the tenth island in the river south of Cairo.

On the Union side, in August of 1861, Brigadier General Ulysses S. Grant assumed command of the Ironton District of Missouri. Over the next few months, General Grant established a solid working relationship with the Flotilla and especially Flag Officer Andrew Foote. As the relationship grew, Grant and Foote began planning an offensive to reduce the Confederate fortifications at Belmont and Columbus.

On November 7th, General Grant led three thousand Union soldiers against Belmont on the Missouri side of the river. Auxiliary transports and two of the Flotilla's timberclads, the Tyler and the Lexington, supported the assault. After landing about three miles upriver from Belmont, the Union force drove a Confederate force back to their encampment. General Polk quickly responded and dispatched additional forces to Belmont and pushed the Union forces back. Supported by the timberclads, the Union forces returned to their transports and departed.

In spite of the fact the raid was not successful, General Grant learned several valuable lessons from the operation. Foremost, the Flotilla was of tremendous value to Union Army operations. Firepower from the Flotilla's ships would support operations and become a major factor in determining the outcome of a battle. Because of his relationship with Flag Officer Foote and other Flotilla officers, General Grant felt comfortable planning and executing operations with the Navy. Finally, General Grant realized the Flotilla's ability to move forces, conduct reconnaissance, and support overall land operations. This would be a critical factor for future success on the Mississippi and Ohio Rivers, as well as on the Cumberland and Tennessee Rivers.

By the time I arrived in Cairo in late January of 1862, the Western Gunboat Flotilla was a formidable naval force. In addition to the three remodeled steamboats, the Tyler, the Lexington, and the Conestoga, the Flotilla included seven "City-Class" gunboats or "Pook's Turtles". These were the St. Louis, the Cairo, the Mound City, the Carondelet, the Cincinnati, the Louisville, and the Pittsburgh. Along with the gunboats and timberclads were a host of smaller supply and auxiliary craft, repair ships, and a makeshift hospital ship.

Cairo proper was a busy place. In addition to the facilities that catered to the needs and desires of soldiers and sailors, there was also a great deal of ongoing construction to fortify the city and protect the Flotilla. Since there was little room ashore, most of the administration, supply, and the limited repair facilities were conducted afloat. For those ships requiring larger repairs, a shipyard and dry dock were located up the Ohio River at Mound City.

General Grant's unsuccessful raid on Belmont set the stage. The pieces were in place for cooperative operations between the Army and the Navy. The Flotilla was prepared for combat. For me, it was a different view of the elephant. The view somewhat obscured by the murky waters of the mighty Mississippi and Ohio Rivers. The view had changed but the elephant was here.

Chapter Twenty-Four

January 1862 – Cairo, Illinois

A lack of sufficient space or quarters ashore forced the Western Gunboat Flotilla to resort to using a receiving ship to house newly arrived sailors and soldiers before assigning them to specific ships. The concept of receiving ships or accommodation ships was certainly not new and was employed by most navies around the world. In olden times, when recruits were not necessarily volunteers, some form of floating receiving ship solved the problem of preventing these unwilling volunteers from trying to escape. It was difficult to covertly depart a ship moored in the harbor without being seen by the topside watch. The desertion problem was further simplified by the fact many of these volunteers could not swim.

In the days of sail, any vessel not deemed seaworthy or considered obsolete, was stripped of all salvageable military equipment. The vessel was then used for a variety of other purposes as long as it could remain afloat. These ships, or hulks as they were called, provided a host of administrative and logistical services besides housing newly arrived sailors. For example, the British Navy was fond of using hulks as prison ships. During the occupation of New York City during the American Revolution, the British housed American prisoners and patriot sympathizers aboard ships in the harbor.

In friendly ports, a navy might use hulks as auxiliary ships, resupply vessels, guard vessels, and powder ships. When a hulk could no longer provide a useful service, the ship would be sold as scrap or scuttled for purposes of harbor defense.

Since the Flotilla had no readily available assortment of hulks to use as a receiving ship, they opted to use one of the newly arrived commercial ships undergoing military modifications. When I reported for duty, receiving and housing newly arrived sailors and soldiers was the secondary task of the USS Maria Denning.

The Maria Denning was a side-wheeled steam ship built in 1858 in Cincinnati. She worked the river trade before being sold to the Union Navy and sent to Cairo in November of 1861. Now, the Maria Denning was undergoing modifications to her superstructure allowing her to serve as a supply ship or as a transport vessel for Union forces. These modifications included adding additional timbers to the ship's structure to protect vital areas such as the pilothouse and the paddlewheels. While not a true timberclad gunboat, the Maria Denning was outfitted with sufficient armament to provide for self-defense but not enough guns or protection to engage in offensive operations.

As I crossed the gangplank, I could hear the sounds of construction going on around the ship. After presenting my orders to the Petty Officer of the Watch, I was directed to a space below that housed the transit office for all incoming Army personnel.

"Welcome to the Western Gunboat Flotilla," a Sergeant behind the desk said. "I'm Sergeant Lane, the Personnel NCO. Drop your gear there and we will get you checked in."

As I put my gear down, the Sergeant began explaining life on the river.

"This is the receiving ship. You'll stay here for a couple of days until we have a need for you to fill. You'll then be sent to an Army detachment aboard one of the other ships of the Flotilla. You won't be a permanent member of the crew however, so if the ship goes into the yards for repairs or is out of commission for other reasons, you may be transferred to another ship depending on the need."

After filling out some paperwork, I was shown to the berthing area for soldiers and given a bunk. There were only two others in the berthing area and they kept pretty much to themselves.

Early on my second day aboard, Sergeant Lane came in with the First Sergeant. The First Sergeant welcomed us and then questioned the three of us about our experiences in the war. My two companions were relatively new to the Army with no combat experience. Spotting my Lorenz rifle, the First Sergeant asked if I had any real experience using it. After listening to my answer and asking a couple more questions about my time in the Third Maine Regiment and the fighting at Manassas, the First Sergeant told the three of us to bring our weapons and come with him.

We were taken to a makeshift rifle range just outside of town in a marshy area next to the river. We were given ammunition and instructed to fire three rounds at targets located about fifty yards away. My associates demonstrated no real proficiency with their weapons as all six of their shots completely missed the target. Firing last, I hit the target with my three shots and earned a well done from the First Sergeant.

The following morning, I was informed that my good shooting qualified me for an assignment as a sharpshooter and member of the ship's self-defense force aboard the USS Lexington, one of the timberclads. I was told to gather my equipment and head down the pier to the Port Captain's office for transportation to the Lexington in Paducah, Kentucky.

January 1862 – Paducah, Kentucky

It took about five hours to travel upriver from Cairo to Paducah. As we moved along, I managed to chat with one of the crewmembers and asked about the area.

"The port side is Illinois and that's Kentucky over on the starboard," the sailor said. This part of the river is fairly quiet now. This time of the year we get a lot of deadfall that floats down the river and can really foul up a paddle or the steering."

"What about the weather?" I asked.

"River runs too fast for ice to build up but occasionally you get a floe that breaks off and can cause some problems."

"Do you ever see the enemy on these trips?" I asked.

"As I said, this part of the river is pretty quiet. Occasionally a Reb patrol or cavalry unit will take a few shots at passing vessels but we usually ignore them or fire one of our guns at them and they depart the area."

As we pulled into Paducah, I noticed a great deal of activity in the harbor and asked the sailor about it.

"They are starting to load some of General Smith's division onto the troop transports. Rumor has it we are making a push up the Tennessee River toward a couple of forts that they found back in the fall," the sailor noted. "That's your ship over there, on the end of the pier taking on supplies."

As far as ships go, the Lexington wasn't much of a looker. Walking down the pier I noted she was not an especially large ship, only about one hundred and seventy-five feet long and thirty-six feet wide. The Lexington was built in 1860 at Pittsburgh and worked the river for a short time until 1861 when she was purchased by the War Department. That summer, all of the necessary military modifications were completed in Cincinnati to make her a steam-powered gunboat and on August 12, the USS Lexington was commissioned into the Western Gunboat Flotilla.

As I approached the ship, I noticed a large gun mounted on the bow. I later learned this gun was one of the two very formidable thirty-two pound guns aboard. A massive piece, the gun was about ten feet long and was capable of shooting a round effectively over nineteen hundred yards. Aside from these two thirty-two pounders, the Lexington was also equipped with four eight-inch guns, each with an effective range of over eighteen hundred yards.

Behind this bow gun were two enormous smokestacks atop the main deck. This deck housed all of the ship's offices as well as the messing and berthing areas. Behind the stacks on the top of the main deck was the pilothouse. Below this main deck was the engine room that housed the two steam engines that drove the two side-wheel paddlewheels at a top speed of seven knots per hour. Also on this lower deck were the coal bunkers as well as other storage areas and the ship's magazine area.

I could see now why the Lexington was called a timberclad. The ship was embellished with what I would call wooden armor plating. The pilothouse, gun mounts, paddlewheels, and other features were encased in five-inch oak planks. More of this planking was arranged to protect personnel working on the main deck. While this oak planking would certainly stop a rifle or musket round, the wooden armor was little protection for any artillery or mortar rounds that struck the ship.

As I boarded the Lexington, I noticed a flurry of activity on the decks. Supplies and ammunition were being loaded and stored below. After checking aboard, I was assigned to a watch section and told to report to the gunnery officer, Mr. Vroon. Samuel Vroon was a career sailor who achieved the rank of Petty Officer First Class in the fifteen years he was on active duty. After reporting to him, I was welcomed and assigned a berth. As the gunnery officer or "gunner", Mr. Vroon was responsible for that portion of the crew who manned the ship's armament and those personnel, like me, on the defense force.

After some time aboard I found the members of the crew to be a rather interesting mix of people. There were soldiers to work the ship's guns and sharpshooters like me to provide for the defense of the ship. There were some career sailors who tended to the duties of the ship but could be counted on to fight when necessary. There were even some civilian volunteers who possessed a skill set deemed desirable to the Navy. Finally, there was a group of individuals who worked the river before the war.

When the brown water navy was created, Navy personnel with riverine experience were at a premium. As a result, the Navy turned to experienced rivermen, most of whom lost their livelihoods as a result of Southern secession. The loss of active duty naval personnel to the Confederate Navy further hampered the manning of the brown water navy. To counter this problem, the War Department started screening soldiers with maritime occupations prior to enlistment. Watermen from Maine, Massachusetts, Rhode Island, and other states were assessed and those qualified were asked to volunteer for riverine service. The Army did something similar when requesting volunteers with experience in artillery. Whatever the method of recruitment, it was an unconventional organizational structure that seemed to work just fine.

The Navy did insist on maintaining command of all riverine vessels and assigned Navy officers to these command positions. Our Commanding Officer was Lieutenant James Shirk, a career Navy officer from Pennsylvania. Lieutenant Shirk was appointed a midshipman in 1849 and served in a variety of billets in the Home Squadron, as well as the West Indies, African, and Pacific Squadrons. He assumed command of the Lexington on January 1st, 1862.

Besides the Captain, there were four other officers that were designated Masters on the rolls. These individuals, as well as the two Pilots, were all former rivermen. Many of the rivermen held positions of responsibility on other vessels before the war and proved themselves invaluable to the brown water navy. The major disadvantage of rivermen was when the ship operated on a part of the river not familiar to them, particularly the pilots, their lack of knowledge often led to navigational and operational problems. The other officers of the crew included the gunner, assistant surgeon, paymaster, carpenter, and armorer. The rest of the ship's complement of about sixty total was soldiers, able seamen, and other volunteers.

I settled into my new routine very quickly. The watch organization allowed for a quarter of the crew to be on duty at all times unless otherwise directed by the captain. Reveille for the crew was at 5:00 am followed by time for cleaning of the ship. The morning meal was served at 8:00 am and the main meal at noon.

When not in port, mornings and afternoons were spent conducting drills or standing watch. If the ship was underway, about 4:00 pm, she would tie up to a quiet part of the riverbank for the evening. If this part of the river was in enemy territory, security patrols and pickets were sent out as necessary. After a light evening meal, those not on watches could relax for a few hours until lights out. When the ship was in port, days were spent conducting necessary repairs, painting, or resupplying stores in preparation for the next operation.

One area of this new life that required serious effort on my part was learning to understand naval vocabulary. For example, in the Navy, as in the Army, Captain was a rank. Aboard ship however, the term Captain was applied to any officer assigned command the vessel regardless of rank. Case in point was our Captain, Lieutenant Shirk.

Port was left and starboard was right when using the front of the ship or bow as a reference. Topside was up and below was down, forward was toward the bow and aft was to the rear of the ship. While it was all so very confusing at first, perhaps the most confusing aspect of the naval vocabulary was the use of the term "head".

In the regiment, the place to perform one's bodily functions was called the latrine or the sinks. On board ship, that area was called the head. When I asked Mr. Vroon why, he just chuckled and explained that in days of sailing ships, the place to conduct one's business was outside the hull and under the ship's figurehead. You literally went "under the figurehead" to an area that seawater kept clean. The phrase was shortened and the term "head" stuck.

On January 30th, the Lexington and the Conestoga received orders to move up the Tennessee River and conduct a reconnaissance near Fort Henry. Earlier in the fall, the timberclads conducted an exploration of the Tennessee and Cumberland Rivers and found evidence of Confederate construction on both rivers. About seventy miles up the Tennessee they discovered the initial stages of what would be Fort Henry. Eight miles further upriver, a Confederate shipyard was observed, converting river craft into gunboats.

About the same distance up the Cumberland, the Union ships found another, larger, and more heavily fortified Confederate position under construction. This was Fort Donelson. General Grant and Flag Officer Foote developed a plan to eliminate these two threats and open the two rivers to Union control. The loss of Fort Henry would split General Johnston's forces and isolate units located in Columbus, Kentucky and along the Mississippi River down to the Tennessee border. They hoped the loss of Fort Donelson would open up central Tennessee and seriously threaten the Capitol at Nashville. Loss of both forts would also remove Confederate control in Kentucky and force General Johnston to consolidate his defenses further south.

Since her commissioning, the Lexington and the other timberclads saw plenty of action on both the Ohio and Mississippi Rivers. As I watched, a somewhat seasoned crew carried out the resupply in preparation for the coming operation. The USS Lexington was once again preparing for battle somewhere on this great river network.

Chapter Twenty-Five

February 2nd, 1862 – The Tennessee River

The two timberclads, the Lexington and the Conestoga, departed Paducah late in the afternoon of January 30th. By dusk, they entered the Tennessee River for the seventy mile trip upriver. The goal of this voyage was a reconnaissance of an area three miles downriver from Fort Henry. This was the area where the transports planned to drop General Grant's assault force for the landward portion of the attack on the Fort.

There was a seasonal January chill in the air that lasted all day and the cloudless Kentucky sky promised a long and bitterly cold night. As the evening wore on, the cold and damp began to seriously affect the topside watch. We started rotating men inside every hour to keep them from developing frostbite. It was a very long night indeed. Finally, at first light we were about a mile from our destination.

The designated area for the offload was downriver from a heavily wooded island in the middle of the river. The channel to the left of the island was virtually impassible from deadfall, muck and other debris. The main channel ran along the right side of the island. In this section of the river, the Confederates placed a series of obstructions to block any further passage upriver. Besides the usual felled trees and other natural impediments, the Rebels anchored a series of torpedoes in the channel itself. I was on watch topside when the torpedoes were discovered and asked Mr. Vroon about them.

"They are a rather crude attempt to sink our ships by filling a cylinder with black powder and either anchoring it to the river bottom or letting it float free," Mr. Vroon explained. "The cylinder is about five feet long with barbs or hooks on the outside that dig into the hull of a ship and ignite a percussion fuse. The idea is to blow a hole below the waterline. They work pretty good sometimes, if the powder doesn't get wet."

"How do we get beyond them?" I asked.

"The auxiliary ships use small boats to 'rake' the water, hook the torpedo cable, and tow it to where it can be safely detonated".

Later that morning I was assigned to the group conducting a reconnaissance of the area behind the riverbank. Our mission was to find useable roads and routes to the Fort. Another patrol was assigned a survey of the riverbank to determine the best locations to land the assault force. We moved to within a mile of the Fort but did not encounter any Rebels. All along our route however, there were signs of recent infantry and cavalry activity. With our patrol and the riverbank survey complete, we returned to the ship and, in the late afternoon, got underway for Paducah.

When we arrived in Paducah on the morning of February 1st, we were greeted by an increase of shipping in the harbor. The lead elements of the transport group started to arrive and the auxiliary ships were resupplying and preparing to get underway.

On February 2nd, the timberclad Tyler arrived with Flag Officer Foote aboard. Three of the armored gunboats, the Carondelet, the Cincinnati, and the St. Louis, accompanied the Tyler along with a new ironclad, the USS Essex.

February 4th, 1862 – The Tennessee River near Fort Henry

As day broke on the morning of February 3rd, the bulk of the transport group arrived and started loading General Grant's assault force. While this was going on, Flag Officer Foote aboard the Tyler, in company with the four gunboats, the other timberclads, and three of the auxiliary ships got underway toward Fort Henry. Their movement was slow as the river level was dropping, exposing new hazards and debris from both winter storms and Confederate axes.

After arriving below Fort Henry, the auxiliary ships commenced clearing the channel of the torpedoes and other obstacles. By the afternoon of February 4th, when the lead element of the transport group arrived, the channel was clear.

February 5th, 1862 – Fort Henry

The plan developed by General Grant and Flag Officer Foote was running smoothly until the evening of February 4th. Around 8:00 pm, a cold rain started to fall and by midnight the rain intensified into a torrential downpour.

Come morning, the offload was severely hampered by both the rain and the slick conditions at the landing site. To make matters worse, the rain turned the road behind the riverbank into a sea of mud, significantly restricting any movement of the assault force toward the Fort. By the end of the day on February 5th, the assault force was ashore, the ships were ready, all preparations were made, and the rain continued.

February 6nd, 1862 – Fort Henry

In spite of slow going, a decision was made to continue along the timeline defined in the original plan. That morning, with Flag Officer Foote now aboard the Cincinnati, the four gunboats began steaming upriver toward the Fort. Behind them, in a second echelon, were the three timberclads.

At 12:30 pm, the Flotilla arrived at Fort Henry and at a range of over seventeen hundred yards, the gunboats opened fire. The timberclads, operating closer to the shore, also opened fire, their shots striking the Fort from the flank. As the gunboats moved forward and closed the Fort, the timberclads were put in a position to fire over the top of the gunboats with their bow guns only.

This brown water armada moved to within six hundred yards of the Fort before the Confederates opened fire. Their fire was accurate and deadly. One round penetrated the Essex causing an explosion in her boilers. The resulting escape of steam caused the ship to go dead in the water and scalded twenty members of her crew to death.

One hour and fifteen minutes after the firing started and shortly after the now incapacitated Essex floated downriver, the Confederate Commander, Brigadier General Lloyd Tilghman, surrendered the Fort to Flag Officer Foote. Unbeknownst to Grant or Foote, General Tilghman sent the majority of his command to Fort Donelson before the assault began, keeping only a force large enough to work the guns.

While none of the timberclads sustained any damage or casualties, the same could not be said for the gunboats. The flagship Cincinnati received thirty-one shots to her casement, the Essex fifteen, the St. Louis seven, and the Carondelet six. Besides the twenty killed on the Essex, the rest of the gunboats suffered three killed, thirty-five wounded or injured, and four missing.

After the Fort surrendered, I went ashore with the defense forces of the three timberclads to provide security until General Grant's troops arrived. From my experience building forts back East, I could see a lot of similarities with those forts and Fort Henry. Abatis on the seaward and landward approaches, clear fields of fire, and gabions and fascines to reinforce the parapets and protect the gun emplacements were all present. What I was not ready for was what we found inside the Fort. Around many of the guns destroyed by the fire of the gunboats were the telltale signs of a battle lost, the broken bodies of dead Confederates. Of the soldiers General Tilghman kept at the Fort, there were only about sixty prisoners left alive. Many of these prisoners were wet from the knees down and, after looking at the gun positions, I understood why. The Fort itself was built on low and very swampy land. When the river rose during the heavy rains, it flooded many of the gun emplacements forcing the gun crews to load and fire in frigid knee-deep water.

With this success at Fort Henry, General Grant pushed for an immediate attack on Fort Donelson. Three key facts discouraged that plan. First, was the state of two of the gunboats, the Essex and the St. Louis. Both were significantly damaged and needed time in the yards for repairs. Second, the soldiers Tilghman sent from Fort Henry before it fell now reinforced the Rebels at Fort Donelson. Third, Fort Donelson was on the Cumberland River and not the Tennessee. From their current position at Fort Henry, Grant's Army had only twelve miles to travel to Fort Donelson; it would be a one hundred and fifty mile voyage for the Navy. In the end, Grant agreed to wait until Foote returned with two additional gunboats and the rest of the naval contingent.

About two hours later, the Fort was turned over to General Grant's forces and we returned to the Lexington. New orders came in for the timberclads to capitalize on the success at Fort Henry and move upriver to seize or destroy Confederate brown water capabilities and further open the Tennessee River.

Back onboard, I stood on the deck and watched as the tugboat Alps towed the Essex away from the Fort. Flag Officer Foote and two more gunboats were preparing to depart the area and return to Cairo. Only the Carondelet remained to provide support for the ground forces. The Tyler, the Lexington, and the Conestoga were preparing to get underway with Lieutenant Seth Phelps of the

Conestoga in charge of our three-ship armada. It was time to move on.

Throughout all the turmoil of the day, I managed to survive my first naval battle. Although the Lexington was not in the line of Confederate fire, metal from exploding shells flew everywhere. The noise of this clash was dreadful. In many ways, the idea of warfare on the water was far more daunting than standing in the regimental line of battle at Manassas. About 4:00 pm, as we moved away from Fort Henry and started to steam upriver, I felt that old seduction bug once again gnawing at my soul. We were now moving deeper into the heart of the Confederacy and I was to be a part of this great adventure.

Chapter Twenty-Six

February 6th, 1862 – Upriver from Fort Henry

It was dark as the small armada of timberclads steamed some twenty-five miles up the Tennessee to a point where a major rail line crossed the river. They were chasing a group of six Confederate boats spotted running upriver about ten miles back. The river was wide at this point and still running high from all the rain. The clear night afforded the opportunity to maintain a visual sighting of the Confederate craft. For the past hour the three timberclads closed on the Rebel boats and, at this rate of closure, would have them in range of their forward guns in another hour.

A decision was made to drop the Tyler at the railroad crossing. Her crew was tasked to dismantle the tracks over the river and either burn or blowup the trestle and bridge approaches. This included appropriating or destroying any materials around the site that could be used to repair the crossing point. The Lexington and the Conestoga steamed on to track the Confederate boats and once the crossing was destroyed, Tyler would continue upriver and rejoin them.

The two timberclads were just about in range when three of the Confederate boats appeared to catch fire. The river was narrowing and the three boats were set ablaze is such a way as to block the main channel. The timberclads reduced speed and approached the burning ships cautiously. Suddenly, as they approached, at least two of the Confederate ships exploded.

"Looks like two of them boats were carrying powder supplies," one of the soldiers on my watch said.

"Must have been a lot of it," the one they called the Old Sailor remarked. "The shock wave blew out the skylights on the main deck."

The explosion was indeed loud. Although the timberclads were not close enough to sustain any damage, the concussion did knock some of the crew down and broke some windows.

"I lost track of the other three," I said. The explosion and the fire pretty much destroyed any ability I had to see in the darkness.

"Won't see those three this side of Hades," the Old Sailor said. "The Rebs have more hiding spots for ships and materials in these little side channels and rivers than you could imagine. We'll never find them now, especially at night."

After towing off the burning hulks, we managed to clear the channel and get back underway. The Old Sailor was right; we never saw those other three Reb boats again.

February 7th, 1862 – Hardin County, Tennessee

The timberclads continued moving upriver all night. Around first light, the river narrowed considerably and started to snake around the countryside. The ships continued on and about midday entered Hardin County, Tennessee. As they approached the Cerro Gordo landing, I could see another Confederate ship wallowing in the mud next to the bank.

"That looks like the Eastport," the Old Sailor said. "She used to move cotton from these parts up to the Ohio and then down the Mississippi to New Orleans. Looks like the Rebs scuttled her."

It was indeed the Eastport and she was in the process of being converted into an ironclad. Fortunately, the ship was scuttled in relatively shallow water and the job poorly done. Sailors from the Conestoga managed to stop the flow of water and, after a time at the pumps, got the ship floating again. The Eastport did not have an operational engine but the shipyard did have a load of very valuable lumber and iron parts that made salvaging her worth the effort.

After we arrived, I was assigned to go ashore as part of the security force. As we got ashore, I learned Cerro Gordo was Spanish for high hill. We climbed the hill and got a good view of the surrounding countryside. No Rebs in sight, just a couple of small villages.

In midafternoon, with the Eastport floating again, the Tyler caught up with the rest of the armada. It was decided that the three ships would remain at Cerro Gordo for the evening and Lexington and Conestoga would continue upriver tomorrow. The Tyler would remain here with the prize, loading the lumber and iron parts, and readying her for a tow back to Fort Henry.

Shortly before dark the ships were struck by small arms fire from the far shore. About twenty-five or thirty Rebs across the river took exception to our being there. A couple of volleys from our bow guns seemed to dampen their enthusiasm and we spent a quiet night.

February 8th, 1862 – Florence, Alabama

Three hours before first light the Lexington and the Conestoga got underway and continued upriver. Around mid-morning we passed Pittsburg Landing and, a short time later crossed the Tennessee/Mississippi border. At a small shipyard in Eastport, Mississippi the timberclads encountered two small steamers and took them captive. The Sallie Wood carried a load of wood and metal parts and the Muscle, a load of iron.

After taking these two prizes, we continued upriver and crossed into the state of Alabama. As the ships approached the end of the navigable river near Muscle Shoals and Florence, Alabama, two shipyards were seen. The Conestoga crossed over to Florence and seized one yard where three steamers were afire.

At Muscle Shoals, the Lexington captured three other small steamers and forced the Rebels to burn six more. We quickly loaded supplies onto our new prizes and rejoined the Conestoga. Since this was the point on the Tennessee River where further upriver movement was not possible, both ships turned and began the return trip to Cerro Gordo and the Tyler.

After arriving back at Cerro Gordo, we learned that the Tyler was given the location of an enemy force by some of the locals. The individuals who fired on us the night before were part of a group of about six or seven hundred soldiers who were "pressed" into service as a form of home guard or militia. Their camp was close enough to the river for one of the timberclads to provide gunfire support for a raid force.

The raid force was composed of the defense forces of the three timberclads with Lieutenant Shirk as the leader of the raiding party. As a member of the Lexington's defense force, my comrades and I joined the others aboard the Conestoga, the timberclad designated to serve as the fire support ship.

We departed the Conestoga for the enemy camp about 10:00 pm and arrived at the site shortly after 1:00 am. We found the camp not long deserted as campfires still burned and tents still stood. We managed to capture some supplies and weapons before destroying the camp and returning to the ship: a very successful raid with no casualties.

February 11th, 1862 – Fort Henry

As our defense forces assaulted the enemy camp, the remainder of the ships' crews loaded the Eastport and the timberclads with the captured supplies. These included lumber, machinery, spikes, nails, and plating. Earlier in the day, the Tyler's crew destroyed the sawmill at the shipyard. Shortly before noon on February 9th, the three timberclads, with all of their prizes in tow, got underway for Fort Henry.

The trip back to the Fort was not without issue. The first problem the armada encountered was with the steamer Muscle. Starting after she was captured, the Muscle began taking on water at an alarming rate. The further downriver she got, the faster the water came in. The fact the Muscle was loaded with iron plating didn't help and, in spite of a tremendous effort to save the plating, the Muscle sank in one of the side channels to the river. The loss of the Muscle did not dampen our spirits. The iron plate, while lost to us, was also lost to the Confederates.

The next issue was difficulty with the Eastport. The Lexington was responsible for towing the Eastport back to Fort Henry. About twenty-five miles from the Fort at the site of the now destroyed railroad bridge, the Eastport got caught between a pier in the water and the bridge abutment and was wedged tight. The crew of the Lexington worked all night to free her and by 10:00 am on February 11th, got her free and past the bridge. The three ships and their prizes continued downriver and about 2:00 pm, the timberclad armada limped back to the area of Fort Henry.

February 13th, 1862 – Fort Donelson

When the Lexington arrived at Fort Henry, the area was a flurry of activity. About ten transport ships were offloading troops for General Grant's coming offensive and loading guns and equipment from Fort Henry.

The Carondelet, left by Foote to support operations at For Henry, departed for the Cumberland River and Fort Donelson by way of

Paducah earlier in the day. Orders for the timberclads also awaited our arrival. The Lexington was to steam downriver to Mound City, drop the Eastport, and then continue on to St. Louis for repairs before returning to Paducah. The Conestoga and the Tyler were ordered to return to Cairo to resupply and join up with Flag Officer Foote and the Flotilla.

Before departing, the Lexington transferred several crewmembers to the Conestoga for the pending operation. I was one of those selected and, with my shipmates, joined our new crew.

On the 12th the two remaining timberclads joined up with Foote and three other gunboats, the flagship St. Louis, the Pittsburgh, and the Louisville in Cairo. After resupplying, the five ships and the auxiliaries departed and headed for the Cumberland River.

General Grant's army started moving for Fort Donelson on February 11th. Bad weather and cold temperatures made the twelve-mile trip extremely difficult. By the 13th, the General arrayed his forces on the landward side of the Fort and was ready for an assault.

On the riverside, the situation at the Fort was much more daunting. Fort Donelson was built on a high bluff some one hundred and twenty feet above the river. From this height, Confederate gunners were shooting down on any attacking Union ships. Downward shots hitting the Union gunboats on their upper deck, where the armor plating and decking was the thinnest, might then pass through critical areas of the ship rendering it unable to continue the fight or even sinking it.

In addition to the main fort, the Confederates built two water batteries facing down the river. The first battery was placed about twenty feet above the river and the second about fifty feet above the water.

Arriving earlier in the day on the 13th, the Carondelet conducted a run against the Fort shortly after noon. Later in the afternoon, with the action already underway on the landward side, General Grant ordered the Carondelet to begin her assault from the riverside.

Commander Henry Walke steamed the Carondelet to a point about a mile from the Fort and opened fire. Slowly moving forward, the ship continued firing against the Fort and the water batteries. When the Carondelet reached a certain point in the river, the Confederates opened fire. After taking several hits, one round managed to penetrate the Carondelet's hull and ricochet around before coming to rest in the engine room. Unfortunately, this forced Walke to retire downriver and affect repairs before continuing the fight.

About 11:30 pm that evening the Flotilla arrived and began preparations for the following day's action. Foote elected to array the four gunboats in the front with the two timberclads as a second line. On the 14th at 3:00 pm the battle was joined on the riverside. As fighting progressed, all four gunboats were repeatedly hit as ship damage and crew casualties mounted.

"Those gunboats are taking a beating," I said to no one in particular. "What on earth are the Rebs doing now?"

"It's an old artillery trick," one of the gunners said. "You fire an artillery round so it bounces along the ground: more casualties that way. What the Rebs are doing is skipping the round over the water, sort of like skipping a rock on a pond. They are trying to hit the ships below the waterline or just above it where the plating is not so thick. Damn effective."

By 5:00 pm it was all over. All four of the gunboats were severely damaged. The Carondelet was dead in the water and floating downriver. One of the Confederate rounds went through the pilothouse of the St. Louis killing the pilot and wounding Flag Officer Foote. His Flotilla in shambles, Foote petitioned Grant to return to Mound City for repairs. As evening fell, the dead and wounded were transferred to one of the auxiliary ships and hasty repairs began on the gunboats.

Union reinforcements from Fort Henry began arriving on the 13th and the Confederate leadership mistakenly felt Grant now had over fifty thousand troops on scene. After an ill planned attack on the Union right on February 15th, the Confederate Generals began to contemplate surrender. On February 16th, after several Confederate commands broke out of the Fort including Brigadier General Nathan Bedford Forrest's cavalry, Brigadier General Simon Buckner surrendered the Fort and over twelve thousand Confederate troops. It was a stunning Union victory.

Chapter Twenty-Seven

February 28th, 1862 – Strategic Overview

The Cumberland River was now open as far east as Clarksville and Nashville. The presence of Union gunboats and General Grant's troops forced Clarksville, Tennessee to surrender on February 20th. Nashville followed suit on the 25th and by the end of February, the strategic picture in the West had dramatically changed.

Major General Henry Halleck commanded the Department of Missouri. His subordinates were Brigadier General John Pope in eastern Missouri, Brigadier General Samuel Curtis in western Missouri, and newly promoted Major General Grant in western Kentucky and Western Tennessee. The eastern portions of Kentucky and Tennessee were under the control of the District of the Ohio, commanded by Brigadier General Don Carlos Buell.

General Albert Sidney Johnston remained in command of the Army of Mississippi with Major Generals Leonidas Polk and William Hardee as his corps commanders. A new player in the Confederate leadership arrived in February in the form of General Pierre G. T. Beauregard, the hero of Manassas. After displaying an inability to work with General Joseph Johnston and a major falling out with President Jefferson Davis, Beauregard was shipped to the Western Theater. General A. S. Johnston promptly named him as the deputy army commander and commander of all Confederate forces between the Mississippi and Tennessee Rivers.

The loss of Fort Henry and Fort Donelson caused General Johnston to move his forces further south. At the end of February, his Army was in Murfreesboro, Tennessee preparing to move to Corinth, Mississippi. General Polk also started moving his Corps out of Columbus, Kentucky for a rendezvous with Johnston in Corinth. To support Confederate operations on the Mississippi River, Polk left small forces in Columbus, New Madrid, and Island Ten to slow

Union advances. Confederate forces also remained along the River at Fort Pillow, Fort Randolph, and Memphis.

Union forces were steadily advancing south. General Pope was in Commerce, Missouri and preparing to move against New Madrid and Island Ten. General Grant was in the Fort Donelson/Clarksville area preparing to move south to Pittsburg Landing and General Buell was in Nashville.

The Western Gunboat Flotilla now controlled Tennessee River traffic as far south as Florence, Alabama and the Cumberland River traffic all the way to Nashville. With most of Kentucky, as well as middle and western Tennessee, now under Union control, the Flotilla's overall strategy shifted. On the Tennessee and Cumberland Rivers, the effort was to be more defensive in nature, including protecting supply lines for the Union army and denying Confederate forces access along the river routes. In the West, operations became more offensive oriented as the Flotilla moved to seize Confederate strongpoints on the Mississippi River and open the "Father of all Rivers" to Union River traffic.

All of the gunboats damaged at Fort Donelson returned to Mound City for repairs. With the new change in strategy, Flag Officer Foote directed the three timberclads to remain in the area of the Tennessee and Cumberland Rivers and support General Grant's forces as required. Foote and the gunboats would now work with General Pope in coordinating the attack on New Madrid and Island Ten.

March 1st, 1862 – Near Pittsburg Landing

Shortly after Fort Donelson surrendered, word came down that the Lexington was returning and the Conestoga was departing for a scheduled yard period. Those of us from the Lexington's crew rejoined the ship on February 24th at Paducah. The Lexington returned to the Tennessee River and on February 28th, met up with the Tyler near Savannah, Tennessee. The Tyler was back from a successful patrol in the vicinity of Florence, Alabama returning with a prize and several tons of wheat.

The timberclads' new mission was to conduct operations against Confederate forces along the river and support General Grant's move south. Grant planned to begin moving his forces on March 5th. The strategic objective for this operation was the railroad hub and resupply center at Corinth. To accomplish this end, Pittsburg

Landing was an ideal area to consolidate his army and resupply his forces.

With the Conestoga gone, the Lexington and the Tyler started actively patrolling the river around Pittsburg Landing as far south as the Mississippi border. After several trips upriver, I was starting to get familiar with the terrain from Cerro Gordo upriver to the border.

Around noon on March 1st, we were patrolling the river in the vicinity of Diamond Island, about five miles south of Savannah. On the western bank near Pittsburg Landing, a Confederate battery of six guns opened fire on the two timberclads. Both ships immediately returned fire and, after a short but intense duel, silenced the Rebel guns.

The Lexington had a company from the Thirty Second Illinois Regiment aboard and another company from that Regiment was on the Tyler. With the Rebel guns either destroyed or moved off, both ships started launching boats and landing the Illinois troops. The timberclads supported the landing by firing canister and grapeshot at the surrounding terrain.

I was assigned a topside watch position with orders to engage targets of opportunity on the right flank of the landing parties. Suddenly, a round came whistling in and crashed into the pilothouse. A short time later the whistling sound returned along with that all too familiar smacking sound of a bullet striking flesh. One of the sailors on the topside watch grasped his chest and slowly toppled over the side into the dark water.

"What was that?" I yelled, looking at the hole in the side of the pilothouse not far from the side opening.

"Get your dang fool head down," screamed Mr. Vroon.

Obediently, I returned my attention to supporting the landing and providing the necessary cover fire until the landing party was ashore. As the Illinois men scrambled ashore, Mr. Vroon came over to see if I was all right.

"What was that?" I asked. "Wasn't like anything ever fired at me before."

"That was a Rebel sharpshooter firing a Whitworth rifle," Mr. Vroon said. "My guess is he was trying to kill the pilot. The round has a very distinctive whistling sound as it comes over. He was probably shooting from about five hundred yards away. Heck of a weapon."

I later learned that Joseph Whitworth developed the Whitworth rifle in England between 1854 and 1857. When fitted with a telescopic sight, the rifle was touted as the first real sniper rifle and extremely dangerous in the hands of a skilled marksman. The Whitworth was a muzzle loaded, percussion lock rifle that fired a .451 caliber round. The rifle weighted nine pounds and had an effective range of eight hundred to a thousand yards, well beyond the capability of my Lorenz. The Whitworth had a maximum range of over fifteen hundred yards: heck of a weapon indeed!

The Lexington and the Tyler continued their supporting fire until the landing parties reached the crest of the ridge where the Rebel battery was positioned. The timberclads remained on watch as the landing party accomplished their mission and began returning to the ships. In addition to the artillery battery, the Illinois men tangled with two infantry regiments and a cavalry regiment approaching on the reverse side of the ridge.

The boats returned the landing party without further incident and the ships moved back downriver toward Savannah, Tennessee. The landing was not without casualties. The Illinois troops and the men from the ships suffered two dead, six wounded, and three missing. One of the missing presumed dead was Seaman Patrick Sullivan, shot off the Lexington by a Reb sharpshooter with a Whitworth rifle. Seaman Sullivan was committed to his eternal rest in the muddy black waters of the Tennessee River.

April 1st, 1862 – On the Tennessee River

Events like the action at Pittsburg Landing on March 1st were pretty much typical of the activities of the timberclads during the month of March. On March 5th, the Army of Tennessee started their movement from Fort Donelson and Fort Henry to Pittsburg Landing. For some unexplainable reason, General Halleck replaced General Grant with Major General Charles Smith. Rumors flew around the army as to the reason why. There was the usual talk of Grant's excessive drinking mixed with other strange stories. The most believable rumor was that Halleck was jealous of the publicity Grant received after Fort Donelson and he was tired of Grant's constant haranguing to move against the enemy. Fortunately, Grant's termination would not last. By the end of the month, he was back in command. Some said it took an intervention by President Lincoln to restore the General.

The timberclads spent the earlier part of March escorting transports and resupply ships from Paducah and Fort Henry. Halleck tasked General Smith to conduct a series of riverine raids to sever Confederate rail lines around Pittsburg Landing and south into Alabama and Mississippi. One such target was the rail bridge over the Bear Creek. The mission was to sever the Confederate line between Polk's forces in Corinth and Johnston's army moving toward Florence.

Unfortunately, river conditions prevented a force from General Sherman's division from reaching the bridge. The raid managed to disrupt rail operations for a short time by tearing up tracks and destroying the engineering assets available to repair the line.

By April 1st, General Grant was back in command of the Army of the Tennessee. and his six divisions were spread around the area of Pittsburg Landing and Shiloh Church. The lead elements of Buell's Army of the Ohio were arriving at Savannah. To the west, Pope's army of Missouri had seized New Madrid, Missouri and was preparing to move on Island Ten.

The riverine raids were over and proved to be only a minor inconvenience to General Johnston's Army of Mississippi. On March 15th the lead elements of his army began arriving in the Corinth area. Polk's corps was arriving from Columbus and Major General Braxton Bragg's Corps from Mobile was marching to join Johnston's forces.

The stage was set. The players were present. What was about to unfold was one of the bloodiest battles in American history and as a member of the crew of the Lexington I was to have a riverside seat to the slaughter.

Chapter Twenty-Eight

April 8th, 1862 – Pittsburg Landing

Spring was in the air on the Tennessee River. Warm days and cool nights replaced the cold and dreary winter weather. Trees bloomed and flowers began to blossom. In the fields, farmers planted the first crops of the new season. As March turned to April, the Lexington was busy guarding transports and resupply ships moving up and down the river.

The river was running high and extremely fast. Fast enough that on April 1st the Lexington was directed to provide a tow upriver from Paducah for the gunboat Cairo. After dropping the Cairo at Cerro Gordo, we steamed to a patrol area near Carrollville. There on the morning of April 3rd, we found and destroyed two ferryboats deemed too small for flotilla use. Later in the day as we steamed upriver past Clifton and Eagle Nest Island, a third ferryboat was located and destroyed. Shortly before dark, the ship returned to the relative safety of Crump's Landing for the evening.

On April 4th, the Lexington steamed upriver to the area of Hamburg and relieved the Tyler. We assumed the river patrol between Hamburg and Pittsburg Landing as the Tyler steamed for Crump's Landing and resupply. The Tyler returned the following morning and assumed the river patrol and we headed for Crumps. The Lexington remained there in support of Major General Lew Wallace's Division until the following morning.

At first light on April 6th the unthinkable occurred. General Johnston's Army of Mississippi attacked on a three corps front in the vicinity of Shiloh Church. General Grant's Army of the Tennessee was caught off guard, believing Johnston's Army still in the Corinth area. General Sherman's Division bore the brunt of the initial Confederate assault and slowly gave ground as the Union forces started to react to the onslaught.

Johnston had consolidated his Army around Corinth on April 1st and began moving toward Shiloh Church on April 3rd. Originally intending to attack on April 4th, conditions forced Johnston to re-evaluate his initial assault time. Narrow roads, bottlenecks, and rain slowed the Confederate advance and the army was not in position until 4:00 pm on the 5th. With the Rebels bivouacking only two miles from Union positions, Johnston issued the order for the attack to begin April 6th at 6:00 am. The initial Confederate assault was successful in pushing the Union army back all across the front.

Reacting to the turmoil of the initial stages of the battle, the Lexington got underway and arrived at Pittsburg Landing at 10:15 am. We joined up with the Tyler and began firing on Rebel positions on the Union left. Early in the afternoon, the Lexington moved back to Crump's Landing as a defensive precaution in support of the last of Wallace's Division moving out and the lead division of Buell's Army of the Ohio crossing the river.

Throughout the day, General Grant orchestrated a series of organized tactical withdrawals. As additional elements of Wallace's Division and Buell's Army prepared to join the fight, General Grant chose to make a final withdrawal to a line along the Hamburg-Savannah Road across to the river at Pittsburg Landing. By the late afternoon, Buell's Army controlled the Union left anchored on Pittsburg Landing while Grant's Army occupied the center and right flank along the Hamburg-Savannah Road.

At 4:00 pm, the Lexington rejoined the Tyler near Hamburg and the two timberclads began engaging Rebel batteries while the ship's defense forces engaged Confederate infantry moving along the riverbank. For two full hours, Rebel artillery shells repeatedly struck the water around the ships. Aboard the ships, infantry bullets chipped off chunks of oak planking but caused little in the way of serious damage. On more than one occasion the Confederate attack closed to within an eighth of a mile of the Union lines. All the while Buell's men, the two timberclads, and the defense forces engaged with elements of Major General Braxton Bragg's Corps. Finally, after heavy fighting, the Rebs fell back to the area of Dills Branch. As night fell, the fighting dropped off and the Lexington returned to Crumps for resupply.

The Confederate army achieved great success on the first day of the battle. The only downside of the day's fighting was the loss of their Commander, General Albert Sidney Johnston. Late in the afternoon General Johnston attempted to rally his forces when he was struck in the knee by friendly fire. The wound and the absence of proper medical care caused the General to bleed to death on the field where he fell. Ironically, the tourniquet that might have saved his life remained in his saddlebags.

Starting at 7:00 pm on the 6th, the Tyler began firing one salvo every fifteen minutes. Around 1:00 am on the 7th, we returned upriver and relieved the Tyler. The Lexington continued that firing cycle until 5:00 am. If we weren't getting any sleep, neither were the Rebs. Day two would not be so successful for the Rebels. At 5:00 am on the 7th, Generals Grant and Buell, reinforced with three fresh divisions, went on the offensive. By 10:00 am Union forces were advancing across the front. The timberclads continued to support the advance along the Union left until the advancing infantry masked their firing. By 2:30 pm General Beauregard, now in command, ordered a general retreat toward Corinth. The Union attack stalled as their forces reached the line of their original camps. This slowdown enabled the Confederate Army to retreat relatively unscathed. A lackluster pursuit was launched on April 8th but easily spoiled by Brigadier General Nathan Bedford Forrest's cavalry.

As the day broke on the morning of the 8th, the battle of Shiloh Church/Pittsburg Landing was essentially over. Besides their Commanding General, the Confederates lost over ten thousand seven hundred killed, wounded, or missing. For the Union, the butcher's bill was much higher: about thirteen thousand seven hundred killed, wounded, or missing. The number of casualties collectively on both sides at Shiloh was greater than the total number of casualties in the American Revolution, the War of 1812, and the Mexican War combined.

The timberclads spent much of the afternoon of the 7th and early the 8th ferrying wounded to the hospital boats. Our losses were minimal: none killed, a few wounded, and none missing. As we steamed downriver toward Paducah, I paused for a moment to reflect on this great battle. I think I fired more rounds in that two-hour period on April 6th, than any other time in the war. Oddly, there seemed to be more hornets in the air than at Manassas. Perhaps this was because the Lexington was a very large target. Even though I was not standing in a regimental line of battle, I was involved and I had survived. The bloodiest battle of the war to date was over and, for now, the seduction bug was satisfied.

June 1st, 1862 – On the Tennessee River

As quickly as General Grant's status rose after Fort Donelson, it crashed dramatically in the aftermath of Shiloh. Since Midwest men did much of the fighting and dying, the Midwest politicians and press crucified the General. In the news and in the halls of Congress, Grant was called a common drunk in uniform, incompetent, and criminally negligent. Receiving no support from Halleck, his case moved up the Army chain of command to the desk of President Lincoln.

As the General's fate was being determined, General Halleck saw an opportunity to raise his own image in the eyes of the American public. Four days after the battle, Halleck arrived at Pittsburg Landing with a plan to reorganize his three armies. His plan also effectively removed Grant from any command position in the event he was retained in the Army.

With the great reorganization underway, on April 12th the Lexington and the Tyler escorted General Sherman and two thousand infantry and cavalry troops as they prepared for a raid on the Bear Creek railroad bridge. Sherman's force landed at Chickasaw Landing and, in short order, destroyed the railroad trestle and the adjacent telegraph lines. Sherman's orders called for his force to move further upriver to Florence and destroy another railroad bridge across the Tennessee River. Unfortunately, river conditions prevented the timberclads from continuing that far upriver so that portion of the mission was cancelled and the raid force returned to Pittsburg Landing on April 14th.

As part of his grand reorganization, Halleck ordered Pope's Army to Pittsburg Landing on April 15th. This put a tremendous crimp in otherwise very successful operations on the Mississippi River. Pope and Flag Officer Foote succeeded in capturing Island Ten on April 8th and started moving against Fort Pillow, some fifty miles downriver. The loss of Pope's army, in effect, suspended land operations on the Mississippi and increased the difficulty in capturing the Fort by the Flotilla alone.

By late April, the reorganization was complete. Major General George Thomas was given Grant's old command and Grant reassigned as the deputy commander under Halleck. Pope's Army remained intact except for the two regiments he left with Foote on the River. Buell's Army was stripped of a division leaving him with only three divisions of green troops. Finally, Major General John McClernand was assigned the commander of the reserve. All totaled, Halleck now commanded a Grand Army of fifteen divisions, over one hundred and twenty thousand men, and more than two hundred guns.

On April 28th, Halleck launched his Grand Army against Beauregard's seventy thousand troops at Corinth. Promising a quick victory, Halleck boasted of engaging the Rebels at Corinth the next day however, that boast turned into four weeks. As May came to a close, the Grand Army was finally in position and on May 28th began an all-day bombardment of Confederate positions. When the initial assault was launched on May 29th, Union forces found Beauregard's Army gone in one of the greatest military deceptions of the war. As Halleck claimed a great victory, Beauregard's intact Army moved into Tupelo, Mississippi. With the fighting now in the Corinth area, the timberclads continued to support Halleck's Army as best they could. They also continued their routine patrols downriver in order to protect the transport and resupply ships.

After Shiloh there was a dramatic change in Rebel tactics throughout Kentucky and Tennessee. With the Reb Army further south, the fighting along the river was left to irregular forces. There were no more traditional engagements between opposing lines of battle. Rather, the Rebs adopted a hit and run, raid type offense using these irregular troops and cavalry. Their tactics toward the timberclads also changed. Instead of pitched battles with artillery batteries and our guns, the new philosophy was to ambush the ships at narrow points on the river. This was accomplished using infantry and dismounted cavalry with the occasional artillery piece. After firing several volleys, the Reb infantry and their artillery pieces would simply disappear into the countryside before the timberclads could react.

On May 19th as the Lexington conducted a patrol downriver to Fort Henry, the ship became the target of one of these Rebel ambushes. Before we could get our guns into action, the ship was hit by fire from dismounted cavalry and a horse drawn artillery piece. The small cannon fired three rounds at the ship and, while doing no real damage, managed to spray oak fragments and splinters at the topside watch.

In addition to three sailors hit by rifle fire, the flying wood shrapnel hit me and six other members of the watch. Only one crewmember was seriously wounded. The rest suffered superficial injuries. My wounds were certainly not life threatening but several long slivers of oak lodged in my right shoulder. After the Rebel ambush was driven off, the ship's medical officer treated the injured crewmembers.

After cutting out the splinters, cleaning the wound, stitching where necessary, and bandaging my shoulder the doctor asked me to perform a simulated shot with my rifle. Unfortunately, most of the damaged area corresponded to the area of my shoulder where the rifle butt was seated. Shooting and reloading would be a painful experience and probably tear out the doctor's stitches. Since my injury precluded me from using a rifle, I was of no value to the ship's defense force. Therefore, the doctor recommended I be sent back to Cairo to recover.

River conditions were becoming very unfavorable as water levels dropped daily. Late on May 20th, the Tyler and the Lexington departed the Corinth area for Cairo. When we arrived, I was sent to the local medical facility for treatment and rehabilitation.

Lately, rumors flourished around the ship about the status of the defense forces. As the war moved away from the navigable parts of the Tennessee and Cumberland Rivers, defense of these portions of the river became the responsibility of the regional commanders. The timberclads and transport ships now carried an appropriately sized force to some trouble spot along the river. The self-defense of the ships assigned to support the operation became the responsibility of an element of that force and effectively eliminated the need for any permanent ship's defense force.

On June 1st, I was cleared to return to duty. The Army liaison office of the Flotilla told me I would not be returning to the Lexington. Instead, I would be assigned to a ship's defense force on one of the vessels providing logistical support to forces on the Mississippi River.

Walking back to my quarters, I started to feel a real sense of anticipation of this posting as operations on the Mississippi River were really starting to heat up. As I walked along, I was also aware of that old seduction bug beginning to gnaw at my soul once again.

The Father of all Rivers

"Here in the dread tribunal of last resort, valor contended against valor. Here brave men struggled and died for the right as God gave them to see the right."

Adlai E. Stevenson

Mississippi River From Cairo to the Gulf of Mexico

Chapter Twenty-Nine

June 1st, 1862 – Cairo Illinois

A great deal changed in the Flotilla since I left Cairo back in January. The harbor was crammed with a variety of ships. Some were new and undergoing modifications before joining the Flotilla. Some were returning from the war to be refitted and re-crewed. Some were loading the supplies needed at the front or the troops bound for one of the forward regiments. Out with the used, broken, or dead parts and in with the new.

As I walked along, a couple of the new vessels caught my eye. One was a barge type boat about sixty feet long and twenty-five feet wide. In the center of the barge was a large cooking pot shaped artillery piece mounted on a circular platform. As I watched the crew loading the boat, a sailor who noted my curiosity approached me.

"That's a mortar barge," the sailor said.

"A mortar barge," I replied. "I have heard of mortars but I've never seen one up close."

"The Flotilla's been getting a bunch of them ready for duty on the Mississippi. Used them fairly effectively at Island Ten and some at Fort Pillow."

The sailor went on to explain that the barge carried a crew of thirteen. Behind the mortar at the bow and stern were storage areas for additional rounds and powder. A bulwark ran around the mortar platform to protect the crew while it was being fired. The barge also had a false bow and stern that made it somewhat maneuverable so it could be moved by a tug or towed by one of the Flotilla ships.

"How does it work?" I asked.

"That there one is a thirteen-inch mortar. Weighs around seventeen thousand pounds. Add another four thousand for the mount," the sailor explained. "It'll take a twenty-pound powder change and fire a two hundred pound ball over two and a quarter miles."

He went on to detail how the crew used bars to install the mortar onto the firing platform. Then they adjusted the direction of fire with a block and tackle system that turned the mortar on the circular platform. When the direction was right, the bars were removed. The crew made any necessary final adjustments, loaded the weapon, and fired it.

The sailor was very informative about many of the ships in the harbor. He described in detail one of the auxiliary ships, the new hospital ship, and one of the transports. As he spoke, I noticed a sternwheel vessel undergoing conversion. The ship was being fitted with oak beams around the engines, boilers, and sternwheel. The unique things about this ship were the reinforced bow and the fact the crew was painting it black.

"What is that ship over there?" I asked.

"That's one of the new boats assigned to the Ram Fleet," the sailor replied. "They built up the bows of the steamships with twelve to sixteen inches of oak beams reinforced with iron rods and bolts to form the ram. The other critical parts of the ship are also covered with oak beams, some two feet thick."

The Ram Fleet was the brainchild of Charles Ellet. Ellet was a civil engineer by trade, designing and building suspension bridges around the country. His specialty was bridges but his side interest was a study of ram ships in naval warfare.

Back in Virginia when the Union abandoned the Gosport Naval Base, they burned and scuttled several ships including a relatively new one, the USS Merrimack. The Confederate Navy raised the wreck and set about building an ironclad from the hull of the Merrimack. In March, the newly commissioned CSS Virginia steamed out into Hampton Roads to do battle with the assembled Union fleet. Before her fateful duel with the USS Monitor, the Virginia sank the USS Cumberland using her ram. As a result of this pivotal battle, the future of naval warfare was forever changed and Charles Ellet got an interview with Secretary of War Edwin Stanton.

In late March, Stanton authorized Ellet, recently appointed an Army Colonel, to purchase seven steamboats and convert them into rams for operations on the Mississippi. While the four sidewheelers and three sternwheelers were being converted, questions arose over command and control of this new fleet. All of the vessels currently working the northern Mississippi were part of the Western Gunboat Flotilla. The Ram Fleet however, was technically under the control of the Secretary of War; a point Colonel Ellet was stubbornly firm about. Additionally, Navy officers commanded all the ships of the Flotilla, while in the Ram Fleet, all of the ship's captains were Army officers and, ironically, all related to Ellet. Although chartered to work in concert with the Flotilla, Ellet generally kept his own counsel and planned all operations for the Ram Fleet.

The timing of the Ram Fleet's arrival was significant as, after Island Ten surrendered on April 8th, a new force emerged on the Mississippi; the Confederate River Defense Force. Since the start of the war, the Confederate Navy attempted to build ironclad ships at shipyards around New Orleans. Before constant pressure from Flag Officer David G. Farragut's fleet forced the Rebels to move their shipbuilding operations upriver, they were successful in converting eight steamboats into rams. These eight ships were dubbed "cottonclads" as they had bales of cotton pressed between thick oak beams to protect the key elements.

On May 9th, the River Defense Force attacked two Union gunboats, the Cincinnati and the Mound City, two miles above Fort Pillow. Before seeking shelter under the guns of the Fort, the cottonclads succeeded in ramming and sinking both gunboats. Although both were eventually raised and returned to service, the Battle of Plum Point convinced Ellet that the rams were indeed effective weapons for riverine warfare.

May was also the time for change within the Flotilla. In April, Flag Officer Foote requested a medical leave from the Secretary of the Navy. Foote's old wound from Fort Donelson was not healing and, in the eyes of the Flotilla medical staff, seriously threatened the Flag Officer's life. On May 8th, Foote turned command of the Flotilla over to Captain Charles H. Davis, his handpicked successor. Although the medical leave was supposed to be temporary, Flag Officer Foote would never see his beloved Flotilla again.

After his medical rehabilitation was completed, Foote was assigned a post in Washington. Promoted to Rear Admiral in July of 1862, he remained in Washington until his assignment to command the South Atlantic Blockading Squadron in 1863. In route to his new duty, Rear Admiral Foote died of Bright's disease on June 26, 1863.

July 1st, 1862 – On the Mississippi River

As May turned to June, many of the command and control issues between the Ram Fleet and the Flotilla came to a head. If tensions between the two commands were high under Flag Officer Foote, they escalated under Captain Davis. Only after Colonel Ellet solicited volunteers from the Flotilla to man the Ram Fleet did the situation rise to the level of the Secretary of the Navy and the Secretary of War. While peace between the two was not declared, tensions eased as both commands prepared to attack Fort Pillow.

Fort Pillow was the gateway to Memphis and the next target for the Union riverine forces. The Confederate commander, Colonel Thomas Rosser, was cognizant of the Union's intentions when word reached him of General Beauregard's evacuation of Corinth. In Rosser's mind, this opened the Fort and all of Memphis to attack from the landward side. On June 3rd, Colonel Rosser evacuated the last of the Fort's personnel, supplies, and ammunition to Memphis and Vicksburg. The Union attack on June 4th drove off the remaining Confederate vessels and, in the absence of any garrison, the Fort surrendered on June 5th.

As Fort Pillow was being evacuated, I was in the process of joining the crew of the USS Great Western, one of the two principal ammunition ships in the Flotilla. The Great Western was launched in 1857 and traveled the river until February of 1862 when she was acquired by the Flotilla. After refitting, the Great Western operated out of Cairo supplying ships all along the Mississippi with ammunition and ordnance. The Captain, Lieutenant Byron Wilson, assumed command of the ship on May 16th. We got underway and on June 4th joined with the rest of the Flotilla at Fort Pillow to begin preparing to move against the next Union objective: Memphis.

Memphis was a vital transportation center for the Confederacy. Railroads and roads connected the West to places like Savannah, Chattanooga, and New Orleans and many of the supplies bound for the Army of Northern Virginia and the Army of the Tennessee flowed through Memphis. Of concern to the Flotilla was the Confederate shipyard in Memphis. This was the shipyard where two Rebel ironclads, the Arkansas and the Tennessee, were constructed.

At dawn on June 6th, Captain James E. Montgomery, the commander of the River Defense Force, positioned his eight cottonclad rams across the river in anticipation of the Union attack. The evening before, the Flotilla and the Ram Fleet anchored some four miles upriver awaiting first light. When the signal was given, the gunboats began moving downriver followed by the rams and the auxiliaries. Along with a couple of thousand Memphis citizens who came out to watch the battle, I had a front row seat for yet another river battle.

As the gunboats opened fire on the Rebel vessels, two of the rams charged forward. Although the smoke from the fight obscured vision, it appeared that three of the Confederate rams were sunk and the remaining five were moving downriver.

For ten miles down the Mississippi, the Flotilla and the rams conducted a running fight with the remaining Confederate rams. I watched in awe as one of Ellet's rams hit a Rebel ram with such force as to drive it onto the riverbank. By the end of the battle, four other Rebel rams were either sunk or captured. Later that afternoon, the Mayor of Memphis surrendered the City to Flag Officer Davis.

The battle over, two of the captured ships from the Confederate River Force were sent back to Cairo to become part of the Flotilla. A third was sent the next day and work was underway to raise a fourth. In spite of the best efforts of the Flotilla and Ram Fleet, one of the original eight managed to escape downriver. The Confederate ram, the CSS General Van Dorn, was still roaming the river network.

Our losses in the battle were minimal, only one casualty of significance: Colonel Charles Ellet. Ellet was struck in the leg by a Rebel sharpshooter and, although the wound initially did not appear to be life threatening, he developed an infection and died two weeks later. Command of the Ram Fleet was passed to his younger brother, Lieutenant Colonel Alfred Ellet.

With Memphis now in Union hands, orders came down from Washington for the Flotilla to support operations in central Arkansas. Major General Samuel Curtis was raising troops to fight as part of the Trans-Mississippi District. These forces were in camps in Eastern Arkansas along the White River. If the river was cleared of Confederate activity, then supplies and equipment could flow freely upriver to the newly established Union camps.

On the morning of June 13th, a task force from the Flotilla departed Memphis for the White River. This force consisted of the recently repaired Mound City, the Saint Louis, and the Lexington. Two days later, the Conestoga, two transports, and the Forty-sixth

Indiana Regiment were sent to augment these three ships. The Great Western was ordered to proceed to the area near the mouth of the White River and provide resupply to the force if needed.

On June 16th, the task force moved up the White River to a point about five miles from Saint Charles, Arkansas. At first light the next morning the ships closed Saint Charles and encountered two Rebel artillery batteries covering the approaches and three hulks sunk in the river to impede traffic.

In the fight that ensued, an artillery shell hit the Mound City. The round penetrated her hull and exploded her steam drum causing major damage and numerous casualties. Although the battle was an eventual Union victory, the casualties aboard the Mound City, eighty-six dead and twenty-five injured, dampened our mood.

While the river was being cleared around Saint Charles, on June 19th the Conestoga and several transports laden with supplies moved upriver and made contact with General Curtis' forces. The remainder of the force with the Mound City in tow, steamed past these ships and continued upriver to a point about one hundred fifty miles from the mouth. Unfortunately, receding waters forced them to return to Saint Charles.

As support operations on the White River continued, the remainder of the Flotilla and the Ram Fleet continued downriver in search of enemy shipping. The Great Western rejoined the Flotilla at White River and we steamed deeper into the heart of the Confederacy toward Vicksburg.

While there was no sign of the General Van Dorn or the Confederate ironclad Arkansas, on July 1st word was passed that the Ram Fleet was in contact with Flag Officer Farragut's fleet at the heavily defended U-shaped turn in the river at Vicksburg. In spite of the fact several locations on the river still belonged to the Rebels and several Confederate gunboats remained, for now, a large part of the "Father of all Waters" was under Union control.

Chapter Thirty

July 1st, 1862 – The Southern Mississippi River

As part of President Lincoln's amended Anaconda Plan, New Orleans became a prime target for Union naval planners. The city was located some ninety miles upriver from the Gulf of Mexico and by 1861, second only to New York in terms of movement of goods and people.

New Orleans had a storied history during the War of 1812. To protect the city from the invading British, Fort Saint Phillip was constructed at a critical juncture some seventy miles downriver. The Fort was instrumental in keeping the British fleet from advancing upriver and set the stage for the epic battle between American and pirate forces led by Andrew Jackson and the British Army.

After the war, Fort Jackson was constructed across the river and down from Fort Saint Phillip. Two additional forts, Pike and Macomb, were also built to guard the eastern approaches to the city.

Confederate naval planners also saw the strategic importance of New Orleans and set about constructing defensive measures and a naval force as a deterrent. A boom was constructed between Fort Jackson and Fort Saint Phillip to block off river access. Additionally, the Rebels built a small fleet of lightly armed gunboats to protect the bayou access and a semisubmersible ram, the Manassas, to patrol the river. The Manassas, while not a true submarine, mounted a sixty-four-pound gun mounted forward behind the ram as its primary armament. The shipyard at New Orleans was also heavily involved in building two new ironclads, the Louisiana and the Mississippi, to counter the Union naval threat.

In September of 1861, as part of the overall blockading strategy, the Union Navy sent five ships upriver to Head of the Passes, the southernmost point of the river before it divides into the delta. For about a month, this Flotilla effectively enforced the blockade of New Orleans from that location. On the evening of October 11th however, the Confederate ram Manassas, selected other ships, and several fire ships attacked the Union position at Head of the Passes. After a short battle, the Rebel ships drove the Union ships back into the Gulf of Mexico and reopened the river to merchant ships that successfully ran the blockade.

In late 1861 the Department of the Navy developed a plan to capture New Orleans and use it as a base for operations further upriver. In phase one of the plan, ships from the blockading force would control the lower river with firepower and mobility. In phase two, mortar schooners would attack the two forts while the capital ships advanced upriver to New Orleans. Finally, an Army force of twenty thousand would land and seize the city. With New Orleans in Union hands, the naval force would then be free to advance upriver toward Baton Rouge and Natchez.

To accomplish this plan, the Gulf Blockading Fleet was subdivided into two separate squadrons, the West and East Blockading Squadrons. Captain David Farragut was designated a flag officer and sent to command the West Blockading Squadron and oversee the capture of New Orleans.

After assembling his force at Biloxi, Mississippi, Farragut began the attack on the Confederate river forts on April 18th. For five days, the mortar schooners poured over sixteen thousand rounds into the two Forts. After one unsuccessful attempt to breech the Confederate boom, on April 24th a second attempt proved effective. As the Squadron began its assault upriver, Confederate ships supported by the Fort's guns attempted to prevent the Union force from advancing. Even the unfinished ironclad Louisiana serving as a floating battery joined the battle. Their efforts proved unsuccessful and the Union ships steamed on.

After landing Major General Benjamin Butler and twenty thousand Union soldiers downriver from New Orleans, Farragut continued upriver and seized the city. In order to keep the City intact, the Mayor of New Orleans agreed to a surrender and Union occupation.

Further downriver, the mortar schooners continued bombarding the river forts and on April 27th, after a brief mutiny in the forts, they surrendered. On May 1st, Major General Butler assumed command of the occupied city. The southern approaches of the Mississippi were now in Union hands.

With river levels dropping, Farragut elected to take the Squadron to Pensacola, Florida to resupply. Soon after his arrival, the

Squadron was directed to return to the Mississippi River and advance upriver to join with the Western Gunboat Flotilla. The two commands would then work together to clear any final Rebel obstacles preventing Union control of the entire river.

On May 3rd, the Squadron was underway for the river and the next Union objective: Baton Rouge. Not wishing to see his City destroyed, the Mayor of Baton Rouge followed the lead of New Orleans and on May 7th, surrendered the Capitol City of Louisiana. A determined Flag Officer Farragut continued upriver to Natchez and in a repeat of Baton Rouge, that City quietly surrendered.

By May 18th the lead elements of the Squadron advanced upriver to Vicksburg. After a Union request to surrender was politely refused, Farragut realized he had neither the manpower nor the firepower to force the City's surrender. On May 30th, the Squadron returned to New Orleans ending the first Union attempt to capture Vicksburg.

After hearing of Farragut's efforts, President Lincoln applied pressure on the Department of the Navy to try again to reopen the river. Left with no other options, Secretary Wells directed Farragut to return to Vicksburg for a second time.

On June 26th, the Squadron arrived at the city and commenced a brisk but ineffective bombardment. After two days, Farragut concluded once again he had too few soldiers to conduct any kind of landward assault. After running several ships past the Vicksburg defenses, these ships met up with elements of the Ram Fleet. The remainder of the Flotilla arrived from Memphis on June 1st and the two commands attempted to solve the vexing problem that was Vicksburg.

August 1st, 1862 – Vicksburg, Mississippi

For the entire month of July, the Flotilla and the Squadron attempted to find a crack in the armor of Vicksburg. The City itself was located at on the southern side of a U-shaped turn in the river some two hundred and ninety feet above the Union ships below. From an area south of the City and running in a northerly direction was Chickasaw Bluffs. All along this natural ridge the Rebels positioned their artillery in locations hidden from the view of Union ships and difficult to hit by any of the Union guns.

The Rebels also positioned artillery at the base of the U turn that commanded any movement on the river in either direction. Any ship attempting to pass was forced to slow down to negotiate the turn and became easy targets for the Confederate gunners. Behind these artillery positions stretching from the Bluffs to the Yazoo River was a large area of swamp impassable even by infantry forces. If these defenses were not enough, the Union forces faced some fifteen thousand Confederate troops under the Command of Major General Earl Van Dorn.

At the center of the U turn was a spit of land called Desoto Peninsula. Part of the Union plan called for troops from General Butler's command to cut a trench across the base of the Desoto Peninsula in order to bypass the city and the Rebel defenses on Chickasaw Bluffs. This task fell to Brigadier General Thomas Williams and over three thousand troops from New Orleans. A thousand slaves from nearby plantations augmented General Williams in his efforts.

A short distance upriver from Vicksburg was the mouth of the Yazoo River. Running southerly, the Yazoo snaked around and through the Mississippi countryside from its origins in Tennessee, past the shipyard at Yazoo City and into the Mississippi.

After linking up with elements of the Ram Fleet, word came down that the Confederate ironclad Arkansas and their remaining ram the CSS General Van Dorn were located at the shipyard at Yazoo City. Flag Officer Farragut requested Ellet send his rams up the Yazoo to conduct a reconnaissance of the upper river and the new commander of the Ram Fleet quickly agreed.

Sixty-five miles up the Yazoo Ellet's two rams encountered a significant obstacle in the river supported by a Rebel battery. Ellet also found the missing ram General Van Dorn and two other Rebel ships, the CSS Polk and the CSS Livingston. As the Union rams approached, the Rebels set fire to the three ships and sent them downriver. The three fire ships and the narrow winding river forced Ellet to terminate his reconnaissance and return to the Vicksburg area.

The USS Great Western arrived at Vicksburg with the auxiliaries and the mortar barges on July 2nd. The mortars were quickly put to work and we spent our time resupplying the barges and protecting them from the periodic attacks by Rebel infantry and cavalry.

Talking with the mortar crews provided some interesting insight into the operation.

"Can't see the dang target," the gunner complained. "Can't see 'em, don't know if we are actually hitting anything. But they keep shooting at us."

"Not to mention the constant harassment by their leg infantry and horse soldiers," another member of the mortar crew added. "They outnumber us soldier-wise about five or six to one."

"And most of our fellas are down digging that dang fool canal," replied the gunner. "Getting sicker by the spade full. A good ten percent of those boys are down with something or other from crawling around in that swamp."

"And you think that pompous ass over in Corinth would send us any support. There he sits with his grand army doing nothing but digging holes and getting sick. Weren't that way when Grant was in charge."

There was some truth to what those two were saying. One evening on watch I overheard the Captain talking with the Pilot. He said Farragut and Davis asked Halleck for troops and they were both denied. The General claimed he had no units to spare as all his troops were refitting or recovering from illness.

On the river there was also a growing concern about the location of the Rebel ironclad Arkansas. So far, the Arkansas had not entered the battle or been seen on the Mississippi River. On July 14th, three ships from the Flotilla and the Ram Fleet steamed up the Yazoo again to search the upper river for the elusive Confederate ironclad.

CSS Arkansas was indeed a formidable enemy. One hundred and sixty-five feet long and thirty-five feet wide, she mounted eight guns, had eighteen inches of armor plate, and sixteen-foot ram ten feet wide. On the evening of the 14th, the Arkansas departed Yazoo City, moved downriver, and anchored at Haynes Bluff as the three Union ships approached.

At 3:00 am on the morning of the 15th, the Arkansas got underway and a short distance downriver encountered the Tyler, the Queen of the West, and the Carondelet. In the short battle that followed the Arkansas quickly gained the upper hand. The Carondelet ran aground in the darkness and the other two Union ships fled back downriver.

Standing watch on the Great Western, I heard the sounds of the battle up the Yazoo. Shortly after day broke, I saw the Tyler and the

Queen of the West come out of the Yazoo and turn upriver on the Mississippi. They were followed a short time later by the Arkansas, her guns blazing. The Arkansas turned downriver and in the reduced visibility of a light morning fog began blasting away at the target rich environment of Union ships.

I watched in sheer fascination as the Arkansas fired salvo after salvo at the Union vessels and received shot after shot in return. After driving completely through the Union ships, the Confederate ironclad reached the relative safety of the Vicksburg defenses. The heavily damaged but still afloat Arkansas tied up to the pier to the cheers of the soldiers on the bluffs and the good citizens of Vicksburg.

July 14th was also the day Flag Officer Farragut received orders for the Squadron to return downriver to the Gulf and await further instructions. Sickness was running rampant through all of the Union forces. By the time Farragut received his promotion to Rear Admiral on July 20th, over forty percent of the Flotilla and Squadron crews were down. General Williams reported that of the thirty-two hundred men in his command, only eight hundred were fit for duty. It was time to go.

On July 23rd, the West Blockading Squadron departed the Vicksburg area. On July 28th, the Flotilla left the area as well for Memphis and Helena, Arkansas. The Great Western traveled upriver with the auxiliaries and the mortar barges. When we stopped for the night at the mouth of the Arkansas River, Confederate cavalry supported by an artillery piece attacked us. In a fierce, one hour fight, we succeeded in protecting the mortar barges and driving off the Rebels at a cost of three dead and nine wounded. This action served as a fitting close to the second Vicksburg campaign.

Chapter Thirty-One

January 1st, 1863 – On the Mississippi River

A s summer gave way to fall there were some significant changes to both Army and Navy organizations in the Western Theater. In July, General Halleck was relieved of duty and transferred to Washington as General in Chief of the Union Army. His appointment came as a result of General McClellan's failed Peninsula Campaign and continued strife with the President and members of the Cabinet. In his place, General Grant was named the Commander of the Western Theater. Halleck's Grand Army was divided between Buell and Grant, as was the territorial responsibility. General Buell was responsible for the eastern area and General Grant the western area to include the Mississippi River.

With regard to Vicksburg, General Halleck received a great deal of criticism for his failure to provide troops. While it was true Halleck was a cautious commander, many of his soldiers were suffering from the myriad of diseases that plagued Union forces during southern summer months: a fact that certainly weighed heavily in the General's final decision. A share of the blame also rested with the War Department for failing to provide Farragut or Davis with sufficient ground forces needed to accomplish the mission. With an adequate amount of ground troops, Vicksburg might have fallen in July. By the end of the year, it was an impregnable fortress.

As a result of the failure at Vicksburg there was great concern in Washington about the situation on the Mississippi River. A few army officers like Generals Grant and Sherman understood what an effective riverine naval force brought to a battle. Most of the other senior officers did not. In their minds the Flotilla was simply a source of supply with no real value outside of the world of logistics and transportation.

Besides the interservice issues involved, within the Navy itself there was a lack of cooperation between blue water sailors and their brown water counterparts. By the summer of 1862 all Navy forces on blockade duty were squadron-sized units commanded by Rear Admirals. The unit that controlled the river networks in the Southern heartland was still commanded by a Navy Captain. In spite of the fact the riverine Navy had several times more ships than any blockading squadron, they were still designated as a Flotilla.

These facts and the failure of a combined operation to capture Vicksburg forced the President and the Secretary of the Navy to make some serious reorganizational changes to the brown water Navy. In August of 1862, Congress passed legislation that finally gave the Navy full control of the Western Gunboat Flotilla. This legislation also upgraded the status and importance of the Flotilla. Effective the first of October, we were designated the Mississippi Squadron.

That fall, Flag Officer Davis was transferred to the Bureau of Navigation in Washington with the rank of acting Rear Admiral. In his place the Secretary appointed Commander David Dixon Porter as an acting Rear Admiral and the first Commanding Officer of the new Squadron. Admiral Porter assumed command on October 5th, much to the chagrin of many senior officers. Some of these officers spent over twenty years in grade waiting for a chance to become Admirals and resented the upstart Commander. While many viewed Porter as arrogant and egotistical, he also possessed the ability to think and plan in a highly unconventional manner, a trait the President and Secretary both admired and desired.

Admiral Porter's first order of business was to develop a new series of gunboats capable of negotiating the shallow water of the river's tributaries. Although Pook's Turtles and the timberclads proved their worth in battle, operations on the White River and the Yazoo River showed these vessels had a difficult time in constrictive waters.

Over the fall when the Great Western returned to Cairo, new ships began showing up in the harbor. Some of these new ships were called "tinclads": smaller sternwheelers with inch and one quarter armor plating and a draft of only four feet. Porter also contacted James Eads for new ideas and designs. Eads turned out two unique vessels, the Neosho and the Osage, both sternwheelers and patterned somewhat after the USS Monitor. These two gunboats had six-inch armor plated turrets like the Monitor, which housed two eleven-inch guns. Around the decks and other key areas were two and one half inches of armor plating.

As part of the reorganization, Admiral Porter managed to solve the problem of how to deal with the Ram Fleet. With Alfred Ellet's approval, a new command was established, the Mississippi Marine Brigade. The Marine Brigade was composed of an infantry regiment and a cavalry battalion that would operate somewhat independently but still under the overall control of the Mississippi Squadron. That fall, Ellet was promoted to Brigadier General and assigned to command it.

On one visit to Cairo in November I spotted a huge sidewheeler being fitted with guns and armor plating.

"What is that," I said to one of the deck sailors.

"She's the New Uncle Sam," the sailor replied. "She was quite a lady in her days on the river. A cruising ship, she made the rounds up to Pittsburgh and down river to New Orleans."

"She is huge," I said.

"Round two hundred sixty feet," the sailor replied. "Gonna be the flagship of Admiral Porter. Even got stables aboard. Quite a ship."

Throughout the late summer and fall, warfare along the Mississippi began to follow the pattern we experienced on the Tennessee and Cumberland Rivers. The newly reorganized main Army of General Grant was operating inland near Corinth and General Buell's Army had moved east in pursuit of Confederate General Braxton Bragg. This allowed Rebel guerillas and irregulars to expand their hit and run and ambush tactics that were somewhat effective in Tennessee and Kentucky. In addition to the Tennessee and Cumberland rivers, Rebel guerilla activity now included the Ohio River and the Mississippi River, including its tributaries.

In July of 1862, Rebels captured the town of Henderson, Kentucky and were spotted establishing camps across the river from Mound City. A hastily organized force from the Flotilla headquarters and a regiment of Union troops finally drove off the guerillas. Along the Mississippi that July, the steamer USS Sallie Wood was sunk in an ambush near Island Eighty-four. In early August, Rebel attacks caused the Flotilla to send a joint expedition up the White River in respond to activities in that area. Further south, a second combined force was sent up the Yazoo River to counter a Rebel buildup just north of Vicksburg.

The Confederate strategy was taking a toll on the ships and crews of the Flotilla. Every bend in the river was a potential ambush site and every night mooring site on the riverbanks forced Captains to provide additional security ashore in case of attack.

By the time Admiral Porter assumed command in October, dealing with the guerilla and irregular Confederate forces was generally defensive in nature. Few, if any, supply or transport ships travelled alone. Ships' captains responded to the threat by organizing convoys supported by gunboat escorts.

Admiral Porter initiated a more offensive approach to the problem. In addition to using the Marine Brigade as an anti-guerilla force, the new tinclads, with their shallow drafts, were capable of chasing the Rebels further up the tributaries and deploying troops to deal with the situation. Porter also issued orders to his captains that when they were fired on from the riverbank, they would return fire and destroy any civilian facilities or homes deemed to be providing aid to the guerillas. The new policies met with little resistance from the captains.

Following the new policy, when Rebel forces assaulted the Great Western, our gun crews returned fire and we landed a security force to burn any barns or dwellings in the immediate vicinity. Since our ship was not designed for shallow water operations, that was where our offensive actions ended. Other ships, and especially the Marine Brigade, were much more violent in their approach. The Marine Brigade went so far as to burn entire towns suspected of harboring or abetting Rebel guerillas. In spite of Porter's proclamations, this type of irregular warfare and the Union response continued until the end of the war.

By November, Union leaders were ready for another try at seizing Vicksburg. General Grant and two Corps of his Army were in Holly Springs, Mississippi, some fifty miles southeast of Memphis and preparing to move against Grenada, Mississippi. General Sherman's Corps was in Memphis and preparing to move downriver to draw out the Vicksburg defenders.

As part of the offensive, the Great Western moved with a majority of the Squadron to Helena, Arkansas. In late November, after establishing a forward position in Helena, we moved downriver with several other ships of the Squadron to a point at the mouth of the Yazoo River. The Great Western remained there with the support ships as two tinclads, the Signal and the Marmora, conducted a reconnaissance of the Yazoo. Their efforts indicated that the deeper draft gunboats were capable of navigating the channel but the Rebels had sunk vessels in the shallower parts of the river and set torpedoes in other areas.

After relaying the information to Admiral Porter and General Sherman, plans were drawn up to use the Yazoo River, particularly the part near Haynes Bluff, as a means of rolling up the Rebel defenses on Chickasaw Bluffs. In early December, we steamed back downriver with the Signal and the Marmora, the gunboats Pittsburgh and the Cairo, the ram, Queen of the West, and several other support ships.

On the morning of December 12th, while we remained at the mouth of the river with the support vessels, the other five ships steamed up the Yazoo. The sounds of the ship's firing at suspected Rebel positions echoed down the river all morning. That afternoon a huge explosion rocked the silence. We later learned that a Confederate torpedo, detonated remotely from the riverbank, sank the Cairo. A landing party from the Pittsburgh found the location of the torpedo factory and destroyed both the site and the stockpile of torpedoes nearby. The four remaining ships returned downriver to our position late that afternoon.

Still intent on using the Yazoo as the gateway into Vicksburg, Admiral Porter directed the gunboats to begin clearing the river of obstacles and torpedoes. By mid-December, the channel was clear to a point near Haynes Bluff.

On December 20th, as the river was being cleared, General Grant and the other two Corps of his Army were moving toward Grenada, Mississippi when disaster struck. Confederate General Van Dorn led thirty-five hundred mounted troops against Grant's supply point at Holly Springs. Almost simultaneously, General Forrest's cavalry tore up about sixty miles of track essential to Grant's movement and resupply. Forrest's raid was also a serious threat to the Union support activity at Memphis. With the supply point at Holly Springs destroyed and Memphis threatened, Grant was forced to fall back on Grand Junction, Tennessee and await any further offensive action by Van Dorn.

Admiral Porter and General Sherman received word of Grant's situation on December 21st and, in the absence of additional orders, elected to continue with their plan to assault Vicksburg from the Yazoo River. On December 23rd, I watched as transport after transport entered the mouth of the Yazoo supported by gunboats and tinclads. By the 27th, Sherman's forces started to land as the gunboats led by the USS Benton moved closer to the bluffs.

There were actually three bluffs between Sherman's forces and main defenses on Chickasaw Bluffs. Rebel defenses extended southerly from Haynes Bluff to Snyder's Bluff before crossing a large swamp called Virginia Bayou and ascending up to Drumgould's Bluff. All three of these geographic features were heavily fortified.

As the ships moved forward, about 2:30 pm, the Rebel guns opened fire on the lead gunboats. The Benton, former flagship of Flag Officer Foote, took the majority of damage as she covered Sherman's troops assaulting the bluffs. At day's end, Sherman's single corps was not enough to win the day. Sherman suffered over seventeen hundred casualties to the Rebel's one hundred eighty-seven. The third offensive for Vicksburg was over as Sherman and Porter retired upriver. As 1862 came to a close, critical areas of the Mississippi River were still under Confederate control.

Chapter Thirty-Two

April 14th, 1863 – Around the Red River

At the start of 1863, Union forces controlled a major portion of the Mississippi River with the exception of a stretch between Vicksburg and Port Hudson, Louisiana, about thirty miles upriver from Baton Rouge. Aside from occasional skirmishes with Rebel guerillas and irregulars, Squadron ships moved up and down the Union controlled portion of the river virtually unimpeded.

After the last attempt to breakthrough the Vicksburg defenses, Admiral Porter and General Sherman, still stinging from their rejection at Haynes Bluff, elected to salvage some small victory from the operation. As the support ships, including the Great Western, waited at the mouth of the Arkansas River, we watched the gunboats, tinclads, and transports that headed upriver to the Arkansas Post. On January 11th, the Squadron's guns silenced the Confederate batteries at Fort Hindman, some fifty miles upriver. As the ships fired, Sherman's troops began their assault of the Fort. This coordinated effort forced the remaining Confederates to surrender the last key obstacle on the Arkansas River. After this brief adventure, by the end of the month, both Army and Navy planners resumed their preparation for offensive operations against Vicksburg.

While Union domination of the northern part of the river significantly affected Rebel operations in Kentucky and Tennessee, Southern forces and cities were still being resupplied through the Confederate controlled sector. Cattle, goods, and other supplies flowed freely from east Texas and western Louisiana, down the Red River, and across the Mississippi to Confederate forces at Vicksburg and further east. Admiral Porter was determined to choke off this vital supply line in an effort to starve out the Confederate garrison and force Vicksburg's surrender.

In the opinion of Navy planners, the Red River was the critical link in stopping the supplies from reaching Vicksburg and beyond. In late January, Admiral Porter directed the ram, Queen of the West, to run the gauntlet at Vicksburg. Once below the city, the Queen was to reconnoiter the lower end of the Red River and interdict any Confederate ships and supplies in the area.

On the moonless evening of February 2nd, we watched from the deck of the Great Western as the Queen began her run past the Vicksburg defenses. The ram had cotton bales attached to the critical areas of the ship to deflect Rebel shells and made the hazardous passage with minimal damage. Once the Queen was downriver, a large barge filled with coal was sent down. The barge floated past the defenses unmolested and was picked up downriver: a truly novel resupply technique.

Commanding the Queen of the West was nineteen-year-old Colonel Charles R. Ellet, the son of the initial commander of the Ram Fleet. The start of Ellet's operation was extremely successful as the Queen captured three steamers loaded with supplies, burned several storage sites, and generally wreaked havoc on the Confederate supply line.

After another coal barge was sent downriver, Admiral Porter elected to augment Ellet with the ironclad Indianola. On the night of February 13th, we watched the Indianola, with two additional coal barges in tow, run the Vicksburg gauntlet. She made the trip with no significant damage and steamed off to join the Queen.

As the Indianola was negotiating the Rebel defenses, Ellet's string of successes came to a close. Operating up the Red River, after the Queen captured another supply vessel, she ran aground under the guns of Fort DeRussy near Gordon's Landing. The fire from the fort was so intense that Ellet was forced to abandon ship and seek refuge on one of his captured prizes. After a second prize ran aground and was set afire, Ellet steamed north and joined up with the Indianola on February 16th.

Unfortunately for Ellet, the Queen of the West was not as damaged as first thought and the Rebels made all of the necessary repairs to get her operational in short order. The repaired Queen, the Confederate ram Webb, and the gunboat Dr. Beatty steamed out of the Red River on February 24th in search of the Indianola. The ships met that night about thirty miles south of Vicksburg and after a fierce fight, the heavily damaged Indianola surrendered. The Rebels towed the Union ironclad to Jefferson Davis' plantation and began making necessary repairs.

The Union Navy leadership was quick to recognize the gravity of the situation. The capture of both the Queen of the West and the Indianola severely impacted any plans to close the vital Confederate supply line and open the Mississippi. If both were made operational again, the threat to Union dominance on the rest of the river increased dramatically.

In a diabolical stunt, Admiral Porter's initial response was to send a "Quaker" gunboat downriver in hopes of having the Confederates destroy the heavily damaged Indianola. I joined the carpenters from our ship and others in fabricating a fake gunboat from a coal barge. Our replica gunboat was even complete with logs representing cannon protruding from the gun ports and had a pirate flag flying from the hastily constructed pilothouse. The deception worked and after running the gauntlet, the Quaker ship came to rest against the bank near the location of the Indianola. Fearing another gunboat would soon attack and recapture their prize; the Rebels blew up the Indianola.

After hearing of the situation, on March 15th, Admiral Farragut attempted to run elements of his Squadron past Port Hudson and occupy the waters south of Vicksburg. Unfortunately, only Farragut's flagship, the Hartford, and one smaller gunboat, the Albatross, were successful in passing the Rebel defenses. Among the casualties of Farragut's effort was the loss of the USS Mississippi with sixty-four members of her crew.

On March 25th, Brigadier General Alfred Ellet sent his flagship, the Switzerland, and a second ram, the Lancaster, past the Rebel guns. The Switzerland was successful in running the gauntlet with minor damages but the Confederate guns disabled the Lancaster and her crew set her afire before abandoning ship. By April 1st, the Hartford, the Switzerland, and the Albatross were actively patrolling the river from the vicinity of Vicksburg south to Port Hudson. Their actions significantly impacted the number of supplies reaching Confederate forces at Vicksburg.

The Confederate Navy had no answer to these three Union ships. Even the refurbished Queen of the West was no match in open conflict with Farragut's flagship. The Rebels chose instead to move the Queen further south on the Atchafalaya River. In the early morning hours of April 14th, as the Queen and two Rebel transports were moving troops south, they were discovered by the Union ships, the Arizona, the Estrella, and the Calhoun. According to witnesses, one shot from the Calhoun's thirty-pound Parrott gun penetrated the Queens upper deck and set her afire. By 7:40 am the fire spread to the magazine area and, in a massive explosion, the Queen of the West was no more.

<h1 style="text-align:center">July 31st, 1863 – Vicksburg, Mississippi</h1>

With winter moving into early spring, it was the time of unconventional thinking throughout the Union Army. As the situation around the Red River unfolded, north of Vicksburg, Union planners set their efforts into bypassing the main Rebel defenses entirely. In their first undertaking, General Grant's engineers attempted to complete the canal across Desoto Peninsula and avoid the city completely. As with the previous effort to cut the peninsula, the swamp, the insects, and the uncertainty of the river bottom soon doomed this effort.

After the failure of the Desoto canal, a second attempt was made some twenty miles upstream near the town of Duckport, Louisiana. The goal of this canal was to use the bayous as a route around the Rebel defenses and come out downriver at New Carthage, well below Vicksburg. Work began on March 31st and the levee between the canal and the Mississippi River was cut on April 11th. Unfortunately, lower water levels on the river caused the water levels in the canal to drop considerably: in some areas to only six inches. After many of the boats assigned to the project were grounded, the effort was abandoned on May 4th.

Undaunted by their lack of success, Union engineers began digging a third canal from the river to Lake Providence. Dubbed the Lake Providence Canal, the proposed route would then follow a series of bayous to the Black River and finally into the Red River. If successful, this route would not only avoid Vicksburg but also a second Rebel defensive area at Grand Gulf. Again, success eluded the Union as lowering water levels and heavy growths of cypress trees in the bayous denied passage to all but the smallest vessels.

While General Grant's engineers wrestled with the bayous on the Louisiana side of the river, Admiral Porter and General Sherman attempted to move forces through the headwaters of the Yazoo River. The next effort, dubbed the Yazoo Pass Expedition, was designed to breach the Mississippi levee and flood the headwaters of the Yazoo. The plan was to make the upper region of the Yazoo navigable and allow ships to travel to an area on the right flank of the Vicksburg defenses. The breach was planned for a section of the levee across the river from Helena, some one hundred and fifty miles from Vicksburg.

The Great Western was assigned to support the engineers at the breach site and I was assigned to the defense force ashore for their protection. On February 3rd, I watched from the levee as the engineers prepared their charges and detonated the breach. A tidal wave of muddy water roared through the break creating a flood of biblical proportions in the Yazoo Basin. Farmers in the area grabbed everything they could and raced for higher ground. Animals of all sorts also ran from the torrent as the river water swelled streams and flatlands for miles around.

After about four days, the water levels finally equalized and on February 12th, we watched elements of the Squadron steam through the breach. Three days later, some six thousand men of Sherman's Corps followed in transports. While the water levels were high enough to support the ships, the surrounding vegetation, both above and below the water level, made the going difficult.

The slow movement of the Union forces gave the Confederates time to construct a hasty defense. About halfway to Vicksburg at a critical junction of the Tallahatchie and Yalobusha Rivers, the Rebels constructed a hastily built, but defensively sound fort that commanded the major approach. The local vegetation, snakes and other critters, as well as Rebel sharpshooters and the fort's guns soon forced the Squadron to retreat back to the Yazoo Basin.

Admiral Porter refused to give up and proposed another expedition to General Sherman. The new route would track down Steele's Bayou and Deer Creek to a point on the Yazoo near Chickasaw Bluffs. On March 12th, Porter and four of the original Pook's Turtles moved down the river. After a successful movement to a point in Deer Creek the lead ship, the Cincinnati, became mired in an impassable thicket of willow trees. Again, the vegetation and Confederate defenses forced Porter and Sherman back to Yazoo Basin.

At this point, after the failure of these expeditions, the idea of bypassing Vicksburg by river was no longer an option. General Grant elected instead to move two Corps of the Army of the Tennessee south along the west side of the river, cross the Mississippi, and attack Vicksburg from the landward side. General

Sherman's Corps would remain upriver and move up the Yazoo in a diversion against Haynes Bluff and the Confederate right flank.

As a secondary diversion, on April 12th, Grant dispatched Colonel Benjamin Grierson to conduct a cavalry raid from Le Grange, Tennessee to Baton Rouge. Grierson's seventeen hundred troopers traveled some six hundred miles tearing up rail lines, burning Confederate supplies, and tying up Rebel cavalry. The combination of Sherman's deception and Grierson's raid tied up Confederate troops and enabled Grant to cross the Mississippi.

On April 16th, eleven ships of the Squadron ran the gauntlet and after making necessary repairs, were poised to support the movement of the Army. North of the City, ships of the Squadron and the mortar barges prepared to support General Sherman's diversion. The Great Western remained near the mouth of the Yazoo River supporting the mortar barges as the gunboats moved up the river followed by the transports.

With winter gone and the land drying out, the two Corps were able to move along the western side of the river and by April 27th, were far enough south for the Squadron ironclads and gunboats to begin their assault on Grand Gulf. The Squadron ships attacked the two Confederate forts located there, Fort Cobun and Fort Wade. Their efforts succeeded in destroying some of the guns of Confederate artillery stationed there but after using up all available ammunition, could not breach either fort's walls without a land assault.

On April 30th, the army was in position to commence the amphibious assault across the river. After receiving new information from a runaway slave, General Grant chose to adjust the landing site to a point six miles further downriver at Bruinsburg. With the diversion at Haynes Bluff completed, Sherman's corps began moving south and by May 1st, the entire Army of the Tennessee was on the same side of the river as the enemy and the final push for Vicksburg was underway.

In November of 1862 there was a major shakeup in the Confederate Western Theater. Beauregard was gone and, in his place, came another familiar Rebel from my time in the Manassas campaign: General Joseph Johnston. Seriously wounded at Malvern Hill in McClellan's Peninsula campaign, Johnston had somewhat recovered and now commanded the Western Theater. That spring there were three operational forces in the theater. Operating in eastern Tennessee was the Army of Tennessee, commanded by General Braxton Bragg. Lieutenant General Joseph Pemberton's Department of Louisiana and Mississippi faced our forces at Vicksburg while Lieutenant General Theophilius Holmes' Trans-Mississippi Department operated in Arkansas.

As winter gave way to spring, Confederate leadership in Richmond sensed the Union desire to finally open the Mississippi River. In early May, Confederate Secretary of War, Joseph Seddon, directed General Johnston to move to Jackson, Mississippi and begin raising troops to augment the six thousand currently in the City. Unfortunately, Johnston's arrival in Jackson on May 13th coincided with the arrival of two Union Corps. The following day, convinced that the city could not be held, Johnston withdrew to the north to find another means of supporting Vicksburg.

One serious flaw in the Confederate military leadership was President Davis' persistent habit of ordering subordinate commanders without first conferring with or advising their military superiors. Such was the case at Vicksburg. In early May, as Grant's army moved to enclose Vicksburg from the landward side, General Pemberton was in receipt of conflicting orders. Directed by the President to hold Vicksburg, Pemberton was also in receipt of orders from Johnston to vacate the City and attack Grant. After an ineffective council of war, Pemberton elected to keep part of his army in Vicksburg while moving the rest east against Grant. As a result of these actions, the Rebels were defeated at Champion Hill and Big Black River Bridge. In spite of urgings from General Johnston to break out of Vicksburg and avoid a siege, Pemberton elected to remain in the City.

By the end of the day on May 19th, Grant's Army cut off all avenues of retreat from the City and began preparing for siege operations. Inside Vicksburg, Pemberton consolidated his forces, evacuating units from the Haynes Bluff area. Sherman's Corps, supported by Squadron ships on the Yazoo River, quickly occupied these abandoned positions. Sherman's primary focus was the Chickasaw Bluffs section of the Rebel defenses but his reconnaissance efforts extended northeast to Canton where General Johnston's twenty-four thousand soldiers prepared to assist Pemberton.

After completing the amphibious assault for the Army of the Tennessee, the Squadron maintained a vigorous operational pace all along the river and its tributaries. After the army moved inland, Admiral Porter directed the ships south of the City to provide support for pending operations against Port Hudson. Later in May, these same ships steamed up the Red River as far as Alexandria to once again cut Rebel resupply from western Louisiana and eastern Texas.

North of the City, the Admiral ordered a six ship force up the Yazoo River to the area of Haynes Bluff. Finding the Bluffs deserted, this force linked up with the lead elements of Sherman's Corps while one ship, the Baron DeKalb, steamed further upriver to Yazoo City. There she found and destroyed a new Rebel shipyard and three ironclads under construction.

With siege operations underway, the Great Western remained busy resupplying the mortar barges and schooners. When stocks were depleted, we headed upriver to Helena, loaded up, and returned with our deadly cargo. These operations were not without a degree of imminent danger. Ships were always subjected to artillery fire and sniping from cavalry and infantry units as well as attacks from guerrilla forces on the west side of the river. The Rebel defenses were also quite capable of firing on any unfortunate ship that came within range. On May 27th, one of the original Pook's Turtles, the Cincinnati, was sunk by artillery fire off Fort Hill, the northern point of the Chickasaw Bluffs defenses.

This hectic pace of siege operations kept up throughout May and June. Towards the end of June word was received that General Johnston was moving to assist Pemberton. Ships of the Squadron once again scrambled to move up the Yazoo River in support of General Sherman. Fortunately, nothing came of this threat and on July 4th, Lieutenant General Pemberton surrendered Vicksburg to General Grant. With the City lost, General Johnston retreated to Jackson followed closely by Sherman's Corps. Unwilling to become involved in another siege operation, on July 16th, Johnston departed Jackson and moved further east.

In the last chapter of the siege of Vicksburg it was the Squadron that suffered the final casualty. On July 13th, the Baron DeKalb was conducting a routine patrol of the Yazoo City area when she struck two Rebel torpedoes and sank. Unlike the Cincinnati, which would be refloated and live to fight again, the Baron was lost to the Squadron.

Vicksburg had long been the key to opening the southern end of the Mississippi River. In spite of the fact operations here would be overshadowed in the newspapers and the history books by the Union victory at Gettysburg, the fight for the City was now over. Five days later, on July 9th, word was received that Port Hudson, under siege since May 24th, surrendered to General Banks. For the remainder of the summer and into the fall of 1863 the fighting moved further east toward Chattanooga and Atlanta. The war on the rivers of the West saw new tactics and strategies and the Squadron was an integral part of it all. But for now, the Father of all Rivers once again flowed freely to the sea.

❧

Chapter Thirty-Three

April 1864 – The Mississippi River

y the late summer and early fall of 1863, the major fighting between the warring armies shifted east to Chattanooga and eastern Tennessee. Vicksburg and Port Hudson were now in Union hands and the entire Mississippi River was open to ship traffic.

Although the Mississippi Squadron weathered the Vicksburg storm, the pace of operations did not diminish. If anything, it increased dramatically. In late 1863, the Squadron was responsible for all of the major rivers and tributaries from the Ohio River, down the Cumberland and Tennessee Rivers, north on the Mississippi to Saint Louis, and south to New Orleans. Squadron ships routinely maintained resupply routes to Union forces in the field, transported troops to and from operational areas, combatted hot spots of Rebel actions, and a myriad of other activities. All of this designed to keep the river networks open and support the overall war effort in the Western Theater.

In my final year on the river, the Great Western spent much of that time on the lower Mississippi supporting operations there. We routinely moved between the supply centers at Cairo and Helena, Arkansas as well as two new centers at Skipwith's Landing, Mississippi and Goodrich's Landing, Louisiana.

As usual, the principal threat to shipping continued to be the Rebel guerillas and irregular forces. Working in small bands of generally less than one hundred soldiers, these Rebel forces routinely ambushed shipping all along the rivers. Usually mounted and in possession of one or two pieces of horse drawn artillery, the guerillas moved quickly after their initial attack to elude the return fire of the ships. If the ships opted to land infantry or cavalry, these troops were at an immediate disadvantage of not knowing the surrounding terrain or ways around the countryside as well as the Rebels.

By 1863, more organized Rebel raids were also becoming commonplace, particularly along the Cumberland and Tennessee Rivers. Confederate cavalry under Major General Joseph Wheeler and Brigadier General Nathan Bedford Forrest routinely attacked into Union held territory. Early on, many of these raids were aimed at the supply lines and rear areas of the Army of the Tennessee or the Army of the Cumberland. As time passed however, the raiding became bolder and further away from the major battle areas in an effort to force Union leadership to pull troops from the fighting to provide additional rear area security.

On February 3rd, 1863 Forrest and Wheeler attacked Fort Donelson on the Cumberland River. Fortunately for the Fort's garrison, Squadron gunboats were escorting a convoy upriver at the time and joined the fight. When the gunboats arrived, they found dismounted cavalry attacking the Fort. The ships engaged the Rebels and the staging area for their horses. After suffering heavy losses, the cavalry forces withdrew.

In another raid rivaling Jeb Stuart's ride around the Army of the Potomac during the Peninsula Campaign, Brigadier General John Hunt Morgan crossed the Ohio River on June 11,1863 in an effort to draw Union forces away from the Vicksburg siege. Attacking through Indiana and Ohio, Morgan's activities forced local governments to appeal for military action. Admiral Porter chose to send gunboats up the Ohio in support of the Union efforts to trap Morgan. At one point, Squadron gunboats intercepted Morgan's forces trying to cross the river into West Virginia, killing many of the raiding party. Although Morgan's raid covered over one thousand miles and involved over two thousand troops, on July 26th, Morgan and what was left of the raid force, some three hundred fifty soldiers, surrendered at Salineville, Ohio. Unfortunately, the raid accomplished very little and had no significant impact on the fighting.

In another spectacular series of cavalry raids, from September to November of 1863, General Wheeler led a force into central Tennessee against the rear areas of the Army of the Cumberland. With the Union reeling from a serious defeat at Chickamauga, Wheeler's raiders destroyed supply centers and rail lines. The raiders also succeeded in overrunning and capturing several Union rear area garrisons before avoiding Squadron gunboats and escaping over the Tennessee River at Muscle Shoals, Alabama.

The only serious Confederate raid against the Mississippi River area occurred in the spring of 1864. In this operation, Nathan Bedford Forrest conducted the last, and probably most controversial raid into Union Territory. On March 25th, Forrest attacked the Union hub at Paducah, Kentucky. In heavy fighting, the Confederate assault was beaten off by the local garrison and two of the Squadron's tinclads. Undaunted, Forrest chose to turn his attention toward Union operations on the Mississippi River and on April 12th, his forces attacked and seized Fort Pillow. Although the USS New Era was on scene providing support to the Fort's garrison, her guns and those of the Fort were not enough to prevent a Confederate victory. In the fighting, Forrest's troopers massacred a large number of Union troops, many of whom were black soldiers from the US Colored Troops.

Forrest's actions at Fort Pillow were condemned at the highest level of government. Lincoln's Cabinet went so far as to recommend enforcing the recently written Order of Retaliation. In this order Lincoln stated that black soldiers were to be afforded the same protection of the law of war as white soldiers and any deviation from this would result in like punishment to Confederate prisoners. While the actions of Forrest's raiders were thoroughly detested, this incidence would not be the last merciless action directed at colored troops in the war.

By the end of 1863 only one military objective remained involving the Mississippi River area. As the new year began, planning was underway to seize the last Confederate stronghold that impacted Union river operations: Shreveport, Louisiana.

Shreveport was located up the Red River and was the connection to Confederate areas in Texas. The city was also a shipbuilding site and the last bastion of Rebel military operations in Western Louisiana. The Red River Campaign, as the plan was dubbed, was designed to gain a Union victory at Shreveport, destroy Confederate forces in Western Louisiana, and isolate Texas from the rest of the Confederacy.

Early in 1864, General Grant departed the Western Theater to assume command of all Union forces as General of the Army. With Grant's departure, command of the Red River operation fell to Major General Nathaniel Banks. The highly complex operational plan called for a three-pronged attack against Shreveport. The twenty thousand soldiers of Major General William Franklin's Corps from

New Orleans were assigned to move up the western side of the Red River while another ten thousand soldiers from Sherman's Corps at Vicksburg attacked along the river itself. These forces were under the command of Brigadier General Andrew Smith. The third axis with seven thousand soldiers from the Department of Arkansas under Major General Frederick Steele would attack Shreveport from the northwest. The Mississippi Squadron was tasked to provide support to the forces operating in the vicinity of the Red River.

In total, Banks had over thirty-seven thousand soldiers and one hundred and four ships at his disposal for the conduct of the campaign. Facing the Union threat was General E. Kirby Smith and some ten to fifteen thousand Rebels of the Trans-Mississippi Department.

The Great Western was included as part of the flotilla of ships assigned from the Squadron. This force included ten ironclads, eleven tinclads, a ram, and a welcome sight for me, the Lexington. I also recognized one of the ironclads that steamed by as the USS Eastport. When I was aboard the Lexington after the capture of Fort Henry, we came upon the Eastport at Cerro Gordo where the Rebels had scuttled her. Sailors from the timberclads managed to get her refloated and we brought her downriver as a prize. Now the USS Eastport was a two hundred and eighty foot gunboat with eight guns and six and one half inches of armor plating.

Also in the flotilla were two Eads-designed, sternwheel monitors, the Neosho and the Osage. Patterned somewhat after the USS Monitor, these two vessels had large turrets up front housing eleven-inch guns. The turrets had six inches of armor plate while the decks and other critical areas had two and a half inches of armor. Rounding out the naval presence were all of the support vessels of the Squadron, the transports and supply ships of the Army Quartermasters, and the rams and support ships of the Mississippi Marine Brigade.

On March 10th, the operation got underway. The forces from Vicksburg and the Squadron ships arrived at the mouth of the Red River on March 11th. After some initial confusion as to the actual entrance to the Red River, General Smith's troops were landed at Simmesport, Louisiana. From there, this force moved north and captured Fort DeRussy on March 14th.

As they moved upriver in support of General Smith's advance, the Squadron gunboats encountered a Confederate dam at Bend of the

Rappiones. There was a delay as the dam was destroyed but the ships managed to rejoin Smith at Fort DeRussy on the 14th. With the Fort secure, Smith's forces re-embarked the transports and, supported by the Squadron gunboats, proceeded upriver to seize the city of Alexandria.

As Union forces neared Alexandria, Confederate Major General Richard Taylor elected to abandon the city and move his force further upriver. Taylor's cavalry was tracking Franklin's movements west of the river and the prudent move was to fall back closer to Shreveport to avoid encirclement. On March 16th, Squadron ships and Union forces took control of Alexandria and prepared for a further push upriver.

To stall Union naval movement upriver, Confederate General Kirby Smith ordered a Rebel ship, the CSS New Falls City, to be strategically placed across a narrow section of the river at the Scorpini Cut, some forty-five miles south of Shreveport. Turned perpendicular to the flow of the river, the New Falls City stretched some fifteen feet up the banks on each side of the Cut. With the ship in this position, Confederate engineers wedged her into the terrain, filled the ship with mud, and broke her keel. Their actions created an impenetrable dam across the river, altered the river bottom, and lower the water levels further downriver. To further prevent movement upriver, General Smith also ordered the destruction of the Hotchkiss Dam at Tone's Bayou. The river water that was so essential to the Squadron's movement now flowed into a vast floodplain before rejoining the river further south near Natchitoches.

By March 31st, Franklin's Corps was some sixty-five miles from Shreveport near the town of Natchitoches and were joined there by General Banks, Smith's forces, and the Squadron. In early April, Banks and Franklin's Corps moved away from Natchitoches and headed toward Shreveport. Some thirty miles south of their final objective, on April 8th, this force engaged Taylor's forces, supported by newly arrived Texas cavalry, at Mansfield. In the battle, the Rebels drove the Union troops back to the town of Pleasant Hill. After another engagement there on April 9th, Banks elected to end the Red River Campaign and ordered a general retreat of his Army to Alexandria.

As Banks and Franklin's Corps were moving toward Shreveport, many of the Squadron's support ships, including the Great Western, moved upriver to Alexandria. Because water levels in the Red River had been dropping since early March, further travel upriver for the supply ships was not possible.

North of Natchitoches, the gunboats of the Squadron moved into a section of the river called the Narrows. Passage for these ships became extremely difficult because, as its name suggested, the channel became a narrow and winding track. Many of the ships, particularly the larger gunboats, were constantly running aground. By April 8th, Porter and the Squadron reached the location of the New Falls City dam. As the Squadron's naval engineers wrestled with how to move the now firmly embedded ship, Porter learned of Banks' defeat at Mansfield and subsequent decision to abandon the campaign and return to Alexandria. Orders were also received for General Smith's forces to return to Grand Ecore near Natchitoches.

If Admiral Porter thought getting up river was difficult, going downriver was to be even worse. The Squadron was packed into the Narrows at the New Falls City dam site and the channel was not wide enough to turn around. With the water level falling, moving downriver was no easy task. Many of the larger ironclads were forced to back down the river to a point where they could successfully turn around without becoming grounded.

Besides having to contend with conditions on the river, Confederate cavalry and their horse drawn artillery further hampered the Squadron's trip back to Grand Ecore. In one case, about forty-five miles their objective, the Lexington, the monitor Osage, and the transport Blackhawk encountered a cavalry brigade. In an hour-long fight, the three ships sustained significant damages but broke through and were able to reach Grand Ecore.

Finally, on April 15th, after running battles with the Rebels and the river, all of the Squadron arrived at Grand Ecore. With river conditions deteriorating rapidly, Porter elected to depart the following day. Unfortunately, three miles downriver, the lead ship, the Eastport, struck a torpedo and settled into the muddy river bottom. The Eastport's crew managed to get her refloated by April 21st, but forty miles further downriver she became hopelessly grounded in the shallow water. After several days of trying to move the ship and the river conditions getting worse, Admiral Porter ordered the Eastport destroyed.

The support ships at Alexandria noted the lowering water levels and, in late April, returned downriver to the safety of Mississippi River. Finally on May 1st, the Squadron arrived in Alexandria but the price of the downriver trip was costly: the Eastport destroyed, two river tugs sunk, and several of the tinclads critically damaged.

The final leg of the voyage proved to be even more costly. Confederate forces in the region began closing in on the river and in heavy fighting south of Alexandria, the Squadron lost more ships and men. To make matters worse, water levels were so low that the larger gunboats became trapped in the muck of the receding river. Only the actions of an engineer Lieutenant Colonel Joseph Bailey of Banks' staff saved the gunboats and enabled them to reach safety downriver. Bailey's background in moving logs downriver enabled him to erect an innovative log dam that allowed the stripped down ironclads to be refloated and steam to deeper waters. By May 15th, the last of the Squadron ships managed to depart the Red River for the safety of the Mississippi.

As the Squadron fought the Rebels and the river, I was called to the ship's office. A message was received directing me to return to Cairo for further transportation back to Maine. Upon my arrival in Augusta, I was to be discharged from the Army as my enlistment was up.

As the gunboats clawed their way out of the Red River, I traveled upriver to Cairo. By the time the last ship reached the Mississippi, I had arrived at the Squadron Headquarters, received my orders, and left for the train station. I was going home.

As I awaited the train, a flood of emotions washed over me. I was certainly overjoyed my enlistment was up and I had survived but, in a way, I was sad to see this chapter of my life end. I reflected on my time in the Western Theater. I recalled those early days aboard the Lexington, the battles at Fort Henry, Fort Donelson, and Pittsburg Landing. I thought of my time on the Great Western, those scores of skirmishes on the Mississippi, the long days at Vicksburg, and my most recent adventures on the Red River.

But those times, like my time in the Third Maine Regiment were behind me. I was going home. As the train pulled into the station and I started to board, an old familiar feeling reappeared. My time in the Army was up but that old seduction bug demanded more.

Once More unto the Breach

"It is not enough that we do our best;
sometimes we must do what is required."

Winston S. Churchill

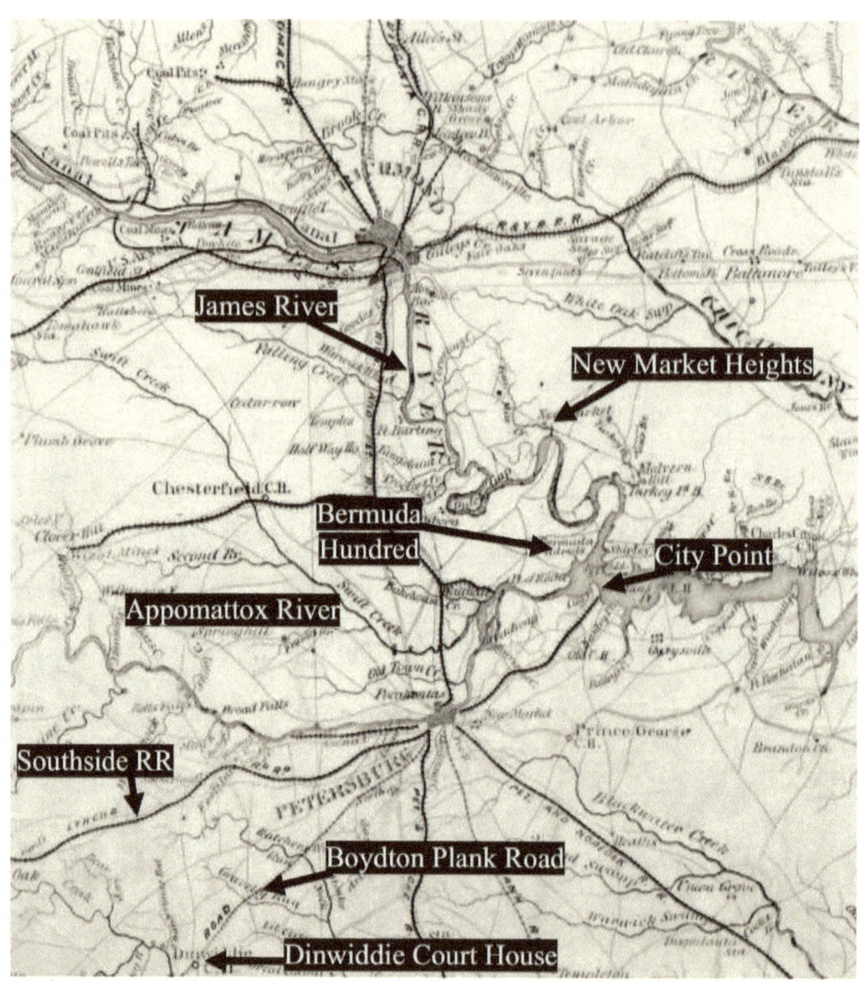

Richmond/Petersburg Area 1864-65

Chapter Thirty-Four

Summer 1864 – Augusta, Maine

I t was a typical Army train ride; overcrowded cars, little room, bad food, and long periods of nothing but time. The heat of the day did nothing except elevate the temperature inside the cars and add the smell of sweat to the noxious atmosphere of engine smoke, tobacco, and coal oil. As we rumbled out of Illinois, through Indiana and Ohio, and into Pennsylvania there was constant movement of people on and off the train.

There were old soldiers like me heading home for discharge at the end of their enlistments. There were new soldiers, in uniform for the first time and wearing the facial expressions so very common to new soldiers and one that I've seen so many times before.

Home: it was difficult to imagine I was actually heading home. After the train chugged out of Pittsburgh, there was a long stretch of time to New York City when memories of the past three years came flooding back. It was hard to remember home and the simpler life I once knew and the place where I was now returning. How much had I changed? What would I do now that my time in the Army was over? It was the seduction bug that brought me to where I was that day and, even after a long reflective time on the train ride home, nagged at me still.

I managed to set aside a bit of money over the past three years. In addition to my one hundred dollar enlistment bonus, I saved some eighty more dollars from my pay. The State of Maine also promised me a piece of land that I might be able to sell and add to this total. I certainly harbored no deep-seated ambitions to return to a life of farming. Before the Army, I envisioned opening my own apothecary shop somewhere but even after three years, my current financial state did support such an effort. In that regard, I felt confident that Mr. Hartwell would take me back to finish my apprenticeship. The few letters we exchanged indicated he was doing well and prospering.

As the train finally rumbled into the Augusta station, I stepped back into the world I left behind what seems like an eternity ago. On the platform were a large number of new soldiers boarding a second train heading south and bound for war. After collecting my things, I joined about fifty other soldiers from various regiments whose enlistments were also expiring. We were transported to a familiar patch of ground on the Capitol lawn and provided a billet.

The next morning, we began the process of turning in our military equipment and weapons, taking another cursory physical examination, and completing a mound of paperwork. Two days later, I saluted the Army captain who handed me my Certificate of Discharge, and still clad in the blue suit I was issued, walked out onto the streets of Augusta to resume civilian life.

After leaving the Capitol area, I boarded the stage for the fifteen-mile ride home. While I was gone, I did exchange letters with the family and tried to keep up with all of the details of life in rural Maine. My homecoming was a joyous event with all of the newest family members present. Planting season was over so I got to spend a good deal of time with my brothers and sisters. We hunted, fished, and worked together fixing up the farm. My father relegated most of the hard work of running the farm to his other sons. In his late fifties, he seemed to have lost a few steps except in his ability to sire offspring. When I arrived home my stepmother was once again in the family way.

As June gave way to July, I prepared to move back to Augusta and resume my apprenticeship with Mr. Hartwell. The Hartwells were more than happy to have me resume my studies but given my three years away, Mr. Hartwell figured it would take another eighteen months to two years to develop the necessary skills to go off on my own. There would be six months to get me up to the level where I was when I enlisted, another nine months to a year to study the advanced skills necessary for a druggist, and three to six more months to learn the business aspects of running an apothecary.

The Hartwells were very excited to see me after all this time. The children had grown so. William was a strapping lad of sixteen who recently completed his studies here in Augusta. Come fall he would move to Brunswick and begin college life at Bowdoin College. Elizabeth was a beautiful fourteen year old who, like her brother, excelled at her studies. There was talk of an academy for young women in Portland once she was of age.

Both children bombarded me with a thousand questions about my time in the Army. Sensing a bit of the seduction bug in William, I avoided many of the details of my great adventure and chose to divert his questions back to discussing his future at Bowdoin College.

Most nights after dinner with the Hartwells, I traveled to the local tavern where I met up with my friends before the Army. I hoped to see one of them or some of the others from Third Maine and catch up. Usually, I spent those evenings pouring through the Kennebec Journal searching for news about the war.

One evening in early August I chanced to meet an old Third Maine man from Somerville, George McDaniel. We were both members of Company I but in different squads. Being from Somerville, I knew him well enough to say hello and talk of home. Over the course of a couple of evenings George brought me up to date on the Regiment and their adventures on the Peninsula, at Second Manassas, Fredericksburg, Chancellorsville, and Gettysburg. I told him about the Western Gunboat Flotilla and what I was doing since my discharge. Like me, before joining the Army, George had no ambitions to farm. His enlistment now up, he was back in Augusta in search of work.

"How much longer are you going to be working at the apothecary?" George asked.

"I got about eighteen months or so of my apprenticeship left but I am in no way set up financially to move out and start my own business," I replied. "I'm actually thinking about reenlisting for the three hundred dollar bonus they're offering."

"Would the bonus cover what you need?"

"Not really. I need a bit more than that. With the bonus and saving a bit from my pay I will still be short."

"You know, the easiest way to get the money you need would be to become a substitute," George said. "A couple of guys from Third Maine got paid a lot more than three hundred dollars for agreeing to enlist instead of some other guy."

"And that is legal?" I asked.

"Sure is. As part of that Enrollment Act, draftees can hire a substitute to enlist for them. It's all perfectly legal. They even give you a form to say you are a substitute."

"What do these people pay for a substitute?" I asked.

"Depends on how bad they want to avoid the draft. Some of those rich fellows are more than willing to pay a lot of money to avoid getting shot at," George chuckled. "And to think we agreed to enlist for a measly one hundred dollars and fifty acres of land."

George's comments that evening got me to thinking. I wasn't in any position financially to purchase a business but with the extra money becoming a substitute would bring and what I could save, opening a business outside of the Augusta area might be in the realm of possibility at some point in the future.

With the ratification of the Enrollment Act of 1863, Congress provided the first real legislation to supply conscripts for the Union Army. States were now assigned enlistment quotas and any state not meeting those quotas with volunteers were required to supplement its numbers with conscripted soldiers. By 1864, most states were not raising new regiments. Rather, volunteers and conscripts were assigned to existing regiments, many of which had been decimated by three years of fighting.

The Enrollment Act also stated that anyone eligible for military service could opt out by paying a qualified substitute a bounty of three hundred dollars. By 1864, the substitute bounty rose dramatically as many sought ways of avoiding the Army. In other terms, the substitute system became a free market business. The current price of a substitute was based on several factors. The first factor was the supply of qualified substitutes and the demand for potential draftees. If the number of volunteers was down, there was a greater demand for conscripts and the price went up.

Also, if there were fewer eligible substitutes, the price went up. It was pure supply and demand. The second factor was the proximity of the potential draftee to his actual reporting date. The closer their actual enlistment date, the higher the price. After checking out some of George's facts I discovered that the process of finding someone who wanted to purchase a substitute was not all that difficult. There were even ads in the newspaper about it.

After discussing the situation with Mr. Hartwell, we both agreed I did not have sufficient capital to buy or start a business. The best I could hope for was to buy into an existing business and look to takeover when the owner retired or died. While Mr. Hartwell was not overly excited about my returning to the war, he did feel the substitute route was best for my financial situation.

Also, his relationship to many of the Maine politicians gave him a unique insight into state and national politics. He felt, based on the war news, discussions with his political friends, and observations about the national political landscape, the war might be just about over. This made the option of my being a substitute much more appealing.

Chapter Thirty-Five

September 1864 – Augusta, Maine

The two major issues facing the nation in 1864 were the war and the presidential election. It looked like the war might be decided militarily in fairly short order or, depending on who was elected, a negotiated peace with the Confederacy might be an option for a new President and the nation.

From the Union perspective, the war news was generally favorable during 1863 and early 1864. Victories at Gettysburg and Vicksburg took a tremendous toll on the South and the Southern armies. In the Western Theater, Grant and Sherman continued to bring the fight to the Confederates and in November of 1863, after bitter fighting, they secured Chattanooga. In March of 1864, General Sherman replaced Grant as the Commander of the Military Division of the Mississippi when Lincoln called Grant to Washington and named him General in Chief of the Union Army. The Mississippi River was now pretty much open to the Gulf of Mexico and with Kentucky and Tennessee secured, Major General Sherman set his sights on the heartland of the South and the railroad hub at Atlanta.

In early May of 1864, Sherman launched his offensive, fighting a series of battles along the rail lines between Chattanooga and Atlanta. By mid-summer, Sherman's Army defeated Confederate forces under Joseph Johnston and John Bell Hood at Kennesaw Mountain, along the Peachtree Creek, and at Ezra Church. In spite of stiffening Confederate resistance, it appeared to be only a matter of time before Sherman's forces captured Atlanta.

As Sherman was cutting across the South, General Grant, traveling with the Army of the Potomac, was actively engaged with the Confederate Army of Northern Virginia around Fredericksburg. In a series of battles in late spring, General Grant took the war to the Confederates at the Wilderness, Spotsylvania Courthouse, and Cold Harbor. By early June, the Union Army drove General Robert E. Lee and his Army toward their Richmond defenses and began a siege of the railroad hub of Petersburg. Over the summer, Grant extended his lines, capturing many of the strategic rail lines into Petersburg and depriving the Confederate government and people of much needed supplies and reinforcements.

By the first of August, the Union Army achieved two of President Lincoln's three stated wartime objectives. They opened the Mississippi River and defeated the Confederate armies in Kentucky and Tennessee. Now, in August of 1864, the Union Army was applying pressure on the economic center of Atlanta and besieging a second economic area south and east of the Confederate capitol.

The war news took center stage in people's minds as the various political parties competed to control the November elections. At the end of May 1864, a group of disenchanted Radical Republicans and War Democrats met in Cleveland and formed the Radical Democracy Party. The Radical Democracy agenda severely criticized the President for being too moderate on the issue of slavery and race relations. At their convention, the Radical Democracy chose John C. Fremont as their presidential candidate and former New York Congressman and New York State Attorney General John Cochrane as vice president.

The Republican Party, in an effort to entice war-oriented Democrats to their ranks, went so far as to rename their national convention, the National Union Convention. Initially, during the early phases of the campaign, the only real threat to Lincoln's reelection came from former Secretary of the Treasury Salmon Chase. Chase and several other political leaders including Radical Republican Senator Benjamin Wade of Ohio and former Congressman and newspaper editor Horace Greeley, opposed Lincoln and the President's ability to bring the war to a swift and successful conclusion.

In March of 1864, Chase withdrew from the election when a large number of Republican politicians, including many from his home state of Ohio, openly supported Lincoln. As a result, when the National Union Convention opened in Baltimore on June 7th, 1864, the delegates quickly nominated the President for a second term.

Throughout the pre-convention period, Maine's own Vice President Hannibal Hamlin displayed a level of ambivalence about remaining on the Republican ticket. Although Hamlin and the President were not close personally, they had a good working relationship. Before the convention, Lincoln announced his desire for a running mate who could assist the nation in healing after the war and aid in the reconstructive effort yet to come. Unfortunately for Maine voters, Hamlin's alliance with Radical Republicans and his indifference toward reelection were strong catalysts for the nomination of Andrew Johnson of Tennessee as vice president. Johnson, a War Democrat, showed his abilities as military governor of Tennessee. Additionally, the Republican Party was very aware of the fact he alone did not resign from the Senate when the rest of the southern states, including Tennessee, seceded. This added strength to future reconstructive efforts and sent a strong message of the administration's desire for national unity.

With the Republican and Radical Democracy conventions concluded, the country waited for the Democratic Party to identify their slate of candidates. Over the summer the war news was not particularly favorable to the Republicans. This was a fact the Democrats hoped to use to sway voters. Sherman was stalled in front of Atlanta and Grant outside of Petersburg. In spite of Grant's aggressive conduct of the war in the East, critics were quick to note the high casualty rates in the Army of the Potomac since he assumed command of the Union Army in March. At the time of the Democratic convention, Lee's Army was heavily entrenched outside of Petersburg, Richmond was still the viable capitol of the Confederacy, and from all appearances Grant was in for a long siege.

Unfortunately, the Democratic Party was divided into two major factions when their convention met in Chicago in late August. On one side were the Peace Democrats who favored a negotiated peace with the Confederacy. This was not a new theme. Moderate Peace Democrats pressed for a negotiated peace after the Union victory at Gettysburg. Their arguments centered on ending the war without the total destruction of the South. The more radical of the Peace Democrats, or "Copperheads", felt the conduct of the war to be a total failure and demanded an immediate end to all hostilities and a return to the prewar status quo in America.

The other major faction of the Democratic Party was the War Democrats. While some switched allegiances to the Republican Party, these were the members who remained loyal to the Democratic Party but still supported the overall war effort. In the end, the compromise position for the Democrats saw the nomination of pro-war Major General George McClellan for president and Peace

Democrat Congressman George Pendleton of Ohio for vice president.

After several discussions with Mr. Hartwell about the national political scene, I realized my window of opportunity as a potential substitute was closing fast. If the military stalemates around Atlanta and Petersburg were resolved quickly, the Confederacy might be favorable to opening discussions for peace. On the other hand, if the Democrats were successful in the November elections, the reverse could be true. It might be the Union who opened the peace negotiations.

I paid a call on the local Provost Marshal's office to become more familiar with the substitute process and confirm what I learned from George McDaniel. The Sergeant I spoke with actually provided me some sound advice about selecting a draftee and what the financial aspects of the arrangement might be. After this discussion, I began the process by contacting three potential candidates.

The first two I spoke with were very adamant they were not going to fight in Mr. Lincoln's immoral war. Both had a tendency to look down at me as some sort of degenerate trying to make a few extra dollars at their expense. Each announced they would not pay any more than the three hundred dollars stipulated in the Enrollment Act. When I bade them each goodbye, both assured me I would be back to take their deals.

The third man I met was William Abbott from Albion in Kennebec County. Abbott was older than most of the draftees but still caught up in the conscript net. He and his aging father operated a family business that hauled freight from Augusta to the outlying communities of Kennebec County. He was also married with three small children. Abbott stated he was a firm supporter of the war effort and the idea of preserving the Union. While not afraid to become a soldier, he felt his freight service to be critical to the well-being of many citizens of Kennebec County and to his family. After weighing these facts against conscription, he believed it to be his Christian duty to serve the citizens of Kennebec County by remaining at home.

I found William Abbott a genuinely sincere individual and, after listening to his financial offer, I agreed to become his substitute. As the Democratic convention began, I stood before the Provost Marshal and the Commissioner of the Board of Enrollment, signed my name, and swore to defend my country for another three years unless sooner discharged by proper authority.

When I talked with George McDaniel, he indicated some of the members of Third Maine who reenlisted were sent to the Seventeenth Maine Regiment. I asked the Provost Marshal about a possible assignment to that regiment but he indicated the Eleventh Maine Regiment was due for end of enlistment discharges in early November and they were the current priority for staffing.

After signing the papers and returning to the Army, I began to realize my reenlistment was not about the substitute money or any reenlistment bonus I would receive. While that money, plus what I already had, would set me up in business if I survived the war, there was more to my decision to reenlist than monetary gain. As a youngster, I had a very strong connection to many of my relatives who proudly served in the military both here in America and in Scotland. How I remembered those great stories I heard about around the family dinner table as a child. In spite of the long odds, they stood tall, determined to finish what they started.

I was there at the beginning of this war. I experienced depression and despair after the loss at Manassas. I experienced an elation moderated by horror after the victories at Pittsburg Landing, Vicksburg, and other points on the river. Now I felt a strong need to be there at the end, to see the final outcome regardless of my chances of survival, and with no remorse. The seduction bug was gone. I was walking into the breach of my own free will for it was the right thing to do.

Chapter Thirty-Six

Five short days after my reenlistment I found myself in coastal Virginia on a ship moving up the James River toward the Union port of City Point. Before leaving Augusta, I received another cursory physical examination on the Capitol lawn. Pronounced fit to serve, I was given a new set of uniforms, some well-worn equipment, and a heavily greased Springfield Model 1861 .58 caliber rifled musket.

In my opinion, the Springfield was a good rifle. At nine pounds in weight, fifty-six inches long, a barrel length of forty inches, and an effective range of two to four hundred yards, the Springfield was, at the time, the most widely used rifle in the Union inventory. After discussing my previous experiences, the armory sergeant told me that if I were selected as a sharpshooter in my new regiment, they would issue me a more suitable weapon. I did miss my old Lorenz rifle. The flip up sights of the Lorenz seemed to be more reliable and more accurate than the fixed iron sights of the Springfield.

Loaded down with new equipment, the next phase of this great adventure was another troop train ride from Augusta to Boston. This was followed by a sea voyage on a contract ship from Boston to Fortress Monroe at the mouth of the James River in Virginia. The weather for the voyage was good and the seas calm so it was possible to spend a good deal of the time above decks. I only went below to sleep and eat. Like all wartime transportation, the accommodations were overcrowded and smelled of rancid air, bilge water, tobacco, and vomit. The food was absolutely inedible and those who did manage to choke some of it down generally found it returning, one way or the other, in fairly short order.

After we arrived at Fortress Monroe there was a short turnaround to the next ship for the sixty some mile trip to City Point. While the accommodations were still crowded, the food was Army issue so at least I could feast on some hardtack. The ship's Captain made it clear that, so long as no one interfered with his sailors' handling of the ship, we could remain above decks in the weather. In the pleasant September weather of Virginia, this was a welcome relief to any time I spent below decks.

As the ship made its way upriver, I took the opportunity to talk to some of the crew about the lay of the land. The north side of the river was referred to as the Peninsula and it was in this area that the Army of the Potomac conducted its major offensive in the spring of 1862. The sailors who were there pointed out various locations where they dropped off this unit or delivered supplies to that unit. One sailor pointed out the mouth of the Chickahominy River and described the various battles that had been fought along its banks.

The James snaked around before the final run into City Point. Along the north bank were several magnificent plantation homes. The first we passed, Sherwood Forest Plantation, belonged to former President John Tyler. Nearby Shirley Plantation was the ancestral home of Anne Hill Carter. Miss Carter and Henry "Light Horse Harry" Lee, a Revolutionary War hero and father of Confederate General Robert E. Lee, were married in the parlor at Shirley Plantation. The last and most magnificent of these homes was Berkeley Plantation, the birthplace of another American President, William Henry Harrison and the site where Brigadier General Daniel Butterfield penned the bugle call "Taps" now used by both sides, Union and Confederate, to mark the end of a burial detail.

After Berkeley Plantation, the river opened up to reveal the roadstead at City Point. While not as large as Boston harbor or New York, City Point was far larger and more active than the Water Street quay in Augusta. As part of the siege of Petersburg, General Grant established his headquarters and logistics hub at City Point.

Sir Thomas Dale established the area known as City Point in 1613. Originally named Bermuda City, the name was later changed to Charles City Point and finally to City Point when the Virginia House of Burgesses annexed the area to Prince George County in 1703. City Point remained relatively unaffected by the Revolutionary War until the spring of 1781 when a British force commanded by Benedict Arnold landed and attempted to capture the Governor of Virginia, Thomas Jefferson. After Arnold departed the area, another British force under Lord Cornwallis returned and attempted to capture French General Lafayette. The General escaped and Lord Cornwallis moved his forces further downriver to the area of Yorktown.

The watch was changing as the ship made its way into the roadstead. One of the old salts I spoke to in the past came on deck and we talked some more about the local geography.

"That's City Point over there," the old salt explained. "Just beyond the point you can make out the mouth of the Appomattox River. Ten or twelve miles upriver is the city of Petersburg."

"Over there," he said, pointing to the right. "The James takes a turn to the north before she starts to snake around the countryside for about eight to ten miles."

"How far upriver is Richmond?" I asked.

"Probably twenty miles or so. The river is tidal all the way to the rapids in downtown Richmond. You can take a small vessel through a series of locks and come out above the rapids. From there it's a pretty smooth sail all the way into central Virginia."

"I imagine the Rebs have the river pretty well defended," I said.

The old man got a faraway look in his eyes before he answered. "Worse now than when we first tried to get upriver during the Peninsula Campaign of 1862. I was aboard the Galena then. We went up river as the lead ship. Made it about ten miles, under fire most of the way. The Galena got to a straight section of the river below Drewry's Bluff before the Rebels opened up with their artillery and naval guns from the heights. It was a pretty brutal time before we turned tail. They've had two years to fortify their river defenses. I know they have another key position at Chaffin's Bluff on the other side of the river and several forts and batteries covering key points where the river makes some wild turns. If those defenses aren't enough, the Rebs have their river fleet above Drewry's Bluff waiting for some action."

The old man turned from his discussion of the rivers to the landmass directly in front of us.

"You might find yourself very familiar with that area there," he said pointing at the area between the two rivers. "That's the area known as the Bermuda Hundred. At the neck of the Hundred, the Rebs constructed some serious defensive works stretching from the James in the north across the peninsula to the Appomattox in the south. The Yankees are in control of the Hundred but there's been some heavy fighting along what is called the Howlett Line. This past summer, the fighting was around the Deep Bottom area at the far north end of the Hundred. The Union Army finally managed to force a crossing of the James at Deep Bottom and establish a pontoon bridge."

As the ship arrived at the mooring and dropped anchor, I said goodbye to the old salt and readied myself to climb into the small boats for the final part of the voyage. Once ashore, all of the incoming soldiers were directed to an administrative area for further processing and transportation to our regiments.

When our transportation arrived, four of us scrambled upon the supply wagon for the trip to Fort Sedgwick and the Eleventh Maine Regiment. I learned that Fort Sedgwick was, in fact, named for Major General John Sedgwick, our former Brigade Commander when I was with Third Maine. Sadly, General Sedgwick was killed in the battle of Spotsylvania Court House.

My three travelling companions were all conscripts, caught up in the draft net in Bangor. As the wagon rumbled into Fort Sedgwick, I caught a glimpse of a sign over the gate that read "Welcome to Fort Hell". Suddenly, people began to crawl out of the ground to gaze in amazement at the resupply wagon. While I recognized them as soldiers, they were covered from head to toe in a thin film of red clay: uniforms, equipment, and exposed skin.

The ground around the Fort was scarred with craters from a variety of weaponry. There were no trees to the front of the Fort, only charred stumps. There was no grass anywhere to be seen. Behind the Fort, some distance to the rear was some woodlands that echoed with the sound of felling trees, no doubt to repair the damages to the Fort inflicted by Rebel projectiles. Nothing in all my experiences in this war to date prepared me for the apocalyptic nightmare that I now beheld. The sign was right. This was truly hell on earth.

After collecting our equipment, we were taken to the Eleventh Maine Regimental Adjutant, First Lieutenant Fox. While my companions were assigned to their companies, I was asked by the Lieutenant to remain. A pleasant sort, Lieutenant Fox asked me some questions about my initial enlistment, my time with the Third Maine, and my time with the Western Gunboat Flotilla. After answering his questions, he afforded me the opportunity to ask any of my own. As he passed a note to a runner, I asked about the past exploits of the Regiment.

The Eleventh Maine Volunteer Regiment was called to service late in October 1861 and mustered into the Army on November 12th. Most of the original members of the Regiment were from the Bangor area but disease and the Rebels whittled that number down considerably. Over the past three years, I learned the replacements the Regiment received hailed from all over Maine.

After their initial training and wintering at Meridian Hill, the Regiment saw service in Virginia with the Army of the Potomac during the Peninsula Campaign. In December 1862, they sailed for the Carolinas and spent all of 1863 fighting around Charleston, South Carolina and in Florida. In early 1864, the Regiment returned to Yorktown, Virginia as part of the Army of the James and in May, landed at the Bermuda Hundred. Over the summer of 1864, Eleventh Maine participated in operations on the Hundred as well as in the First and Second Battles of Deep Bottom as part of Major General Winfield Scott Hancock's Second Corps. At the end of August, the Regiment returned from across the James and took up positions at Fort Sedgwick.

When Lieutenant Fox finished his historical sketch of the Regiment, another officer joined us. He was introduced as Second Lieutenant George Payne of Company G. Lieutenant Payne was a tall, lanky officer much older than the second lieutenants I knew. His mannerisms were purely military and his face bore the expression of one who was not to be trifled with.

Lieutenant Payne questioned me about some of the same things Lieutenant Fox did but focused more on my abilities with a rifle. After a while, he indicated he was the head of the Regimental sharpshooters and asked if I would be willing to shoot a little so he could evaluate my skills.

We went out the rear side of the Fort, through a trench line, and into a sheltered area away from the front lines to a makeshift rifle range. As I fired my first round, I was pleasantly surprised to find the sights on the Springfield rifle to be fairly accurate. After firing two marking rounds to evaluate the sights and clear the bore of any residue and grease, I fired three more rounds in a very tight group. The two marking rounds were close enough together to allow me to apply some "Kentucky windage" before firing the final three. "Kentucky windage" involved observing the marking rounds and adjusting the aiming point to move the bullet strike on the target. While not necessarily the best method for serious sharpshooting, this method of shooting was acceptable in the absence of any tools to adjust the sights between shots. The Lieutenant seemed to be satisfied with my shooting abilities.

"Have you ever shot this Springfield before today?" He asked.

"No sir," I replied. "In the Third Maine I had a Lorenz with flip sights. I used it a lot for longer distances as part of the ship's defense force on the river."

The Lieutenant nodded. "The Lorenz was a good choice given the situation you were in at the beginning of the war. Now that they are mass producing Springfields I think you would be better served with that rifle and adjustable sights. Did you ever fire a Sharps?"

"Yes sir. The Navy used both the Sharps rifle and carbine on one of the ships I was on to arm their defense force. I fired them a few times. I thought the rifle to be an exceptional weapon but I didn't like the accuracy of the carbine at longer distances. One of the ships I was on used Spencer rifles and carbines. The Spencer rifle was a good weapon but I found the Sharps more accurate at longer distances."

"Did you ever fire a Whitworth rifle?" The British made Whitworth rifle was a single shot, muzzle loaded, sharpshooting rifle that fired a .45 caliber round. In the hands of a skilled marksman, the Whitworth was extremely accurate at distances of over a half mile. The Whitworth was one of the weapons employed by Southern sharpshooters.

"Never fired one, sir. We had a few fired at us. The Whitworth was easy to recognize. It made a very distinctive sound when it was fired at you."

The Lieutenant smiled. "It sure does. What did you do when it was fired at you?"

"We generally hunkered down behind something and prayed the ship could get out of range before the son of a bitch could reload. We really sweated those Reb sharpshooters. There weren't many places to hide in the middle of the river."

Still smiling, the Lieutenant said, "It was a Reb with a Whitworth that killed General Sedgwick at a range of about a thousand yards. One hell of a shot." I couldn't disagree.

He continued, "I think your marksmanship abilities make you a prime candidate to be one of the Regimental sharpshooters. All of the sharpshooters are veterans, like you, who have proven they can shoot and have done so under fire. I give the boys the option of weapons. You can use either a Springfield with adjustable sights or one of the Sharps rifles. Once you are settled, I will arrange for you to fire both weapons and decide for yourself. Here at Fort Sedgwick, our boys take turns out on the picket lines.

It's not glamorous shooting but having skilled marksmen around keeps the Rebels from looking around at our defenses or planning any surprises. When the Regiment is on the move we also serve as skirmishers. We can engage the Rebs at a greater distance and give the Regiment more time to react. If you are in agreement, I will speak to Lieutenant Fox and have you assigned to Company G as a sharpshooter."

Chapter Thirty-Seven

September 1864 – Petersburg, Virginia

y introduction to Company G of the Eleventh Maine was much different from my introduction to the Army. The difference between the soldiers of Third Maine in 1861 and the soldiers of Eleventh Maine in 1864 was like day and night. These men were real soldiers, many hardened by three years of fighting. They were not the puppets that played at being soldiers on the Capitol lawn at Augusta. There were no shirkers here, no malcontents, dandies, or Sunday soldiers. They were gone; dead or released from active service. Those who remained were battle-hardened veterans well versed in the art of war and I was accepted as an equal.

I was welcomed to the company by Captain Lewis Holt and First Sergeant Thomas Tabor. The First Sergeant was from the Augusta area and knew many of the haunts I frequented before the war. I was assigned to a Squad and settled in for my first night in the field.

The next morning, I went back to the makeshift rifle range with my new Squad Leader, Sergeant Luther Robbins of Augusta, and Lieutenant Payne. Sergeant Robbins seemed to be a likable enough fellow who worked the Augusta docks as a longshoreman before enlisting.

The Lieutenant carried two weapons, a Sharps rifle and a Springfield Model 1861 with adjustable sights. The Sharps was about the same weight as the Springfield but some nine inches shorter overall with a barrel length of thirty inches, ten inches shorter than the Springfield. Unlike traditional muzzleloading rifles like the Springfield, the Sharps rifle employed a falling block design. A solid metal breechblock slid along grooves manufactured into the breech and is activated by a lever below the trigger housing. When the breech was closed, the chamber was sealed so the cartridge could be fired. Pulling down on the lever lowered the breechblock and allowed the spent cartridge to be extracted and ejected.

A new cartridge was then positioned in the chamber, the lever was returned to the closed position, and the breechblock closed and sealed the chamber. This enabled the shooter to fire the next round. This system permitted a soldier armed with a Sharps rifle or carbine to fire eight to ten rounds per minute. In addition to the increased rate of fire, the Sharps rifle was easier to reload. The reloading process could also be accomplished quicker and easier than a muzzleloader from either the prone or kneeling positions. After firing both weapons, I decided I preferred the Sharps to the Springfield. I spent the rest of the day familiarizing myself with my new weapon, cleaning it and the Springfield, and getting acquainted with my new comrades and Fort Hell.

When Lieutenant General Grant took command of the Union Army in March, his battle plan was to apply continuous pressure on the Army of Northern Virginia, forcing General Lee to withdraw closer to his defenses around Richmond. By June, in spite of few significant victories and a high casualty count, Grant and two Union Armies, the Army of the James and the Army of the Potomac, sat poised on the doorstop of the Confederate Capitol and threatened one of the South's major railroad and logistics hubs at Petersburg. Realizing the extent of the Confederate defenses, Grant began a siege campaign directed against Petersburg in an effort to capture this key Confederate city.

Confederate defenses around Petersburg were formidable. Beginning in 1862, their engineers constructed a series of fifty-five forts and artillery positions that stretched some ten miles from the Appomattox River on the east side of the city to the Appomattox River on the City's west side. These defenses were named the Dimmock Line after Captain Charles Dimmock, the chief architect of the Richmond defenses.

As part of the siege campaign, Grant conducted a series of offensive operations to break the Confederate defenses. In their first attempt in mid-June, Union forces failed to concentrate enough units to affect a complete breakthrough of the Confederate defenses. However, as a result of this offensive, the eastern side of the Dimmock Line was broached by elements of the Union Seventeenth Corps on June 15th forcing the Rebels to retreat to an inner line of defensive positions closer to the city.

A second Union Offensive began on June 21st when Grant sent Major General Hancock's Second Corps and Major General Horatio

Wright's Sixth Corps to the south and west of Petersburg in an attempt to capture the Weldon and Southside railroads. While this second venture proved to be unsuccessful, the incursion forced General Lee to stretch his lines further to the west to avoid being flanked.

In July, a third Union offensive sent Hancock's Second Corps and Major General Phillip Sheridan's cavalry across the James to threaten the forces guarding one of the avenues of approach into Richmond. This undertaking forced Lee to shift forces from the defense of Petersburg to protect the Capitol. As part of the attack, Union forces exploded a large mine under Confederate positions in what was called the Battle of the Crater. While the mine exploded as planned, poor exploitation of the ensuing chaos allowed the Confederates to counter the attack and maintain their lines.

"I remember that attack quite well," one of my new comrades recalled. "Even though we were across the James, we felt the blast from that mine. I'd bet the folks back in Bangor probably felt it too. Dirt and smoke filled the sky. When all was said and done, a lot of casualties and no real change in the lines."

The Union's fourth and final offensive of the summer began on August 14th and stretched the Confederate line to the north and southwest. By the 25th of August, Union forces gained a foothold across the James as a result of the Second Battle of Deep Bottom. They also pushed further to the south and west capturing the Weldon railroad. Union engineers promptly fortified the area around the rail line and the Globe Tavern and connected these new fortifications to existing ones along the Jerusalem Plank Road. By capturing new ground and fortifying it, Grant forced Lee to extend his lines even further than they already were and forego sending reinforcements north to support Confederate operations in the Shenandoah Valley.

At the onset of siege operations, Union engineers began construction on two lines of fortifications that would eventually ring the City of Petersburg. Fort Sedgwick was one of those fortifications built astride the Jerusalem Plank Road and adjacent to the rail line from Petersburg to Norfolk.

Fort Sedgwick was unlike any I ever experienced. Certainly, the Fort was not built to the specifications of any of the forts Third Maine worked on as part of the Washington defenses. The overall shape was almost rectangular with the exception of a bastion-like protrusion that housed the main artillery battery. The Fort was about four hundred and fifty feet long, about one hundred feet wide at its widest point, and generally oriented to the northwest. The Jerusalem Plank Road ran through the left side of the Fort about seventy-five feet in from the outside wall. The Fort consisted of a front line of works that ran perpendicular to the road down to the artillery bastion. On the right side of the front line were two batteries of mortars. A second line or rear line of works ran somewhat parallel to the front line and was designed to repel any force that attempts to attack the Fort from the rear.

The part of the Fort split by the Jerusalem Plank Road housed the parapets and fighting positions for three infantry companies. The other seven companies of the Regiment were across the road along the rear line of works. Another trench line started at the center of the rear line of works and extended to a wooded area where the administrative and logistics support services were located. On the left side of this trench, close to the Jerusalem Plank Road, was where the sutler's store was located. The area to the right of the trench was a landing area for overshot artillery and mortar rounds that was dubbed Hell's Half Acre.

As I looked across the engineered obstacles and the desolation of the forward area I could see the Confederate positions at Fort Mahone and the Rivas' Salient less than a half mile away. This made Fort Sedgwick the Union position in closest proximity to the Confederate lines. From my vantage point on the parapet, it appeared that our pickets could easily shake hands with the Rebel pickets.

Later I asked some of my comrades about our proximity to the Rebels.

"It's a bit nerve-racking," said Freeman Flint, one of my squad mates. "On occasion, the Rebs actually talk to you. Of course, the officers discourage it, but it does happen more often than not. One night, just after we arrived here, I struck up a conversation with some Rebs from Georgia. They had just arrived as well to the Reb fort over yonder." Flint pointed at Fort Mahone. "Those boys called the place Fort Damnation. Got a big kick out of it when we told them we called this little piece of heaven, Fort Hell."

Another member of the squad, Frank Johnston added, "Just remember, there are a lot of ways to die here. There is the sickness that comes either from the infernal swarms of critters that abound in the trenches or from drinking the foul water we are provided. And, of course, there is always the opportunity to be the next target for some Reb sharpshooter or mortar crew."

"Remember that one old boy from Company C," Freeman stated. "Fell off the dang parapet and broke his fool neck."

"Even if the mortar rounds or the artillery doesn't kill you outright," Frank continued. "Some have been killed by the concussion of the blast when the mortars or artillery hit their bombproof or landed near their trench."

It didn't take me long to adjust to life at Fort Hell. We lived a basic subterranean existence. Our off-duty hours were spent in the bombproofs dug into the ground and covered with earth, railroad iron, gabions, and thick wooden beams. Our living quarters and fighting positions were often linked together by a series of trench lines or covered ditches. It didn't take long for the red clay of the Fort to coat me as it did to those soldiers I spotted from the wagon when I arrived.

The routine for the Regiment called for one twenty-four hour day of duty on the picket lines. Another full day was spent on the parapets and the third day was taken up participating in fatigue duty or working parties. The manpower required for these details generally ranged from one hundred to two hundred fifty men daily. Some days nearly all the able men in the Regiment who were not on picket duty or on watch were involved in some form of labor detail.

A good percentage of fatigue duty was devoted to the task of repairing the Fort's defenses that were damaged by the enemy or by the weather. This proved, on occasion, to be a difficult task if the enemy chose to fire on the repair parties. Therefore, certain components of fort repair were accomplished under cover of darkness so the repair parties could avoid observation or targeting by the enemy.

The best labor details were the ones that required us to go to the rear echelon to gather trees and branches to repair parapet walls. We felled trees, constructed gabions and fascines, and generally spent the day in relative safety before returning to the Fort. Once our day of fatigue duty or labor details was complete, the cycle reset and we were back on the picket line.

For those of us in the infantry this truly was hell on earth. The worst thing about our daily routine was standing picket duty. Time spent on the picket line was, without a doubt, what Dante referred to as the ninth ring of hell itself. Pickets, like the rest of the Fort's inhabitants, lived a very dangerous and subterranean existence. On the picket line, we were literally a stone throw from the enemy pickets. The basic task of the pickets involved observing the Confederate lines and engaging any targets of opportunity on the enemy picket line or in their main defenses.

Picket duty was a twenty-four hour posting. Soldiers assigned to the picket line were posted and relieved only during hours of darkness. A series of trench lines and covered ditches connected the pickets with the front line of works. We moved quickly and quietly through those labyrinths of trenches to reach our assigned posts. During the day many of the open trench lines were under constant observation by the Rebels at Fort Mahone and Rivas' Salient. As a result, any attempt to cross between the Fort and the picket line during daylight often proved to be fatal.

Once in our assigned picket, no one raised a head or other body part to observe the enemy. We used a series of loopholes in the parapets to observe and fire our weapons. Loopholes were small, protected openings in the parapet that enabled a soldier to see and fire his weapon while providing a degree of cover and concealment. In order to fire a weapon, the rifle was held so it was actually fired from inside the trench line and through the loophole. This cut down on the muzzle flash that could be seen by the Rebels, especially at night.

Daily, our pickets and theirs engaged in this dance of death. Often, random shots escalated into an outright skirmish between the pickets. The air was filled with the "chew" sounds as the enemy bullets whizzed past or the occasional "chug" sound when one found a flesh covered target. Most of the wounds and deaths on the picket line involved some form of head, neck, arm or upper torso injuries. Wounded soldiers were not moved to the rear until after dark. This forced many a seriously wounded man to lie in the trench of a picket post and wait to meet his maker.

Another enemy of all soldiers here at Fort Sedgwick was Virginia itself. When not actually on watch, soldiers attempted to sleep, eat, or carry on a second war with Virginia's insect population. While most of us were all too familiar with the problems of lice, what were formerly the woods of Virginia added a few other interesting critters into the mix. Chiggers and ticks routinely attacked resting soldiers and feasted on their flesh. When the rains left ponds of stagnant water on the battlefield, mosquitoes flourished and gorged themselves on the blood of Maine men. The dead and dying provided a habitat for flies, maggots, and other insects with insatiable appetites for the carnage of war.

Virginia's weather also posed its own set of problems. Daytime temperatures were still hot in September and the humidity hung like a wet blanket over the battlefield. These hot, humid days inevitably gave way to an afternoon shower or thunderstorm. If the rain was heavy enough or long enough, it played havoc with the earthen works of the Fort. Trench lines and bombproofs filled with water making living and moving difficult. The rain also washed away sections of the parapet and other earthworks that required repair before the next round of rain.

The standard tour for units assigned to Fort Sedgwick was a month. Shortly before we were due to be relieved, I was standing picket duty with Freeman Flint and Frank Johnston. It was a black and moonless night when, about eleven o'clock we heard voices calling to us from the Rebel picket line.

"Hey Yank! Yank!" the voice called. "Don't shoot. We're coming over. Don't shoot."

The voice continued to beseech us not to shoot until two figures materialized out of the darkness. Their hands were in the air and they carried no weapons that we could see.

"Don't shoot Yank. We're unarmed and coming in."

As the two scrambled over the parapet, the familiar "chew, chew, chew" of Rebel bullets passed overhead. The two Rebs, now in our picket, were deserting. Since I arrived here there were several Confederate soldiers who wanted to desert. They would start running from Fort Mahone or Rivas' Salient and most of the time be killed by their own side. These two were lucky. They were Georgia soldiers who planned their desertion to coincide with a moonless night and their assignment to picket duty.

Shortly after this incident, the Eleventh Maine Regiment was formally relieved of duty at Fort Sedgwick. In the early evening of September 24th, the Regiment turned over responsibility for the Fort to elements of Second Corps and marched off to rejoin the rest of our Brigade in the rear area. The Regiment was posted to Fort Sedgwick for a total of thirty-one days. During that time, Eleventh Maine suffered a total of four soldiers killed and two wounded. Rebel sharpshooters killed two of the soldiers while they were on picket duty. One of the other soldiers was killed in an artillery barrage. Spent bullets struck the fourth dead man and the wounded soldiers while they slept.

Once in the rear area, we realized our time in this portion of a soldier's hell was over. Word was passed we would rejoin our Brigade the next day and into a new hell in some other God forsaken part of this war. At least we were safe and away from the bombs and bullets of Fort Sedgwick. For one night we could sleep the interrupted sleep of the dead.

Chapter Thirty-Eight

September 1864 – Deep Bottom, Virginia

The morning after we marched away from Fort Sedgwick, the Eleventh Maine Regiment established a formal camp in the rear area near a place called Friendly's Farm in close proximity to the other units of our Brigade. The next day, September 26th, word came down that the Brigade would engage in a series of drills and training sessions. After what we just experienced at Fort Sedgwick, a couple of days of rest seemed to be what everyone wanted.

Consequently, the idea of marching around a parade ground was not met favorably, especially by the veterans. Their three-year enlistments almost up, many of these men would be leaving the Regiment in the not too distant future, bound for Maine and discharge. On the other hand, as the officers and noncommissioned officers noted, a large number of replacement soldiers joined, fought, and died in this Regiment without ever having any formalized training about what was expected of them or how to do it.

Regardless of any personal feelings on the subject, the Regiment fell out for company drills that very afternoon. The next day was spent on more company drills in the morning followed by battalion and regimental drills in the afternoon.

During this period, I learned a bit more about the command structure of the Army of the James. Our Regimental Commander, Lieutenant Colonel Jonathan Hill, was wounded in the Second Battle of Deep Bottom and recovering in hospital. In his absence, the Regiment was under the temporary command of Captain Simeon Merrill.

Eleventh Maine was brigaded with the Tenth Connecticut, the Twenty-fourth Massachusetts, and the One Hundredth New York. The Brigade Commander was the former commanding officer of the Eleventh Maine, Colonel Harris Plaisted. Before the war, Colonel Plaisted practiced law in Bangor. He was commissioned as a lieutenant colonel in 1861 and assigned as the second in command of the Eleventh Maine. The Colonel assumed command of the Regiment in 1862 and fought with them in South Carolina and Florida before being named the Brigade Commander when the Regiment returned to Virginia.

Our Brigade was designated the Third Brigade of the First Division of the Tenth Corps. Colonel Francis Pond of Ohio commanded the First Brigade and Colonel Joseph Abbott of New Hampshire commanded the Second Brigade. Our Division Commander was Brigadier General Alfred Terry of Connecticut. Another lawyer by trade, General Terry had been the first commanding officer of the Second Connecticut and fought with that regiment in the First Battle of Manassas. Promoted to division command in April of 1862, General Terry led the Division in operations around Charleston, South Carolina in 1863.

Tenth Corps was under the command of Major General David Birney. General Birney was commissioned a lieutenant colonel and commander of the Twenty-third Pennsylvania in 1861. He commanded a brigade during the Peninsula Campaign of 1862, Second Manassas, Fredericksburg, and a division at Gettysburg. In July of 1864, General Grant appointed him the Corps Commander of Tenth Corps assigned to the Army of the James.

Tenth Corps consisted of two full infantry divisions, an artillery brigade, and a partial division consisting of one infantry brigade. Besides General Terry, Brigadier General Robert Foster of Indiana commanded the Second Division. The Brigade from the partial division was under the command of General Birney's brother, Brigadier General William Birney, and composed of the Twenty-ninth Connecticut Regiment and four regiments of the U.S. Colored Troops.

The Army of the James was established in April 1864 with Major General Benjamin Butler as its Commander. The Army was composed of the Eighteenth Corps, Tenth Corps, and a Cavalry Division. In many people's eyes, General Butler owed his status as commander more to political favor than any degree of military prowess. Before the war he was a lawyer, a member of the Massachusetts legislature, and a member of the Massachusetts militia. Early in the war, Butler was assigned as commander of Fort Monroe and served in North Carolina before being appointed as the military governor of New Orleans.

During Butler's tenure as military governor, there were several controversial issues involving his governing of and interactions with the city's citizens, all of which inflamed the South and earned him the nickname of the Beast. As a result of these and other incidents, General Butler was recalled in December of 1862. In November of 1863, President Lincoln gave him command of the Department of Virginia and North Carolina out of Fort Monroe. In April of 1864, the forces assigned to this command were re-designated as the Army of the James with Butler as its commander.

As the soldiers of Eleventh Maine were busy drilling and taking our rest, General Grant was planning his next offensive against the Army of Northern Virginia and the defenses of Petersburg. Drawing on past successes that entailed stretching General Lee's Army in multiple directions, Grant's plan called for an assault by the Army of the Potomac south and west of Petersburg to capture the Southside Railroad. Simultaneously, the Army of the James would attack Confederate positions north of the James and, if feasible, move against Richmond itself.

The topography east and southeast of Richmond was basically rolling hills peppered with farms, woodlands, and swamps. Seven major road networks branched out from Richmond to points down the Virginia peninsula. To the far north was Nine Mile Road, coming out of the Capitol as far as the Chickahominy River before turning and joining the Williamsburg Road. The Williamsburg Road was the main avenue from Richmond to Virginia's former capitol, Williamsburg. Branching off the Williamsburg Road was the Charles City Road that extended southeast to the Long Bridge Road in Charles City County. Long Bridge Road was one of the main crossing roads that connected these major arteries out of Richmond. Parallel to Charles City Road was the Darbytown Road that also stretched from Williamsburg Road to Long Bridge Road.

The fifth major road network, the Osborne Turnpike, ran from Richmond south along the James about eight miles to a point just below Chaffin's Bluff. There the Turnpike joined the other main crossing route in the region, Kingsland Road. Branching off Osborne Turnpike was New Market Road that ran southeast and intersected Kingsland Road and Long Bridge Road before continuing along the James toward Williamsburg. The final avenue of consequence was Varina Road that split off New Market Road to the south and met the James River at Aiken's Landing. While these seven major arteries and the two crossing roads were critical to the local farmers and planters of the region, Southern military planners recognized, before the Peninsula Campaign, they would be of tremendous value to the Union Army in any future move to capture Richmond.

By September of 1864, three primary lines of defense ringed these major road networks and the Confederate Capitol. The closest to the city proper was the Interior Line. This defensive line consisted of a series of twenty-four forts and artillery positions encircling the city. Outside of the Interior Line was a second series of works called the Intermediate Line. Primarily oriented north and east, the Intermediate Line stretched from the east bank of the James west of Richmond, around the north side of the city, and south to the east bank of the James some seven and a half miles downriver. An offshoot of this line ran from the intersection of New Market Road and the Osborne Turnpike south to the river at Chaffin's Bluff. The Exterior Line was the farthest from the city proper and the one least developed. This line ran from Chaffin's Bluff generally northeast, across the major road networks to the Chickahominy River just north of Nine Mile Road.

These three lines of defense were constructed in response to General McClellan's Peninsula Campaign of 1862. In 1864, the Confederates began construction of two additional defensive lines in the area. The New Market Line was planned to run from the Exterior Line at Chaffin's Bluff, east to New Market Heights, the high ground just north of Deep Bottom, and then northeast to the White Oak Swamp. In early September, in response to Union offensives north of the James over the summer, Confederate engineers began work on the second defensive line stretching from New Market Heights southwest to Signal Hill at Dutch Gap on the James River overlooking the area of Aiken's Landing.

Besides these defensive preparations, the defenses of the James River approach to Richmond were pretty much as the old salt described them on my trip up to City Point. The Howlett Line ran across the Bermuda Hundred from the Appomattox River north to Dutch Gap on the James. In addition to several smaller forts and artillery positions along the James, the two principal river defensive works were Drewry's Bluff on the west side of the river, and Chaffin's Bluff on the east side.

The major problem with the Richmond defenses was the number of people required to adequately man them. Confederate military planners figured it would take Robert E. Lee's entire army and then some to adequately man these defenses. Consequently, this lack of manpower saw many of the outlying defenses falling into disrepair or subject to erosion by the elements. Only the area around Chaffin's Bluff and New Market Heights were considered adequately manned and maintained.

Word came down from the Brigade of our pending movement late in the afternoon of September 27th. The Brigade was directed to move out no later than three o'clock in the afternoon of the 28th. Since our final destination was not mentioned, rumors began to circulate by last call that evening. Some said we were being withdrawn to Fortress Monroe to prepare to discharge our veterans and await replacements. Others suggested we were heading back to North Carolina to reinforce General Sherman's Army and his efforts in the deep South.

As directed, our Brigade stepped off at three o'clock following the other two brigades of the Division. As we marched along, we passed two regiments of the U.S. Colored Troops assigned to the Brigade of the Third Division. These regiments were awaiting our passing before joining the line of march. This was my first real chance to observe colored troops up close and what I saw was certainly positive. They looked and acted like soldiers.

In May of 1863, the War Department established the Bureau of Colored Troops and began actively recruiting and training free men of color for the Army and Navy. By the end of the war, colored troops accounted for nearly ten percent of the total strength of the Union Army. The four regiments assigned to Tenth Corps were all organized in the fall of 1863 and participated in operations in South Carolina and Florida before moving north to Fortress Monroe where they were brigaded with the Twenty-ninth Connecticut as part of the Army of the James.

As the day wore on, our destination became more apparent. We were not heading to City Point and the transportation that was rumored. Instead, when the Regiment took the turn onto the Bermuda Hundred, it became clear our destination was the area around Deep Bottom.

In my experience, night marches were the worst. Compounding the blackness of the evening was the level of inactivity of the Regiment over the past month. In spite of the fact it was a clear and dry evening, when it became apparent where we were actually heading, many began to drop out. It was a bone-tired group that crossed the pontoon bridge at Deep Bottom and moved up to the Kingsland Road. About two o'clock on the morning of September 29th our Division assumed a line of battle in a wood line along the north side of the road, set out skirmishers, and awaited daylight.

The task of the Army of the James was to attack the Confederate positions north of the river. Beginning in June, General Lee started moving forces from the defense of Richmond south to support operations around Petersburg. Now, the area around Deep Bottom was perceived to be the point where Rebel defenses north of the James were the weakest.

After crossing the river, Tenth Corps' initial objective was the Confederate positions on New Market Heights. Once the Heights were secure, Brigadier General August Kautz's Cavalry Division would sweep to our right and move out to the Darbytown Road. With New Market Heights secure, Tenth Corps would then move up New Market Road as the Cavalry Division moved up Darbytown Road screening the flank.

While Tenth Corps was moving across the pontoon bridge to attack the eastern side of the Confederate lines, Major General Edward Ord's Eighteenth Corps was crossing a second pontoon bridge at Aiken's Landing at the end of the Varina Road. General Butler's operational plan called for Ord's Corps to attack the main Confederate works at Chaffin's Bluff, cut any Confederate bridges on the James to prevent reinforcements, and drive up the Osborne Turnpike toward Richmond.

Confederate forces north of the James were indeed spread thin. Front line troops on the New Market Heights and Chaffin's Bluff areas numbered about six thousand from two separate and distinct commands. The forces occupying New Market Heights were under the command of Brigadier General John Gregg of Texas and part of the Army of Northern Virginia. The soldiers on Chaffin's Bluff were part of the Richmond Defense Force under the command of Lieutenant General Richard Ewell. Facing these two commands were over twenty-six thousand soldiers of the Army of the James.

Terry's divisional line of battle extended from the swampy area around Four Mile Creek in the west, along New Market Road to Bailey's Creek in the east. The initial task for our Division was to provide a show of force to the Rebels on the Heights forcing them to spread their lines to match ours. The real assault on New Market

Heights would occur on our left by members of Brigadier General Charles Paine's Third Division of the Eighteenth Corps. This Division was composed of three brigades of U.S. Colored Troops and handpicked by General Butler to spearhead the attack against the Heights.

Unfortunately, as the sun rose, the Confederates on Signal Hill observed and reported Eighteenth Corps' crossing the James and moving up Varina Road. Likewise, their scouts also reported Tenth Corps' crossing and movement up to Kingsland Road. When word of this reached New Market Heights, General Gregg saw the folly of trying to hold both his position and the Chaffin's Bluff area. After conversing with General Ewell, Gregg planned to withdraw his troops from New Market Heights to the northwest and the Confederate works at Fort Gilmer.

Our Third Brigade formed the far right of Terry's Division. To our right was Bailey's Creek and to the front were New Market Road and the eastern side of the Heights. As part of the skirmish line, I was positioned forward of the battle line. As sunrise broke, we began a spirited exchange of gunfire with the Rebels on the Heights. While we continued to demonstrate against the left flank of the Confederate forces, elements of Paine's Division began their assault. The Confederate line stiffened at the point of attack and Paine's brigades were stopped with heavy casualties.

As luck would have it, just as Tenth Corps' attack bogged down, General Gregg chose that moment to begin his withdrawal of forces off the Heights. Sensing a lull in the action, the brigades of Paine's Division renewed their assault. This time their attack was successful and Union forces began cresting the top of the Heights into the Confederate works.

As soon as General Terry saw elements of the Colored Troops seize the left side of the Heights, he ordered a general advance of the First Division. The fight, while not as spirited as before, was still ongoing. We were engaged with the withdrawing Rebel rear guard. After a final firefight, the Heights were ours. The battle over, Colonel Plaisted ordered out skirmishers to the front and right flank to protect against any Rebel counterattack. Off to our left we could hear the sound of heavy fighting from the Eighteenth Corps area of operations. General Ord's forces were heavily engaged with the Confederate forces at Fort Harrison and along the unfinished New

Market Line. About 7:00 am, after a series of attacks and bitter fighting, Eighteenth Corps succeeded in capturing Fort Harrison.

The early morning fight was over. We succeeded in capturing our primary objective and stood poised to continue the assault to the very doorstep of the Confederacy. Just a few more critical engagements and this war could very well be over. I allowed myself to think that all I needed to do was endure this hell of battle for a short time more and we would be in Richmond. It all seemed so simple, at least in my mind.

$$\clubsuit$$

Chapter Thirty-Nine

October 1864 – Deep Bottom, Virginia

My renewed optimism was quickly dashed as the morning of September 29th wore on. Although the seizure of both New Market Heights and Fort Harrison was indeed a great psychological victory for the Union, the cost of this victory was quite high. From my vantage point atop the Heights I could see the dead, dying, and wounded from the colored troops that littered the field. For some reason, the Rebels seemed to fight harder when they knew their opponent to be the colored troops. Across the way, I could also make out the area of Fort Harrison and the blue jackets lying in the field before the engineer obstacles of the Fort. Among the seriously wounded was General Ord. Several of his key commanders also lay dead or wounded. Command of the Eighteenth Corps fell to Brigadier General Heckman, the Second Division commander.

About ten o'clock I was sitting with Sergeant Robbins atop the Heights when Lieutenant Payne and the other squad leader of the sharpshooters came over.

"General Grant is at Fort Harrison now assessing the situation", the Lieutenant stated. "He has directed Tenth Corps to push further up New Market Road and out toward Darbytown Road to link up with the cavalry."

"What's going on over at Fort Harrison?" Sergeant Robbins asked.

"Eighteenth Corps owns the fort but the attack has stalled. The Rebs now control the area of Chaffin's Bluff on a line from Fort Maury down by the river south of the Bluff generally northeasterly to Fort Gilmer," was the reply. "More importantly," the Lieutenant continued, "the Rebs still control the pontoon bridges across the James. Might only be a matter of time before Lee's whole Army comes over."

"What do you want us to do?" the other Sergeant asked.

"We are going to move over behind Birney's colored troops. Them and Foster's Second Division are tasked to seize Fort Gilmer. If we can, we will provide them some support. Try to pick off the officers, gunners, and the like. Hopefully, give the Rebs something else to worry about besides the coloreds."

In preparation for the next part of the operational plan, our Brigade moved into the woods astride the Mill Road between Varina and New Market Roads. Lieutenant Payne's sharpshooters moved across Varina Road to the edge of the woods near the home of Mrs. Throgmorton. The woman refused to leave her home and that home was now smack between two warring armies. The Lieutenant ordered four men to return to the supply train and bring food for Mrs. Throgmorton. We all figured that since we were going to shoot up her property, the least we could do was feed her.

As we approached the edge of the wood line, both Foster's Division and Birney's troops were visible. Off to our right, Foster's three brigades formed in a line of battle facing south. Directly to our front, Birney's four colored regiments were formed in a vee formation facing west. Across the field from Birney's troops lay Fort Gilmer, sticking out onto the field at a bend in the Intermediate Line.

From our current position it would be very difficult to provide any kind of support to Birney's forces. All we could do was watch as the battle began to unfold. Foster's Division began their assault just as we observed Confederate reinforcements moving into the Fort. Rebel artillery was locked into the Second Division's attack and as Foster held up his forces in the ravines between his initial position and the Fort, the troops were pummeled by shells exploding all around them. Charging from the final ravine, the Second Division soldiers were greeted by the direct fire of canister shells and volleys of rifle fire. By 2:30 pm, the Division was done and withdrew to the north leaving its dead and wounded behind.

As Foster's Division was withdrawing and Birney's Regiments began their assault, we were ordered to return our Regiment. General Grant directed General Butler to push Terry's Division out to the northeast and attempt to link up with Kautz's Division. Plaisted's Brigade moved out at 3:00 pm and rejoined the Division at Clyne's Farm.

The Division's route of march took us along the Strath Road on the north side of and parallel to the Exterior Line up to Darbytown Road. We then moved up Darbytown Road to a point where our lead elements became engaged with the Rebel pickets and skirmishers just south of the Intermediate Line. My vantage point of the fighting up front was a piece of high ground at the intersection of Darbytown Road and a side road near the now abandoned Powell Farm. From here, I could clearly see the Intermediate Line about a half mile ahead. I could observe the Rebels in the process of reinforcing this line with newly arrived infantry units and artillery batteries.

Freeman Flint, Frank Johnson, and I were so engrossed with our examination of the Rebel defenses, we failed to see Captain Trumbull, our Regimental Chaplain, arrive.

"Good afternoon, lads," the Chaplain called. "It's a glorious day for a visit to Richmond. Wouldn't you agree?"

We laughed. "It sure is, Sir," Freeman said. "Only about two divisions standing in our way."

"And another twenty miles to walk," Frank added.

"I don't think it's that far," Chaplain Trumbull replied. "Do you see those spires on the horizon and the roofs on either side of them?"

We all acknowledged we did. "Those spires and rooftops belong to the good citizens of Richmond. By my reckoning, those buildings are just up the hill from the James River." Looking at those rooftops and spires I figured we were no more than three or four miles from having our evening meal in Jefferson Davis' dining room. If only we could affect some kind of breakthrough of the Rebel positions on the Intermediate Line, the city might very well be ours.

Unfortunately, my wishes would remain unfulfilled, at least, for the time being. Our mission was to link up with the cavalry and, if feasible, attempt to move on Confederate positions. While Generals Grant and Butler gave us the latitude to capture Richmond, there was no sign of the illusive Cavalry Division.

Born in Baden, Germany, the Cavalry Division Commander, Brigadier General August Kautz, was raised in Ohio and enlisted in the Army to fight in the Mexican War. After the War, he enrolled at West Point, graduating in 1852. After tours of duty in the northwest, when this war started Kautz was reassigned to the Army of the Potomac. He saw service in the Peninsula Campaign before transferring to the Western Theater. Although Kautz demonstrated some prowess in military administration, authoring several duties and customs manuals, his egotistical nature and arrogant attitude far exceeded any tactical competence.

"We should have known Kautz wouldn't be anywhere around here," Frank said.

"He's probably riding around the countryside as far away from the Rebels as he can get," Freeman added in a rather disgusted tone. "I wish we had a decent cavalry commander. One who actually wanted to fight, like Pleasanton or Phil Sheridan. I think if Jeb Stuart were on our side, we'd be in Richmond by the end of the day."

My two companions began swapping stories of General Pleasanton's routing of Stuart's cavalry at Brandy Station and how effective he was at Gettysburg. I remembered Pleasanton from the Western Theater. His troops defeated General Sterling Price and brought an end to Confederate Army resistance in Missouri.

Off to our left there was a great deal of commotion from the vicinity of Fort Gilmer. Our artillery was pounding the Fort from all angles. Word was passed that General Lee was seen at the Fort, sparking the firestorm. Later, as I relaxed under the warm, gray skies of the day and listened to my comrades argue about this commander or that one, I began to think about the mystique that surrounds some military leaders.

Robert E. Lee was one of those commanders who had an unmistakable aura about them. For the past two years, under his leadership, the Army of Northern Virginia ran circles around a series of inept Union commanders. Soldiers on both sides spoke of the man who led the mission to retake Harpers Ferry and captured John Brown in respectful, almost reverent, tones.

I tried to imagine other commanders throughout history who commanded such respect and loyalty from their troops. Some, like Wellington, were sound militarily, but the Duke's aristocratic air alienated many in his Army. Admiral Nelson was of a similar ilk, militarily superb but personally aloof and distant. On the other hand, King Leonidas of Sparta, Julius Caesar, and Napoleon seemed to possess both the military expertise and the leadership qualities that endeared them to their troops.

I do believe President Lincoln chose such a leader to command the Union Army. General Grant not only exhibited sound tactical expertise; he possessed a solid grasp of the strategic implications of the war. I did have the opportunity to observe the General during my time in the Western Theater. While certainly not without his faults, Grant was a simple man with a tremendous understanding of what needed to be done and how best to do it.

There was a story starting to circulate around the Regiment about Grant's visit to Fort Hamilton earlier today. The General arrived at the Fort about the time the Rebs decided they wanted it back. Confederate artillery and naval gunfire raked the Fort as a precursor to the infantry assault that would follow. Throughout the hail of lead that rained down on the Fort and its occupants, General Grant sat calmly and drafted a series of messages and orders, seemingly oblivious to the hell that surrounded him.

After considerable time searching for Kautz's Cavalry Division, General Terry ordered the Division to return to the vicinity of Clyne's Farm and establish defensive positions on the now vacated Exterior Line. Plaisted's Third Brigade was assigned positions astride the New Market Road and tied into the Third Brigade of Foster's Division on our left and Pond's Brigade on our right.

Since the current defensive orientation of the Exterior Line focused on the direction from which we initially attacked, our major task became reversing the defenses to face the retreating Rebels. The better part of the late afternoon and evening was spent rebuilding the Exterior Line and preparing picket and skirmisher positions in front of these new defenses.

Rain began to fall early on September 30th. As of this morning, the defensive positions of Eighteenth Corps now stretched from Fort Harrison south to the area of Signal Hill and northeast to Varina Road. Units of Tenth Corps linked up with Paine's Division at Varina Road and their defensive positions extended out to the end of our division, well past New Market Road. General Terry also established pickets from the end of our lines to Doctor Johnson's farm on Darbytown Road. Kautz's Division, now returned from their raid, was tasked to screen the right flank beyond the Darbytown Road.

Around 9:00 am, word came down that General Grant decided not to renew offensive operations north of the James River. The main focus would now be on the Army of the Potomac who were heavily engaged south of Petersburg. Their goal was to capture the South Side Railroad and extend Union lines toward Boynton Plank Road.

General Grant directed the Army of the James to assume defensive operations at their current locations along the Exterior Line and conduct heavy reconnaissance out toward the Williamsburg Road to determine enemy intentions in that sector. It went without saying that the Army had to be prepared for continued Rebel counterattacks as part of their efforts to recapture Fort Harrison.

Around 11:00 am Rebel attacks appeared to begin as Confederate gunboats on the James began shelling Fort Harrison. Around noon reports came in of heavy Rebel reinforcements moving toward the James River bridges. This shelling and the report of arriving units added to an already high level of anxiety all along the Union line that day. In spite of the rain soaked, horrid working conditions, soldiers continued in earnest to erect defensive works for the anticipated Rebel attack.

By early afternoon, already having to deal with the heavy rain and the mud, our situation was further aggravated by periodic artillery firing and skirmishes with Rebel pickets and scouting parties. The main Rebel assault of Fort Harrison began about 3:00 pm. Heavy fighting centered on the Fort but spilled over to other units until about 5:00 pm. The skirmishing continued until after 6:00 pm when heavy rains effectively drowned out any further desire by either side to continue fighting.

The heavy rains continued all evening, letting up only after dawn and leaving us in a sea of mud. Orders came down just after the morning meal. General Terry would be taking two Brigades, Abbott's and Ponds', up the Darbytown Road for the purpose of conducting a reconnaissance in the area between Darbytown Road and Charles City Road. Our Brigade, less the Tenth Connecticut, would extend our current positions to the right and fill the gap left by the other two Brigades. The Tenth Connecticut was tasked with demonstrating in front of the Exterior Line in order to force the Rebels to remain in place and not exploit the reduced manpower along the Division line. All of the sharpshooters of the Brigade would be deployed in support of Tenth Connecticut's demonstration.

About 11:00 am the cavalry began moving out to the vicinity of the Charles City Road. Terry's forces followed shortly after as Tenth Connecticut began their demonstration. Early in the afternoon we started hearing the sounds of fighting from the vicinity of Darbytown Road. Colonel Samuel Spears' Cavalry Brigade, moving up Charles City Road, began driving back the Confederate cavalry outposts. As the troopers approached the Intermediate Line, Rebel infantry joined the fight.

As Spears' Brigade skirmished with the Rebels, Abbott's First Brigade moved up Darbytown Road to a piece of high ground just north of Roper's Farm. From this vantage point Abbott could see the intersection of Charles City Road and Williamsburg Road as well as the Confederate works on the Intermediate Line. The mud from the previous day's rains did little to support Abbott's efforts and only served to slow the deployment of his Brigade. This delay provided the Confederates with the necessary time to begin reinforcing the area.

As events unfolded, Terry's efforts managed to find a potential weak spot in the Intermediate Line. However, the cursed mud and a lack of sufficient forces to exploit the Rebel weakness forced the General to recall Abbott and the Cavalry Brigade. About 5:00 pm, Terry directed his forces to return to their previous positions along the Exterior Line.

The Battle of Roper's Farm signaled the end of General Grant's Fifth Offensive although some limited attacks by both sides would continue until the end of the month. During this offensive, the Army of the James managed to capture some key ground, notably Fort Harrison and New Market Heights. Following initial successes, subsequent operations kept the Confederates from retaking this lost terrain but failed to break the Intermediate Line or pose any significant threat to Richmond. At the end of the offensive, operations north of the James proved to be mostly indecisive.

South of the James, the Army of the Potomac also achieved limited success. While General Meade realized some small level of success by capturing some key areas south of Petersburg and lengthening the Union defenses, his forces failed to seize either the South Side Railroad or the Confederate supply route along Boydton Plank Road. Overall, while the offensive caused the Army of Northern Virginia to shift forces to the defense of Richmond and further stretch out an already overstretched Army, in the end, General Lee's Army was able to defend both Richmond and Petersburg.

This phase of the hell on earth was over. All that remains is to wait as the two great commanders plotted their next moves in this bloody chess match, moves that would hopefully take us closer to the final chapter of Armageddon and, ultimately, toward our own personal redemption.

Armageddon

"How am I supposed to believe that there is a heaven and a hell when all I see now is hell?"

Aaron Powell

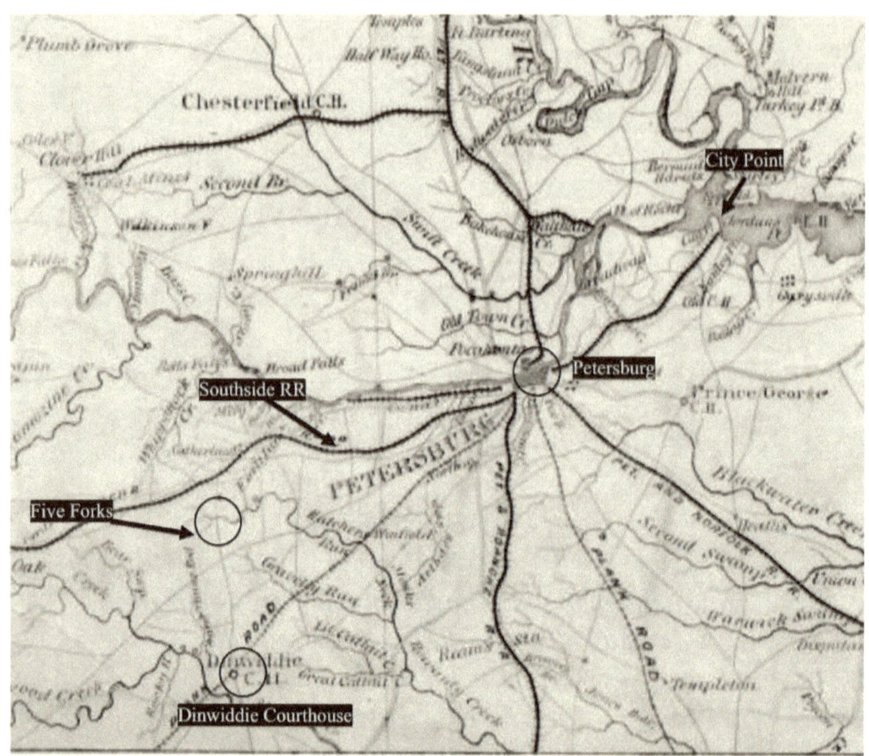

Petersburg Virginia

Chapter Forty

November 1864 – Petersburg, Virginia

The "chew, chew, chew" of bullets rang all around our picket position.

"I distinctly heard the captain say that this offensive was over," Freeman muttered.

"Apparently that rumor has not reached the Butternuts yet," Frank replied. "There must be something powerful important about this position."

"I think it stands to reason that since they went and built this whole defensive line and we went and took it from them, they would be a might sore about it," I answered.

Looking from one to another and then at me, Freeman and Frank could only shrug. They did have a point. It had been five days since Grant's Fifth Offensive supposedly ended but the Rebs continued to maneuver forces along the Intermediate Line. Their pickets were acting in an overly aggressive manner and routinely exchanged fire with our pickets. These exchanges, more often than not, generally escalated into a full-blown skirmish complete with artillery fire.

Since the Battle of Roper's Farm on October 1st, most of our time was spent on the picket line or working to improve the defenses of the Exterior Line. Our situation was such that the long absent baggage train could finally reach us. For a change, we got to eat hot meals, change clothes, and sleep in the comfort of our tents.

In addition to our routine duties, we also conducted scouting parties and demonstrations against the Rebel positions to evaluate their defenses. Confederate infantry reciprocated and conducted their own scouting parties and demonstrations to evaluate our positions with an eye toward possibly turning a flank. The activities all seemed to confirm what Confederate prisoners and deserters all indicated. A large Rebel force was scheduled to arrive and an attack was planned for as early as the morning of October 7th.

On October 6th, the Third Brigade's lines stretched along the Exterior Line from New Market Road toward Darbytown Road with pickets and skirmishers as far out as the intersection of Darbytown Road. We were the far right of Terry's Division. Beyond our positions was Kautz's Cavalry Division. Behind the Exterior Line and between Kautz's positions and our rear area was a large swampy area running southeast along Four Mile Creek.

Shortly after dawn on the morning of the 7th, we heard the sound of heavy fighting echoing from Kautz's positions on Darbytown Road. Later we learned two Confederate divisions, supported by cavalry, attacked Kautz's front and right flank. Our Cavalry was simply overwhelmed and beat a hasty retreat toward New Market Road through the swamp.

General Terry quickly recognized the enemy's intentions and as Kautz's Cavalry flailed its way through the underbrush toward our rear area, Terry realigned two Brigades at right angles to their current position on the Exterior Line. Eleventh Maine was on the far left of the Third Brigade and positioned along New Market Road. We were tied into Second Brigade on our left and Twenty-fourth Massachusetts on our right. To the right of the Twenty-fourth were Tenth Connecticut and One Hundredth New York.

As we readied a hasty defense, a Rebel infantry brigade was seen preparing to move against our position and that of Second Brigade. The enemy was attacking in line formation with no skirmishers in front of the assaulting line. We allowed them to come in close before the command to open fire was given. The fight was over in relatively short order leaving stacks of Rebel dead and wounded to our front and the enemy brigade withdrawing.

As the first Rebel brigade fell back, scouts reported a second Confederate line forming on our right. Their goal appeared to be locating and turning our right flank. This second Confederate brigade ran headlong into the Tenth Connecticut and the One Hundredth New York. There was heavy fire from the advancing infantry augmented by their famous Rebel yell. While Tenth Connecticut stood like a granite wall during the Confederate barrage, under the onslaught of flying lead, the New Yorker's line started to collapse. We all held our collective breath as the officers of the One Hundredth attempted to rally their troops. After a period, the New Yorker's rejoined the fight and the Rebel brigade was beaten off.

In the aftermath of the fight, I surveyed the area. The Rebel dead and wounded filled the field, some only a few yards from our lines. As I examined the Brigade, I realized that Third Brigade held off the Rebel charge with only about six hundred men total in the four regiments.

As the second enemy brigade fell back, skirmishers were sent forward but after a short distance we were met with stiff resistance from what appeared to be a third Rebel brigade. Fearing another assault, we prepared ourselves for the next charge. When no attack came, the command collectively breathed a sigh of relief and prepared to send skirmishers back out.

"Get yourselves ready," Sergeant Robbins called. "We are moving out. Skirmish order. Prepare to take prisoners."

As I moved through the bloodstained field, I chanced upon a gut-shot Confederate soldier in a small grove of trees. He was lying next to the bodies of two captains and sobbing quietly.

"Stay with him," Sergeant Robbins said.

I acknowledged his order and knelt beside the wounded soldier.

"Could I trouble you for a drink of water," the young soldier asked. "We can't get any good drinking water here. At least, not as good as the water back home."

As I handed him my canteen I said, "This water isn't much better, but it's wet."

He nodded, thanked me, and took a few swallows.

"Where's home?" I asked.

"Outside of Mobile, Alabama," he replied. "And you?"

"Maine."

"Reckon I never been to Maine before. Is it pretty there?"

"Sure is, especially this time of year when the trees start turning colors. It's truly grand. What unit are you with?"

"Forty-fourth Alabama, Laws Brigade, Field's Division," he replied.

As he lay there, we talked a bit of home, of good drinking water, the war, and other things. He told me one of the dead captains was his regimental commander and his parson back home. As he spoke, he held the hand of the other captain. In addition to being his company commander, this officer was also his father.

"Do you smell that?" he asked quietly. "Smells like Ma is baking bread again. Nothing better than fresh bread and newly churned butter."

"I agree. My stepmother always baked bread for our Sunday dinner. It was the best, with butter or honey, fresh from the oven."

Somewhere in our discussions of bread and Sunday dinner, the young man went to meet his God: no screaming, no hollering or crying: just a dignified and peaceful death as he held his father's hand. The Alabama lad was fifteen years old.

The rest of October was pretty much more of the same; limited objective attacks on our part, demonstrations by both sides, and countering Rebel advances. Of course, there were the inevitable scouting parties and picket duty. During this time there were also some serious changes to the command structure within Tenth Corps. Major General Birney was forced to relinquish command of the Corps due to an illness. The General returned to his home in Philadelphia to recover, but sadly, on October 18th, he died.

General Terry assumed command of the Corps and Brigadier General Adelbert Ames of Rockland; Maine took over the First Division. A West Point graduate, General Ames commanded the Twentieth Maine earlier in the war and came to us by way of General Meade's staff.

The biggest loss to the Regiment occurred during early November. On the first, those members of the Regiment who enlisted in 1861, and had not reenlisted, prepared to depart for Augusta and discharge. Among the veterans departing was Colonel Plaisted. On November 2nd, with the Colonel in the lead, our veterans marched away.

After the departure of our comrades, our new acting Regimental Commander, Lieutenant Maxfield, mustered the 1861 re-enlistees and the rest of the Regiment. There were scarcely two hundred of us left. The Regiment was promised that new recruits were staging in Augusta to augment our dwindling numbers and keep us from being reassigned to other regiments. The muster complete, we were directed to pack up all of our equipment, load the baggage train, and prepare to move out. Two hours later, Lieutenant Maxfield marched the Regiment, or what was left of it, to Deep Bottom to board ship for Fortress Monroe.

Chapter Forty-One

November 1864 – New York, New York

On the morning of November 2nd, what was left of the Eleventh Maine Regiment arrived at Deep Bottom. By noon, the Regiment was aboard a coastal freighter and rumors abounded about our final destination.

"I heard it on good authority we're sailing to North Carolina to join up with Sherman's Army," Frank said.

"That's rubbish," Freeman replied. "We're heading back to either South Carolina or Florida."

When the ship arrived at Fortress Monroe late that evening, we disembarked and found our billet. As the sun rose the next morning, I discovered we were not the only regiment here. Walking around that morning I saw the insignia from three Connecticut regiments, two New Hampshire regiments, and one each from Indiana and New York. I even spotted a battery from the First United States Artillery and scores of support troops.

That afternoon all of the rumors were put to rest and our final destination was revealed. We were to be a part of a provisional division that would proceed to New York City to help keep the peace during the forthcoming Presidential elections. After spending the rest of the day cleaning our equipment, our uniforms, and ourselves, we boarded the steamer, the General Lyon, for the trip to New York.

Joining Eleventh Maine on the General Lyon were the Sixth Connecticut, the Tenth Connecticut, and the One Hundred-twelfth New York. We set sail the next morning bound for New York City.

The General Lyon was a chartered steamer used by the Army to ferry troops along the east coast. The ship had participated in several campaigns over the course of the six months since her charter. These included the attacks on Fort Wagner in South Carolina and Fort Fisher in North Carolina as well as the fighting along the Bermuda Hundred in Virginia.

The seas were calm and the trip was relatively comfortable for a charter vessel. The weather was pleasant at the start but grew progressively colder the further north we traveled. On November 6th, the General Lyon passed through the Narrows between Staten Island and Brooklyn. As we entered the Hudson River, we caught sight of the island of Manhattan and the rest of New York City. We remained on board until the next morning when we disembarked at Fort Richmond on Staten Island.

New York City was certainly no stranger to violence as a result of this war. The largest, and arguably the most influential city in the North, the New York business community did not welcome the war and the loss of Southern commerce that moved through the port. Cotton was an important commodity for both the port and the textile industries of upstate New York and New England.

When war was declared, the City's mayor, Fernando Wood, a Southern sympathizer, suggested that New York also secede from the Union and form the Free State of Tri-Insula. Wood's goal was to keep the cotton trade with the Confederacy and maintain the revenue and jobs that trade with the Southern states brought to New York.

The first of the New York protests to turn violent occurred after President Lincoln's announcement of the emancipation of slaves. New York's anti-war advocates managed to churn up emotions among the white working class citizens. Many of these workers were German and Irish immigrants and a goodly number of these citizens were unemployed. Workers throughout the City were led to believe that emancipation of the slaves would cost them their jobs. They feared thousands of free slaves would descend on New York to flood an already saturated job market and work at a cheaper wage than white workers.

Protests over emancipation were not limited to New York's work force. Many of the officers and soldiers serving in New York regiments also protested what appeared to be a shift in national strategy from preservation of the Union to the abolishment of slavery.

In July of 1863, following the passage of the Enrollment Act, New York's streets once again erupted into one of the most violent and bloody riots in American history. In addition to the new conscription standards for white men, the protesters were extremely upset over the three hundred dollar substitute clause of the Act. Three hundred dollars represented a year's salary for the average New York worker making it impossible for a run-of-the-mill worker to buy their way out of the draft. To add insult to injury, the Enrollment Act failed to consider any black men for the draft as they were not considered citizens.

On July 11th, 1863, New York City held its first draft lottery. Two days later the rioting broke out as white workers attacked government offices and facilities, overwhelming the small number of policemen and military personnel that City officials gathered to quell the rioting. Later in the day the rioters turned their attention to black citizens and businesses especially around the port area.

The new mayor and political associate of President Lincoln, Republican George Opdyke, bypassed the anti-war Governor of New York, Horatio Seymour, and wired the War Department directly to request military troops. On July 15th, four thousand New York troops, fresh from the battlefield at Gettysburg, arrived to put down the riot. When the draft riots, as they came to be called, were officially over, New York suffered millions of dollars in property damage and upwards of one thousand of its citizens dead.

Now, with the Presidential elections looming, officials feared another round of protests, rioting, and violence. Compounding matters, word was received that Confederate agents operating in New York were planning an attack against the City on Election Day.

One day before the election, our Regiment landed at Fort Richmond on Staten Island. The Fort sat on the western shore of the Narrows, the main approach into New York from the Atlantic Ocean. Various fortifications had occupied the present site of the Fort since the early 1800's. Work began on the present Fort in 1847 on, what was, the site of the former Battery Weed. Rumors quickly spread throughout the Regiment that General Robert E. Lee developed the initial designs of Fort Richmond during his time here as the post engineer at Fort Hamilton.

On the evening of November 7th, the Eleventh Maine, Third New Hampshire, Thirteenth Indiana, One Hundred-twelfth New York and the artillery battery from the First U.S. Artillery were ferried across the bay to Pier 42 on the southeast side of Manhattan Island. When the citizens of Lower Manhattan woke on Election Day, they found their streets being patrolled by soldiers of the Provisional Division.

"I don't think these folks much like our being here," Frank said.

"You can say that again," Freeman replied. "Hard to believe this is a Northern city."

"Kind of reminds me of the reception we received as we marched into the City of Alexandria back in the summer of 1861," I commented. "Except the good citizens of Virginia were much more vocal in their opinions about our presence."

"I sure hope nothing happens today," Frank said. "I wouldn't feel right about having to shoot any of these people."

"Me too," Freeman added. "But if it comes down to them or me, there really isn't much choice. I'll worry about the consequences later."

Fortunately for us, and the good people of New York, there were no howling mobs crying for blood on Election Day or for three days after the election. The President was reelected and on the afternoon of November 11th, New York officials were satisfied a military presence was no longer required. We departed Pier 42 and returned to Fort Richmond for another two and a half days. Late in the day on November 14th, the Regiment embarked the steamer North Point and that evening, the ship departed for Virginia and the war.

We arrived back in Fortress Monroe on November 16th where the Provisional Division was disbanded and the regiments were returned to their parent commands. Early on the 17th we boarded another coastal steamer for the trip upriver to Deep Bottom. By late afternoon we reached Deep Bottom, disembarked and marched back to our rear area along the Exterior Line.

When we arrived, waiting for our return were over two hundred new recruits fresh from Maine and ready to fill our depleted ranks. Five days later, Lieutenant Colonel Jonathan Hill, minus the arm he lost at the First Battle of Deep Bottom, returned to assume command of the Regiment.

Colonel Hill was one of the original officers of the Regiment when Eleventh Maine was mustered into the Army in November of 1861. Initially serving as the Company Commander of Company K, Colonel Hill assumed command of the Regiment when Colonel Plaisted became the Brigade Commander. In hospital since August, Colonel Hill chose to remain in command of the Regiment when the rest of the veterans returned to Maine for discharge.

The Eleventh Maine was, once again, a fully functional regiment. There were now over four hundred on the rolls and present for duty. Some two hundred and eighty more were listed on the rolls but absent for duty for a variety of reasons. While we were indeed a fully functional regiment, the fact remained that over half our numbers were raw recruits who had never heard a shot fired in anger and were as green as a newly cut tree.

By the end of November, the fighting was pretty much over for 1864. Much of the Army of the James was preparing to go into winter quarters here on the Exterior Line. Hopefully, there would be time to train our new recruits before the fighting began in earnest yet again.

Chapter Forty-Two

Winter 1864/5 – Petersburg, Virginia

By December, when the Army of the James went into winter quarters, their battle line stretched from the Darbytown Road, along the Exterior Line, down to the James River below Chaffin's Bluff, across the river, through the Bermuda Hundred to the Appomattox River.

The Army of the Potomac's section of the Union line extended from the Appomattox River, along the east side of Petersburg, and around the southern side of the city to Hatcher's Run in the vicinity of Boydton Plank Road. Taking the total of both Armies together, the cumulative length of the Union line was over thirty-seven miles long.

On the Confederate side, the Army of Northern Virginia knew they needed to keep pace with the Yankees. Their lines now extended from the area of White Oak Swamp in the north, across the Bermuda Hundred on the Howlett Line, through Petersburg along the Dimmock Line, and as far west as Boydton Plank Road. Additionally, Confederate cavalry and infantry controlled the approaches to the South Side Railroad from Five Forks down Courthouse Road to Dinwiddie Court House.

General Lee's Army was stretched thin all along the front. Compounding this fact, disease, death, and desertion dramatically reduced the overall manpower available for duty. Essentially cut off from the rest of the Confederacy, Lee's Army now depended solely on the South Side Railroad for what meager supplies that came in. Grant's chokehold on all other rail lines around Petersburg and the Union Navy's blockade of Southern ports were having their effect on not only on the Army of Northern Virginia but the rest of the South as well.

For the individual soldier, there was a renewed level of confidence that winter. With Rebel defenses stretched well beyond their limits, we began to look forward to the spring offensives with a hope that the Army of the Potomac could break the siege at Petersburg and the Army of the James could crack the Intermediate Line and capture Richmond.

In December, there was a major shakeup in the structure of the Army of the James. With the rest of the Army in winter quarters, General Butler was assigned command of the Expeditionary Force and ordered to travel to North Carolina to participate in offensive actions against Fort Fisher, an impressive Confederate fortification that guarded the mouth of the Cape Fear River at Wilmington.

General Terry was also assigned to the Expeditionary Force as commander of a modified Tenth Corps. Two divisions were identified to travel with General Terry: the Second Division of Tenth Corps with General Ames in command, and General Paine's Division of colored troops from Eighteenth Corps. Additionally, Abbott's Brigade from the First Division was assigned to the Expeditionary Force. As a replacement for General Ames, Brigadier General Foster, formerly the Second Division Commander, was reassigned as commander of the First Division.

The Expeditionary Force sailed in early December with over nine thousand troops. In response, General Lee dispatched Brigadier General Robert Hoke's Division to reinforce Confederate forces in the Fort. The Union naval bombardment began on December 24th and as the Expeditionary Force troops landed, Hoke's newly arrived Division intercepted them.

The assault stalled and on December 27th, General Butler ordered the withdrawal of his forces from the beach. Butler's actions were in direct disobedience to General Grant's original orders that called for siege operations if the initial attack on the Fort failed. As a result of his actions, Butler was relieved of command and sent home.

Butler's dismissal set off a series of organizational shockwaves in the Army of the James. To replace General Butler, General Terry assumed command of the Expeditionary Force and although Fort Fisher eventually fell to the Union, Terry's force would not return to Virginia. Rather, the Expeditionary Force linked up with Brigadier General John Schofield and later with General Sherman, and remained in North Carolina.

On January 1st 1865, command of the Army of the James fell to Major General Ord, now recovered from the wounds he received at Fort Harrison in September. In the past, Butler's combat organization mixed the white regiments with those of the colored troops. With this structure, Butler hoped to create an identity for the colored troops and a level of trust among the white troops with the goal of creating a cohesive fighting force. Based on some of the previous problems associated with Butler's organization, one of General Ord's first tasks was to reorganize the Army by creating an all white Twenty-fourth Corps and an all black Twenty-fifth Corps. In addition to all of the colored regiments from both Tenth Corps and Eighteenth Corps, the newly formed Twenty-fifth Corps also included colored troops from the Ninth Corps of the Army of the Potomac. With the creation of these two new Corps structures, the Tenth Corps and the Eighteenth Corps were officially disbanded.

The Eleventh Maine Regiment was now part of the Third Brigade of the First Division of Twenty-fourth Corps. Our new Corps Commander was Major General John Gibbon of Pennsylvania. A career Army officer, Gibbon was an 1847 graduate of the Military Academy. The loss of the Second Division to the Expeditionary Force saw a Third Division added to the Corps' organization under the command of Brigadier General Charles Devens of Massachusetts. Devens' Division was made up of some of the regiments from the old Eighteenth Corps. Later, word came down that an Independent Division would be joining the Corps when they arrived from the Shenandoah Valley. Brigadier General John Turner commanded that Division.

Major changes also happened to the First Division's organization. Since Abbott's Brigade was off in North Carolina, Colonel Harrison Fairchild's Brigade from the Eighteenth Corps took their place. This Brigade was identified as the Fourth Brigade and composed of three New York regiments, a Pennsylvania regiment, and the Eighth Maine Regiment from Augusta. The First Brigade was now under the command of Colonel Thomas Osborn. In the new organization, the First added another Pennsylvania regiment to their former configuration. With the departure of Colonel Plaisted, the Third Brigade was now under the command of Colonel George Dandy, former Commanding Officer of the One Hundredth New York. Our Brigade still included the Tenth Connecticut, Eleventh Maine, Twenty-fourth Massachusetts, and One Hundredth New York, and we added the Two Hundred-sixth Pennsylvania.

The last major change to the Army of the James was to the Cavalry Division. Brigadier General Kautz was reassigned as a Division Commander in the Twenty-fifth Corps. In his place,

General Ord named Brigadier General Ranald Mackenzie as the Cavalry Commander.

While all of these organizational changes were occurring to the Army of the James, the lives of the individual soldiers changed very little. Since the Regiment was in winter quarters, we constructed log houses complete with canvas-covered roofs to keep out the rain and snow. There were two of these log houses for our Squad, each capable of housing eight soldiers. Each soldier had a wooden bunk covered with pine boughs that served as a rather comfortable alternative to a mattress. It was certainly better than sleeping on the plank floor. Besides a bunk, our equipment and spare clothing was stored in hardtack boxes that did double duty, serving as both cabinets and tables.

Each log house was kept warm by a small sheet iron stove. Generally, while the inside of the house retained a degree of smoke, the stove was vented to the outside by a chimney extending out the roof. We were careful to keep the fire at a safe level in case the stovepipe heated up to a point that the canvas roof would catch fire. Over the course of the winter, more than a couple of log houses lost their roofs this way.

The company cookhouse was also a log structure. Food was plentiful with fresh bread and meat arriving regularly from City Point. The camp was also laid out with concern for sanitation. Latrines were dug and filled away from all sources of drinking water and the garbage dumps were far enough away to discourage wild animals from running through the camp. The Regiment spent a rather tolerable winter without the levels of disease seen in previous years.

Early December did mark a significant change in Virginia's weather. For the most part, the days were usually overcast and cold. Even when the sun was out, the temperatures were chilly. Strong winds often blew from the north or northwest throughout the afternoon, dying off only as the sun set and adding to our daily discomfort. The overcast skies did manage to keep the nighttime temperatures at a respectable level however, if we could see stars, the night temperatures usually plummeted.

Our daily activities were pretty well defined. Picket duty, duty on the line, or drill filled our time. Picket duty during the cold Virginia winter was the toughest and pickets were rotated with regularity to keep the soldiers warm. In spite of this rotational arrangement, the cold, stormy nights proved to be the times that tried even the heartiest of Maine men. When we were forced to endure these conditions, Colonel Hill authorized a hearty breakfast complete with a ration of spirits for the watch coming off the line.

As part of our winter routine, the Regiment was subjected to daily drills and training. For the two hundred plus new recruits, this training was their introduction to the hard times that lay ahead. Veteran officers and noncommissioned officers oversaw the training of both the new recruits and the rest of the Regiment. Once the training noncommissioned officer felt the recruits were ready, they were assigned to duties on the Exterior Line and eventually, on the picket line. The recruits were now ready to join the rest of the Regiment in the more advanced drill we were all accustomed to.

Thanks to the fact that General Grant was more concerned about how well a soldier fought rather than how he turned out for parade, we did not participate in any of the extravagant ceremonies or reviews other commanders had routinely scheduled. That said, there were occasions when protocol dictated honors be rendered to a visiting dignitary. These ceremonies generally involved a small number of soldiers and were usually held in a field in the rear area.

Back in the fall, part of the Brigade was involved in a Corps review for Secretary of War Edwin Stanton. Fortunately, our Company did not have to participate and remained on the lines. On March 20th, the word was passed that the whole Regiment would participate in a review on March 23rd.

No mention was made of who the dignitary was so, once again, the rumors began to fly as to who our visitor might be. Some said it was a foreign general or statesman visiting the United States to determine if his country would support the Union cause. Others thought it was Secretary Stanton returning for a repeat performance. Still others thought, since we were requested, it was the Governor of Maine dropping by to see how his soldiers were doing.

After the appropriate degree of preparation and the customary inspections that preceded any review, we stood in Regimental formation with three other regiments in a field on the Bermuda Hundred. At the appointed time, an escort of officers preceded the visiting dignitary. From my position in the front rank of Company G, I could see General Grant and the visitor arrive on horseback. Behind them was an open carriage carrying two women. The General and his aide assisted the ladies from the carriage as the visiting dignitary adjusted his clothing. Only after he donned a stovepipe hat did I realize our guest of honor was President Abraham Lincoln. When the ladies joined the President and General Grant, I also realized one was Mrs. Lincoln and the other Mrs. Grant.

Murmurs of the President's arrival quickly spread across the assembled regiments. The President and General Grant remounted their horses and rode along the assembled line of troops as the band played "Hail to the Chief". After the President reviewed the formations, he and General Grant rode to the reviewing area and rejoined the ladies. When the proper commands were given, the four regiments marched past the President and across the pontoon bridge back to the Exterior Line.

A second review, this one involving units from the Army of the Potomac, was scheduled for March 25th. Unfortunately, General Lee had other ideas for welcoming the President. Early the morning of the 25th, three divisions of Major General John B. Gordon's Second Corps, Army of Northern Virginia slipped across no man's land from the Colquitt Salient and attacked Fort Stedman. Supporting Gordon's attack was a division from Major General George Pickett's First Corps from along the Howlett Line, two brigades from Major General Bushrod Johnson's Fourth Corps, and two brigades from Major General Cadmus Wilcox's Third Corps. Major General Rooney Lee's Cavalry Division was assigned to exploit any breach of the Union lines. General Robert E. Lee was taking a tremendous gamble with this early morning assault. While the area around Fort Stedman was not as heavily fortified with engineer obstacles, the Army of Northern Virginia was committing almost one half of its available infantry to this venture.

Although the initial assault was successful, the Union's Ninth Corps, under the command of Major General John Parke, managed to stabilize the line and begin a series of counterattacks to reclaim the lost ground. By noon, Ninth Corps succeeded in regaining Fort Stedman and the other areas that had been overrun by the Rebels. Outnumbered and outgunned, General Gordon's forces were compelled to return to the Colquitt Salient. When the butcher's bill was tallied, Union losses were only seventy-two dead and about a thousand wounded or missing. Confederate losses, on the other hand, were significant. Over six hundred killed and another nineteen hundred wounded or missing. It went without saying, the Army of the Potomac's review for the President was cancelled.

Once the lines were again stabilized, President Lincoln took the opportunity to tour the Fort Stedman area. Since his arrival, the President and General Grant met regularly to discuss the main purpose of the President's visit to City Point, the upcoming spring offensive. General Sherman was also scheduled to arrive from his headquarters in the Goldsboro, North Carolina area sometime on March 27th to hear Grant's strategic plan for the coming offensive. It didn't take much time for the pre-offensive preparations to start. On March 24th, after our review, General Ord began pulling units from off the Exterior Line and moving other units around to confuse the Rebels as to his actual intent. Our Regiment did not return to the line. Rather, we began to strike the camp, load the baggage train, and prepare to move out.

"Where do you suppose we are going?" Frank asked.

"I'm not sure," I replied. "If I had to guess, given all the secrecy and movement of troops along the line, I figure we don't want the Rebs to know we are heading south."

"Sounds about right," Freeman said. Those Second Division boys have been running up and down the line all day. And several of the colored troop regiments are moving around as well."

"I also heard that Sheridan and his Army have arrived on the south side of Petersburg," Freeman added. "With the way the roads have been drying out, the next offensive can't be too far off."

"Yeah, I heard he licked a Reb army in the northern part of the Shenandoah Valley before starting down here," Frank said.

If some of these rumors were actually true, it meant there were three Union Armies in the Petersburg area. Spring was in the air and, in spite of the rain, there was hope the weather would clear and the roads would dry out. A million questions filled the minds of the men of the Regiment. Fortunately, we didn't have long to wait for the answers. On the evening of the 26th, the Regiment moved out of our current rear area and joined the rest of the First Division down at Deep Bottom. The Army of the James was relocating south to join what all of us hoped would be the final offensive of the war.

$$\sim \diamondsuit \sim$$

Chapter Forty-Three

March 27-29, 1865 – Army of the James

It would be yet another night march. On the evening of March 27th, General Ord and his staff, two divisions of the Twenty-fourth Corps, our Division and the Independent Division, and Brigadier General Mackenzie's Cavalry Division began crossing the pontoon bridge at Deep Bottom. At the same time, Brigadier General William Birney's Division of colored troops began crossing the pontoon bridge upriver at the end of Varina Road. As we began our movement, the troops who remained on the Exterior Line started a demonstration up at Darbytown Road to draw Confederate attention away from the James River area.

On top of the pitch-blackness of the evening, it was raining. Not a misting, gentle rain but a downright deluge. It was the kind of rain that caused low-lying areas to turn into lakes and roads into virtual quagmires of mud. Mud that stuck to everything and added ten pounds to a soldier's body weight. Yet, into that wet, dark, night the Regiment set off.

The Independent Division led the march followed by our Division. Just after dark, we crossed the pontoon bridge at Deep Bottom and moved out onto the Bermuda Hundred. We marched all night and just around 6:00 am arrived at the pontoon bridge across from the supply depot at Broadway Landing. The depot and pontoon bridge were located about three miles up the Appomattox River from City Point and about eight miles downriver from Petersburg.

When Thomas Broadway settled the area in the late seventeenth century, he established himself along the Appomattox River naming his land and the adjacent town, Broadway Landing. In 1781, the British used Broadway Landing as a base of operations against the Continental Army in the Richmond area. Now with the arrival of the Union Army in June of 1864, a series of supply points along both the James and the Appomattox Rivers were established to support operations at Petersburg. While City Point became the largest and best known, Broadway Landing became a critical secondary supply point due to its location and the depth of the river, which allowed larger ships to travel further upriver.

The Broadway Landing supply depot handled a large number of artillery pieces, artillery ammunition, and gunpowder that led to the site becoming a key target for Confederate military planners. As the ground situation around Petersburg and Richmond began to deteriorate, the Confederate Navy started to assault Union supply positions all along the two rivers. On January 25th, 1865, Rebel gunboats and ironclads attacked the supply depot at Broadway Landing. Fortunately, coastal artillery and Union Navy gunboats beat off the attacking force with no damage to the site.

When we arrived at the pontoon bridge at Broadway Landing, we found Brigadier General Birney's Division of colored troops from the Twenty-fifth Corps waiting. By 7:30 am on the 28th, all three Divisions of the Army of the James were across the Appomattox River and moving south. The lack of marching and other activity over the winter made it hard for our Division and Birney's to keep up the pace. General Ord recognized this and once past Broadway Landing, around 8:00 am, he allowed our two Divisions to move off the road to regroup and recover until noon. The Independent Division, who was fresh from operations in the Shenandoah and somewhat accustomed to forced marches, continued on.

"That had to be the worst trek I have ever experienced," Frank exclaimed. "And it isn't even over."

Frank made a valid point. In addition to the night and the rain, the roads were in absolutely terrible condition. Already soft from the unusually wet winter and spring, the roads were also severely furrowed by heavy artillery wheels and the weight of wagon trains. Coupled with last night's heavy rain, the roads appeared to be glassy smooth ribbons of mud. However, these ribbons of mud often concealed knee-deep channels in the road that we were forced to negotiate.

For those who tried walking along side of the road to avoid the mud, the darkness of the evening hid the presence of large trees and brambles that grew next to the road. The choice boiled down to flailing through knee-deep mud or knocking yourself unconscious by walking into a tree. Now that morning had dawned, the choices of where to walk improved greatly.

Somewhat refreshed after our morning breather, the Division set out to rejoin the Army of the James. The rest of the day was spent passing by the rear area of the Ninth Corps. Major General Parke's Corps was responsible for the area from the Appomattox River south to Fort Davis, the next fort south of Fort Hell. During one of our afternoon rest breaks, the Regiment found itself located near a holding compound for prisoners of war.

As the siege around Petersburg continued and resupply routes for Confederate forces dwindled, more and more Confederates deserted or were taken prisoner during the fighting. In spite of efforts to make Union soldiers of these prisoners, Union leadership acknowledged most Confederate prisoners were averse to the option of taking up arms against their comrades. As a result, in August of 1864, General Grant issued a special order that exempted Confederate prisoners and deserters from service as Union soldiers.

As part of this order, Grant further offered incentives to any Rebel contemplating desertion. The order stated, any Confederate soldier who deserted and signed a loyalty oath not to return to the fighting would be given food and transportation home, if that home was within Union occupied territory. If home was not under Union control, the soldiers would be fed and offered transportation anywhere in the North. Deserters who took the oath could also be given work in various noncombat Army departments as paid civilian employees. This included work in the supply and logistics areas or as stevedores or longshoreman at depots along the river.

While the Regiment did capture a few prisoners and deserters in our time north of the James, I never saw such a multitude of Rebels in one place who weren't actually charging at us. This fact was not lost on my comrades.

"Do you think a lot of them are deserting for the money?" Frank asked.

"Either the money or the thought of a good meal," Freeman replied. "Looks like some of those boys haven't eaten in a fortnight."

As we marched on, my friends continued their discussion of the relative merits of General Grant's special order and the rain continued. Our route that night took us past the campfires of the Sixth Corps. Major General Horatio Wright's Corps stretched out from the Ninth Corps position at Fort Davis through the line of Union forts to the Arthur Swamp area. Just beyond the Sixth Corps area was our final objective, the rear of Second Corps. Second Corps now held the section of the line from the Sixth Corps positions on the Arthur Swamp to the point where Hatcher's Run crossed Vaughn Road in Dinwiddie County.

We trudged on through the night and during the afternoon of March 29th, the three divisions of the Army of the James began arriving in the rear of Second Corps. The march was indeed a grueling one of over thirty-six miles. Over the entire duration of the march the rain pelted down, soaking everyone and everything. The Independent Division arrived first and around 4:30 pm, began replacing Second Corps units on the front line. The other two divisions were told to make camp and be prepared to move up in the morning.

After a long winter, finally the pieces were moving into position for General Grant's Spring offensive. In addition to the Army of the James and the Army of the Potomac, Major General Sheridan's Army of the Shenandoah was here. It seemed like the only thing holding up the final push for Petersburg was the weather. Perhaps this would be the beginning of the end.

March 27-29, 1865 – Army of the Shenandoah

As the Twenty-fourth Corps, Army of the James slogged along the muddy roads heading for the southern end of the Union battle line, other pieces in the grand chess match were already set in motion. To Union planners, the key to a successful conclusion of this siege was stopping supplies from coming into the Army of Northern Virginia. Since arriving here in June of 1864, the Union Army succeeded in closing most of these supply channels. The final two supply routes for the Confederate resupply remained the South Side Railroad and Boydton Plank Road. In early February, General Grant ordered a winter offensive directed at these two supply routes.

The battle plan called for a cavalry division under Major General David Gregg to move on Dinwiddie Court House to prevent further resupply up Boydton Plank Road. Warren's Fifth Corps and Humphrey's Second Corps would support Gregg's cavalry. After the cavalry moved out, Fifth Corps took up positions halfway between Hatcher's Run and Dinwiddie Court House along Vaughn Road. Second Corps assumed positions along Vaughn Road and Duncan Road to prevent a Confederate attack from the north.

For three days beginning on February 5th, the Army of the Potomac engaged Rebels in an action that became known as the Battle for Hatcher's Run. In the end, some supplies were seized coming up Boydton Plank Road but the South Side Railroad was unaffected. When Gregg's cavalry withdrew from Dinwiddie Court House and the other two Corps returned to their previous positions, the supply wagons again, began rolling up Boydton Plank Road.

As part of the spring offensive, General Grant ordered the Army of the Shenandoah to seize the Dinwiddie Court House area and cut supply routes up Boydton Plank Road. General Sheridan was then to cut the final rail line into Petersburg, the South Side Railroad

On March 29th, the Cavalry of the Army of the Shenandoah departed Hancock Station on the Union Army's military rail line out of City Point. Their route of advance took them east of Twenty-fourth Corps' track, down through Ream's Station, west across Dinwiddie County, to Dinwiddie Court House. By the end of the day, with minimal fighting, Sheridan controlled the Court House area, effectively putting an end to the Confederate supply route along Boydton Plank Road.

March 27-29, 1865 – Army of the Potomac

While Sheridan was moving on Dinwiddie Court House, Fifth Corps of the Army of the Potomac started their advanced down Vaughn Road, turned north on Quaker Road, and were attempting to reach Boydton Plank Road. As Twenty-fourth Corps continued its movement south toward Second Corps' area, the sound of heavy fighting could be heard from the southwest. The lead division of Fifth Corps was engaged with three Rebel brigades in the vicinity of Lewis Farm on Quaker Road. When Fifth Corps succeeded in reinforcing their lead division, they were able to drive the Rebels back to Boydton Plank Road and eventually, to their initial positions on White Oak Road.

Late in the afternoon of the 29th, when the lead elements of Twenty-Fourth Corps began to replace Second Corps' units along Vaughn Road, the lead division of Second Corps started its move toward the right flank of Fifth Corps. By the end of the day, after skirmishing with the Rebels, fighting the weather, and trudging through the mud, Second Corps tied into Fifth Corps along a line that now extended from the vicinity of Boydton Plank Road back along Dabney Mill Road to Armstrong's Mill on Duncan Road.

March 30th 1865 – Army of the James

Dawn on the morning of March 30th saw no relief from the weather. At 6:00 am that morning, as General Gibbon's forces moved up on the line to replace Second Corps, the rain continued to fall and showed no signs of stopping. In spite of the weather, all along the Union battle line hopes were lifted even as the rain fell. Unfortunately, the rain-soaked roads hampered any major movements by Union Army units. With Twenty-fourth Corps now in place between Sixth Corps' positions along Arthur Swamp and the point where Hatcher's Run crossed Vaughn Road, the southern section of the Union battle line now extended from Sixth Corps positions, along Vaughn and Dabney Mill Roads to Boydton Plank Road.

Shortly after noon, Lieutenant Payne called the Brigade sharpshooters together to review the current situation and give us our orders.

"Our present location is along Vaughn Road. Directly to our front is the Rocky Branch and beyond that is Duncan Road," the Lieutenant said. "We are going to send out scouting parties to find ways across the river so the whole Brigade can move up to Duncan Road."

Freeman, Frank, and I were assigned to Sergeant Robbins' team and we were tasked to scout the right front of the Brigade's current position. As we moved along the Rocky Branch, what was normally a meandering creek was now a raging torrent surrounded by swamp. Near the right flank of the Brigade, the river took a marked turn to the northwest with high ground along both sides.

We climbed up the bank to find ourselves looking across Duncan Road at the Rebel fortifications on the other side. The Rebel pickets noticed us as well and we began a spirited exchange of gunfire before Sergeant Robbins ordered us to fall back. In spite of the rain, the river, and the swamps, that afternoon the Brigade sharpshooters succeeded in locating several potential crossing points over the Rocky Branch in addition to the route our patrol uncovered around the right front of the Brigade.

March 30th 1865 – Army of the Shenandoah

As we searched for a route out of the swamp, General Sheridan was moving his Cavalry up Courthouse Road and Crump Road in an effort to seize the South Side Railroad. Cavalry patrols on Crump Road reported a division-sized force moving west on White Oak Road toward Five Forks. The patrols on Courthouse Road became engaged with elements of Major General Fitzhugh Lee's Cavalry Division just short of Five Forks and were forced to fall back.

The day ended with the Rebels holding a line along White Oak Road from Boydton Plank Road out toward Five Forks. The Union Fifth, Second and Twenty-fourth Corps matched the White Oak Road line with the right flank of the Twenty-fourth Corps tied into the Sixth Corps. General Sheridan's cavalry occupied positions on both Crump and Courthouse Roads. Through it all, the rain continued.

Chapter Forty-Four

March 31st 1865 – Army of the James

In the morning, the weather remained overcast with periods of heavy rain followed by periods of steady drizzle. Around 9:30 am, the lead elements of our Regiment crossed the Rocky Branch over some improvised bridges and began moving toward Duncan Road. Our skirmishers quickly became engaged with a Rebel force behind makeshift fortifications in the vicinity of Duncan Road. As more of the Regiment crossed the river, we managed to gain some momentum and, over the course of the next few hours, forced the Rebels back to their defensive positions west of Duncan Road. Skirmishers were sent out again as the rest of the Regiment began preparing our own defensive positions on the north side of the Rocky Branch.

March 31st 1865 – Army of the Potomac

Due to the weather conditions, General Grant called off any offensive operations along the White Oak Road around 7:40 am on the 31st. Unfortunately, the Rebels did not get the message. Instead, General Lee directed Major General Bushrod Johnson's Division to drive against the center of the Fifth Corps. Gaining the element of surprise, General Johnson's Division succeeded in driving part of Fifth Corps back to Gravelly Run. Support from two brigades of Second Corps enabled General Warren to regroup his Corps and drive the enemy back into its White Oak Road emplacements.

March 31st 1865 – Army of the Shenandoah

In a second offensive action, General Lee ordered Major General George Pickett to attack General Sheridan's forces on Crump and Courthouse Roads. While General Pickett's Division did achieve some degree of initial success in driving Sheridan's units back toward Dinwiddie Court House, when the situation along White Oak Road stabilized, General Warren dispatched two brigades toward Crump Road. The appearance of these two brigades posed a direct threat to Pickett's rear and left flank. Under cover of darkness, General Pickett recalled his division back to the area of White Oak Road and Five Forks.

Evening of March 31st/April 1st 1865 – Army of the James

Throughout the night the Rebel units west of Duncan Road conducted a series of probing attacks against our Brigade's positions. The firing was somewhat unnerving, especially for our newest soldiers who were experiencing their first real battle. We heard a flurry of firing from the pickets on one part of the line followed by a lull, and then on another part of the line, a flurry of firing followed by a lull. For my friends and I, the sound of firing to our left and right was disturbing, but in spite of the noise we managed to sleep. Shortly before sunup the situation changed. There was an outburst of gunfire across the Brigade front and the ominous Rebel yell of a charging Confederate attack.

The Rebels were conducting a night attack against our lines. Everyone was now wide awake and set in our hastily constructed defensive works. In the blackness of a moonless night, the Rebels had crept within a short distance of our picket lines without being seen. As they charged and began firing, many of our pickets were overrun. Although I was only involved in a few such attacks, I found night attacks were the worst form of offensive or defensive operations. Confusion reigned supreme as both sides maneuvered and fired. The Brigade began to gain the upper hand and as the Rebels approached our positions we counterattacked, surprising them and driving them back toward Duncan Road.

At first light on April 1st, all of Foster's Division pushed forward, driving the Rebels out of their defenses on Duncan Road and back to their main lines east of Boydton Plank Road. As the Division moved out, a goodly number of Confederate soldiers stepped out of their defensive positions and surrendered. While still possessing arms and ammunition, these men seemed to lack the physical strength to fight. Many were skin and bones from a lack of food and physically incapable of retreating with their comrades.

That morning, the rain finally stopped and at dawn the sun broke through the clouds. We all realized, Union and Confederate alike, dry weather would greatly improve the mobility of the three Union Armies and set the stage for a final push against Petersburg. The rest of the day of April 1st was spent lying behind the earthworks previously occupied by the Rebels. Our skirmishers moved out toward Boydton Plank Road. They didn't get far before becoming engaged with Rebel pickets and skirmishers in the vicinity of the main road. The sun was fully out and the gentle breeze seemed to dry out the area as we watched. It would not be long now before the final battle started.

April 1st 1865 – Army of the Potomac

A couple of days before, the Sixth Corps Commander presented a potential plan to Generals Meade and Grant. The plan called for a massed night attack by Sixth Corps against Confederate positions further up Duncan Road. While the Generals approved the plan, the wet weather hampered any actual implementation. Twice the plan was postponed as the slow going and muddy roads would impede any follow up operations if Sixth Corps managed to breach the Confederate lines. With the weather clearing and the roads drying out, General Grant sensed Sixth Corps' plan might be a foregone conclusion

April 1st 1865 – Army of the Shenandoah

Down at Dinwiddie Court House, General Sheridan was unwilling to wait for the roads to dry. Reports coming in from his cavalry patrols indicated General Pickett's Division held a section of White Oak Road about a mile and a half long. Rebel lines extended from just west of Five Forks down White Oak Road toward the main Confederate positions a mile or so further up the road. Both ends of Pickett's position were marked by a ninety degree turn to the north creating an angle on the flank of the line designed to thwart an envelopment or attempts to attack the Division's rear area.

Based on these reports, General Sheridan recognized that Pickett's Division was isolated from the White Oak Road defenses and the rest of the Army of Northern Virginia. In Sheridan's mind, now was the time for action as only one Confederate division stood between the Army of the Shenandoah and the South Side Railroad. Orders were sent out for Brigadier General George Custer to move his Division up Scotts Road to the west of Five Forks and attack the right flank of the Confederate line. Brigadier General Thomas Devlin's Division would hold the center of the Union battle line from Scotts Road across Courthouse Road toward White Oak Road. Two divisions of Fifth Corps would attack the left flank of Pickett's Division at the angle. These divisions would swing out to White Oak Road and roll up the left flank while driving for the Rebel rear area.

The sloppy conditions created by the weather of the last few days slowed Fifth Corps' movement so it was after 4:00 pm before their divisions were in position. As Fifth Corps attacked the left flank of Pickett's Army, Custer's Division turned Major General Fitzhugh Lee's cavalry on the right flank. The battle was short-lived. At 5:45 pm General Lee ordered Pickett to withdraw to Petersburg along the South Side rail line. The Army of the Shenandoah's victory at Five Forks effectively sealed off all supply routes for General Lee's Army and started both sides moving toward what would be the beginning of the end.

April 1, 1865 – General Grant's Headquarters

In the afternoon, General Grant established his headquarters at the former site of Dabney's steam driven sawmill. With the weather improving and the roads drying out, Grant believed this to be the location to best direct the coming operations. About 7:30 pm, as Grant's staff assembled around the campfire after the evening meal, Colonel Porter, who the General had dispatched to General Sheridan as a headquarters liaison, arrived with the news of the victory at Five Forks. As the jubilant staff reacted to the news, the ever stoic General asked the excited Colonel a series of questions about the battle.

Grant listened quietly to the retelling of the battle and the assessment of casualties on both sides. Initial estimates indicated Pickett's Division suffered about six hundred killed and wounded and another twenty-four hundred prisoners. The Army of the Shenandoah suffered eight hundred and thirty killed or wounded. Reports reaching General Sheridan also indicated that Pickett and Fitzhugh Lee were able to regroup further up the South Side Railroad at Sunderland Station.

General Grant was in receipt of similar reports indicating units from Anderson's Corps around the Burgess Mill area of Boydton Plank Road were moving west presumably to join Pickett at Sunderland Station. After questioning the Colonel, Grant retired to his tent with no comment. Ten minutes later, the General emerged and passed a series of dispatches to his orderly.

"Gentlemen," the General said quietly. "I have ordered a general assault along the lines. I have sent General Meade a telegram approving the night attack proposed by Sixth Corps for 4:00 am tomorrow. Ninth Corps will begin to move their pickets and sharpshooters forward as soon as possible tonight and evaluate whether General Lee intends to pull all of his forces from Petersburg. If Lee is retiring, Sixth Corps and Ninth Corps are to pursue."

"We will commence operations this evening with an artillery barrage all along the front. The artillery will conduct a three-hour bombardment of Confederate positions starting about 10:00 pm. My main concern this evening is to prevent General Lee from mustering sufficient forces in order to overwhelm Sheridan's troops. The Army of the Shenandoah is presently isolated and vulnerable to an attack by Confederate forces massing at Sunderland Station."

Evening of April 1st/2nd 1865 – Army of the James

As the orders for the morning's action were being disseminated, the Eleventh Maine Regiment occupied defensive positions along Duncan Road. For the past two days the Regiment sparred with the Rebels in the worst of conditions. Today, the sun came out, the skies cleared, and the roads began to dry out. The evening air was also warm and dry, a far cry from the past few nights. Around 10:00 pm, we were rudely awakened by the sound of artillery firing from the forts to our northeast. Shaking off sleep, I realized this artillery firing wasn't just from the forts but even from the batteries operating with Second and Fifth Corps to our west. Shortly after the firing started, Sergeant Robbins appeared with our orders for the morning.

"The artillery firing is the beginning of what we hope will be a push to Petersburg tomorrow," the Sergeant said. "Sheridan licked the Rebs at a place called Five Forks, so we now own the South Side Railroad. Tomorrow at first light the whole Corps is going to move forward to the area of Boydton Plank Road near Burgess Mill and wait for further instructions."

"How much longer will the artillery keep firing?" Freeman asked.

"Word has it, about three hours," Robbins replied.

For three solid hours the ground shook and the night were filled with shots flying through the air and delivering their deadly cargo on the Rebel defenses. While the Rebel artillery offered some counterbattery fire, it was predominately a Union artillery show. For us, it was like watching a meteor shower in the middle of an earthquake for three hours.

"I pity the poor boys that are under that fire," Frank said.

"Yeah," I replied. "Being in that nightmare certainly represents another level of this hell on earth."

As the artillery barrage roared in the night, we also noted some extensive movement in the Sixth Corps area to our right. With the guns blazing and Sixth Corps moving, it was difficult to get any sleep that night. At 1:00 am, as predicted, the guns fell silent.

Suddenly, around 4:30 am, we awoke to a tremendous fight from the vicinity of Sixth Corps area. The sounds of the fighting from that sector were intense. Shortly after the sounds of that battle started, we were rousted from our sleep and told to prepare to move out.

About 6:00 am, our division and one Brigade from Turner's Independent Division moved out toward the sound of the fighting. Word was passed that the three divisions of Sixth Corps massed their forces and attacked Rebel positions further up Duncan Road. Their lead elements were successful in breaking through the Rebel defenses and were now inside the Confederate lines.

April 2nd 1865 – Petersburg, Virginia

About the time Sixth Corps reached Boydton Plank Road, we were busy trying to navigate the swampy ground to reach the Confederate works east of Boydton Plank Road. That Confederate line stretched southward from the breakthrough parallel to Duncan Road about halfway between Duncan and Boydton Plank Roads.

While Sixth Corps was exploiting their breakthrough of the Confederate line, Twenty-fourth Corps was further south and pushing against the Rebel works from the east. Second Corps was also driving north from their positions against the end of the White Oak Road line. When we arrived at the Burgess Mill area, Twenty-fourth Corps established hasty defenses and awaited developments. As the morning wore on, the sound of fighting to our north grew louder and increased in intensity.

The Brigade sharpshooters were located in front of our defensive positions with the skirmishers as the Rebels who occupied the defensive works began firing on us. Realizing there was a heavy Union presence to their south as well as Sixth Corps pushing down from the north, the Rebels either turned and started fleeing west or laid down their arms and surrendered.

"There are troops moving down on us from the north," a soldier of the sharpshooters called out a short time later.

In the distance we could make out the gleam of bayonets in the sunlight as a large force moved south toward our position.

"Don't shoot!" Lieutenant Payne shouted and the word quickly spread. "That's Sixth Corps."

By 9:00 am, Sixth Corps and Twenty-fourth Corps were in control of over four miles of the Confederate works from Hatcher's Run north to a position near Church Road, north of the breakthrough point. As the last of the Rebel resistance to our front ended, we linked up with Sixth Corps. We got a breather as the Generals conversed. Our blood was up as we all felt the end of the siege was at hand. It was time to go.

A short time later, Twenty-fourth Corps began moving up the east side of Boydton Plank Road while the three divisions of the Sixth Corps moved up the west side. One brigade of Sixth Corps remained at the breakthrough site, sealing off the penetration to the north. The other two Brigades of Turner's Independent Division were moving up Duncan Road toward their position to assist these efforts.

Shortly before noon, we pushed past the breakthrough point, past the Duncan Road intersection, and halted at the intersection of Boydton Plank Road, which tailed off to the east, and Long Ordinary Road, which headed northeast. Ahead we could see two Confederate Forts, Gregg on the right and Whitworth on the left. While small in size, these two Forts guarded the final approaches to Petersburg. To the right of Fort Gregg, remnants of Rebel infantry were setting up hasty defenses along Boydton Plank Road.

When the order was passed to form a line of battle, two Brigades of Foster's Division deployed on a low ridgeline about eight hundred yards from Fort Gregg. Osborn's First Brigade established their line on the right of Boydton Plank Road just down from Church Road.

Dandy's Third Brigade formed on the left of Osborn with Tenth Connecticut and One Hundredth New York on line. Fairchild's Fourth Brigade formed a second, reserve line behind Dandy and Osborn.

On the other side of the field, Colonel Thomas Harris' Third Brigade of the Independent Division formed in line opposite Fort Whitworth. Colonel Dandy detached Eleventh Maine to support Harris. Lieutenant Colonel Andrew Potter's First Brigade and Colonel William Curtis' Second Brigade, both of the Independent Division, formed in the space between the two forts and behind the forward line.

About 1:00 pm, General Gibbon issued the attack order to General Foster. The two lead Brigades, Osborn's and Dandy's, began to move against Fort Gregg.

As part of the Brigade sharpshooters, my friends and I watched our comrades from Eleventh Maine move away toward Fort Whitworth. The sharpshooters were assigned to support the two regiments in the assault of Fort Gregg. As the regiments moved, shot and canister from the fort began to wrack our Brigade and Osborn's. As the two lead Brigades moved forward under the deadly fire, Potter's Brigade moved into position behind our Brigade.

After moving across a natural glacis in front of the Fort, the lead regiments encountered the fourteen-foot moat in front of the parapet. Sliding down into the muck filled moat, soldiers from six regiments began clawing their way up the side of the parapet, all the while under tremendous Rebel fire.

The loopholes in the walls of the Fort and the log top of the parapet made it difficult to select targets. Even the artillery pieces were positioned so as to prevent clear shots from the sharpshooters. Around the Fort, Union soldiers were scaling the parapet. Others were moving around the moat to an unfinished trench line on the northeast corner that ran out toward Fort Whitworth. A third group was attacking the fortified sally port in the rear of the Fort. By my calculation, Union forces outnumbered the Rebels in Fort Gregg by about twenty or thirty to one. In spite of these overwhelming odds, the Rebels refused to surrender and kept up a murderous volume of fire. Their actions reminded me of Leonidas and his brave Spartans at "Hell's Gate", an apt description for Fort Gregg.

With the regiments of three brigades already in the moat, two more regiments from Fairchild's Brigade started to move forward.

As they moved, Lieutenant Payne assembled a few of the sharpshooters on the northeast corner of the Fort and we began moving into the unfinished trench line. Following some of the soldiers from the One Hundredth New York, the Lieutenant charged across a narrow foot bridge and up the side of the parapet. As he reached the top of the parapet, the Lieutenant swung his cavalry saber like a wild man before a Rebel minie ball dropped him.

As we moved to follow the Lieutenant, Union soldiers were scrambling over the parapet on three sides of the Fort like angry ants attacking a pile of sugar. Regimental flags billowed in the wind atop the parapet as the soldiers fought their way into the Fort. Still the Rebs refused to surrender.

As I crossed the narrow footbridge and climbed to the top of the parapet, I could see the Lieutenant lying on the banquette tread writhing in pain from a leg wound. From my position on the parapet wall, I could see the inside of the Fort was awash with pools of blood. Union wounded and dead fell from the parapet onto piles of Confederate wounded and dead in the courtyard.

I jumped down to the banquette tread and found a spot on the wall where I could support the soldiers breaching the parapet and fighting their way into the Fort. I started firing at a group of artillerymen who were loading a cannon in the center of the Fort. As I fired my second shot, my lower left leg gave way as if hit by a sledge. I fell onto the tread in excruciating pain.

Looking down, I could see blood flowing freely and bone protruding from the wound. As the curtain started to fall on the assault of Fort Gregg and the siege of Petersburg, I gasped from pain as shock set in. Determined not to scream, I gave way to the curtain of blackness that sought to encompass me. Mercifully, as the pain intensified, I fell into blessed unconsciousness.

Survival and Salvation

"I cannot be awake for nothing looks to me as it did before, or else I am awake for the first time, and all before has been a mean sleep"

Walt Whitman

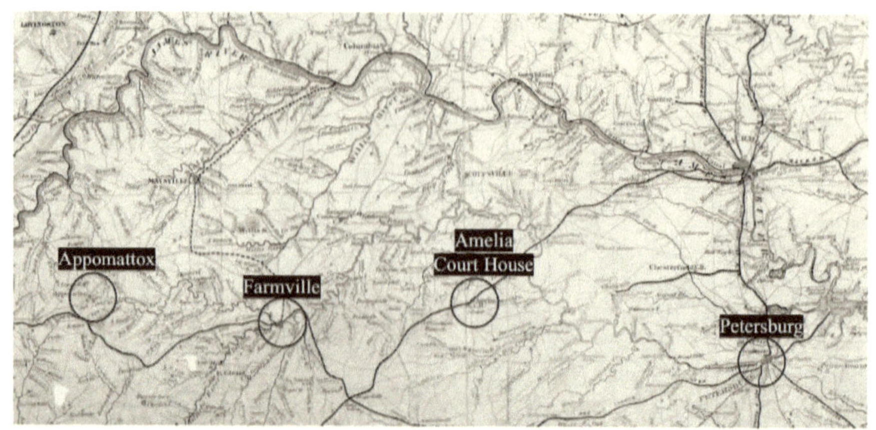

The Final Days – April 1865

Chapter Forty-Five

April 2, 1865 – Petersburg, Virginia

As I was about to find out, the quality of medical care in the Union Army had improved greatly in the four years since the onset of hostilities. After Fort Sumter, no one in the Army in general, or Army medicine in particular, was prepared for the scale and intensity of wartime casualties. Army medicine was not even prepared for the influx of the seventy-five thousand men who answered President Lincoln's call for volunteers. At the highest levels of the Medical Department, no one saw any need to provide more than a reasonable number of medical services for a conflict that would not last more than a couple of months.

As a result of the Medical Department's shortsightedness, when volunteers began to arrive, the Army was forced to rely on the individual states to weed out those unfit for military service. While some states, like Maine, did a fair job in the initial physical examination process, other states did not. There were more than a few stories around the campfire of this regiment or that regiment about women who actually passed the initial physical and were serving in the ranks.

By July of 1861, the house of cards that was Army medicine came crashing down. The sheer number of casualties on both sides at Manassas simply overwhelmed inexperienced doctors and their wholly undermanned staffs. The contracted ambulance services, driven by civilians, led the retreat from Centerville, empty of any of the critically wounded that lined the battlefield. The general retreat of the Army of Northeast Virginia left in its wake hundreds of critically wounded men. Those doctors who did remain on the battlefield and chose to attend the wounded found themselves taken prisoner, separated from those who needed their services the most, and sent off to prison camps in Richmond.

Before the medical travesty of Manassas, the government did make a modest gesture to those calling for medical reform in the military. In June of 1861, a reluctant President Lincoln signed the order to create the United States Sanitary Commission. This new organization patterned many of its reform-oriented activities after the highly successful British Sanitary Commission and their activities in the Crimean War. While not in favor with many in the medical field, including Surgeon General Clement A. Finley, the Commission assumed responsibility for reforms needed to improve the quality of life for the individual soldier and the quality of medical response and care for the Army.

I definitely remember those early days of camp life in the Third Maine Regiment. Little, if any, concern was given to the sanitary conditions of the camps or the food and water the soldiers were forced to consume. Drinking tainted water from local sources or downriver from latrine sites was commonplace and felled more soldiers than Confederate bullets. As I recollect, the Regiment was down over forty percent of its total strength as we marched from Centerville to Manassas that hot July day. Not a single one of those casualties was from encounters with the Rebels.

April of 1862 saw the first of many positive changes to Army medicine and the care and welfare of Union soldiers. Surgeon General Finley, a veteran of the War of 1812, was retired and in his place, Congress named Doctor William Hammond. After serving as a surgeon in the Indian Wars, Hammond's papers and articles on military medicine and the time he spent in Europe studying their military medical systems and hospitals further bolstered his reputation. Although he left the Army for a short stay as a professor of medicine at the University of Maryland, Doctor Hammond answered the call at the outbreak of the war.

Recommended by Major General George McClellan, Hammond was nominated by the Sanitary Commission as Surgeon General. The new Surgeon General immediately began a series of sweeping changes and reforms to the Army's medical system. These new initiatives included improving patient administration, redesigning and redefining the structure of field medicine, and constructing permanent military hospitals.

By the time of my return to the Army and assignment to the Eleventh Maine Regiment, many of Surgeon General Hammond's reforms had taken hold and the physical welfare of the individual soldier improved greatly. As seen in the Eleventh Maine's winter camp across the James, the overall cleanliness of the camp was markedly better. Latrines were dug the proper distance from the sites of drinking water. Any water taken from local streams or ponds was boiled before soldiers were allowed to drink it. There was also an increased emphasis on the personal hygiene of the individual soldier. We were expected to groom ourselves regularly, change our bedding periodically, and generally keep our shelters clean.

Another of Surgeon General Hammond's initiatives was the introduction of professionally trained cooks for the field messes. We not only ate food that tasted better, our diets were supplemented by the distribution of fruits, vegetables, and fresh meat.

These reforms also impacted the constant harassment by the lice, mosquitos, and flies that plagued the individual soldier. The new initiatives dramatically reduced the numbers of soldiers lost to insect related maladies and other diseases not associated with combat related wounds. Now, lying in the blood and the mud of Fort Gregg, I was about to experience some of the other reforms to Army medicine.

In one of my more lucid moments after being shot, I noticed the fighting inside the Fort had stopped and soldiers from the various regiments began rounding up Confederate prisoners and tending to the wounded. Now that the battle was over, Freeman found me and stayed with Lieutenant Payne and I until the medical orderlies prepared us for evacuation.

At Manassas, the individual regiments assumed responsibility for the wounded of their respective units. Care varied depending on the expertise and experience of the regimental medical staff. During the Peninsula Campaign of 1862, this old organizational structure displayed many of its inherent shortfalls. This included care for the thousands of sick and wounded that routinely bogged down the Army of the Potomac. For those in need of treatment, the system proved unable to reach many soldiers who were wounded on the battlefield. In some cases, this delay in transportation was up to a full week after a battle ended. Even those who could reach help found there was a severe shortage of medicine. Surgeon General Hammond sought to reform this system and appointed a like-minded thinker, Doctor Jonathan Letterman, as the medical officer for the Army of the Potomac.

Doctor Letterman drew on his experiences and those of General Grant's medical officer, Doctor John Brinton, to redesign and restructure medical support for the Army of the Potomac. The individual regimental field hospitals were consolidated into a single field hospital at the division level. The doctors and medical personnel at the division field hospital were drawn from the regiments based on ability and not on rank. Immediate aid would remain with the regimental medical teams but major surgeries would now be conducted at the division field hospital.

Transportation to these division field hospitals was also reorganized. The responsibility for transport of the wounded fell to the newly created ambulance corps. All of the ambulances from all of the subordinate commands were now organized at a central location or depot controlled by military officers and consisting of military medical personnel. Many of these medical personnel included regimental band members who assumed these duties during and after battle. By 1864, each Army corps with more than two divisions was authorized one ambulance corps. These ambulance corps normally provided a portion of their ambulances to the individual divisions. At the division level, the ambulances could be kept under division control in the division trains or sent out to the brigades and regiments. Regardless of the organization, the vehicles and their associated medical personnel could be quickly reorganized and sent to the area of the battlefield with the greatest need.

When the medical orderlies arrived, I was loaded onto a litter and readied for movement to a waiting ambulance. In spite of their concern for my comfort, the lift onto the litter was more pain than I could bear. I was handed down off the Fort's banquette tread and, once on the ground, the medical orderlies prepared to move me to the ambulance. As we moved, I noticed this medical duo did their version of the litter dance; a technique designed to keep the patient from bouncing around and the litter somewhat level. The lead man would step off with his left foot while the rear man stepped off with his right. In all my time in the Army, this was the only time I can remember where being out of step was the preferred method of movement.

At the forward medical area, a doctor examined my wound and ordered me to be loaded into a waiting ambulance. The ambulance was a modified horse driven wagon with a canvas covering to keep out the weather. Inside, there were seats for six wounded soldiers or the seats could be folded down to accommodate four litter patients. I joined three other soldiers in the back and the driver began moving toward the Division field hospital.

Although the ambulance was fitted with springs on the axles to absorb some of the shock, the trip from the front to the field hospital was a painful experience. Boydton Plank Road was drying out from the recent rains but the movement of heavy wagons and artillery pieces tore up the muddy roadway.

My three travelling companions and I moaned and groaned as the ambulance drove up the rut filled road. The soldier next to me was from the Tenth Connecticut. He was critically wounded in the fighting at the moat in front of the Fort. As the ambulance moved on, he gasped for air and frothy red bubbles began to appear around his mouth. His eyes wide open and his breathing labored, as we approached the hospital, he gave up his fight and went peacefully to his God.

The field hospital was located about a mile back up Boydton Plank Road near the site of Sixth Corps' breakthrough. There was a plantation home there that was taken over by the Division medical personnel. Several large tents were being erected on the grounds to serve as hospital wards. Several other large tents were used as surgeries for incoming patients.

Another team of medical personnel, led by a doctor, met the incoming ambulance. I was evaluated and moved to one of the surgical tents. My comrade from the Tenth Connecticut was quietly and reverently taken away. Many of the soldiers, myself included, did not want to die on the battlefield as a nameless, unknown soldier. For this reason, I carried a piece of cloth pinned to the inside of my coat that contained my name, unit, and next of kin back in Maine. Other soldiers purchased pins or identification bracelets with similar information inscribed. While it wasn't a guarantee that we would be identified or our next of kin notified, it did provide many with some peace of mind.

Inside the surgical tent I saw three teams of doctors working. Still on the litter, I was placed on a table and one of the doctors recorded my information. I recognized one of the doctors as our Regimental Surgeon, Doctor Richard Cook from Bangor.

"Always glad to see a fellow Eleventh Maine man," the doctor said. "Let's see what we are dealing with."

Doctor Cook carefully cut away my bootie and then my trousers above the knee. Another doctor cleaned away some of the mud and dried blood in order for Doctor Cook to make a better evaluation.

"You have a serious lower leg wound," Doctor Cook said. "One of your lower leg bones was shattered by the bullet. I'm afraid we are going to have to remove your leg below the knee."

"Please do a good job, Sir," I responded.

"I always try to do my best for a Maine man," the Doctor replied.

He smiled and patted me on the shoulder as he nodded to the other doctor. The second doctor held a cloth covered cone over my nose and mouth and began pouring some liquid into the cone. As the medicine took effect, I got a bit agitated and tried to sit up on the litter. Two medical orderlies held me down as the doctor continued to hold the cone near my face. Slowly, I began to relax and felt my body go limp. As the doctor spoke to me quietly, I felt my whole body become completely unresponsive. Finally, the blackness closed in and I fell into a blissful state of pain-free unconsciousness.

Chapter Forty-Six

April 1865 – Petersburg, Virginia

T he peace and serenity of the blackness that surrounded me started to slip away as light began invading my dreams. As I awoke, the medical orderlies were putting me into a bed in one of the tents set up as a recovery ward. My head ached, I felt nauseous, and my mouth was dry. I dared not take any water for fear of vomiting. I still wore parts of a muddy uniform, although the trousers and long underwear were cut off above the left knee. The uniform jacket, cap, and the equipment I was carrying were placed on the floor beneath the bed. My rifle was gone.

The area below my left knee was covered with bloody bandages that wrapped over the knee and onto my thigh. That part of my leg covered by the bandages ached something awful, but this pain was much different than before the surgery. Below the bandage was nothing. My lower leg and left foot just were simply not there anymore and that was a bit alarming.

Later, I found out that headaches and nausea were common side effects of chloroform used as an anesthetic during surgery. Chloroform was developed in 1831 by an American chemist, Doctor Samuel Guthrie. Doctor Guthrie combined whiskey with chlorinated lime in an effort to create a more effective pesticide. In 1847, a noted London surgeon, Sir James Young-Simpson recognized the value of chloroform as an anesthetic during surgery. As a result of this and other medical advancements, chloroform became the anesthetic of choice for British Army doctors who used it with great success during the Crimean War. After its introduction in America in 1849, chloroform was quickly adopted by the Army Medical Department and became the principal anesthetic for all field hospitals.

At the time, a second choice of anesthesia was ether. In 1846, Doctor Crawford Williamson of Georgia performed the first surgery using ether as the anesthesia. By 1865 however, chloroform proved to be more effective and efficient than ether and less flammable, making it the anesthesia of choice for most doctors in field hospitals where time was of the essence. Ether, on the other hand, was used more frequently in general hospitals where surgeons had the necessary time and when the surgery was less demanding. Although ether was slower to act than chloroform and had a very unique smell, it did not have the aftereffects of nausea, vomiting, and headaches common to chloroform.

By this point in the war, the amputation of my leg was a relatively straightforward procedure and over in a matter of minutes. Since the majority of wounds on the battlefield involved limbs, Army surgeons were forced by sheer repetition to become extremely proficient at performing amputations. The nature and size of Civil War bullet wounds often involved compound fractures of bones, fractures of limb joints, or lacerations of major peripheral blood vessels that could not be repaired surgically. All of these scenarios dictated immediate amputation of the affected limb. Any wound left exposed for twenty-four hours was sure to become inflected, a certain death sentence for the injured soldier.

For a soldier requiring a limb amputation, there were two methods of removing the damaged appendage: a circular amputation or a flap amputation. A circular amputation severed the limb perpendicular to the main axis of the bone. This type of surgery took the doctor more time and the recovery time for a patient was often longer than for a flap amputation.

In 1837, another noted British surgeon, Doctor Robert Liston, developed the flap amputation as an alternative to the traditional circular amputation. By 1865, for most limb amputations, Army doctors preferred the flap type amputation. In my case, since the wound was located on the lower leg, a single flap method was employed. After cleaning the amputation site and shaving any hair, a tourniquet was place on the leg compressing the major arteries against the leg bones. With the tourniquet in place, the surgeon performed an oblique incision severing the skin and muscles down to the bone. The cut took on an oval shape and the surgery was often called an oval amputation. After the initial cut, a second doctor retracted the skin and muscle as the surgeon used a bone saw to cut the two bones of the lower leg leaving the lower portion of the initial cut to serve as a flap to cover the wound.

With my lower leg and foot cut away, the surgeon turned his attention to tying off the blood vessels and bringing the flap of skin up and over the sawn bone. The flap was then stitched in place with stitches wide enough apart to allow for drainage of any materials from the surgery or any postoperative infection. Finally, the site was secured with adhesive strips and bandages that were changed regularly until the limb healed.

In addition to being faster to perform, the single flap amputation allowed for a thick padded surface to rest against the newly severed bones. This was important when it came time for fitting and wearing of prosthetics devices. The single flap amputation was also a less agonizing approach for the patient when it came to managing postoperative pain.

As I lay in the recovery tent, one of the doctors came by and gave me a shot for pain. The use of opiates for pain management was commonplace in the war and, while I welcomed the relief, I was keenly aware of the addictive property of the drug. For the Civil War doctor, opium came in several forms. There was the opium pill, easy to swallow and gave relief, although it took a while to enter the blood stream. There was laudanum, a mixture of opium and alcohol available almost anywhere for almost any aliment you may have. Additionally, there was a relatively new medical innovation that involved injecting an opium derivative called morphine directly into the veins using a device called a hypodermic syringe.

Ancient Greek and Roman physicians used syringes of various forms for various medical purposes but not the injection of medicine directly into the patient's veins or under the skin. It wasn't until 1844 when Francis Rynd invented a hollow needle and made the first subcutaneous injection of a drug. In 1853, Charles Pravez and Alexander Wood, both working independently, developed medical syringes with fine needles for piercing of a patient's skin. Pravez's syringe was made of silver and used a screw mechanism to dispense the medicine. Similar in design, Wood's syringe was made of glass so the contents could be seen and measured. The medicine was then dispensed by use of a plunger that moved the liquid medicine up the needle and into the patient.

I remember my days in Mr. Hartwell's apothecary. Scarcely a single doctor who came in for liquid opium or morphine was without a hypodermic syringe or two in his bag. When dispensing any opiates, Mr. Hartwell was careful to issue a warning about the addictive properties of the drug to the customer. Unfortunately, Civil War doctors were not as diligent as Mr. Hartwell about their opiate addiction warnings. I often heard stories of soldiers during and after the war that became dependent on the drug long after the reason for the opiate was healed.

As I lay in my bed, the war still raged around me. Fortunately, most of the news reaching the recovery tent was favorable. The Army of Northern Virginia had suffered significant losses both in manpower and territory. A short distance from the hospital, members of the Sixth Corps killed one of General Lee's most trusted corps commanders, Lieutenant General Ambrose P. Hill, shortly after the initial breakthrough. Later in the day along the South Side Railroad, a division from Second Corps under the command of Brigadier General Nelson Miles routed the beleaguered forces of General Fitzhugh Lee and Major General Henry Heth at Sunderland Station.

Shortly after the breakthrough, General Lee telegraphed President Jefferson Davis to apprise him of the situation and advise the President to move the government out of Richmond. By 8:00 pm that Sunday evening the situation deteriorated to a point where General Lee notified his commanders to begin an immediate withdrawal from the Richmond and Petersburg battle lines. All Confederate units would then rendezvous at Amelia Court House. General Lee's intentions were to move what was left of the Army of Northern Virginia towards Danville with the hope they could eventually link up with General Johnston's Army of Tennessee in North Carolina.

North of the James, Lieutenant General Ewell and Lieutenant General James Longstreet began pulling Confederate forces off the Interior Line, Drewry's Bluff, and the Howlett Line. South of the river, Major General Gordon's forces on the eastern side of Petersburg and Lieutenant General Richard Anderson's on the south and west side were also on the move. As the sunset on the evening of April 3, 1865, Petersburg and the Confederate Capitol of Richmond were in Union Hands.

Chapter Forty-Seven

For almost two weeks, the President of the United States absented himself from his regular duties in Washington and remained at City Point. His original itinerary called for a sea voyage to Virginia and time to discuss strategy with General Grant and General Sherman before returning to the White House. When the President met with his Generals, the mood of the session was very positive. The weather was starting to clear and the final push was only days away. Following these strategy sessions, Lincoln chose to remain in Virginia for what was hoped to be the final operation against Petersburg and Richmond.

On April 1st, the President sent Mrs. Lincoln and Secretary of State William Seward back to Washington. With their Navy ship underway, Lincoln returned to the sidewheel steamer, the River Queen. The rest of the day was spent at Grant's City Point headquarters awaiting news of the battle. Late in the evening, he was notified by General Grant of Sheridan's victory at Five Forks and Grant's intentions for a general attack on the morning of April 2nd.

As Sixth Corps began their night attack, President Lincoln paced the deck of the River Queen, pausing occasionally to look into the darkness for a sign. As Dandy's Brigade assaulted Fort Gregg, the President moved from the River Queen to Admiral David Porter's flagship, the USS Malvern to await news of the day's battles. Later that evening, as General Lee was withdrawing the Army of Northern Virginia, President Lincoln received news from General Grant that Petersburg had fallen and Union forces had captured over twelve hundred Confederate prisoners.

As I lay in the recovery ward of the field hospital, the President was traveling from City Point to a modest home on Market Street in downtown Petersburg. The purpose of his visit was to meet with General Grant and discuss Grant's plans for the next phase of the operation. Both men were anxiously awaiting news from Union forces north of the James about the fate of Richmond. When no word arrived, General Grant returned to his field headquarters and the President returned to City Point. Shortly after his arrival back on the Malvern, a message reached him from General Weitzel of the Twenty-fifth Corps stating that those elements of the Army of the James remaining north of the river now occupied Richmond.

The following morning, April 4th, as the President prepared to travel up the James to the Confederate Capitol, those of us in the recovery tent received a visit from Doctor Cook.

"The Division is preparing to move against the remnants of the Army of Northern Virginia," the Doctor said. "Unfortunately, the hospital must follow the Division. We will be moving some of you to the hospital at City Point. Others will be transported back to hospitals in the Washington area."

Those in the tent with the ability to recover from their wounds and return to the Division and the more critically wounded would remain to convalesce at City Point. All of the recovering amputees were designated to travel to a general hospital in Washington.

My comrades and I were loaded into ambulances for the eight mile ride from the hospital to the Patrick rail station. As we moved out, President Lincoln was being rowed ashore in downtown Richmond. When word of the Confederate Government's evacuation of Richmond spread, a small fire was set to destroy some warehouses before Union troops arrived. Left unattended, the fire raged out of control and by the time the President arrived, a three-quarter mile section of the City between Main Street and the river had burned.

The ambulance ride to the rail station was brutal. In spite of the medication we received before departing, the bumping and jostling along the heavily rutted roads only served to exacerbate the agony. As we arrived at the station, the President was being hailed as the great emancipator by a group of black laborers in downtown Richmond.

After his greeting at the waterfront, Lincoln began the walk to President Davis' residence for a meeting with General Weitzel. As Lincoln moved along the two mile route to the Presidential Mansion, curious Richmonders watched from windows and porches. As the President walked the streets of Richmond, the medical orderlies began transferring the wounded onto the hospital cars for the ride to City Point.

Railroads were a common means of transportation for wounded soldiers moving from field hospitals to general hospitals. Early in the war, this meant the wounded soldiers were loaded onto contracted trains. Packed into boxcars strewn with filthy hay or straw, these soldiers often endured a one hundred plus mile ride to the closest general hospital. In 1862, when the Federal Government authorized a military takeover of all Northern rail lines, the Sanitary Commission was quick to insist on better accommodations for wounded soldiers. Doctor Elisha Harris and his team began converting sleeping cars into fully functional hospital cars, in many cases, complete with medical personnel.

Wounded soldiers were brought onboard on stretchers fitted with rubber rings on each handle. These rings were then hung from hooks on the support beams creating a three-tiered bed system or a four-tiered bed system if a stretcher was laid on the floor beneath the lowest bed. Each of the fifty foot hospital cars was capable of carrying thirty-six wounded soldiers comfortably, forty-eight, if the floor space was used and the trip was short.

Our train was equipped with three such hospital cars and, once loaded, began moving toward City Point. As the train chugged along, President Lincoln toured Jefferson Davis' home before conversing with General Weitzel. He then met with the Confederate Assistant Secretary of War, John Campbell. As part of their discussion, Lincoln offered to allow the Virginia House of Delegates to reconvene. This offer carried with it a significant stipulation: the legislature must repeal its decision to secede and recall all Virginia troops from the fighting.

After his meeting at Jefferson Davis' mansion, Lincoln took a coach ride around the city before returning to the wharf for the voyage back to City Point. As the President was being rowed back to the Malvern, our hospital train arrived at the docks at City Point. Tied to the pier was the Hospital Ship J. K. Barnes.

Early in the war, the Army relied primarily on contracted shipping to deliver supplies and evacuate wounded from the battlefield to general hospitals. Unfortunately, these coastal freighters were better equipped to handle cargo than evacuate wounded soldiers. The lack of concern for the cleanliness of these vessels often resulted in wounded passengers developing infections needing more surgery or worse. In early 1862, the Sanitary Commission received a rusted out hull that was refurbished as the Hospital Ship Daniel Webster.

Although hospital ships were used routinely out West along the Mississippi River, the Daniel Webster became the first of its kind to operate along the East Coast. By 1865, fourteen such ships, including the J. K. Barnes, worked along the Atlantic Coast ferrying wounded to and from general hospitals.

The J. K. Barnes was named for the current Surgeon General, Doctor Joseph Barnes. In May of 1863, Surgeon General Hammond's banning of certain mercury-based drugs for front line hospitals met with displeasure by many doctors and other enemies of both Hammond and the Sanitary Commission. Counted among Hammond's legion of enemies was Secretary of War Edwin Stanton. By the summer of 1863, Hammond was gone and, in his place, Stanton appointed Joseph Barnes.

From initial appearances, the J. K. Barnes looked like an average two hundred twenty-three foot, steam driven, paddlewheel freighter. That is where the similarity ended. In addition to the normal ships' spaces such as the bridge, engine room, and crew quarters, the largest part of the ship was dedicated to the five hospital wards capable of carrying four hundred and forty-nine wounded soldiers. Inside the individual wards there were a series of three-tiered beds securely fastened to the ship's bulkheads. Each ward was ventilated by a series of skylights eliminating the dank, musty smell so common to other ships' lower decks.

As the afternoon came to a close, the USS Malvern reappeared from the James River and tied up to the quay. As President Lincoln stepped off the Malvern, he waved at those of us awaiting loading onto the J. K. Barnes. The President then disappeared in the direction of General Grant's headquarters. With the last of the wounded aboard, the Barnes began moving away from the pier at City Point, steering a course to the southeast for Fortress Monroe and the Chesapeake Bay.

Almost seven months after I raised my hand and agreed to support and defend our country, I was once again leaving the war. My first evening aboard the J. K. Barnes was one of mixed emotions. There was a sense of anger at the loss of my leg. In spite of the promise of rehabilitation and a prosthetic device, I still raged every time I looked at what was a whole leg only two days before. Between these bouts of anger were periods of relief that I was actually leaving the war behind. There were also periods of pure frustration at leaving my friends and comrades behind. I enlisted in this war at the beginning, reenlisted to remain to the finish, but I failed to see the final outcome of this soldier's hell.

Finally, there was the remorse that is so common to any soldier with half a soul. I saw men die. I was responsible for many on the other side losing their lives, most all of them, men just like me, fighting for what they believed, and the freedom to live and die as they wanted. When these periods of remorse blossomed, I often thought back to that fifteen year old Alabama soldier who went to meet his God with dignity and grace believing what he was doing was just. I hoped to meet him again in another life.

Finally, with all these emotions spent, I listened to the ships' heartbeat. The noises coming from the engine room beat a soothing rhythm in harmony with the paddlewheel slapping at the dark waters of the James River. For me, this chapter of hell on earth was over. I have survived. All that is left is to find the acceptance that comes from the reminiscences of old men.

Chapter Forty-Eight

April 1865 – Washington D.C.

A s the Hospital Ship J. K. Barnes made its way down the James to the Chesapeake Bay and the Potomac River, the battle continued to bring the war to a successful conclusion. Richmond was ours, as was Petersburg. The only remaining objective of three Union Armies became General Robert E. Lee and the Army of Northern Virginia.

When Lee's Army pulled out of Petersburg and Richmond, the retreating Confederates set off a series of cavalry engagements and rearguard actions all along the line. The Union cavalry attempted to track the Confederate movement while the Confederate cavalry attempted to mask their movements.

By the morning of April 3rd, The Army of the Potomac's Second, Fifth, and Sixth Corps, as well as General Sheridan's Cavalry, were in pursuit of the Confederate Army. During that day, General Fitzhugh Lee fought a rear guard action against elements of Sheridan's Cavalry at Namozine Church. This effort netted the Union three hundred and fifty new prisoners. On April 4th, as the hospital ship beat its way down the James River, Confederate units fought rear guard battles at Deep Creek, Tabernacle Church, and Beaverpond Creek.

For General Grant, the chase now focused on keeping the pressure on the Army of Northern Virginia while shifting forces to the Confederate flanks in an effort to deny Lee's Army much needed supplies. To avoid Grant's persistent tactics, the Army of Northern Virginia left Amelia Court House and made a night march toward Farmville.

To counter this move, on April 5th General Grant sent General Sheridan's Cavalry to Jeterville to seize the Richmond to Danville Railroad. General Ord's Army of the James was also on the move along the South Side Railroad toward Burkesville. Behind the Army of the James, the Ninth Corps realigned the South Side Railroad to accommodate Union railcars and supply trains. On April 6th, as Second Corps was engaged in a running fight with Lee's rear guard near Amelia Springs Resort, General Ord sent two regiments to destroy the High Bridge over the Appomattox River. As the fighting continued, the J. K. Barnes pulled to the pier in Washington and began unloading wounded.

There were twenty-four of us from Dandy's Brigade assigned to the Carver General Hospital in Washington. After the Bull Run campaign, both North and South saw the need for the creation of a general hospital plan. While the idea seemed novel, it was not, as general hospitals in America dated to Revolutionary War times. Doctors long realized that housing wounded soldiers in separate, uncrowded, and well-ventilated buildings could minimize many of the maladies that affected them. They also realized that emphasis must be placed on facility cleanliness and quality of food, as well as adequate garbage and sewage disposal.

Following the battle of Manassas, the Army commandeered hotels, churches, and even, warehouses in an attempt to serve all of the wounded returning to Washington. To alleviate some of the problems, Surgeon General Hammond and the Sanitary Commission became the driving force behind implementation of a general hospital plan. By 1865, over two hundred hospitals nationwide served as general hospitals with a total of over one hundred and thirty thousand beds. In Washington alone there were sixteen such hospitals and about thirty thousand beds. Over the course of the war, nationwide, these hospitals treated over one million soldiers with a mortality rate of about eight percent.

Once we were loaded, the ambulances rumbled across the Washington streets, past the National Mall, and up a large hill that seemed very familiar to me. We were heading up Meridian Hill to the former site of the camp of instruction. No longer training regiments for the war, the camp facilities were turned over to the Medical Department in the spring of 1862. The camp of instruction was renamed the Carver Medical Hospital, after First Lieutenant James Carver of the One Hundred-fourth Pennsylvania. Carver was the supervising officer when the hospital facilities were constructed.

As the ambulance pulled up to the hospital, I could see the hospital was arranged with clean, airy, wards. After checking in, I was assigned to one of the amputation wards. Most of the soldiers on this ward were single or double amputees in various phases of recovery and rehabilitation. The soldiers were from a variety of different units, some wounded near Petersburg, some from the Shenandoah, and a few from Sherman's command in North Carolina. Each ward was overseen by a medical ward officer, generally a military surgeon or civilian physician. The medical ward officer was assisted in his duties by a noncommissioned officer who served as ward master, and a variety of enlisted specialists such as quartermasters or hospital stewards. Often, these hospitals would also have medical students on the staff. While students could not perform surgeries, they served as medical assistants, changed dressings, or oversaw ward dispensaries. Additionally, I was very surprised by the number of female nurses that worked on the ward.

Female nurses were not new to either general hospitals or the fighting. When the war broke and the first batch of Union volunteers rushed to the defense of Washington, a short but extremely determined woman banged on the acting Surgeon General's door demanding an audience. Her name was Dorothea Dix, a well-known reformer for the mentally ill and prisoners. Miss Dix emerged from the meeting as the new Superintendent of Army Nurses. By 1865, over three thousand females had joined Dix in her campaign to aid wounded soldiers.

After I was assigned a bed, bathed, and given a clean hospital gown, an older gentleman approached.

"Hello. I'm Walt, one of the volunteer aides here," he said. He was a nice enough individual who offered to get me some reading materials so I might keep abreast of the war news. This offer generated many more academic discussions. As it turned out, Walt was a bit of a writer and enjoyed talking about all kinds of literature. I was scheduled for more surgery but he promised to get me a couple of good reads from the hospital library.

One of the major problems of amputations was the risk of secondary infection. My situation was further compounded by all of the jostling I was exposed to since leaving the field hospital. General inflammation of long bone wounds left over time became infected to the point where, at best, a second amputation was required. At worst, the patient developed blood poisoning that was, more often than not, fatal. My situation was not that severe but the traveling created an inflammation requiring a secondary surgery to clear out any wound ulcerations, bone fragments that remained, or infectious discharge.

Once inside the operating theater, I was sedated, this time with ether, as the doctor made an examination of my leg and performed any corrective surgery required. If there was an issue with the bone splitting, the operation was conducted using a chain handsaw. This tool was a flexible chain with serrated teeth to cut away any splintered bone. The surgeon attached a long, threaded needle to the saw and inserted the needle below the bone to be cut. The saw was then pulled through the needle hole. Once the saw teeth positioned properly and a handle attached to each end of the chain, the saw could then cut out the offending bone splinters and the inflamed tissue.

My leg did not require so complex a procedure, just some cleaning and re-stitching of old sutures. When I returned to my bed, I found two volumes from the library to help me pass the time. Unless something else happened, I was pretty much out of the woods as far as the amputation was concerned. My leg could now begin the final healing process. When the limb was healed to a certain point, I could then be fitted for a prosthetic device and begin the rehabilitation process of learning to walk all over again.

Chapter Forty-Nine

April 9, 1865 – Washington D.C.

"I t's over!!! The war is over!!! Lee surrendered to Grant!!!" Just before taps on the evening of April 9th, the Ward Master burst into the ward and began shouting that the war was over. Most of us sat or lay somewhat dumbfounded until we heard the din and clamor from the other wards. Still somewhat in a state of disbelief and shock, I looked around the ward at my fellow amputees. Some were cheering, some were laughing, some were praying, some were crying, but, to a man, all of us felt a sense of relief; the war was over.

For those who refused to believe the news, the proof came shortly after dawn the next morning. Five hundred guns from the defenses of Washington opened up in a series of salvos that lit up the sky and shook the earth. Windows were broken, people were cheering, and church bells rang. It was over. The war in Virginia was truly over.

On April 6th, after the Army of Northern Virginia made a night march to Farmville, the three Union armies began, once again, to nip at the Rebels all along the front. Early in the morning, advanced forces of Ord's Army of the James battled with forces from Richmond and the Howlett Line under the command of Lieutenant General James Longstreet. Moving to assist the Army of the James, Sixth Corps, Army of the Potomac, became heavily engaged with Ewell's Corps at a place called Sailor's Creek. Farther east, Anderson's Corps clashed with Major General Wesley Merritt's Cavalry while the Union Fifth Corps assaulted Gordon's Corps. By days end, over seven thousand, seven hundred Confederates lay dead, wounded or prisoners. This number included eight general officers taken prisoner, among them Lieutenant General Ewell and Major General Custis Lee.

On April 7th, the Army of Northern Virginia reached Farmville and settled in around Cumberland Church. General Lee ordered a third consecutive night march to Appomattox Station. The following morning, sensing an opportunity to end the conflict without additional bloodshed, General Grant opened a dialogue with General Lee.

By the afternoon of April 8th, the Army of Northern Virginia was virtually surrounded at Appomattox Court House. Earlier that day forces from the Army of the James thwarted an attempt by General Gordon's Corps to break out to Danville. The Second and Sixth Corps were once again pressing the Confederate rear. Realizing the situation to be hopeless and further fighting to be futile, General Robert E. Lee asked to meet General Grant to discuss the surrender of the Army of Northern Virginia.

In the afternoon of April 9th, Grant and Lee met in the Appomattox home of Wilmer McLean. Mr. McLean was one of the more remarkable civilian figures of the war. A retired Major of the Virginia Militia, McLean was a wholesale grocer living outside of Manassas when the war broke out. On July 21st, 1861, Confederate Brigadier General Beauregard commandeered his home as his headquarters. After the battle, McLean found it easier to peddle his wares to his Southern customers if Yankees did not surround his home. In the spring of 1863, he packed up his family and moved one hundred and twenty miles west to the sleepy hamlet of Appomattox Court House. Now, on April 9th, 1865, the war visited him again in the form of Ulysses S. Grant and Robert E. Lee. In the years after the surrender, Mclean was fond of saying "the war started in my front yard and ended in my parlor".

It was over!

The war in Virginia was now officially over. General Grant telegraphed the news to President Lincoln at City Point and Secretary of War Stanton in Washington. Although General Lee had indeed surrendered, the fighting still festered in other parts of the country. General Joseph Johnston still commanded a formidable force in North Carolina. General Richard Taylor, the son of former President Zachary Taylor, still commanded forces in the Department of Alabama, Mississippi, and East Louisiana. Additionally, General Kirby Smith was still in control of the Army of the Trans-Mississippi. It would take until the end of May 1865 before the war east of the Mississippi was finally over.

April 15, 1865 – Washington D.C.

It's been almost two weeks since that Confederate mini ball shattered my lower leg and transformed my life. Initially, I guess I chose to deny the incident ever happened or downplay the severity of the wound. In spite of bones sticking out, I convinced myself it was only a through and through wound and I would be up and about in quick order.

After waking from the amputation, as I looked at the bloody bandage and the empty space where my foot was supposed to be, I began to feel a growing sense of rage deep in my soul. I felt rage at the doctors who cut my leg off. I felt rage at those in my chain of command who actually ordered such a foolhardy assault. Interestingly, I felt rage at just about everyone and everything except for the Confederate soldier who actually pulled the trigger. He, like me, didn't really want to be where he was and, like me, was only doing his job.

Aboard the hospital ship, as this internal rage burned, I began playing the "what if" game. What if I hadn't volunteered to become a substitute? What if I hadn't become a sharpshooter? A myriad of these scenarios ran through my mind. The longer I lay in my bunk the more the "what if" scenarios and the questions continued to mount. Then, ever so slowly, the questions and the "what ifs" that ran through my mind began to change. The change was ever so subtle starting as a glimmer of reality and a realization that my current situation was what it was. I could now accept that most of the "what if" scenarios were things I could not go back and undo.

I began to believe that what happened really did happen. From these admissions, my concerns about things that happened in the past morphed into "what will" type questions and scenarios about what lay ahead. Will I wind up in a raggedy uniform armed only with a tin cup on some street corner in Augusta? Obviously, planting a field with only one leg would be increasingly difficult, so what exactly would I do? Could I still hop around an apothecary store without knocking everything off the shelves or scaring the small children? What will happen to me now? Can I learn to walk again? What will be my future?

As my mental state shifted from past events I had no control over to future events I had no answer for, I recognized the impact of time on my current emotional state. In the Regiment, my time was rarely ever my own. There was always picket duty, duty on the line, working parties, forage parties and the thousands of other sundry things that filled my days. There were times on sentry duty, particularly in the middle of the night, when I could think of other things besides being a soldier, but for the most part, my free time was devoted to resting, sleeping, or writing home to the family.

In the hospital however, aside from brief sessions with the medical staff, my time was my own. There was more than enough time to ponder past events or question future ones. The only breaks in this routine were the periodic visits from Walt. Often, he would bring me new reading materials and we would spend some time discussing this book or that one. Sometimes he would read me a new piece he was working on. It was a wonderful interruption from my own, somewhat dismal thoughts and time I actually looked forward to.

During the evening of April 14th, we noticed a good deal of commotion around the hospital. Shortly after taps, medical personnel began running around and moving equipment and beds. A short time later the Ward Medical Officer came in and told us the grim news: President Lincoln had been shot.

Since Carver General Hospital was one of the closest hospitals to downtown Washington, there was speculation that the wounded President might be brought here for treatment. The hospital medical staff went on full alert to prepare the facility should it be necessary. Soldiers from the facility began preparing defensive positions at key points around the hospital. Soon, soldiers from other units began arriving to bolster the defense force.

Around 1:00 am the Ward Medical Officer returned to provide an update to the situation.

"President and Mrs. Lincoln were attending a play at Ford's Theater when, shortly after ten, an assassin entered the Presidential box and shot the President in the head. The assassin then jumped onto the stage and disappeared out the back door. Onlookers identified the gunman as John Wilkes Booth, an actor with intimate knowledge of the theater layout.

"What is the President's condition?" asked a one-armed soldier from Ohio.

"Severely wounded," the Doctor replied. "He has been moved to a boarding house across the street and is being tended to there."

"What happened to Booth?" one-legged Williams from Indiana asked.

"Currently on the run," the Doctor replied. "A cordon has been established at all points entering and leaving the City. Booth may have accomplices as a rumor is circulating that Secretary Seward was also attacked."

On the ward, the remainder of that night was spent in a state of agitation, anxiety, and disbelief. No one slept as my ward mates talked quietly among themselves or prayed to their God for President Lincoln's recovery. Those of us still able to shoulder and fire a weapon appealed to the Ward Master for permission to join the defense force. Since the President would not be coming, our requests were denied.

Outside of the hospital grounds, thousands of Washington residents took to the streets in a vigil for the President. The Washington military garrison blocked off all access and egress points to the City in an effort to maintain security while searching for Booth and his fellow accomplices.

Around 8:00 am on Saturday, April 15th, as church bells tolled throughout Washington, the Ward Medical Officer returned with an update.

"About 7:25 this morning President Lincoln succumbed to his wound at the boarding house across from Ford's Theater," the Doctor stated. "Secretary Seward, who was gravely wounded by a second assassin, remains in guarded condition at his home. Apparently a third assassin was tasked to kill Vice President Johnson but this effort was thwarted."

"What about the assassins?" one of my ward mates asked.

"It appears Booth and one other conspirator have managed to escape the city. As we speak, the Army has initiated a manhunt for the fugitives."

The ward fell into a somber silence as the news of the President's death sank in. Some sat in stunned silence. Some were visibly emotional with tears running down their cheeks. Others prayed, but no one spoke.

The day continued in a state of disbelief. All of us on the ward had previously experienced loss. For some that loss was personal or family oriented. For all of us that loss was of comrades on the battlefield. This however, was a totally different experience. This was the loss of our President. This was the loss of the man who became synonymous with the Union cause in the war. This was the loss of the man who had bested the odds and rose to the highest office in the land in a time of great turmoil. This was the loss of the man whom many felt was the only one capable of putting this great nation back together.

Later in the afternoon, Walt came on the ward and we had a chance to talk. He was visibly upset about the loss of the President and spoke openly about the greatness of the man. Walt was working on a poem about Lincoln's death and its effect on the nation.

"Oh Captain! My Captain! Our fearful trip is done,"

In the days following the assassination of the President, facts began to surface about the breadth of the conspiracy against the government. John Wilkes Booth was the leader of the conspirators and, after careful preparation and planning, carried out the attack on the President. Booth's co-conspirators included Lewis Powell and David Herold, assigned to kill Secretary Seward, and George Atzerodt tasked to kill the Vice President. The group routinely met at a boarding house owned by Mary Surratt, a known Confederate sympathizer.

While Booth was successful in his efforts, Powell and Herold only managed to severely wound Secretary Seward. The Secretary was at home recovering from a recent carriage accident. Vice President Johnson was unharmed as George Atzerodt chose to get drunk rather than participate in the assassination plot. In an ironic twist, only that morning, April 14th, 1865, President Lincoln signed legislation creating the United States Secret Service, the agency responsible for the security of the President.

"The ship has weathered every rack, the prize we sought is won,"

On April 15th, upon the death of Abraham Lincoln, Andrew Johnson became the seventeenth President of the United States.

"Johnson will be no friend to the South," Walt said.

"Why so?" I asked.

"In his second inaugural address, Lincoln spoke of 'malice toward none' and 'charity for all.' I don't think that will be the case now. In spite of his southern upbringing, Johnson will not be so charitable toward the former Confederate states," Walt replied.

Shortly after our discussion, Walt's prediction came to pass. By Presidential Directive General Sherman and other Union commanders were ordered to deal harshly with the remaining surrendering Confederate forces. Union malice also took the form of a bounty for the capture of President Jefferson Davis. Unfortunately, the South would feel the full wrath of their secession in the Reconstruction era to follow. This would be a sad period of time in our history that could have been more benevolent under the guidance and influence of Abraham Lincoln.

"The port is near, the bells I hear, the people all exulting,"

Lincoln's death also promised no bright future for the former slave population of the South. Although the Emancipation Proclamation freed the slaves and the Thirteenth Amendment to the Constitution abolished slavery, the road to economic prosperity for the descendants of former slaves would be a long and harsh one. Even with passage of the Fourteenth Amendment to the Constitution, which guaranteed citizenship rights and equal protection under the law to all, it would be decades of turmoil and bloodshed before the families of those enslaved would be recognized as equals.

"While follow eyes the steady hull, the vessel grim and daring,"

For twelve days Union forces pursued the conspirators around the Maryland and Virginia countryside. John Wilkes Booth and his co-conspirator David Herold managed to escape Washington before the military cordon was fully established. The pair traversed the southern Maryland area in an effort to escape patrols and cross the Potomac into Virginia.

After stopping at Surratt's Tavern to resupply, the two fugitives continued on to the home of Doctor Samuel Mudd. Doctor Mudd treated the injury to Booth's leg caused by his jump to the stage of Ford's Theater. For his assistance to Booth, Doctor Mudd was tried by a military court and sentenced to life imprisonment. President Johnson pardoned Doctor Mudd in 1869.

Booth and Herold reached the Virginia side of the Potomac on April 23rd and held up at the Garrett farm near Bowling Green. Shortly before dawn on the 26th, Union soldiers cornered the pair in Garrett's tobacco barn. Their situation hopeless, Herold chose to surrender but Booth refused. After soldiers set fire to the barn, Booth attempted to avoid the flames and fight off the attacking forces. He was fatally wounded and taken to the porch of Garrett's house where he died some three hours later.

With Booth dead, the other conspirators, David Herold, Lewis Powell, George Atzerodt, and Mary Surratt were all tried by military court and sentenced to hang for their roles in the assassination plot. On July 7th, 1865, the four were taken to the courtyard of Arsenal Penitentiary at Fort McNair in Washington and the sentence was carried out. At 1:15 pm on that July day, Mary Surratt became the first woman executed by the United States Government.

"But O heart! heart! heart!
O the bleeding drops of red,
Where on the deck my Captain lies,
Fallen cold and dead."

Chapter Fifty

May 25, 1865 – Augusta, Maine

After his death, President Lincoln's remains were taken to the East Room of the White House where his body was prepared for the funeral events. On April 18th, the East Room was opened to the public for a daylong viewing before the private funeral service was held on the 19th. At the close of the service, the President was transported to the Rotunda of the Capitol where he laid in state on April 20th for the public to again pay their respects. Thousands lined the funeral route to the Capitol and thousands more passed the President's coffin in the Capitol Rotunda. After a private prayer service for members of the Cabinet on the morning of the 21st, the President was taken to the funeral train for his final trip back to Springfield, Illinois.

On April 19th, as the funeral service was conducted for Abraham Lincoln in the White House, I was taken to the rehabilitation ward and fitted for my artificial leg. As part of a federal government subsidized program, wounded soldiers were given the option of receiving prosthetic devices or seventy-five dollars for each amputation if they chose not to receive the artificial limbs.

In the early days of the war, artificial limbs were poorly constructed, cumbersome, and ill-fitting contraptions made of leather, wood, and iron. Because few of the early models fit correctly, many lower limb amputees like me chose to receive the seventy-five dollars and a set of crutches.

By 1863 however, many cosmetic and mechanized improvements were made to these prosthetics by the burgeoning artificial limb industry. When a government sponsored prosthetic subsidy was initiated in 1863, one of the first to compete was James Edward Hanger. Hanger was a former Confederate officer who lost his leg seven inches below the hip at the Battle of Philippi in 1861. He was treated and fitted for an artificial limb by Union doctors. Dissatisfied with his new appendage, Hanger began the development of a better artificial limb. Hanger's design turned out to be not only lighter than what the government was currently offering but hinged at both the knee and ankle to allow a degree of flexibility.

The company Hanger formed was just one of several businesses that competed for a share of the amputee market. During the course of the war over thirty thousand Union soldiers and more than forty thousand Confederates lost limbs in the fighting. The Manufacturing of artificial limbs quickly became a growth industry.

The year 1863 saw the first use of rubber in the prosthetic industry with the development of an artificial rubber hand. Rubber was an attractive alternative to iron and wood, more cosmetic in design, resilient, flexible, and significantly more lifelike. There appeared to be no limits to the lengths these companies went to in order to garner government contracts. Aside from the cosmetic considerations, some companies even advertised removable accessories that allowed the wearer to replace the hand with various attachments such as hooks, knives, saws, or brushes.

When the day arrived for my first rehabilitation session, I was excited to be fitted for my new limb and, once again, be allowed to walk around freely. While my new leg fit well enough, my excitement was soon dashed as I tried to walk. Almost immediately, I realized rehabilitation was not going to be as simple or easy as I suspected. After stumbling and almost falling several times, I experienced the first of many amputation related issues that plagued wounded soldiers. The truth was I would now have to learn to walk all over again and this would be a long and painful process.

By the time I returned to the ward after this first session, my leg ached from wearing the prosthetic device and my leg muscles were sore from trying to maintain an upright position. However, unlike many of my fellow amputees who chose to give up rather than endure the therapy, I was determined to stay the course. While some felt a pinned up sleeve or trouser leg to be a badge of honor, I chose to work at returning to a level of mobility close to what I had before that Confederate bullet changed my life forever.

As my rehabilitation continued, I began to comprehend many of the other physical and mental issues that my fellow amputees and I faced. After discharge from the Army, we were expected to be the primary means of support for our families. Although I was determined to gain a degree of self-sustainment, the reality of this issue was that many amputees were forced to depend on others for their livelihood and care of their families. This situation carried with it a serious negative repercussion on the individual soldier's morale and character as well as his sense of self-worth and value to his family and community.

Regarding the post war fate of these wounded soldiers, the federal government was not as supportive as it could be, to the point of creating additional obstacles that amputees needed to overcome. The Federal Pension System, created in 1862, was specifically designed to assist wounded soldiers returning to civilian life. A pension, based on rank, was offered to the wartime wounded with the stipulation that the pension recipient must not have the ability to work. Any discharged soldier who wanted a pension faced another moral crisis, as he would be dependent on the federal government to support his family. As a result, many chose to refuse the pension and prove they could work to support their families rather than accept a government handout.

Finally, the society we fought to preserve also placed additional hurdles on these combat wounded veterans. Members of the community often viewed a wounded and disabled veteran as just another burden on society. This was especially true as time passed. As the war became a distant memory, many Americans chose to look to the future and not at the relics of the past. In this regard, to many of his countrymen, being a combat wounded soldier carried with it the stigma of not being a productive or effective member of society.

President Lincoln's funeral train chugged along the eastern countryside at twenty miles per hour, reversing the route Lincoln took on his trip to Washington some four years earlier. Thousands lined the rail route and thousands more attended viewings at scheduled stops in the major cities along the way. After almost two weeks on the road, the train arrived in Springfield on May 3rd and the President was laid to rest in Oak Ridge Cemetery on May 4th.

As Lincoln's train traveled across the country, I continued my rehabilitation activities. By the time of Lincoln's interment, I was able to walk fairly well. The amputation site was becoming accustomed to the new artificial limb although not without some discomfort after long periods of wear. My leg muscles were also adjusting to the new leg and my new way of walking. The muscle soreness I had experienced early in the rehabilitation cycle slowly faded as the muscles responded to changes created by the new appendage.

On May 10th, as President Andrew Johnson was declaring hostilities to be effectively over, I was learning to climb stairs and other more advanced walking skills. With his declaration of peace at hand, the President also directed a formal review to be held on May 23rd and 24th to honor the victorious forces before most of the soldiers would be discharged and sent home.

Since the beginning of May many of my fellow amputees had completed their rehabilitation and were receiving their discharges. On May 15th the Ward Medical Officer approached me after one of my rehabilitation sessions.

"You are making great progress in your rehab," the Doctor said. "In fact, you have progressed to a point where we feel comfortable in recommending your discharge. If you are interested in attending the Grand Review, I can arrange for your discharge to be effective after the Review is complete. Otherwise, I can have the paperwork started and you can be on your way home in about a week."

I thought about the Doctor's offer before responding.

"I appreciate the offer to allow me to stay for the Review sir, but Third Maine Regiment already disbanded back in Maine last summer and Eleventh Maine Regiment is still in Richmond as part of the Army of the James. If you think I am ready to leave, I guess I would just rather go home."

"Of course," the Doctor replied. "If you don't get out soon, no telling when you would get home once they start discharging all those other boys. I'll tell them to get started on your discharge paperwork right away."

The Grand Review was scheduled for two full days. May 23rd was devoted to the Army of the Potomac, and the 24th featured the Army of Tennessee and the Army of Georgia. These three armies were close enough to Washington to participate in the Review. The Army of the Potomac, under the command of Major General George Meade, began arriving in the Washington area on May 12th and encamped at various sites on the north side of the Potomac. As the Army of the Tennessee and the Army of Georgia, both under the command of Major General William Tecumseh Sherman, reached the Washington area, they encamped on the south side of the Potomac in Virginia. The Army of Georgia recently completed operations in the Carolinas where Sherman accepted the final surrender of General Joseph Johnston's Army of Tennessee.

With my equipment turned in and my discharge paperwork complete, as the signal gun announced the start of the Review on May 23rd, I climbed aboard a military train with just my personal effects, a crutch, and wearing my new artificial leg. The military train was crowded but, as an amputee, I was given a seat in one of the cars. Six hours later the last of the one hundred eighty infantry regiments, twenty-nine regiments of cavalry, and thirty-three batteries of artillery from the Army of the Potomac passed in review before President Johnson and General Grant. By the end of the day's Review, our train departed Baltimore and headed for Philadelphia.

The train was filled with military personnel recently discharged and heading home. When we arrived in Philadelphia a good number of these soldiers got off, mostly from Pennsylvania and New Jersey regiments. This freed up a bit of space so I was able to move around and stretch my leg. After a lengthy break and a locomotive change, the train departed for New York City. By the time the signal gun announced Day Two of the Grand Review, our train was fast moving toward New York.

Another group of soldiers got off in New York from the New York and northern New Jersey regiments. As we departed New York I noticed more and more civilians filling the seats. Only a few soldiers like me remained. The trip across Connecticut and Rhode Island was spent in relative comfort and as we pulled into Boston, I began to look forward to returning home.

I was required to change trains in Boston and got some time to eat and stretch my aching leg. Finally, I boarded the new train for the final leg of the journey back to Augusta. The busy city of Boston and its surrounding towns soon disappeared behind us. As we crossed the Piscatagua River from Portsmouth, New Hampshire into Kittery, Maine I could smell the fresh sea air of southern Maine mixed with the woodsy scent of the Maine wilderness. I was actually going home.

Three hours after leaving Kittery behind, I stepped down off the train and onto the platform of the Augusta Station. I was home. Now, as I stood looking over the city, the trip from Washington seemed somewhat anticlimactic. The war was over. We had won. Lincoln, the great architect of our victory, was dead, but I was home.

The trip gave me time to contemplate everything that happened over the past four years. It really was four years and twenty-three days since I first raised my hand and swore to protect and defend the

Constitution of the United States. I thought about my time in Third Maine and the metamorphosis from civilian to soldier at the camp of instruction. I remembered the horrors of our baptism of fire in the Virginia countryside at Manassas. That period of my life seemed so very long ago. The men from that Regiment are now home after their enlistment ended, serving with other regiments after reenlisting, or filling graves in countless battlefields from Virginia, across the South, and into Pennsylvania.

The trip also gave me ample time to reflect on my time in the Western Gunboat Flotilla and living and fighting on the mighty Mississippi. Fighting in battles along the river or assisting those who fought their battles inland. New names for my memory, new graveyards for so terribly many on both sides: Pittsburg Landing, Island Ten, and Vicksburg. Different fights, same outcomes.

Finally, there was time to deliberate on my last nine months in Virginia. The siege of Richmond north of the James River, Fort Hell, the break through along the southern line in Petersburg, and, of course, my life-changing incident on the ramparts of Fort Gregg.

All of that was behind me now. The only things now left behind were memories: memories of friends made and comrades served with over the four years. Memories of my commanders good and bad and of sergeants caring and uncaring I had experienced from the beginning. There would be time for more memories, more old and new emotions, and a lifetime of nightmares that will haunt my dreams for the rest of time.

But it was over. I survived. I was saved. While I sacrificed a portion of my body to the cause, over the past four years I achieved a level of salvation that comes only to those who have served. I really had survived.

With these final thoughts, I picked up my gear and my crutch, and began walking to the stage depot for my final ride home.

Epilogue

"Only the dead have seen the end of war."

Plato

Strafford, New Hampshire 1921

October 1921 – Strafford, New Hampshire

I t has been fifty-six years since the guns went silent. Fifty-six years since Private John Williams of the Thirty-fourth Indiana Regiment fought in a battle at Palmito Ranch, Texas. Private Williams became the last soldier killed in that dreadful war. The very last one of over six hundred and twenty thousand killed or missing on both sides. Given the number of soldiers and sailors involved over the four years of the war, that equated to one out of every four who never returned home. They were buried at sea or in some distant graveyard at the site of some forgotten battle: many known only to their God.

Not all of these men died from combat related wounds. For every three men killed on the battlefield, five more died from disease, many which are easily cured or prevented by today's standards. In total, there were over a million and a half casualties of that great period of hell on earth. One and a half million men were killed, wounded, or taken prisoner. Many were wounded multiple times, over seventy thousand who returned, like me, missing an arm or a leg, or multiple limbs. Upon returning, their injuries served as validation for their inability to work and earn a living, their failure to support their families, or even to support themselves. For these individuals, the hell endured on the battlefield was transferred to a new and different kind of agony. And still, the United States rolled on like a juggernaut, finding new people to subdue and new ways to kill.

Early in those fifty-six years we managed to subdue an entire race of people in the western states and claim their lands as part of our country; Manifest Destiny, from sea to shining sea. Many of these indigenous peoples killed by the very men who only a short time before were killing each other.

Then, late in the last century, our country began to emerge as a global power. Merchant ships roamed the seven seas delivering

American materials and products to the world. To keep the economy growing, we evoked the rule of the Monroe Doctrine. We fought a war with the Spanish to proclaim our dominance in the Western Hemisphere and, once again, sent our soldiers to Mexico to keep the peace. Most recently, our soldiers fought in that "war to end all wars" in Europe, a truly horrible conflict replete with new and improved methods of ending life. New weapons like machine guns, tanks, and dreadful gases enabled us to kill and maim in large numbers. In addition, our technical dominance grew exponentially. Flying machines or airplanes promise to take war to a whole new level, death from above but death nevertheless.

Now in the eighty-first year of my life, I have finally reached the end of all things. As I lay here eaten by the cancer, I take time to remember. I especially remember all of those comrades who have shed this mortal coil, both on the battlefield and here at home. Remembering has grown to consume all of my waking moments. Some of their fates still remain a mystery, but some are front-page news, both in Maine and around the country.

It was not hard to follow the further activities of General Grant. After the war, he became the General of the Army, the first four star general in American history. Disillusioned with President Johnson's plan for Reconstruction, Grant accepted the Republican nomination and was elected the eighteenth President of the United States in 1869. After serving two terms as President, the second riddled by scandal and turmoil, the General retired to travel and write his memoirs. On July 23rd, 1885, at the age of sixty-three, President Grant succumbed to throat cancer in New York City.

Another individual to achieve national prominence was Walt, the volunteer orderly at the Carver Medical Hospital. Walt was already a published author, journalist, and poet at the outbreak of the war. After the war, Walt's literary star rose dramatically to the point where he was hailed as one of the greatest poets of the nineteenth century. I managed to collect all of his published works and read them with enthusiasm over and over again. Sadly, the great Walt Whitman died in 1892 at the age of seventy-two.

Our Regimental Commander in Eleventh Maine, Colonel Jonathan Hill, and our Brigade Commander, Colonel Harris Plaisted, both Maine men and lawyers before the war, continued their wartime successes after the conflict ended. After his discharge, Colonel Hill was promoted brevet Brigadier General for service to the Country and to Maine. He continued to practice law and even chaired a group who wrote the definitive history of the Eleventh Maine Regiment. Colonel Hill passed away in 1905 at the age of seventy-five.

After his service, Colonel Plaisted was appointed Brigadier General of Volunteers for the state of Maine, and later, brevet Major General. Plaisted served in the Maine House of Representatives and as Maine's Attorney General before his election to the U.S. House of Representatives in 1875. In 1881, he was elected governor of Maine and continued active in Maine politics until his death in 1898 at the age of sixty-nine.

The Platoon Commander of the sharpshooters, George Payne, survived his wounds at Fort Gregg. In October of 1865, he was promoted to First Lieutenant and remained in the Army after the war. After retiring from active service, Lieutenant Payne lived in Newport, Maine until his death in 1882.

Our Squad Leader in the sharpshooters, Sergeant Luther Robbins, also survived the war but was not so lucky in civilian life. After moving to Boston to work in the construction industry, Robbins was killed in 1871 when a load of lumber fell on him.

The fate of my two friends from Eleventh Maine, Freeman Flint and Frank Johnson, remains a mystery. Freeman supposedly moved to California but Frank remained in Maine. I have heard nothing of either of them since the end of the war.

I also learned the fate of many of my comrades from the Third Maine Regiment. Oliver Otis Howard, the first Commanding Officer of the Third Maine Regiment, had a long and illustrious career. After losing his right arm in the Battle of Fair Oaks during the Peninsula Campaign of 1862, Howard went on to command a division at Antietam, a corps at Gettysburg, and the Army of the Tennessee in 1864. After the war, Howard was assigned as Commissioner of the Freedman's Bureau, an organization designed to integrate former slaves into mainstream society. In 1874, General Howard commanded the Army of the Columbia during the Nez Perce War before retiring from the Army. He died in Burlington, Vermont in 1909 at the age of seventy-eight.

The first Company Commander of Company I, Captain Moses Lakeman distinguished himself during the Peninsula Campaign. In November of 1862, Lakeman was promoted Colonel and given command of the Regiment. Despite issues with alcohol, Colonel Lakeman remained in command of Third Maine until the Regiment was disbanded in June of 1864. Lakeman lived in Melrose, Massachusetts until his death in 1907 at age seventy-eight.

Sergeant Henry Lyon, the gentile giant and lumberman who was our first Squad Leader, fell in battle on the second day of the Gettysburg Campaign. He is buried in the National Cemetery in Gettysburg.

Four headstones down from Sergeant Lyon is the grave of my friend John Lewis. Both Sergeant Lyons and John died in an area of the battlefield called the Peach Orchard. I had the occasion to visit their graves in 1912.

One of my other friends, Jim Ross, survived the war and returned to a life of farming. He purchased land near his family's farm in Androscoggin County and lived the rough life of a Maine farmer until his death in 1904.

The last of my friends from before the war, Charlie Clark, also survived the war and returned to Augusta. Charlie, who wrote stories of the Regiment's activities hoped to become a reporter after the war. He also hoped to write the great American war novel based on his exploits, however the war managed to change something in Charlie. After Gettysburg, he never wrote another line or story about his experiences. Charlie returned to Gardiner, Maine and opened a printing shop. The times we visited he chose not to reminisce about the war and remained very closed about what happened. Charlie passed away in 1909.

As for me, after my discharge and some time at home, I returned to my apprenticeship with Mr. Hartwell. Shortly after my arrival back in Augusta, on September 17th, 1865, a tremendous fire broke out in the early morning hours. By the time the fire was brought under control eighty-one buildings along Water Street and the docks were destroyed and another twenty severely damaged. Mr. Hartwell's apothecary was spared, as were many other homes and businesses thanks to the efforts of the fire departments involved and the initiative of local citizens. The area was later rebuilt with granite and brick buildings that are still part of the Augusta waterfront.

After two years of apprenticeship with Mr. Hartwell, I stayed on with him for another three years as an employee. By 1870, Mr. and Mrs. Hartwell were anxious to sell the business and move to Bangor to be closer to their children and grandchildren. William graduated from Bowdoin College and law school. He opened a law practice in Bangor, married, and fathered three children. Elizabeth also finished her schooling, married a fine young man and lived in Bangor as well. The Hartwell's bought another apothecary in Bangor and kept it until Mr. Hartwell's retirement in 1902. He passed away in 1915 and Mrs. Hartwell in 1919.

Although Mr. Hartwell's business was well out of my price range, he did help me find an apothecary in Strafford, New Hampshire whose owner, James Scott, was planning to retire. Mr. Scott agreed to take me on as a partner for a period of two years. He retired from the business in 1873 and moved to upstate New York to be near family.

I became a small business owner in a small town in southeast New Hampshire. It was a beautiful area with friendly people who accepted me as one of their own. I met a young lady, Martha, and shortly after Mr. Scott left, we began courting. Maddie, as she was called, was a widow whose husband died suddenly a year or so before. In spite of the difference in our ages, we were married in 1878.

By 1884, we had two small children, Herbert and Lynne. Tragedy struck in 1886 when young Herbert died of dysentery. After his death I experienced what so many fathers had during the war, the pain that comes from the loss of a child. Lynne grew to be a fine young lady. By 1900, she had completed her schooling and married George Kelley. They live with my two grandchildren in Rochester, New Hampshire.

Maddie and I continued to work in the apothecary until 1909 when I decided to sell the business and retire. We did some traveling, mostly to visit relatives who had moved away. My father passed on in 1866 leaving my stepmother with the farm and a herd of young children. One by one they grew and married or moved away. My stepmother joined my father and mother in Sand Hill Cemetery in 1872.

Now, in the winter of my life, I lay in this bed with only my memories. It is October and that means fall here in New Hampshire. As in Maine, the fall in New Hampshire is the very best time of year. It is that time of the year when the green shades of the pines and cedars mix with the reds, oranges, yellows, and browns of the hardwoods to create a palate of incredible beauty on the surrounding landscape. Warm, brightly lit days marry with cool, crisp nights and serve as the harbingers of the cold harsh winter yet to come.

The fall in New Hampshire is that time after the crops have been harvested, the orchards picked, and the cooking, salting, smoking, and preserving complete. County fairs are in full swing and the air is filled with a general mood of thanksgiving for another successful season.

The fall in New Hampshire is a time for hunting and fishing. Beautiful spring fed lakes and rivers and the proximity of the ocean provides a bounty of fish and other seafood. The woods and fields are a wonderful source of animals to hunt.

As in Maine, the fall in New Hampshire really is the closest thing to paradise on earth. Looking out my bedroom window I can take in the entire splendor of the region. I can see everything about the area: my family, the wonderful people, and the beauty of the landscape.

As the lights are extinguished, my room is drenched in the ebony darkness of a moonless, New Hampshire night. Once again I am left with my memories. As my eyes close I can feel a deep-seated sense of inner peace and a release from the pain and suffering the cancer brings. Slowly, as I start to open my eyes, the blackness is replaced by a grayish hue and the vision of a large conical shaped ceiling.

"It's about time you woke up," a voice calls out.

"You better hurry or we'll be late for assembly," a second voice said.

As the sleep fades from my eyes, I realize I am inside a Sibley Tent and the voices I hear are my friends: Charley Clark, Jim Ross, and John Lewis. They look as I remember them in my dreams, as they did before the war in the time of our great innocence.

Sitting now on the edge of the bed, I discover my left leg, long since turned to dust at Petersburg, is as it was in my youth, intact and strong. A body devastated by the pain and anguish of cancer is once again, whole and healthy.

After dressing quickly in a pair of Jefferson boots and a blue, single-breasted, sack coat with four brass buttons, I step outside to join my friends. The day is pleasant and bright, the sky a beautiful shade of blue, and all around, the beauty of nature flourishes. As we walk along I notice groups of soldiers dressed in blue and gray. Some are playing cards, others are playing baseball, and still others just sitting and talking. Two Confederate soldiers approach me. I recognize one as the young Alabama lad from the fighting at Deep

Bottom. The other one, dressed in a Captain's uniform, introduced himself as the young soldier's father.

"I wanted to meet you and thank you for the respect and caring you showed my boy that day," the Captain said. The young lad just smiled and shuffled his feet.

"It was an honor to be with him at that time Sir. I have seen a lot of men meet their maker over the years but he demonstrated a degree of dignity and poise in death that I have never seen before or since. I was proud to be there for him and I have never forgotten him."

As I walk along, I realize this is the place of my dreams. I greet family, friends, and former comrades in an environment that is utterly surreal. Later, as I reflect on recent events, I begin to realize that in addition to the burdens of life in general, I have experienced that version of hell created specifically for a soldier. I lived in that nightmare world for four years of my life. I was seduced into it as a child and a young man. The seduction bug that ate away at my soul guided my decisions and put me on the path to becoming a soldier.

My metamorphosis was complete through the drill and training at the camp of instruction. I first saw the elephant in the Virginia countryside and then again on the rivers of the West. More campaigns followed around Richmond and in Petersburg. I have seen and lived a soldier's hell on the battlefields of our Country and in my dreams and memories for over sixty years. I have carried the ominous burden of lives lost and lives taken and sought the salvation and forgiveness that only comes with time. A salvation finally revealed in the dreams and memories of an old man.

And now it is done. The burdens of my life are lifted. The soldier's hell I created during that life is over. The experiences that I dreamed about for so many years are now just fading memories.

I am at last, free.

It is truly over.

319

About the Author

Bill King is a graduate of the University of Massachusetts and holds advanced degrees from Boston University and Old Dominion University. In this his first novel, the main character is loosely based on the real-life Civil War experiences of the author's great-great uncle. A retired Marine, a retired defense contractor, and former adjunct college professor, Dr. King and his wife reside in Dinwiddie County, Virginia.